Praise for
Hitler's War

"Turtledove is always good, but this return to World War II, one of his favorite turfs, is genuinely brilliant." —*Booklist*

"The author's mastery of the ever-widening ripples that small changes make in history is unchallenged, his storytelling always gripping, and his research impeccable." —*Library Journal*

"One can rely on Turtledove. He writes well and with confidence. He develops strong plots. Delivers well considered storylines. Take the most recent entry, *Hitler's War*. The novel is predicated on a single question: what would have happened if Britain's Prime Minister Neville Chamberlain had refused to allow Hitler to annex the Sudetenland? Again, change one thing and, like a kaleidoscope, everything looks different. One piece falls another way and all things are altered. . . . [*Hitler's War*] is solid writing and classic Turtledove."

—January Magazine

"[Turtledove] brings the deprivations of war to life in this vision of a very different WWII. . . . American Peggy Druce, caught behind the lines, gets a firsthand look at the period military hardware and nationalistic mindsets that Turtledove so expertly describes."

—*Publishers Weekly*

"Not for the squeamish . . . *Hitler's War* would qualify as realistic war fiction except for the alt-history setting. No generals, strategists and such here, just regular people. . . . If you like 'real war' novels the book is for you." —Fantasy Book Critic

BY HARRY TURTLEDOVE

Hitler's War

THE WAR THAT CAME EARLY

Hitler's War

HARRY TURTLEDOVE

BALLANTINE BOOKS | NEW YORK

2010 Del Rey Trade Paperback Edition

Copyright © 2009 by Harry Turtledove

Excerpt from *The War That Came Early: West and East* copyright © 2010 by Harry Turtledove.

All rights reserved.

Published in the United States by Del Rey, an imprint of The Random House Publishing Group, a division of Random House, Inc., New York.

DEL REY is a registered trademark and the Del Rey colophon is a trademark of Random House, Inc.

Originally published in hardcover in the United States by Del Rey, an imprint of The Random House Publishing Group, a division of Random House, Inc., in 2009.

This book contains an excerpt from the forthcoming book *The War That Came Early: West and East* by Harry Turtledove. This excerpt has been set for this edition only and may not reflect the final content of the forthcoming edition.

Library of Congress Cataloging-in-Publication Data
Turtledove, Harry.
  Hitler's war / Harry Turtledove.
    p.   cm.
  ISBN 978-0-345-49183-1
  1. World War, 1939–1945—Fiction. I. Title.
  PS3570.U76H58 2009
  813'.54—dc22   2009021287

Printed in the United States of America

www.delreybooks.com

9 8 7 6 5 4

Book Design by Mia Risberg

Hitler's War

Chapter 1

General José Sanjurjo was a short, heavyset man in his early sixties. He looked from the light plane to the pilot and back again. "Is everything in readiness?" he asked, his tone saying heads would roll if the pilot told him no.

Major Juan Antonio Ansaldo didn't tell him anything, not right away. Ansaldo was pacing back and forth, his agitation growing with every stride. He watched as Sanjurjo's aides shoved two large, heavy trunks into the airplane. "Those look heavy," Ansaldo said at last.

"They hold the general's uniforms!" an aide said, as if to a simpleton. "On the eve of his victorious march into Madrid, he can't arrive in Burgos without uniforms!"

Nervously, Ansaldo lit a cigarette. Who was he, a major, to tell Spain's most senior—and most prestigious—general what to do? He'd placed himself at the disposal of the Spanish state . . . which Sanjurjo would embody, once he flew from Portugal to Burgos to take charge of the rising against the Spanish Republic.

When he flew to Burgos? If he flew to Burgos! The city, in north-central Spain, was a long way from Lisbon. The plane, a two-seater, had only so much fuel and only so strong a motor.

"General . . ." Ansaldo said.

"What is it?" growled the man people called the Lion of the Rif because of his victories in Spanish Morocco.

"*¡Viva* Sanjurjo!" the general's men shouted. "*¡Viva España!*"

Sanjurjo preened . . . as well as a short, heavyset man in his sixties could preen. "Now I know my flag is waving over Spain," he boomed like a courting grouse. "When I hear the Royal March again, I will be ready to die!"

That gave Major Ansaldo the opening he needed. "General, I don't want you to die before you get to Spain, before you hear the Royal March again."

"What are you talking about?" Sanjurjo demanded.

"Sir, those trunks your men put aboard—"

"What about them? They're my uniforms, as my aides told you. A man is hardly a man without his uniforms." At the moment, Sanjurjo was wearing a light gray summer-weight civilian suit. He looked and acted quite manly enough for Ansaldo.

"They weigh a lot." The pilot gestured. "Look at the pine trees all around the airstrip. I need the plane's full power to take off. I have to make sure I have enough fuel to fly you to Burgos. I don't want anything to happen to you, *Señor*. Spain needs you too much to take chances."

General Sanjurjo frowned—not fearsomely, but thoughtfully. "I can't fly into Burgos like this." He brushed at the gray linen of his sleeve.

"Why not, your Excellency? Why not?" Ansaldo asked. "Don't you think the people of Burgos would be delighted—would be honored—to give you anything you need? Aren't there any uniforms in Burgos? God help the rising if that's true!"

"God help the rising." Sanjurjo crossed himself. Major Ansaldo followed suit. The general took a gold case from an inside jacket pocket and lit a cigarette of his own. He smoked in abrupt, savage drags. "So you think we'll crash with my uniforms on board, do you?"

"When you're flying, you never know," the pilot answered. "That's why you don't want to take any chances you don't have to."

Sanjurjo grunted. He took a couple of more puffs on the aromatic Turkish cigarette, then ground it out under his heel. "Luis! Orlando!" he called. "Get the trunks off the plane!"

His aides stared as if they couldn't believe their ears. "Are you sure, your Excellency?" one of them asked.

"Of course I'm sure, dammit." By the way José Sanjurjo spoke, he was *always* sure. And so he probably was. "Spain comes first, and Spain needs me more than I need my uniforms. As the pilot here says, there are many uniforms. *Por Dios, amigos,* there is only one Sanjurjo!" The general struck a pose.

The aides didn't argue any more. They did what Sanjurjo told them to do. Wrestling the trunks out of the plane's narrow fuselage proved harder than stuffing them in had been. It took a lot of bad language and help from three other men before they managed it.

Major Ansaldo wondered how many kilos he'd saved. Fifty? A hundred? He didn't know, and he never would—no scale was close by. But now he would fly with the kind of load the light plane was made to carry. He liked that.

"If your Excellency will take the right-hand seat . . ." he said.

"Certainly." Sanjurjo was as spry as a man of half his age and half his bulk.

After Ansaldo started the motor, he ran through the usual flight checks. Everything looked good. He gave the plane all the throttle he could. He needed to get up quickly, to clear the trees beyond the far edge of the bumpy field.

When he pulled back on the stick, the nose lifted. The fixed undercarriage left the ground. The bumping stopped. The air, for the moment, was smooth as fine brandy. A slow smile spread across General Sanjurjo's face. "Do you know what this is, Major?" he said. "A miracle, that's what! To fly like a bird, like an angel . . ."

"It's only an airplane, sir," said Ansaldo, as matter-of-fact as any pilot worth his pay.

"Only an airplane!" Sanjurjo's eyebrows leaped. "And a woman is only a woman! It is an airplane that takes me out of exile, an airplane that takes me out of Portugal, an airplane that takes me away from the hisses and sneezes and coughs of Portuguese. . . ."

"*Sí, Señor.*" Major Ansaldo knew how the general felt there. If a Spaniard and a Portuguese spoke slowly and clearly, or if they wrote things out, they could generally manage to understand each other. But Portuguese always sounded funny—sounded *wrong*—in a Spaniard's ears. The reverse was also bound to be true, but the pilot never once thought of that.

And his important passenger hadn't finished: "It is an airplane that takes me back to Spain, back to my country—and Spain will be *my* country once we settle with the Republican rabble. It is—what does Matthew say?—a pearl of great price." He crossed himself again.

So did Juan Antonio Ansaldo. "You have the soul of a poet, your Excellency," he said. General Sanjurjo smiled like a cat in front of a pitcher of cream. Ansaldo did, too, but only to himself; a little judicious flattery, especially flattery from an unexpected direction, never hurt. But he also had a serious point to make: "I'm glad you chose not to endanger the plane—and yourself, a more valuable pearl—with those trunks. Spain needs you."

"Well, yes," Sanjurjo agreed complacently. "Who would command the forces of the right, the forces of truth, against the atheists and Communists and liberals in the Republic if anything happened to me? Millán Astray?"

"I don't think so, sir!" Ansaldo exclaimed, and that wasn't flattery.

Astray, the founder of the Spanish Foreign Legion, was a very brave man. Colonial fighting had cost him an arm and an eye. He still led the Legion, whose war cry was *"¡Viva la muerte!"*—Long live death! Men like that were valuable in the officer corps, but who would want such a skeletal fanatic leading a country?

"*Bueno.* I don't think so, either." Yes, Sanjurjo sounded complacent, all right. And why not, when he held the rising in the palm of his hand? He couldn't resist throwing out the name of another possible replacement: "Or what about General Franco?"

"Not likely, your Excellency!" Again, Major Ansaldo meant what he said. No one had ever questioned Francisco Franco's courage, either, even if he wasn't so showy about displaying it as Millán Astray was. But the plump little general was no great leader of men. With Sanjurjo's personality, he could stand beside—could, at need, stand up to—Mussolini and Hitler. Franco? Franco had all the warmth, all the excitement, of a canceled postage stamp.

"No, not likely at all," General Sanjurjo said. "Once I get to Burgos, the true business of setting Spain to rights can begin."

"*Sí, Señor,*" Ansaldo said once more. The light plane droned on: toward Spain, toward Burgos, toward victory, toward the birth of a whole new world.

29 SEPTEMBER 1938—MUNICH

Adolf Hitler was not a happy man. Oh, yes, he was going to get Czechoslovakia. The British and French had come here to hand him his hateful neighbor—what an abortion of a country! one more crime of Versailles!—all trussed up on a silver platter, ready for the slaughter.

But, for all the fuss the Sudeten Germans had kicked up inside Czechoslovakia (fuss orchestrated from the *Reich*), to Hitler the Slavic state wasn't an end in itself, only a means to an end. The end was dominating Europe. Had that required dropping the Sudeten German Party he'd fed and watered for so long, he would have dropped it like a live grenade.

Getting his hands on Czechoslovakia would be nice, yes. What he really wanted, though, was war.

He was ready. He was convinced the enemy wasn't. Chamberlain and Daladier wouldn't have been so pathetically eager to sell their ally down the river if they were.

The trouble was, they were *too* damned eager. They kept falling all over themselves to make whatever concessions he demanded. The more they yielded, the less excuse he had to send in the *Wehrmacht*.

His generals would be relieved if he got what he wanted without fighting. He wasn't happy with the halfhearted way so many of them were readying themselves and their units. And Mussolini, while a good fellow, had more chin than balls. The *Duce* kept insisting Italy wasn't ready to take on England and France, and wouldn't be for another two or three years.

"*Dummkopf,*" Hitler muttered under his breath. The real point, the point Mussolini didn't get, was that *England and France* weren't ready. Not only did they not want war, their factories weren't geared up for it. And the Russians were in even worse shape. Every day, it seemed, Stalin knocked off a new general, or a handful of them. When the Reds laid on a purge, they didn't fool around.

General Sanjurjo got it. Spain stood foursquare behind Germany. Well, actually, Spain stood about two-and-a-half-square behind Germany; the Communists and anarchists of the Republic still hung on to the rest of the battered country. But Sanjurjo had a proper Spanish sense of honor and obligation. He would do what he could against his benefactor's enemies.

The time was *now*. The *Führer* could feel it in his bones. Of all the gifts a great ruler had, knowing when to strike was one of the most vital.

He'd shown he had it when he got rid of Ernst Röhm in the Night of Long Knives, and again when he swallowed Austria in the *Anschluss.* (Oh, all right—the Beer-Hall *Putsch* hadn't quite worked out. But that was fifteen years ago now. Back in those days, he was still learning which end was up.)

He was ready to fight. The *Wehrmacht* and the *Luftwaffe* were ready, even if some generals tried dragging their feet. Even if the French and English did declare war when he hit Czechoslovakia, he was sure they wouldn't do anything much in the West. They'd wait, they'd dither . . . and then, as soon as he'd stomped the Czechs into the mud, he'd turn around and smash them, too.

Yes, he was ready. But tall, stork-necked Chamberlain—with Daladier scuttling along in his wake like a squat, swarthy little half-trained puppy—was also ready: ready to hand him Czechoslovakia without any fighting at all. The British Prime Minister was so abject about the whole business, even the hard-bitten *Führer* would have been embarrassed to order the panzers to roll forward and the bombers to take off. Chamberlain, damn his gawky soul, gave away so much, Hitler couldn't very well demand more. There was no more to give.

And so they played out the charade here in Munich. Hitler and Mussolini, Chamberlain and Daladier sat down together and calmly arranged for the transfer of the Sudetenland—and its mountain barriers and its fortifications, second only to those of the Maginot Line— from Czechoslovakia to Germany. Without those works, the Czechs hadn't a prayer of being able to fight.

They knew it, too. They'd sent a couple of nervous observers to Munich to learn their fate. The Czechs cooled their heels at a distant hotel; the *Führer* wouldn't let them attend the conference. The Soviet Union was similarly excluded.

On with the farce, then. The *Führerbau* was the National Socialists' chief office building in Munich. Hitler had taken a major role in its design, but it wasn't a full success. A hundred yards long and fifty deep, it was only three stories high. To an uncharitable observer, it looked like nothing so much as an overgrown barracks hall.

Nevertheless, Hitler thought the big bronze eagle over the entryway particularly fine. Mussolini, Chamberlain, and Daladier were already there by the time the *Führer* and the interpreter, Paul Otto Schmidt, came in. So was Göring, in a fancy white uniform—he'd motored in with Daladier.

The *Duce* spoke with Chamberlain in English and Daladier in French. He spoke German, too, after a fashion. Hitler, who knew only his own language, envied his fellow dictator's linguistic skills. He consoled himself by noting how plain the handful of British and French aides in civilian clothes appeared in contrast to his uniformed henchmen, and Mussolini's.

Hitler led the heads of government into his office. The big oblong room had a fireplace at one end, with a portrait of Bismarck above it. Light-colored chairs and a matching sofa faced the fireplace. There were no name tags—not even any pads and pencils for taking notes. There was no agenda. Discussion darted where it would. Everyone already had a good notion of how things would end up.

"Now that we are all here, we must decide soon," Hitler said, and smacked one fist into the palm of the other hand.

But things moved more slowly than he wanted them to. The heads of the two leading democracies had to get their views on record. The *Führer* supposed that was for domestic consumption. It wouldn't change anything here.

His temper began to fray. "You know nothing of the dreadful tyranny the Czechs exert over the Sudeten Germans," he said loudly. "Nothing, I tell you! They torture them, showing no mercy. They expel them by the thousands, in panic-stricken herds. They have even forced the Sudeten Germans' leader, Konrad Henlein, to flee from his native land."

"One jump ahead of the gendarmes, I shouldn't wonder," Daladier said dryly.

"Joke if you care to, but I—" Hitler stopped in surprise at a loud knock on the door.

"What's going on?" Neville Chamberlain asked.

"I don't know," Hitler answered after Dr. Schmidt translated the question. "I left clear orders that we were not to be disturbed." When he gave orders like that, he expected them to be obeyed, too.

But, even for the *Führer,* expectations didn't always match reality. The knock came again, louder and more insistent than before. Hitler sprang to his feet and hurried toward the door. Somebody out there in the hallway was going to regret being born.

"Whatever he's selling, tell him we don't want any," Mussolini said in his inimitable German. Daladier and Chamberlain both smiled once the interpreters made them understand the crack. Hitler didn't. He'd never had much of a sense of humor, and the interruption pushed him towards one of his volcanic eruptions of fury.

He flung the door open. There stood Colonel Friedrich Hossbach, his adjutant. "Well?" Hitler growled ominously. "What is the meaning of this—this interruption?"

Hossbach was a stoic man on the far end of middle age. "I'm sorry to bother you, *mein Führer,* but—"

"But what?" Hitler demanded. "Whatever the devil it is, it had better be important."

"Yes, sir. I believe it is." Hossbach took a sheet of flimsy yellow paper from his left breast pocket. "Here is a telegram we have just received. You will know *Herr* Henlein has had to take refuge in the *Reich* because of Czech outrages. . . ."

"Of course, of course," the *Führer* said impatiently. "I was just now talking about his plight, as a matter of fact. What's going on with him?"

Colonel Hossbach licked his lips. "Sir, he has been shot. Shot dead, I should say. The murderer is in custody. He is a certain Jaroslav Stribny: a Czech, sir. His passport shows a Prague address."

Hitler stared at him in astonishment, disbelief, and then sudden crazy joy. "*Ich bin vom Himmel gefallen!*" he blurted. *I've fallen from heaven!* was what the words meant literally, but what they really conveyed was his utter amazement.

"What shall we do, *mein Führer*?" Hossbach asked nervously.

A moment later, it was his turn to be amazed, because Hitler bussed him on both cheeks like a Frenchman. "Leave that to me, my dear Hossbach," he answered. "Oh, yes. Leave that to me!"

He was almost chortling as he turned back to the statesmen and officials and interpreters inside his office. He'd thought about getting rid of Henlein to give himself a *casus belli* against Czechoslovakia. He'd thought about it, yes, and put it aside. It would have been too raw, too unlikely, for anyone to swallow.

But *Herr* Jaroslav Stribny had just handed him that *casus belli* in a fancy package with a ribbon around it. The *Reich* would have to execute Stribny as a murderer. Hitler understood the need, and he'd never been shy about disposing of anyone who needed disposing of. All the same, what he wanted to do was pin a medal on Stribny's chest. Talk about advancing Germany's cause . . . !

"What is it, *Führer*?" Mussolini asked. "By the look in your eye, it is truly important, whatever it is."

"*Ja*," Hitler said, and the pause that followed gave him the chance to pull his thoughts together and figure out how best to use the extraordinary opportunity that had fallen into his lap. "Truly important, indeed. Colonel Hossbach brings me word that Konrad Henlein, whom I mentioned only a few minutes ago, has been viciously and brutally assassinated. Assassinated by one Jaroslav Stribny, of Prague. Not content with forcing him out of the Sudetenland, the Czechs followed him into Germany and finished him off here."

"*Dio mio!*" Mussolini exclaimed, eyes bulging in astonishment.

Dr. Schmidt translated for Chamberlain. Daladier had his own interpreter. The leaders of the two democracies gaped at the *Führer*. Chamberlain murmured something. Hitler looked sharply at Schmidt. "He says he can hardly believe it, *mein Führer*," the translator said.

"Well, I can hardly believe it, either," Hitler said. "I can hardly believe the perfidy of the Czech government, the perfidy of the whole Czech race, that has brought things to such a pass. You can surely see that we in the *Reich* did everything we could to be reasonable, to be generous, toward Czechoslovakia. But what thanks do we get? Murder! And I am afraid, gentlemen, that I see no choice but to avenge the insult with blood."

Edouard Daladier frowned. Hitler almost told him how ridiculous he looked, with a few long, pathetic strands of hair combed over a vast bald pate. "This seems too convenient for words," Daladier said. "Too convenient for you, too convenient for your aggression."

Hitler almost told him he hadn't rubbed out Henlein for just that reason. But, while he might have been so frank with Mussolini, whom he esteemed, he felt only contempt for the miserable little Frenchman. "Before God and before the spirit of history, I had nothing to do with it," he declared.

"*Monsieur* Daladier is right," Chamberlain said. "The advantage you gain from this almost surpasses belief."

"Believe whatever you please." No, Hitler hadn't arranged for Henlein's elimination. But he intended to use it. Oh, yes! Warming to his theme, he went on, "I have said all along that these Slavs are not to be trusted. I have said all along that they do not deserve nations of their own. Look what happened to Archduke Franz Ferdinand in 1914. Those murderous Serbian maniacs plunged a continent into war. And now the Slavs have done it again!"

"This need not be," Neville Chamberlain said urgently. "As a result of this most unfortunate incident, I am sure we can extract more concessions from Mr. Masarik and Mr. Mastny." The Foreign Ministry counselor and the Czech minister to Germany waited to hear what the great powers would decree for their country. The British Prime Minister continued, "And I do not see how the government of Czechoslovakia can fail to ratify whatever agreement we reach."

"No," Hitler said. "Not a soul can claim I was unwilling to meet you halfway, your Excellency. My thought all along was that Czechoslovakia deserved punishment for her arrogance and brutality. But I restrained myself. I convened this meeting at your request. You persuaded me the Czechs could be trusted far enough to make it worthwhile. In this we were both mistaken."

He paused to let Dr. Schmidt translate. Schmidt was an artist, keeping a speaker's tone as well as his meaning. Hitler's tone, at the moment, had iron in it. So did the interpreter's when he spoke English.

"You could overlook the enormity if you chose," Chamberlain insisted. When turning his words into German, Schmidt somehow sounded like a fussy old man. "Henlein was, after all, a citizen of Czechoslovakia, not of the German *Reich*—"

"*He was a German!*" Hitler thundered, loud and fierce enough to make every pair of eyes in the room turn his way. "He was a German!" he repeated, a little more softly. "That is the whole point of what we have been discussing. All the Germans of the Sudetenland belong within the *Reich*. Because the Czechs will not allow this and go on persecuting them, we see disasters like this latest one. I am very sorry, your Excellency, very sorry indeed, but, as I said, blood calls for blood. As soon as I leave this office, Germany will declare war on Czechoslovakia."

"May *Monsieur* Daladier and I have a few minutes to confer with each other?" Chamberlain asked, adding, "The situation has changed quite profoundly in the past few minutes, you understand."

Would they throw Czechoslovakia over the side because of what Stribny had done? If they would, Hitler was willing to give them as much time as they needed. Their turn would come next anyhow. "You may do as you please," the *Führer* said. "I must ask you to step outside to talk, though; as I said, I shall not leave the room without declaring war."

Chamberlain, Daladier, and their flunkies almost fell over one another in their haste to leave. As soon as they were gone, Mussolini asked, "Did you—?"

He left the question hanging, but Hitler knew what he meant. "*Nein,*" he said roughly. As he shook his head, a lock of hair flopped down over one eye. Impatiently, he pushed it back. "The Czechs did it themselves. They did it to themselves. And they will pay. By God, they *will* pay!"

"Italy still is not truly ready for this struggle," the *Duce* warned.

"When the Czechs murder the leader of an oppressed minority, will you let them get away with it?" Hitler asked in astonishment. Full of righteous indignation that the *Untermenschen* should dare such a thing, he forgot for the moment all his own murders.

"They shouldn't," Mussolini admitted. "Still, England and France and Russia . . ."

"Russia? What good is Russia?" Hitler said scornfully. "She doesn't even border Czechoslovakia. Do you think the Poles or the Romanians will let her ship soldiers across their territory? If she tries, we'll have two new allies like *that.*" He snapped his fingers.

"I suppose so. . . ." Mussolini still didn't sound convinced.

Hitler was ready to argue with him all day, but didn't get the chance. Chamberlain and Daladier returned to the office. Both heads of government looked thoroughly grim, their aides even grimmer. Daladier spoke for them: "I regret to have to say that, if Germany attacks Czechoslovakia, the French Republic and the United Kingdom will honor their commitments to their ally. We cannot believe that the murder of *Monsieur* Henlein is anything but a trumped-up provocation. Peace and war, then, lie entirely in your hands."

Hitler almost screamed wild laughter. He wanted war, yes. But to have the leaders of the democracies ready to fight him because they were sure he'd done something of which he was entirely innocent . . . If that wasn't irony, what was?

"I must tell you, you are making a dreadful mistake," he said. "That Czech, that Stribny, murdered *Herr* Henlein on his own. I had nothing to do with it. Germany had nothing to do with it. Henlein left Czechoslovakia and entered the *Reich* because he feared for his own safety. And now we see he had reason to fear. If anyone inspired Stribny, it was the wicked Slavs in Prague, just as the wicked Slavs in Belgrade inspired Gavrilo Princip a generation ago."

Every single word of that was the gospel truth. But it fell on deaf ears. He could tell as much even while Dr. Schmidt was translating. Chamberlain and Daladier had made up their minds. If he told them the sun was shining outside, they would call him a liar.

Chamberlain murmured something in English. "What did he say?" Hitler asked sharply.

"He said, 'And then you wake up,' *mein Führer*," Schmidt replied.

"What does that mean?"

"It's slang, sir. It means he doesn't believe you."

"*Donnerwetter!*" Hitler could see the Allies' propaganda mill spewing out endless lies. They would shout that he was a murderer, that he'd got rid of his own henchman to start a war. They would make him look bad to all the neutrals in Europe and Asia and the Americas. The Allies had trounced Germany and Austria-Hungary in the propaganda war during the World War. Now they had a great chance to do it again.

"If you are truly innocent of this crime, then do not assume the guilt of plunging the world into battle because of it," Daladier said.

"This is madness!" Hitler cried. "If I had ordered Henlein killed, maybe a guilty conscience would keep me from taking advantage of it. But my conscience is clean." *Of this, anyhow* he added, but only to himself. He got angrier by the word as he went on, "Konrad Henlein must have vengeance. The Sudeten Germans must have vengeance. Germany, to which they were about to return, must have vengeance. Czechoslovakia must be punished. If you want to line up behind a pack of skulking, cowardly assassins, go ahead—and be damned to you!"

"*Mein Führer*—" Göring began.

"No!" Hitler roared. He was in full spate now. Nothing could stop him, or even slow him down. "They want war? They can have war! They will have war! War! . . . War! War! War!"

He threw open the doors to his office. "Is everything all right, *mein Führer*?" one of the guards asked. "We could hear you shouting. . . ."

So even the thick oak doors hadn't muffled him? Well, too bad! "It is war!" he bellowed. "Colonel Hossbach!"

"*Ja, mein Führer?*" his adjutant said.

"Begin Case Green. Immediately! War with Czechoslovakia! Now!" Yes, Hitler had what he most wanted, handed to him by, of all people, a Czech.

GUNS THUNDERED ON BOTH SIDES of the Ebro. General Sanjurjo's Fascists had modern German and Italian pieces, guns that could put a shell on an outspread blanket five miles away. The Republic had a few Russian howitzers that weren't bad. The rest were the artillery pieces the Republicans had started the fight with. After more than two years of civil war, they kept only vestiges of their original rifling—and they weren't such hot stuff back when they were new.

Crouching in a foxhole west of the Ebro, Chaim Weinberg decided he feared his own side's guns more than the Fascists'. When the enemy Spaniards or their German advisers opened up, at least you had a good notion of what they were shooting at. If it wasn't you, you could relax.

But when the Republican artillery started shooting, you always needed to be on the jump. Those shells might come down on the Fascists' head . . . or they might come down on yours. You never could tell. Neither could the poor, sorry bastards firing the guns.

"Aren't you glad we came from the States?" asked Mike Carroll, another volunteer from the Lincoln Battalion.

Before Chaim could answer, somebody's shell burst much too close. Shrapnel and shards of shattered stone screamed through the air. He listened for shrieks, but didn't hear any. Luck. Nothing but dumb frigging luck.

"Aren't you?" Carroll persisted.

"*Chinga tu madre,*" Chaim told him. He wouldn't have said anything like that even in English before he sailed to Spain. Well, he was a new man now. That new man needed a shave (at the moment, he also needed a razor). He was scrawny and hungry. He was filthy. He was lousy. But damned if he wasn't new.

He'd never fired a rifle before he got to Spain. Hell, he'd never even handled a rifle. He could field-strip his Mauser blindfolded now. He'd started out with a crappy French piece, and got this much better German one off a dead Nationalist soldier. Keeping it in cartridges was a bitch. But keeping the French rifle in ammo would have been a bitch, too. Logistics was only a bitter joke to the Republicans.

The shelling went on, but none of the other rounds burst close enough to make him pucker. He lit a cigarette. The tobacco was allegedly French. It smelled like horseshit. It tasted the way he imagined smoldering horseshit would taste, too.

"*No pasarán,*" Mike said, and then, "Gimme one of those."

"Here." Chaim handed him the pack.

Mike took a smoke from it. He leaned close to Chaim to get it going. After his first drag, he made a face. "Boy, that's rotten."

"Uh-huh." Chaim held out his hand, palm up. Reluctantly, his buddy returned the cigarettes. Chaim stuck them back in the breast pocket of his ragged khaki tunic. "Only thing worse than rotten tobacco's no tobacco at all."

"No kidding," Mike said.

Chaim took a cautious look out of the trench. Nothing special was going on in the Nationalist lines a few hundred yards away—everybody here talked about meters, but they seemed like play money to him. The shelling was just . . . shelling. A few people on both sides would get maimed or killed, and it wouldn't move the war any closer to the end, not even a nickel's worth.

"*No pasarán,*" Chaim echoed. "They'd fucking better not pass, not here, or we're butcher's meat." He sucked in more smoke. "Hell, we're dead meat anyway, sooner or later. I still hope it's later, though."

"Yeah, me, too." Mike Carroll sounded like Boston. Before he came to Spain, he'd worked in a steel mill somewhere in Massachusetts. That was what he said, anyway. A lot of guys had stories that didn't add up. Chaim didn't get all hot and bothered about it. He didn't tell the whole truth and nothing but the truth about himself, either. The only thing that really mattered was that you hated Fascism enough to hop on a boat and try to do something about it.

"Amazing thing is, the Republic's still in there kicking," Chaim said. Mike nodded. General Sanjurjo and his pack of reactionary bastards must have thought their foes would fall apart in nothing flat. Who could have blamed them? They had the trained troops, and they had Mussolini and Hitler—which meant Italian and German matériel and soldiers—on their side.

But it didn't pan out that way. The brutal farce of noninterference kept the Republicans from getting munitions and reinforcements. Like the rest of the men in the Lincoln Battalion, Chaim and Mike had to sneak over the border from France, dodging patrols every step of the way. Russia sent arms and advisers, though not enough to offset what the Fascists fed Sanjurjo.

And the Republicans squabbled among themselves. Did they ever! Anarchists and Trotskyists didn't like admitting that, since Stalin was paying the piper, he could call the tune. They also complained that Communist units got the best weapons. Chaim was a Party member, even if he'd left his card in New York City when he sailed. Most (though not all) of the foreign volunteers—men from every corner of the Earth—were. But the Spaniards themselves did the bulk of the fighting and dying.

An airplane buzzed by overhead. Chaim automatically started to duck; German and Italian aircraft ruled the skies. But this was a Republican plane: a Russian biplane fighter. Its blunt forward profile made the Spaniards call it *Chato*—flat-nosed. It dove to shoot up the Nationalists' trenches, then scooted off to the east.

" 'Bout time those mothers caught it for a change," Mike said.

"Yeah," Chaim agreed doubtfully. "But now we'll get it twice as hard to make up, you know?" The Spaniards on both sides thought like that and fought like that. It made for a rugged kind of combat.

Mike started to answer. Before he could, a runner came up from the rear yelling, "War! War!"

Mike and Chaim started laughing like maniacs. "The fuck ya think we're in now?" Chaim said. "A ladies' sewing circle?"

"No, goddammit—a big war," the runner said. "The Munich giveaway just fell apart. A Czech murdered some Sudeten Nazi big shot inside Germany—that's what Hitler says, anyway. And he's gonna jump on Czechoslovakia, and England and France can't back down now. And if they get in, the Russians do, too."

"Holy Jesus!" Mike said. Chaim nodded. If the gloves came off in the rest of Europe, they'd have to come off in Spain, too . . . wouldn't they? No more noninterference? Hot damn! Maybe things here just evened up.

Chapter 2

Corporal Vaclav Jezek crouched in a hastily dug trench just in front of Troppau. If the Germans came—when they came—this was one of the places they'd hit hardest. Slice through here in the north, push through from what had been Austria till a few months ago down in the south, and you would bite Czechoslovakia in half. Then you could settle with the Czechs in Bohemia and Moravia—the important part of the country, as far as Vaclav was concerned—at your leisure.

The Czechoslovakian General Staff wasn't blind, or stupid. Some of the heaviest fortifications in the whole country lay along this stretch of the border. If Vaclav stood up in the trench, he could see them: big, rounded, squarish lumps of reinforced concrete that had good fields of fire from high ground and plugged valleys through which tanks might otherwise charge freely.

He didn't stand up. His khaki uniform and brown, bowl-shaped helmet offered good camouflage, but they weren't perfect. Somewhere on the other side of the border, some bastard in a field-gray uniform and a black coal-scuttle helmet would be sweeping the area with heavy-duty field glasses. Vaclav didn't want him marking this position.

Trucks and teams of horses rushed machine guns and cannon and ammunition to the Czechoslovak forts. Not all of them were done yet. The government hadn't really got serious about them till the *Anschluss*. But with Nazi troops in Austria, Czechoslovakia was surrounded on three sides. Without fortifications, it wouldn't last long. It might not last long with them, but they gave it the best—likely the only—chance it had.

Maybe the German with the field glasses wouldn't be able to see too much. It was cool and overcast, with a little mist in the air: autumn in Central Europe, sure as hell. But some of the Sudeten shitheads were bound to be sneaking over the border to tell their cousins on the other side what was going on here. If Vaclav ran the world, he would have shipped them out or shot them to nip that crap in the bud. But would the big shots listen to a corporal who drove a taxi in Prague before he got called up? Fat chance!

The air might be cool and moist, but he smelled burning bridges all the same. Diplomats were going home by plane and train. Armies that hadn't been mobilized were getting ready for the big plunge. The Poles, damn them, were concentrating opposite Teschen (spelled three different ways, depending on whether you were a German, a Czech, or a Pole). Didn't they see they were the next course on Hitler's menu? If they didn't, how stupid were they?

"Got a smoke on you, Corporal?" asked Jan Dzurinda, one of the soldiers in Vaclav's squad.

"Sure." Jezek held out the pack. Dzurinda took a cigarette, then waited expectantly for a light. With a small sigh, Vaclav struck a match.

Dzurinda leaned close and got the cigarette started. He took a deep drag, then blew out two perfect smoke rings. "Thanks a bunch. Much obliged."

"Any time," Vaclav said. Dzurinda puffed away without a care in the world, blowing more smoke rings. Just hearing his voice made Corporal Jezek worry. Jan was a Slovak, not a Czech. Czech and Slovak were brother languages, but they weren't the same. Czechs and Slovaks could tell what you were as soon as you opened your mouth.

And Czechs and Slovaks weren't the same, either. Czechs thought of Slovaks as hicks, rubes, country bumpkins. Before the World War, Slovakia had been in the Hungarian half of Austria-Hungary, and the Hungarians made a point of keeping the Slovaks ignorant and down on the farm. Things had changed since 1918, but only so much. The Czechoslovakian Army had something like 140 general officers. Just one was a Slovak.

If Slovaks were rubes to Czechs, Czechs were city slickers to Slovaks. A lot of Slovaks thought the Czechs, who were twice as numerous, ran Czechoslovakia for their own benefit. They thought Slovakia got hind tit, and wanted more autonomy—maybe outright independence— for it.

Vaclav had no idea whether Jan belonged to Father Hlinka's Slovak People's Party, the main nationalist outfit. Hlinka had died six weeks before, but another cleric, Father Tiso, was heading the party now. The Nazis had brownshirts; the Slovak People's Party had Hlinka Guards.

If the shooting started, how hard would Jan Dzurinda and thousands more like him fight for Czechoslovakia? A lot of Slovak People's Party men figured Berlin would give them what they wanted if Prague didn't. If you thought that way, how loyal would you be toward your nominal country?

Since Vaclav didn't know and didn't want to ask straight out, he lit a cigarette of his own. The harsh smoke relaxed him . . . a little. He said, "At least we've weeded most of the Germans out of the Army." The Sudetens damn well *weren't* loyal. They'd made that plain enough.

"Well, sure," Jan Dzurinda said, which might mean anything or nothing.

Corporal Jezek decided to push a little harder. If the Slovaks were going to run off or give up first chance they got, how could the army hope to defend Czechoslovakia? The noncom said, "Now we have to run off the buggers on the other side of the frontier, eh?"

"Reckon so." Dammit, Dzurinda *did* sound like a hick. He went on, "Anybody tries to shoot me, I expect I better nail him first."

"Sounds good to me." Jezek decided he had to be content with that. He could have heard plenty worse from a Slovak. Up and down the lines, how many worried Czech noncoms and lieutenants and captains *were* hearing worse from Slovaks right about now? How many who weren't hearing worse were being lied to? He muttered to himself and lit another cigarette and wished his canteen held something stronger than water.

"FORWARD!" SERGEANT LUDWIG ROTHE CALLED softly. He laughed at himself as the Panzer II crawled toward the start line through the darkness of the wee small hours. With all the motors belching and farting around him, he could have yelled his head off without giving himself away to the Czechs on the other side of the border.

He rode head and shoulders out of the turret. He had to, if he wanted to see where he was going. They said later models of the Panzer II would boast a cupola with episcopes so the commander could look around without risking his life whenever he did. That didn't do him any good. All he had was a two-flapped steel hatch in the top of the turret.

Engineers had set up white tapes to guide panzers and personnel carriers to their assigned jumping-off points. The whole Third Panzer Division was on the move. Hell, the whole *Wehrmacht* was on the move, near enough. Oh, there were covering forces on the border with France, and smaller ones on the Polish frontier and inside East Prussia, but everything that mattered was going to teach the Czechs they couldn't mess around with good Germans unlucky enough to be stuck inside their lousy country.

Other panzers—more IIs and the smaller Panzer Is—were dim shapes in the night. Ludwig affectionately patted his machine. The Panzer II was a great improvement over the I.

The driver's voice floated out through the speaking tube: "Kinda hate to leave Katscher. Found this little waitress there—she doesn't know how to say no."

"Jesus, Fritz!" Rothe said. "D'you pass shortarm inspection?"

Fritz Bittenfeld chuckled. "Doesn't hurt when I piss, so I guess everything's all right."

"Wonderful," the panzer commander muttered. Fritz only laughed. The third member of the crew—the radio operator, Theo Kessler—sat in the back of the fighting compartment. The only way he could see out was through peepholes. Ludwig wasn't sure whether he couldn't hear the conversation or just ignored it. But then, he wasn't sure about Theo a lot of the time.

"Halt!" The command floated out of the night. Rothe relayed it to Bittenfeld, who was driving buttoned up. The panzer stopped. They were where they were supposed to be . . . unless some Czech infiltrator was screwing them over. Rothe shook his head. Natural to be nervous before the balloon went up, but that was pushing things.

Nothing left to do but wait. Ludwig pushed back the sleeve of his black panzer coveralls to get a look at the radium-glowing hands on his watch. A quarter to four. Right on time. Everything was supposed to start at 0600. That gave him something else to worry about. It would still be almost dark. If the clouds overhead lingered, it might really be dark.

And if the clouds lingered, the *Luftwaffe* wouldn't be able to do as much as it was supposed to. How could you see what to bomb and shoot up if low clouds and fog blotted out the landscape?

This kind of weather was normal for this time of year. Ludwig hoped the fellows with the General Staff's red stripes on their trousers knew what the hell they were up to. If they didn't, a lot of good *Landers* would get buried in makeshift graves with only a rifle and a helmet for a headstone.

As if picking that thought out of his head, Fritz said, "The *Führer* knows what he's doing. Those dirty Czechs, they deserve everything we'll give 'em. They can't go murdering people inside Germany."

"Sure," Ludwig said. He thought the Czechs had a lot of nerve bumping off Konrad Henlein, too. But he was fretting about how much the *Wehrmacht* would take, not what it would dish out.

Again, Theo didn't say a thing. Well, he didn't have a speaking tube to Fritz. And he'd been wearing his earphones. Rothe wondered why. Radio silence was bound to be tighter than Fritz's waitress' works. The only signal that might come was one calling everything off because peace had broken out. The panzer commander didn't expect that. Nobody else did, either.

Ludwig looked at his watch again. 0400. At this rate, he'd feel as if he'd aged a year before things started happening. He couldn't even smoke. Somebody out there would skin him alive if he showed a match. And you had to be even more desperate for a butt than he was to light up inside the turret, what with all the ammo in there. Nothing to do but wait and fidget.

As 0600 neared, the sky slowly began to get light. A few minutes before the hour, he thought he heard thunder in the air. Then he realized it was nothing of the sort: it was untold hundreds or thousands of airplane engines, all of them roaring toward Czechoslovakia.

Fritz heard them, too. You'd have to be deaf not to. "Boy, those Czech assholes are really gonna catch it," he said happily.

"*Ja*," Ludwig said, and let it go at that.

Behind them, artillery started bellowing. Red flares leaped into the sky—the go signal! Without waiting for an order, Fritz put the Panzer II in gear and started forward. Other panzers were heading for the bor-der—heading over the border—too. Half-seen German soldiers trotted along with them, clutching Mausers and hunching low to make them-selves smaller targets.

A shell burst a couple of hundred meters away. Maybe it was a short round. More likely, it was the goddamn Czechs shooting back. Dirt and a couple of men flew up into the air. *Poor bastards,* Ludwig thought. He wondered what would happen if a 75 or a 105 hit his panzer. Then he wished he hadn't.

More shells fell on the Germans. He'd thought the opening bom-bardment would silence the enemy guns. Evidently not. One shell did hit a little Panzer I. It slewed sideways and started to burn. Machine-gun ammunition inside started cooking off—*pop-pop-pop!* It sounded ab-surdly cheerful.

Somebody in a khaki uniform—almost brown, really—popped up from a hole in the ground and fired at the Germans. They were over the border, then. Ludwig traversed the turret and squeezed off a burst of machine-gun fire at the Czech soldier. He didn't know whether he hit the man. If he made him duck and stop shooting, that would do.

Things inside Czechoslovakia didn't look much different from the way they did on the German side of the line. The terrain was rugged. One reason the Czechs didn't want to give back the Sudetenland was that the rough ground and the forts they'd built in it gave them their best shield against attack. Best or not, it wouldn't be good enough . . . Ludwig hoped.

The panzer clanked past a house. It looked like the ones inside the *Reich,* too. Well, why not? Germans were Germans, on that side of the frontier or on this one. Past the house was a forest. Ludwig thought it seemed wilder than woods in Germany would have. The Czechs proba-bly didn't care for it the way they should.

Or maybe they wanted it all jungly and overgrown. A machine gun in there started spraying death at the German infantry. When a bullet cracked past Ludwig's ear, he realized that machine gun could kill him, too. He ducked reflexively. He almost pissed himself. The Czechs were playing for keeps, all right.

They had more than machine guns in the woods, too. An antitank gun spat a long tongue of flame. A Panzer II just like Ludwig's caught fire. A perfect smoke ring came out through the commander's hatch. Ludwig didn't see any of the crew get away.

"Do we go into that, Sergeant?" Fritz asked.

Ludwig understood why he hesitated. Open country was best for panzers. Out on the plains and meadows, you could see trouble coming. But somebody'd forgotten to issue a whole lot of plains and meadows to this part of Czechoslovakia. "Yes, we do," Rothe answered. "Our job is to smash through their defensive lines. Once we do that, the rest of the country falls into our lap."

"If they don't blow our balls off first." That wasn't Fritz; it was Theo. So the radioman was listening after all. Ludwig would have come down on him for sounding defeatist if he weren't so likely to be right.

Into the woods. Other panzers were pushing forward, too. Things were better—or seemed better, anyhow—when you had company. There was, of course, the saying about misery.

A bullet struck sparks as it spanged off the panzer's hull. That left Ludwig with a couple of really unpleasant choices. If he stayed where he was, he was much too likely to get shot. But if he ducked down inside the turret and shut the hatch, he would have the devil's own time seeing where he was going. All kinds of bad things were liable to happen to the panzer then.

He stayed where he was. Every so often, he fired a short burst from his machine gun. The other panzer commanders were doing the same thing. Foot soldiers banged away, too. With enough lead in the air, the Czechs would be too busy taking cover and dying to shoot back much.

He hoped. Boy, did he!

The Panzer II emerged from the woods onto open ground that had taken a beating from bombs and artillery. As soon as it did, Ludwig wished it hadn't, because there sat a Panzer I, burning like nobody's business. The commander had tried to get out of the turret, but he hadn't made it. Something nasty lurked in the next stretch of trees.

"There it is!" Fritz screamed. "One o'clock! Panzer! Goddamn Czech panzer!"

The Czech LT-35 was a light tank, as its initials suggested. It was still bigger and heavier and better armored than a Panzer II. And the bastard carried a 37mm gun: a real cannon that could fire a real HE round as well as armor-piercing ammo. The Panzer II's 2cm main armament had decent AP rounds, but they just weren't big enough to carry a useful amount of high explosive.

One good thing about the Panzer II's little gun, though: it was an automatic weapon, firing from ten-round magazines. Ludwig traversed the turret toward the LT-35, all the while wishing for a power assist. He'd just about brought the gun on target when the Czechs fired. Their AP round chewed a groove in the field a few meters to his left. They'd be reloading as fast as they could. . . .

His 2.5X sight brought the target a lot closer. The trigger was on the elevating wheel. He squeezed off a four-round burst. Smoke rose from the Czech tank. "Hit!" Fritz yelled. "You hit the son of a bitch!"

"Do you have to sound so surprised?" Actually, Ludwig was surprised he'd hit the panzer at all. The gun was noisy enough to make him glad he was sober. "Come on—put the beast back in gear. We don't want to hang around in one spot, or some other bastard'll draw a bead on us."

He breathed a sigh of relief as the panzer raced toward the cover of the woods. He hadn't wanted to go into the first belt, but he'd discovered being out in the open was dangerous, too. It was a war, for Christ's sake. Everything was dangerous. He just hoped it would be more dangerous for the Czechs.

BOMBS STARTED FALLING ON MARIANSKE LAZNE—Marienbad, if you liked the old German name better—at six o'clock in the morning. Peggy Druce hadn't gone to bed till three. Just because you were here to take the waters (which smelled like rotten eggs, tasted almost as bad, and kept you on the pot like you wouldn't believe) didn't mean you couldn't do other things, too. Peggy'd been playing fiery bridge with an English couple and a young man who might have come from almost anywhere.

Everyone thought she was crazy for coming over from Philadelphia with the war clouds thickening by the day. Even after Henlein got shot, she'd pooh-poohed the idea that things would actually go boom. "We already had one war this century," she'd said. She remembered very precisely, because she was squeezing every trick from a small slam in diamonds. "Wasn't that enough to teach the whole world we don't need another one?"

Well . . . no.

The first explosions might almost have been mistaken for thunder. The couple right after that burst much too close to the Balmoral-Osborne Hotel de Luxe to leave any doubt about what they were. They knocked Peggy out of bed and onto the floor with a bump and a squawk. She said something most unladylike when she scrambled up again, because she'd cut both feet on shards of glass that hadn't been there a moment before.

People were yelling and screaming and—probably—jumping up and down. Peggy threw a robe over her silk peignoir. She made as if to rush for the door, then caught herself. Her feet would be raw meat and gore if she tried. The only shoes she could grab in a hurry were last night's heels. They'd have to do.

Out she went—but not without her handbag, which held passport and cash and traveler's checks. Everybody else in the hall was in the same state of dishabille. People dashed for the elevator: the lift, everyone called it here, in the English fashion. Peggy was almost there when the lights went out.

Shrieks filled the air as darkness descended. She turned around and went the other way, against the confused tide. If the lights weren't working, the goddamn elevator wouldn't, either. The stairs were . . . that way.

Peggy liked to think she looked ten years younger than her forty-five. She hadn't put on weight, and peroxide kept her hair about the same color it had always been. But, in spite of her misplaced optimism the night before, she had a coldly practical streak. When she was Peggy Eubank, growing up a devil of a long way from the Main Line, her mother told her, "Kid, you're eleven going on twenty-one." If Mom had been half as smart as she thought she was, she would've been twice as smart as she really was. But she'd hit that nail right on the head.

And so—the stairs. Peggy found the door as much by Braille as any other way. The stairwell wasn't very light, either. Somebody bumped into her and said, *"Excusez-moi."*

"Don't worry about it," Peggy said, and then, *"C'est la guerre."* And wasn't that the sad and sorry truth?

Gray early-morning light spilled out of the door that led to the lobby. Three flights of stairs had made Peggy's feet start to hurt, but more broken glass crunched under her soles. She would hurt worse if she took off the heels.

The lobby looked like hell, and smelled pretty bad, too. It reminded her of a butcher's shop with a whole bunch of fresh meat. Some of this meat came in trousers and dresses and nightclothes, though. Stewards and bellhops—they had different titles here, but basically the same jobs—were doing what they could to help the wounded. One of them was noisily sick on the floor, which only made the stink worse.

And, in what looked at first like a scene from a Three Stooges two-reeler, a couple of men near the front desk were punching and kicking each other and poking each other in the eye. Even with more bombs going off not terribly far away, they went at it hammer and tongs. But one of them swore in Czech, the other in guttural German. The big war had started, and so had their own little private one.

"*Mon Dieu!*" exclaimed a man standing next to Peggy. His voice said he was the fellow who'd bumped her on the stairs. "*C'est*—" He broke off, at a loss for words.

"It's hell on wheels," Peggy said. "You understand? *Comprenez?*"

"Yes. But what am I to do?" He spoke good British English. "I was for two years a prisoner in the last war. If the *Boches* come here, they will intern me again, as an enemy alien. I do not wish this at all."

If the Germans came to Marianske Lazne? No, *when* they came. The border wasn't more than a long spit to the west. Peggy had her passport. The United States was neutral. The Nazis would treat her better than that poor Frenchman . . . if they or the Czechs didn't blow her to the moon while they were bashing each other over the head. Right this minute, that looked like a pretty big if.

"Maybe you can get a train out of town if you hustle," she said.

"It could be, *Mademoiselle*," he said, not noticing the ring on her finger. Herb was still in Philadelphia. He'd been set to join her in Paris in a couple of weeks. Well, *that* wouldn't happen now. All kinds of things wouldn't happen, and all kinds of worse ones would. The man went on, "Will you accompany me? This is no more—no longer—a good place to be."

He was dead right—no, live right—about that. "Let's go," Peggy said.

As soon as she got her first look at a bomb crater, she wasn't sure outside was the best place to be. Marianske Lazne sat in a valley with pines and firs all around. The hotels and other buildings were mostly Austro-Hungarian leftovers from before the war (*before the last war,* she thought). They had more architectural gingerbread than the wicked witch's house in the Grimm fairy tale.

Right now, Peggy was trapped in a grim fairy tale of her own. Some of those buildings had chunks bitten out of them. Several were burning. Wounded people, bodies, and pieces of bodies lay in the streets. And everybody who wasn't wounded or blown to bits seemed to be running toward the train stations.

All kinds of people took the waters here. Some were ordinary Czechs and Slovaks. Some were Germans. Some came from other European countries. Peggy spotted half a dozen Jews in long black coats and wide-brimmed black hats. If the Frenchman beside her didn't want to deal with the Germans, they *really* didn't want to—and who could blame them?

There was a shriek in the air, getting louder by the moment. The Frenchman knocked her down and lay flat on top of her. She started to scream. Then more explosions shook Marianske Lazne, and she realized he hadn't gone mad and wasn't trying to assault her right out in the middle of the street.

"Artillery!" he bawled in her ear. "When you hear that sound, for God's sake *get down!*"

Peggy did scream then, but on a note different from the one she might have used a moment earlier. Through the shell bursts she heard more shrieks, men's and women's and Lord only knew whose. Something warm and wet and sticky splashed her hand. She looked at it. It was blood—not hers, or she didn't think so. With a little disgusted cry, she wiped it off her robe. No, not hers: no more welled out.

More and more shells landed on and around Marianske Lazne. How many guns did the Germans have, anyway? "Make it stop!" she yelled to the Frenchman. "Jesus, make it stop!"

"I wish I could, *Mademoiselle*," he replied.

Peggy heard guns going off, too, in the woods around the spas. The Czechs were making a fight of it, anyhow, or trying to. But Marianske Lazne was within artillery range of the border, as she knew much, much too well. How long could this little country hold off Hitler's armored legions?

After what seemed forever, the bombardment eased. Peggy raised her head and looked around. She wished she hadn't. Her husband had fought in the Great War. He'd never talked much about what he'd done and what he'd seen. If it was anything like this . . . Peggy understood why not. She would spend the rest of her life wishing she could forget what artillery did to the civilians in Marianske Lazne. She remembered one thing Herb had said, talking to someone else who'd seen the elephant: "Artillery—that's the killer." Jesus, he wasn't kidding.

As politely as she could, she tapped the Frenchman on top of her on the shoulder. "Could you move, please? You're squashing me." He had to weigh close to 200 pounds, and there was nothing between her and the sidewalk but two layers of silk.

"I do apologize," he said, and rolled to one side. "This is . . . very bad. Very, very bad. But if you hear that sound in the air, you must get down at once, without hesitation. It is your best chance to save yourself."

"God forbid I ever hear it again," Peggy said. The Frenchman crossed himself.

No trains went out. No trains came in. Maybe the Germans had bombed the tracks. Maybe Czechoslovakia was using the railroads to haul troops around. Peggy saw no dun-colored Czech uniforms in town. Every so often, though, the guns in the woods boomed. What kind of forts lay between the border and Marianske Lazne? How long would the Germans take to break through them. Two good questions. Peggy had no good answers.

The town was full of clinics. They weren't equipped for carnage like this, but they did their best. Unhurt people did what they could for the wounded. Peggy carried stretcher after stretcher. She got more blood on her robe, but hardly noticed. The hotels set out the usual massive spread of cold cuts for breakfast. She ate . . . somewhere.

About ten o'clock, the mist retreated and a wan sun came out. Airplane motors throbbed overhead. Peggy looked up. She'd never seen anything like those ungainly vulture-winged planes before. One after another, they peeled off in dives. It was fascinating to watch. But the shrieks they let out as they dove reminded her of incoming artillery. She got down, as the polite but portly Frenchman had said she should.

People gave her funny looks—for a few seconds, till the first bomb went off and the vulture-winged planes started machine-gunning the town as they zoomed away.

Half a dozen Czech biplane fighters showed up then. They looked like last year's models next to the vulture-winged jobs with the swastikas on their tails, but they shot down two of them. Peggy wasn't the only one cheering her head off.

She went on lugging stretchers till her feet started to bleed. Somebody gave her a pair of flats. They were too big, but still an improvement. She moved more casualties, and more, and more yet.

By midafternoon, she heard small-arms fire off to the west. It kept getting closer. She feared she knew what that meant: the Germans were pushing the Czechs back. She spotted more of the Nazi dive-bombers. Now that they'd delivered their terror message, they were doing serious work, pounding Czech positions.

The hotels kept putting out food. It was about all they could do. One displayed a sign in several languages: WE HAVE LOCKED UP OUR GERMANS. That was brave. It might also have been stupid. If the Nazis rolled into town, they wouldn't be happy.

When the Nazis rolled in, Peggy feared. That evening, she got a blanket and a chair and counted herself lucky. Sleep wouldn't come, no matter how exhausted she was. She would have looked to play more bridge, but fireplace and candles didn't give enough light. The electricity stayed off. She sat there and listened to the advancing gunfire.

About midnight, Czech soldiers fell back through Marianske Lazne. One of them, dirty, weary, harried—peered into the hotel. He shook his head and walked on. The Czechs didn't try to fight in the town. Peggy supposed she should have been grateful to them for not causing more civilian casualties. She hoped it wouldn't hurt their defense.

Rattling, clanking German vehicles entered Marianske Lazne at

3:17, Czech cuckoo-clock time. Peggy went out to look. She almost got shot. A peremptory wave from a tough-looking, black-uniformed man in a tank sent her reeling back into the hotel. *Under new management,* she thought, and finally started to cry.

LUC HARCOURT DIDN'T LIKE SERGEANT DEMANGE. What private in his right mind *did* like his sergeant? Demange was little and skinny and tough, with a tongue sharper than a bayonet. He looked unwontedly serious now as he gathered his squad together. Without preamble, he said, "The French Republic is at war with Germany."

Along with the rest of the men, Luc stared at the sergeant. He was just a conscript himself. All he'd ever wanted to do was serve his time and get out. The first thing he found out when he put on the uniform and the Adrian helmet was that nobody gave a damn about what he wanted.

Demange paused to light a Gitane. He even smoked like a tough guy, with the cigarette hanging down from the corner of his mouth. "England is with us," he said. "And the Russians have declared war on Germany, too."

"Oh, joy," Paul Renouvin said. He wasn't a bad guy, but he'd been at a university somewhere before the draft got him, and he liked showing off how much he knew. "That would matter a lot more if Russia bordered Germany. Or even Czechoslovakia."

Sergeant Demange looked as if he wanted to spit in Renouvin's eye. He contented himself with blowing smoke in the college kid's face. "Shut up, punk," he rasped. "The point is, we've got allies, dammit. So when we march into Germany, it's not like we're marching in all by ourselves."

We? Luc wondered. *We as in France, or we as in this squad?* He wanted to know—it was his neck, after all. But he didn't ask. One way or the other, he figured he'd find out pretty damn quick.

And he did. "We move out in half an hour," the sergeant said. "Remember, we're doing this for the poor goddamn Czechs." He sounded like a guy telling his girl they'd be doing it for love. Who cared why? They'd be doing it.

"What happens if the *Boches* shoot at us?" somebody asked.

"Well, we're supposed to be cautious," Demange said. "But we're supposed to move forward, too, so we will. And we'll shoot back, by God."

"My father did this in 1914," Luc said. "Red kepi, blue tunic, red trousers—there are photos at home. Not color photos, of course, but you know what the colors were." Several of the other soldiers nodded.

So did Sergeant Demange. "They were targets, that's what," he said. "I did it myself in 1918. We wore horizon-blue by then. Not as good as khaki"—he tapped his sleeve—"but Christ, better than red. How many times your old man get wounded?"

"Twice," Luc answered, not without pride.

"Sounds about right. He was luckier than a lot, that's for goddamn sure." Demange glanced at his watch. "Twenty minutes now. If we aren't marching at 0630 on the dot, I'll be in trouble. And if I'm in trouble, you sorry assholes are in *big* trouble."

Luc wondered why 0630 was so sacred. Would the war be lost if they started five minutes late? As far as Czechoslovakia was concerned, they were starting three days late. The Czechs said they were still fighting hard. The Germans claimed enormous victories. Somebody was lying. Maybe two somebodies were.

The border bulged south below Saarbrücken. At 0630 on the dot—Sergeant Demange and his ilk knew how to get what they wanted—French soldiers started moving into the bulge. A few French guns fired at the German positions ahead. A few German guns shot back. Both sides seemed halfhearted. Lou had been through much scarier drills.

Fields on the German side of the border looked—surprise!—just like fields on the French side. The only way Luc could be sure he'd crossed into Germany was by looking over at a German frontier post, abandoned now, that lay athwart a two-lane macadam road a few hundred meters off to the southeast.

Soldiers from another company poked through the frontier station as if they'd just occupied Berlin. Then, without warning, something over there went *boom!* Sergeant Demange hit the dirt. For a moment, Luc thought he'd been hurt. But then he got up and brushed wheat stubble off himself, altogether unselfconscious. "You hear a noise like that, you better get flat," he remarked. "I bet those Nazi cocksuckers booby-trapped the station."

Something had blown out part of one wall. Now the French soldiers over there scurried around like ants in a disturbed hill. Luc saw one man lying in the roadway. Even from this distance, he would have bet the poor bastard wouldn't get up again.

"Lesson number one," the sergeant said. "If it looks like they want you to pick it up, they probably do. Wouldn't be surprised if there are mines in these fields, too."

"*Merde alors!*" Luc muttered. The very ground under his feet might betray him. He tried to walk like a ballerina, on tippytoe. It didn't work very well in army-issue clodhoppers with a heavy pack on his back. Feeling foolish, he gave up after a few steps.

A belt of trees lay ahead. Did Germans lurk there? Sure as hell, they did. A spatter of rifle fire came from the woods. After the first bullet cracked past him, Luc needed no urging to flatten out. Prone, he fired back. His MAS36 slammed against his shoulder. In between rounds, he dug a scrape for himself with his entrenching tool.

Very cautiously, the French advanced. They took a few casualties, which made them more cautious yet. The Germans didn't make much of a fight, though. They melted back toward their fancy Westwall. It wasn't supposed to be as good as the Maginot Line—nothing was, not even the Czech forts—but everybody said it was tough even so.

When Luc finally reached the woods, he found several countrymen exclaiming over a dead German. The redheaded guy in field-gray had taken one in the chest. He didn't look especially unhappy—just surprised. Luc wondered if he'd killed the *Boche* himself. Not likely, but not impossible, either. He felt like a warrior and a murderer at the same time.

Chapter 3

It was six in the morning in Peking, which meant it was yesterday afternoon back in New York City. Corporal Pete McGill and several of the other Marines at the American Legation clustered in front of a shortwave set, listening to the World Series. The Yankees were up on the Cubs, two games to none. They were leading in game three, too. Joe Gordon had already singled with the bases loaded and homered, and Hoot Pearson was cruising along on the mound.

"Cubs are history," McGill said happily—he was from the Bronx. "Three straight Series for the Yanks, it's gonna be. Nobody's ever done that before."

None of the other leathernecks argued with him. He would have liked to see them try! When the Cubs got done losing today (or yesterday, or whatever the hell day it really was), they would have to sweep four to take the championship. Nobody did that, not against the Bronx Bombers!

A Polack named Herman Szulc—which he insisted was pronounced *Schultz*—said, "I bet they won't be as good next year."

"Oh, yeah, wise guy? How come?" McGill had brick-red hair, freckles, and the temper that went with them. And if you affronted his team, you affronted him, too.

"Only stands to reason. Shit, look at Gehrig," Szulc said. "He didn't even hit .300 this year. He's getting old, wearing out."

"Nah, he'll be back strong. You wait and see," McGill said. "Sheesh! A little bit of an off year for one guy, and you want to write off the ballclub."

Before the argument could go any further, a Chinese servant brought in a tray with coffee and sausages and rolls stuffed with this and that for the Marines. None of it except the coffee was what McGill would have eaten in the States, but it would all be tasty. Duty at the Legation was as sweet as it got.

"*Sheh-sheh,* Wang," Szulc said as the servant set the tray down on a table. That meant *thank you* in Chinese. McGill had learned a few phrases, too. They came in handy every once in a while.

Wang grinned a toothy grin. Several of his front teeth were gold. A twenty-four-carat smile meant you were somebody here. "Eat," he said—he knew bits of English, the way the Marines knew bits of Chinese. He waved at the tray. "*Hao.*" That meant it was good.

And it was. "Wonder what's in the sausages," somebody said with his mouth full.

"Your mother," somebody else came back, which almost made Pete squirt coffee out his nose.

"The Missing Link," Szulc suggested. That wasn't even so far-fetched. They'd found prehistoric human bones in these parts that were God only knew how old.

It also wasn't so far-fetched for another reason. Chinamen would cook and eat damn near everything. You could get snake. It was supposed to be good for your one-eyed snake. You could get dog, which was also supposed to make John Henry perk up. You could get fried grasshoppers. McGill had eaten one once, on a bet. It wasn't even bad, and he picked up five bucks crunching it.

Out went the Cubs again. A singing commercial came on. Szulc fiddled with the radio dial. "What the hell you doing?" McGill asked.

"Seeing if I can find some news between innings," Szulc answered. "Check what's up with the war."

"Oh. Okay," McGill said. The war was as important as the Series. Back in the States, people wouldn't have believed it. McGill was sure of that. But back in the States, people weren't right around the corner from the Japanese Legation and its garrison of tough bastards—not as tough as Marines, McGill was sure, but tough. Back in the States, people were doing their best to forget the Japs had bombed the crap out of the *Panay* the December before, even though she was flying the American flag.

Japan apologized, didn't she? She paid an indemnity, didn't she? That made everything all right, didn't it? Maybe so—back in the States. Not in Peking. Not even close.

Back in the States, people forgot the Japs had a zillion more soldiers sitting in Manchuria. Manchukuo, they called the puppet state there these days. If they decided they wanted a war with the USA, how long would this garrison last? Hell, back in the States, most people didn't know it existed.

If the balloon goes up with the Japs, it's my ass, McGill thought.

Szulc got a couple of bursts of static. Then he found the BBC. The announcer had a much posher accent than most of the Royal Marines at the British Legation. They called themselves leathernecks, too, and they made damn fine drinking buddies even if they did talk funny.

"—vakia continues to offer stout resistance to Hitler's aggression," the announcer said. "Russian volunteers and aircraft have begun appearing in Ruthenia and Slovakia. Both Poland and Romania deny consenting to their crossing."

"Fuck, I would, too," Szulc said. "Picking between Hitler and Stalin's gotta be worse'n the devil and the deep blue sea."

"Shut up already, if you want to listen to the news," somebody told him.

That supercivilized-sounding BBC announcer was continuing: "—another day of fierce air raids against Prague. Civilian casualties are said to be very heavy. The Czechoslovak government has condemned what it calls 'the barbarous German onslaught against defenseless noncombatants.' "

"Nice war," McGill muttered. Blasting the crap out of anything that got in your way wasn't anything the Marines hadn't heard about and seen before. The Japs did it all the time here, now that their war against China had heated up. But you expected better from Europeans, somehow. Then again, the difference between what you expected and what you got made a pretty good measure of how fucked up the world was.

"Czechoslovakia insists that reports of unrest in Slovakia are greatly exaggerated. Uprisings by the so-called Hlinka Guard"—the announcer read the name with fastidious distaste—"are being suppressed in Bratislava, Radio Prague declares, and elsewhere in that area."

"C'mon—put the ballgame back on," said a big, burly PFC named Puccinelli and inevitably called Pooch.

"In a second," Szulc said. "He'll get to the rest of the shit, and then we'll go back." Pooch muttered to himself, but didn't reach for the tuning dial himself.

"France continues its advance into Germany. German resistance is termed light," the BBC newsman said. "France has occupied the Warndt Forest, and seized the towns of Lauterwald and Bübingen."

"Wherever the hell those are," McGill put in. He'd never heard of either one of them before. That probably meant you could piss across them.

The limey's voice grew stern. "For the second night in a row, air pirates from Spain bombed Hendaye and Biarritz in southwestern France. It is not yet known whether the bombers were flown by native Spanish Fascists of the Sanjurjo junta or by Nazis of the Condor Legion mercenary group. In any case, French aid to the rival Spanish Republican government, including men, munitions, aircraft, and tanks, continues to flood across the Pyrenees."

"Yeah, it floods now, after the frogs and the limeys spent years keeping it out." Max Weinstein was a rare duck: a pink, almost Red, Marine. He wasn't real big, but he was tough. With politics like his, he had to be. He got into more than his share of brawls, and won more than his share, too.

"Prime Minister Chamberlain was in Manchester today, reassuring anxious citizens that, despite the long, difficult road ahead, victory will inevitably—"

Herman Szulc turned back to the World Series. The Cubs had one out in the seventh. They were going down the drain, all right, the same way the Giants had in '36 or '37.

"Wonder whether the Japs are listening to the Series or the BBC," McGill said. It wasn't obvious. Japan was crazy for baseball. On the Fourth of July in '37—three days before the fighting between Japan and China broke out for real—a Marine team had played a doubleheader against a squad from the Japanese garrison. They'd split two games rougher than any John McGraw's Orioles played back in the '90s.

"Wonder whether Japan will go after Russia like she means it if the Russians start going at it hot and heavy with Hitler," Szulc said.

"That would be just like the damn Japs," Max said, and for once nobody wanted to argue with him. Japan and Russia had been banging heads for a couple of years now, up on the border between Manchukuo and Mongolia. Most of the official bulletins talked about Manchukuan and Mongolian soldiers, but anybody who knew anything knew better. The puppets wouldn't dance that way without their masters pulling the strings.

"Hey, I hope the Japs do go north," Pete said. Weinstein gave him a furious look. Before the champion of the Soviet workers and peasants could start screaming, McGill went on, "If they don't, they'll hit the USA, and everybody here is fucking dead meat if they do."

Max opened his mouth. A moment later, he closed it again. Nobody could say Pete was wrong there. Japan occupied northern China these days. She occupied all of Peking except the Legation Quarter. If she went to war with the United States, the few hundred Marines in the garrison wouldn't last long.

Japanese soldiers were little and scrawny. Their equipment was nothing to write home about. But they were rugged sons of bitches, and there were swarms of them. Oh, America would eventually kick the snot out of them. Eventually, though, was way too late to do anybody here any good.

SERGEANT HIDEKI FUJITA HATED MANCHUKUO. He hated Mongolia even more. And getting sent to the border between the Japanese puppet state and the one the Russians propped up combined the worst of both worlds.

Japan claimed the border between Manchukuo and Mongolia lay along the Halha River. The Mongolians and Russians insisted it belonged a good many kilometers farther east. Japan and Russia had banged heads along Manchukuo's borders before: here, and along the Amur River, and near Korea, where Russian territory dipped down as far as Vladivostok.

The Mongolians had found a new game to get on their neighbors' nerves. They would light grass fires near the frontier—wherever the hell it was—and let the prevailing westerlies sweep the flames into Manchukuan territory. Naturally, that made the locals come running to the Japanese, screaming that they should do something. When you set up a puppet, you had to hold him upright or else he wasn't worth anything.

Not that Fujita thought the Manchukuans *were* worth anything. But their country—to give it the benefit of the doubt—had more timber than anybody knew what to do with. It raised lots of rice and wheat and millet, too. And it drew ever more Japanese colonists, people who wanted more land and a better chance than they'd ever get in the overcrowded home islands. Whether the Manchukuans did or not, real Japanese people needed protecting.

Trouble was, even if the border lay on the Halha, the way Japan said it did, the Mongolians and Russians still had the better of it. The land west of the Halha, on the Mongolian side, stood fifty or sixty meters higher than it did over here. High ground counted, same as always.

Only a couple of days earlier, on October 4, the Mongolians had fired from the high ground at two dozen Japanese surveyors riding through what was plainly Japanese territory . . . if you accepted the Japanese view of the frontier, anyhow. Sergeant Fujita did, of course.

One of the other men in his little detachment, a corporal named Masanori Kawakami, asked, "Excuse me, Sergeant-*san,* but would the Mongolians harass us if the Russians didn't want them to?"

"Not bloody likely," Fujita said with a snort. He was short and squat and tough—the kind of noncom whose men hated and feared him but couldn't help respecting him, too. "The Mongols can't wipe their raggedy asses unless some Russian commissar says they can."

"*Hai.*" Kawakami nodded. He was younger than Fujita, a conscript rather than a career soldier. "That's what I thought."

"Funny they would do it with the war in Europe heating up," Superior Private Shinjiro Hayashi said.

"What's that got to do with anything?" Fujita rumbled ominously. He wanted to boot Hayashi around, but sometimes even a sergeant in the Imperial Japanese Army had to be careful. Yes, Hayashi was a conscript, with no rights or privileges to speak of. Yes, he was clumsy and four-eyed, and so deserved thumping more than most of the other soldiers.

But he was also a university student. He talked like a damn professor. A guy like that was bound to have connections. If he complained, Sergeant Fujita was too likely never to see anything but the dusty Mongolian frontier for the rest of his days.

Hayashi smiled now. He liked explaining things. "If the Russians really are fighting in Czechoslovakia"—a name that sounded very strange in Japanese—"why would they also want to fight us? A man with two enemies at the same time has trouble."

"Maybe," Fujita said with a grudging nod. "You can see that—but you're almost as smart as you think you are." He wouldn't give any praise without putting a sting in its tail. "Are the dumb foreigners clever enough to see it, too?"

"I think so, Sergeant-*san*." Hayashi knew better than to piss Fujita off on purpose. "Lots of countries know the rules of diplomacy and war."

Corporal Kawakami pointed west. "I think I just saw something move, Sergeant. . . . There, about one o'clock."

"I'll check it out." Fujita wore binoculars on a leather strap around his neck. Japanese optics were some of the best in the world. He'd looked through captured Russian field glasses, and they were crap. Pure junk. He'd also seen fancy German binoculars—from Zeiss, no less. Those were okay, but not a sen's worth better than his own pair.

He scanned the plain on this side of the Halha. Yellow dirt, yellowish-green grass, the occasional bush—that was about it. The steppe rolled on for countless kilometers. Then he spotted the horseman.

A Mongolian, he thought at once. He had trouble knowing how he was so sure. Manchukuan cavalrymen rode the same kind of shaggy little steppe ponies. They carried carbines slung on their backs, too, and wore the same mix of uniforms and native garb. Then Fujita realized why he knew. The horseman kept glancing back over his shoulder, toward the east. If he expected trouble, it was from this direction, yet he was the only man in sight.

"Let's reel him in," Fujita said. "Hayashi! Fire two shots in the air."

"Two shots. Yes, Sergeant-*san*." Superior Private Hayashi obeyed without question. *Bang! Bang!* The reports rolled across the steppe.

Fujita kept the field glasses on the rider. When the fellow heard the gunshots, he jerked in the saddle, looked around wildly in all directions, and started to grab for his weapon. Then he checked himself. "Two more shots, Hayashi," the sergeant said. "And we'll show ourselves. If he comes in, fine. I think he will. But if he doesn't, we just have to deal with him."

Bang! Bang! The sergeant and the men from his squad stood up. He waved. He hoped the shots wouldn't draw artillery fire from the other side of the river. If the horseman was what Fujita thought he was, the bastards over there might want to see him dead even if he was on this side of the line . . . not that they admitted the Halha *was* the line, anyway.

The Mongolian looked back toward the other side of the river again, too. He wore a fur cap with earflaps up right now—the day was mild. After reaching under it to scratch his head, he rode slowly toward the Japanese soldiers.

As he got closer, he waved his hand to show he was friendly. Then he must have decided that wasn't enough, because he threw down the carbine. He shouted something in his own language. It sounded like dogs barking to Fujita.

"I don't know what the devil you're talking about," the Japanese sergeant yelled back. "Come ahead anyhow, though." He gestured emphatically.

When the Mongolian called again, it was in a different tongue. "That's Chinese, Sergeant," Hayashi said.

"You understand it?" Fujita asked. Maybe the four-eyed guy was good for something after all.

And Hayashi nodded. "I studied it in school."

"All right. Talk to him. Find out what's what."

Whatever Hayashi said was only singsong gibberish to Fujita. But the Mongolian understood it. He answered eagerly. He and Hayashi had to go back and forth and round and round—neither was exactly fluent. After a bit, the senior private turned back to Fujita. "About what we would have guessed, Sergeant. He thought they were going to purge him, and he figured he'd better bug out while he was still breathing."

Fujita grunted. "The Mongolians are crazy, and they caught it from the Russians." Russia had been purging its officer corps for a couple of years now. People just disappeared. Captains, colonels, generals . . . It didn't matter. And, since Marshal Choibalsan's Mongolia imitated Stalin's Russia in all things, Mongol officers started disappearing off the face of the earth, too. More and more of the ones who feared they might be next fled to Manchukuo instead—which made Choibalsan look for still more new traitors.

This fellow said something else in his hesitant Chinese. Fujita looked a question to Hayashi. "He says—I think he says—he can tell us a lot about their dispositions on the far side of the Halha."

Hearing that improved Fujita's disposition. "Can he? Well, he'll get his chance. We'll take him in, and he'd better sing like a cricket in a cage. Tell him so, Hayashi."

"I don't know if I can say that in Chinese, Sergeant-*san*."

"Shit. Tell him we'll cut his balls off if he doesn't talk. That ought to do it."

Hayashi spoke slowly. The Mongolian officer's face didn't show much. He was darker than most Japanese, maybe because he was born that way, maybe just because he was weathered, which he certainly was. *Left in the oven too long,* Fujita thought scornfully. The Mongolian did gnaw on his lower lip for a moment before answering. "He says he'll tell us whatever we want to know," Hayashi reported. "He says he knew all along he'd have to do that."

"All right. Good. You and Kawakami take him back to our officers." Fujita held up a hand. "Wait! Ask him one thing first. Ask him if the Russians and Mongols aim to jump us any time soon."

Hayashi put the question. The deserter shook his head. He said something. Hayashi translated: "No, Sergeant. He says they're just hoping we leave them alone. The Russians are almost pissing themselves about what's going on in Europe, he says."

"*Ichi-ban!*" Fujita said enthusiastically. "That's good intelligence. If they're afraid we'll jump on them, maybe now's the time to do it, *neh?*"

Senior Private Hayashi shrugged. He wasn't about to argue with a superior. He and Corporal Kawakami just took the Mongolian back toward battalion headquarters.

ARMORERS WHEELED BOMBS TOWARD LIEUTENANT Sergei Yaroslavsky's Tupolev SB-2. The medium bomber would hold half a dozen 100kg bombs or one big, hefty 500kg firework. The big bombs were in short supply, though. Yaroslavsky was glad the armorers had enough of the smaller ones to fill up the bomb bay.

He was a stolid, broad-faced blond, getting close to thirty. He'd had a tour against the Fascists in Spain. Now he was doing it again, flying out of a field near Poprad in eastern Slovakia. Officially, he was a volunteer, aiding the people of democratic Czechoslovakia against the Nazi invasion. And, in a way, he supposed he *had* volunteered. They would have shot him if he'd said no. They were shooting lots of officers these days. They were jumpy as cats in a rocking-chair factory. They'd shoot you without any excuse if they felt like it. If you gave them one, you were dead for sure.

Of course, the Germans were liable to shoot him, too. Things were simpler and safer in Spain. Back in early 1937, the SB-2 could outrun anything the Spanish Nationalists, the Condor Legion, or the Italians put in the air.

It wasn't like that here. The Messerschmitt 109 was a very nasty piece of work. It was faster than both Russian flat-nosed Polikarpovs and biplane Czech Avias. It was a hell of a lot faster than an SB-2. The best recipe for not getting shot down was not getting seen.

The armorers were Czechs. When they talked with one another, Sergei could almost understand them. He really could follow Ruthenian, which was just Ukrainian with another name. Slovak? He didn't know about Slovak. Sentries around the airstrip kept Slovaks away. The squadron was flying out of Slovakia, but the place wasn't exactly loyal to the country of which it was supposed to be a part.

Clanging noises said the bombardier was closing the bomb bay. "We ready, Ivan?" Yaroslavsky called.

"*Da*, Comrade Lieutenant," Ivan Kuchkov replied. He was dark and stocky and muscular and hairy. People sometimes called him "Chimp." Not very often, though, not after he broke a man's jaw for doing it. He had the right slot—a bombardier needed muscle.

"Start them up, Anastas," Sergei told the copilot.

Anastas Mouradian nodded. "I will do it." His throaty Armenian accent grated on Yaroslavsky's ears. Damned swarthy bastards from the Caucasus . . . But you couldn't say that, not when Comrade Stalin was a Georgian. Better not even to think it.

At least the Georgians and Armenians were Christians, not Muslims like the Azerbaijanis and Chechens. In the officially atheist USSR, you weren't supposed to think things like that, either. But, while Sergei might be a New Soviet Man, he was also and always a Russian.

The two M-100A radial engines thundered to life. The props blurred into invisibility. Yaroslavsky checked the instruments, one after another. Everything looked good. The mechanics were Czechs, too. They were better than any Russian mechanics he'd ever had. They seemed to care more about the work they did.

Five more bombers were also warming up on the airstrip. They were going to give the Nazis one right in the eye. Sergei hoped so, anyhow. More than a week into the war, and the Germans still hadn't cut Czechoslovakia in half. Lots of the Czech army was pulling back into Slovakia to keep up the fight here—and to sit on the pro-Fascist Slovaks.

Down the runway bounced the SB-2. It was made for taking off from grassy fields. Paved runways were as rare as capitalists inside the Soviet Union.

Sergei pulled back on the stick. The bomber's nose came up. No more bouncing—he was airborne. He'd shake again soon enough, when they started shooting at him. Best to enjoy the calm while he could.

If running didn't help, he could shoot back. Mouradian was in charge of two machine guns in the SB-2's nose. Kuchkov had a machine-gun blister on the back of the airplane and another in its belly. Those looked like a good idea. Bombardiers were rapidly discovering, though, that you had to be lucky to hit anything with either gun. If you *weren't* lucky, you might use the dorsal gun to shoot off your own tail. At least one intrepid bombardier had already done that.

If he'd lived, they would have court-martialed him and then shot him. As things were, he saved them the trouble.

"All good," Mouradian shouted, pointing to the instruments. He wasn't in the front glasshouse yet. With 840 horsepower roaring away to either side, you had to yell to make yourself heard.

"I see 'em." Sergei nodded. "Let's hope they stay that way." The SB-2 was a robust warplane. It could take a beating. Sergei didn't want it to this time around.

On he flew with his buddies. Down below, bursting shells and bombs told when they entered the combat zone. The Czechs were still pulling back through the gap between the Nazi armies advancing from the north and south. If the Czechs got enough men and matériel into eastern Moravia and Slovakia before the Germans finally sealed that gap, they could keep fighting a while longer.

When Sergei said as much to Anastas Mouradian, the copilot—who also served as gunner and bomb-aimer and navigator—nodded. "*Da*," he said, for all the world as if he were a real Russian. Then he added, "If they don't, they're fucked." Any Russian might have said that, too. He sure wouldn't have been wrong if he did.

Antiaircraft fire started bursting around the bombers. Yaroslavsky jinked, going up and down to the left and right at random and slowing down and speeding up to keep the German gunners from being able to lead him like a duck. When a shell filled the air with nasty black smoke close by, it was as if he drove over a big pothole. His teeth came together with a click.

Mouradian growled something in what had to be Armenian. Then he came back to words Sergei could understand: "Too damn close."

"No kidding," the pilot said. Just then, another shell went off even closer to the SB-2. A fragment clanged off—or, more likely, bit through—the fuselage. Yaroslavsky checked the controls to the rudder and elevator. They answered—no cables cut. He yelled into the speaking tube to the bombardier: "You all right, Ivan?"

"*Khorosho*," Kuchkov answered. "A little draftier, but no damage."

"Get ready," Sergei told him. "We're almost there."

They were almost there if Mouradian's navigating was worth a kopek, anyway. He'd got them where they were supposed to go before. The target this time was just outside of Brno, the biggest factory town in Moravia. The Czechs were still holding out there, still holding up the Nazis. If 600 kilos of high explosive could help them hang on a little longer, Sergei would deliver the goods.

That thick cloud of smoke ahead had to be Brno. *Who needs navigation?* Sergei thought wryly. The Germans were bombing the crap out of Czechoslovakian civilians. Thousands and thousands were supposed to be dead in Prague. Brno was catching it, too.

"So where's our target from here?" Yaroslavsky asked.

"Southwest, Comrade Pilot," Mouradian answered from the nose— he was ready to fight now.

That made sense: it was the direction from which the Nazis were advancing. Sergei didn't want his bombs coming down on the Czechs' heads. He spotted something ahead that looked like a division HQ. "Aim for those tents," he ordered. "I'll bring us in low and straight."

"We'll get 'em," Ivan Kuchkov said. And maybe they would, and maybe they wouldn't. But they'd scare the crap out of the Nazis if they didn't.

The bomb bay opened. The extra drag slowed the SB-2 and made it sluggish in the air. At Mouradian's shouted command, the bombs tumbled free, one after another. The plane would be livelier with them gone: they made up about a tenth of the weight it was carrying.

And the Tupolev bomber would need to be livelier, too. German fighters jumped the Russians just as they were finishing their bombing runs. These Messerschmitts were terrifying. They could have been more maneuverable, but they were well armed and fast as the Devil's godson. And diving down on the SB-2s made them faster yet.

One of the bombers fell out of the sky. By the way it dove, the pilot was dead at the controls. Fire filled the left wing. Another SB-2 fled east with smoke trailing from one engine. Maybe it could get down safely in Czech-held territory. Maybe the Germans would hack it down first.

Sergei couldn't worry much about the other SB-2s. He had to worry about his own. The Chimp started blazing away from the dorsal turret. Tracers snarled past the bomber from behind.

But Ivan made the 109 pull up. From the nose, Mouradian squeezed off a long burst at the lean, predatory shape. The enemy fighter didn't catch fire or go down. But it didn't try another attack, either.

With all the throttle he could use, Sergei got out of there. Then he had another bad moment, when two Czech Avias buzzed up in what might have been another attack. At the last second, they saw he was no Nazi and swung away. One of the pilots waved from his cockpit. Yaroslavsky returned the compliment.

Then he had to find the airstrip again. Mouradian came back to help him. Between them, they figured out where the hell Poprad was. They got down smoothly enough. One other plane from the flight came in a few minutes later. Sergei could hope some of the rest had landed elsewhere. The one that had plummeted to the ground . . . He shuddered. Better not to think of such things.

He had to, though, because he needed to report to his superiors. "One of our planes damaged, one definitely lost," he said.

They nodded. All part of the game, as far as they were concerned. "We'll keep banging away," one of them said. *Till you're expended, too,* Sergei thought, and made himself nod.

VACLAV JEZEK DUG LIKE A MOLE. What was left of his company was trying to hold the Germans out of Kopecek, a little town six or eight kilometers northeast of Olomouc. In and of itself, Kopecek hardly mattered. But Olomouc did. Olomouc was the last surviving northern rampart against the Nazi flood. The Czech army was pulling back to the east between Olomouc and Brno. If Hitler's bastards closed off that passageway . . .

Then we're fucked, Jezek though, making the dirt fly with his entrenching tool. Czechoslovakia was probably fucked anyway. No, scratch *probably*. Czechoslovakia *was* fucked anyway. But the stubborn Czechs were making Germany pay a hell of a high price.

Artillery came down in and around Kopecek. The Nazis were shelling the pilgrimage church. It stood on a hill a couple of hundred meters above the plain, and made an observation post dangerous to them. Vaclav would have been surprised if his side didn't have some guns of its own around the church.

"Hey, Corporal! Got a smoke?" Otakar Prsemysl asked.

"Everybody bums cigarettes off me," Jezek grumbled, but he gave the private one. Back just before the shooting started, Jan Dzurinda had scrounged a butt from him. Vaclav didn't know where Dzurinda was now. Maybe he'd got killed when the Germans dropped everything and the kitchen sink on the Czech lines by the border. Or maybe he'd just bugged out. A hell of a lot of Slovaks had. The miserable rubes didn't think this was their fight—or else they thought they were on the wrong side when they wore Czech brown.

"Tanks!" somebody shouted. Everyone who heard that yell grew fearfully alert. Without tanks, the Nazis would still be banging their heads against the Czech lines. But they had them, and they had more of them than Czechoslovakia did. Breakthrough machines, that's what tanks were.

A machine gun chattered. That was wasted ammo. Machine-gun bullets wouldn't pierce a panzer's steel hide. Tanks could kill you, and you couldn't kill the sons of bitches inside them. Was that fair?

Then Vaclav heard the bigger boom of an antitank rifle. Those fired heavy, large-caliber, armor-piercing bullets out of a long barrel that gave high muzzle velocity. They could get through . . . sometimes, anyhow. The rifles weigh a tonne and kicked like a jackass, but so what? They worked . . . again, sometimes.

One of the panzers up ahead stopped. Smoke poured from the engine compartment. The two-man crew bailed out. Vaclav didn't think either Nazi in black coveralls made it to shelter. *Too bad*, he thought. *Yeah. Toooo bad.*

Avias and Messerschmitts dueled overhead. The German fighters were faster, but the Czech biplanes seemed more nimble. People cheered like maniacs when a 109 spun out of control and went down. It was like watching a football match, except you counted lives instead of goals. Score one for our side!

Trouble was, not many Avias were left. The Nazis kept pounding the airfields from which they flew. The Messerschmitts came out of Germany, of course. A few Czech air raids on German soil had made Hitler and Goebbels scream and squeal, but the *Luftwaffe* had a big edge there.

"Wish the French would push harder, take some pressure off us," Private Prsemysl said.

"Yeah, me, too," Jezek agreed. "Wish for the moon while you're at it." He supposed the Czechs had to count themselves lucky France had moved at all. *Great. Some luck.*

No sooner had that gloomy thought gone through his mind than cries of alarm came from the west. "They're through! They're through!" somebody howled, which sounded bad. Then someone else shouted, "They're into Olomouc! Get away while you can!"

Otakar Prsemysl crossed himself. That looked like a good idea to Vaclav, so he did the same thing. It couldn't hurt, anyhow.

"South and east! South and east!" That was an officer's authoritative shout. "We pull back farther into Moravia and keep fighting. They haven't whipped us yet, by God!"

No, but how much longer will it be? And what good will keeping up the fight do except get more of us killed? Still, Corporal Jezek had no better ideas. The only other choices were surrendering, which he couldn't stomach, and dying in place, which also struck him as unattractive.

He got out of his foxhole and stumbled through the streets of Kopecek. To his surprise, trucks—mostly commandeered civilian jobs—waited on the southern edge of town. He piled into one of them. A moment later, he saw Otakar and pulled him into it, too. A moment after that, the truck rattled away.

"Where are we going?" Prsemysl asked.

"Beats me," Vaclav answered. "But did you want to stay where we were?" The other man shook his head. This couldn't be worse. . . . *Unless we get bombed, of course.* One more thought Jezek could have done without.

Chapter 4

Another gray day in Münster. People in the Westphalian town said it was either raining or the church bells were ringing. Sarah Goldman could hear the bells, but it was raining anyhow. That didn't seem fair.

Of course, for Sarah the past five years had seemed gray and gloomy and weepy even when the sun did come out. Since she was only seventeen, that seemed like forever. She hadn't understood why the Nazis decided they had to clamp down on Jews—she and her family weren't hurting anybody. She still didn't understand, not really. But the time since Hitler took over had been plenty to teach her that people could act like vicious idiots without having any good reason for it.

Her mother had the radio on. She was listening to a German station. Listening to foreign broadcasts was illegal for everybody. But ordinary Germans who did something like that might escape with a warning if they got caught—the first time, anyway. Any infraction at all would send Jews straight to Dachau or Buchenwald.

"German storm troops fight today on the outskirts of Prague!" the announcer shouted. He had a hoarse, braying voice and a strong Berlin accent. Sarah thought he sounded like a Prussian jackass, which he probably was. "Czech air pirates dropped bombs on a school in Dresden, murdering seventeen innocent children at play!"

"Why were children playing during an air raid?" Hanna Goldman asked. The same question had formed in Sarah's mind. She wondered how many people thought that way. Not very many, evidently, or the announcer couldn't have got away with spewing such nonsense.

"Farther east, our victorious soldiers advancing from north and south have met in Moravia, sealing the fate of the Czech army and of what was the vicious bandit state of Czechoslovakia!" he trumpeted. "Now we can help the Slovaks achieve their national aspirations and whip the Bolshevik dogs back to their Russian kennel."

"Do you hear that, Sarah?" her mother called from the kitchen. She was trying to make meager, bland rations into something worth eating for supper. Most of the time, she did it, too.

"*Ja,* I hear it," Sarah answered.

"Such rubbish," her mother said. "Listening to that crap makes me embarrassed to be a German."

"I know what you mean." And Sarah did, too. In spite of everything, she still felt like a German. Why shouldn't she? Her father had fought in the World War (the First World War, she supposed you would have to call it now) like every other German man his age. He'd won an Iron Cross, too. And he had an amazing scar on his arm where a French bullet had gouged a furrow in his flesh.

Her older brother was such a good football player, the Aryans didn't want him taken off their team. They cared more about winning than about whether Saul was circumcised. That made nothing but sense to

Sarah, but it had scandalized a lot of people in Münster. Tough men in black uniforms had paid some unofficial visits. Saul didn't play for the Foresters any more.

But he still thought he was a German, too, in spite of everything. He and Samuel Goldman were doing their best to prove it today. Sarah didn't know whether to hope they would fail or succeed.

The braying announcer didn't say anything about the fighting on the Western Front. He hardly ever did. The Czechs were giving the war everything they had in them. The French and the English didn't seem to have their hearts in it.

After an almost tearful appeal to buy war bonds, the newsman finally went away. The radio started playing music again. That was a relief. Music was—mostly—harmless. But you never heard jazz any more. The government said it was degenerate, like modern art. If the government didn't like it, Sarah thought she should.

She was working on an essay on Goethe—Münster's Jewish school naturally taught the German poets—when the front door opened. She put down her pen and dashed downstairs.

One glance at her father's face, and her brother's, told her everything she needed to know. "They wouldn't take you?" she blurted.

"Bastards!" Saul seemed ready to kick something that wasn't a football.

He towered over Father, who looked more sad than angry. "I had my discharge papers. I had my medal. I had my wound certificate. I had a letter from Max Lambert, who was my captain during the war. I had everything," he said. "And we went into *Wehrkreis* headquarters, and they wouldn't let us joint the *Wehrmacht*."

"Bastards!" Saul said again.

Wehrkreis—Military District VI—was centered on Münster. It drew in recruits from all over Westphalia and from western Hanover. But it didn't want a couple of Jews, even if one was a veteran and the other a fine physical specimen.

Sarah's mother came out of the kitchen. "What did they tell you?" she asked.

"They told us no, that's what. There's a law, it seems, from 1935, that says Jews can't join up," Samuel Goldman answered. One corner of his mouth curled up in a wry smile. "Even so, I don't think they expected to see us sticking our heads into the lion's mouth."

"We didn't," Saul said. "If we'd tried to join the SS, now . . ."

In spite of five years of ever harder times, in spite of a day of crushing disappointment, Father started to laugh. When he did, the rest of the Goldmans did, too. He lit a cigarette. German tobacco smelled nastier than it had a couple of years before. Sarah didn't smoke, but Father said it tasted worse, too. Fewer imports . . .

Father blew out a gray cloud. "In fact, I'm sure they didn't expect anyone like us," he said.

"Why are you so sure?" Mother asked, as she was supposed to.

"Why? I'll tell you why." Samuel Goldman's mouth quirked again, but this time it was more grimace than smile. "Because the *Feldwebel* we talked to wasn't even mean to us. He just said it was impossible, and he kept on saying it, and he finally went and got a captain who said the same thing. The captain was polite, too—turns out he knows Max. If they had orders about how to deal with Jews trying to volunteer, they would have screamed at us and called us filthy Jewish pigdogs and maybe said we'd just volunteered to clean toilets—"

"With our tongues," Saul broke in.

"That's disgusting!" Sarah exclaimed.

"That's why they do it," her brother said, and then, "Bastards!" again.

"Anyhow, they looked at my papers. I showed them my scar," Samuel Goldman said. "I showed them the letter. I showed them the Iron Cross, but it was only Second Class, not First." He shrugged. "I was a corporal. Almost impossible for an enlisted man to get an Iron Cross, First Class, in the last war."

"The *Führer* did," Sarah said. He was proud of it, too. He wore it on his left breast pocket all the time.

Father sighed. "I know. But he was one of a handful. The *Feldwebel* told me to be sure to hang on to the papers. 'You can't wear the uniform again,' he said, 'but that stuff may save your bacon anyway.' Then he laughed like a loon, because he thought saving a Jew's bacon was funny."

"What do you think he meant?" Sarah asked.

"Well, things aren't *as* bad for us because I'm a veteran," Father answered. "Even the Nazis respect that some. Not enough, but some."

"I can't say I'm really sorry they did turn you down," Mother said. "Now I won't have to worry about the two of you off at the ends of the earth with nasty people shooting at you."

Father only sighed. "Plenty of things closer to home to worry about. Where are we going to find money? What will they do to us? We should have got out before the war started. Too late now. One of the things I thought was—" He broke off.

"What?" Sarah asked it before Mother could. Or, more likely, Mother already knew.

Samuel Goldman looked at her. "If your brother and I—or even one of us—got into the *Wehrmacht*, nobody could say we weren't proper Germans. Nobody would do anything to the family because we weren't proper Germans, either." He gave Mother an ironic nod. "We might have been safer at the front than here in Münster, you know."

Mother's mouth twisted. "Don't talk about such things."

"Why not? It's not as if talking about them makes them come true." But then Father was the one who looked as if he'd bitten down on a lemon. Hitler had spent years talking about all the things he wanted to do to Jews. He talked about them, and talked about them, and talked about them—and the more he talked, the more of them did come true.

That was why Father didn't teach Roman history at the university any more. Jews were forbidden from holding academic positions. Father still made some money writing articles for the monumental Pauly-Wissowa *Real-Encyclopädie der klassischen Altertumswissenschaft*: basically, a multivolume encyclopedia of everything that was known about ancient Greece and Rome, up to the sixth century A.D. Samuel Goldman wasn't the only displaced Jewish professor putting cash in his pocket and bread on his table that way. If you had an Aryan academic friend who would steer things your way—who would, sometimes, put his name on what you'd written . . . You wouldn't get rich, but you might get by.

Editors paid by the page, too. Jewish scholars had written some monumental articles because of that. Scholars of the next generation would have a hard time finding anything more to say about quite a few topics.

If, of course, the next generation cared a pfennig's worth about classical antiquity. Maybe all the Aryan scholars would study Goths and Vandals and Vikings instead of Greeks and Romans. But even then, Sarah knew, Pauly-Wissowa would help.

If anything helped, anyway . . .

FROM CALAIS, ALISTAIR WALSH COULD look across the Channel and see the white cliffs of Dover smudging the northeastern horizon. He'd been in France before, in 1918. He'd been a private then, an unhappy conscript. But he'd discovered he liked soldiering, even if getting shot in the leg meant he spent Armistice Day flat on his back in a military hospital.

So here he was again, this time with the three stripes and crown of a staff sergeant on his sleeve. He'd come as far as he was likely to. They wouldn't make him an officer even if the sky fell. He'd got what little education he owned in the army, and he had a buzzing Welsh accent.

Still, staff sergeant wasn't bad. It beat the hell out of a lifetime in a factory or a coal mine, which he would have had if he hadn't stayed a soldier. He could break in new men. And he could talk back to lieutenants, a lot of whom weren't much more than half his age.

He also had the pleasure of the company of his own kind. The British army would have come to pieces without its senior sergeants, and was smart enough to know it. Lying right across the Channel from Blighty, Calais had a better notion of what made a proper pub than most foreign places. In fact, the fellow who ran the Green Duck was an Englishman. He'd got wounded during the war, too, and ended up marrying his pretty French nurse and staying behind here.

Since the British Expeditionary Force crossed, the Green Duck had become the unofficial headquarters for people like Alistair: men who'd been through the mill, who wanted a place where they could get a pint or three and sit around and drink them and have a smoke without getting bothered by officers or yapping soldiers. If they thought they knew more about what was going on than the General Staff did . . . well, sergeants have had such thoughts since the days of Caesar, if not since those of Hammurabi.

Walsh lit a Brutus and blew smoke up toward the dim ceiling. He turned to the man sitting next to him. "I tell you, Joe, it's not like it was in the last go-round."

"Too bloody right it's not." Joe Collins' clotted speech said he came from London's East End. He was a wiry little fellow, tough as a rat-catching terrier and about as sentimental. He held out a hand. "Gimme one o' them."

"Here you go." Walsh handed him the packet, then leaned close to let him have a light. "It's not, I tell you."

"I said the same fing myself." Collins blew out smoke, then whistled respectfully. "Bastard's strong as the devil. Turkish blend?"

"That's right. If you aren't going to taste it, why smoke it?" Walsh said.

"Knocks the socks off Navy Cut Gold, it does," Collins said.

"I should hope so." Alistair took a pull at his pint. Some places on the Continent, they sold beer by the half-liter, which wasn't enough. None of that nonsense at the Green Duck, though. Walsh repeated, "If you aren't going to taste it, why smoke it? And if you aren't going to fight, why send the bloody Expeditionary Force over here?"

"Politics." Joe Collins turned it into the filthiest word in the world. "The froggies, they'd break out in arseholes if we wasn't here, so we bleedin' well are."

"Sounds right to me," Alistair agreed. "But say what you please about the frogs, last time around they *wanted* to have a go at the *Boche*. So did we. Everybody was dead keen to get in there and mix it up. Not now."

"No, not now. Sufferin' Jesus!" The other senior sergeant drained his pint and waved for another one. "The way those sorry sods are tippy-toeing into 'Unland . . . and they 'aven't moved us up towards the front at all."

"Don't I know it!" Alistair said. "We just sit around soaking up beer and pinching the barmaids' bums. . . ."

"You try it, dearie, and you'll draw back a bloody stump," said the broad-shouldered blonde who brought Collins his refill. The words carried a bit of a French accent. The sentiment could have come from any British barmaid from Londonderry to Dover.

"Don't pay him no mind, sweet'eart," Joe Collins said. "If *I* get my mitts on you, now, you'll love every minute of it."

"And then you wake up," she retorted. Away she went, with a little extra roll to her hips to show the soldiers what they were missing.

Collins chuckled. "She'd be a 'andful and a 'alf, she would."

"You might say so." But Alistair wanted to talk about the war, not women. They could always come back to women, and they probably would. For now, though . . . "Only ones who fight like they mean it are the Czechs—and the Germans in Czecho, too."

"Fat lot of good it does the bloody Czechs," Collins said. "They'd be better off if they lay down for old Adolf."

"Tell that to the next Czech you see," Walsh said. "Go on—I dare you. But make sure I'm there, mind, on account of I want to watch him wallop the snot out of you. And he will, too. You're a tough bugger, Joe, but these blokes from the middle of Europe, they bloody well mean it. Tell me I'm wrong."

"Oh, I could lick a Czech or a Pole," Collins said. "But if I turned me back 'arf a mo', 'e'd bloody well pull a knife out of 'is boot top and give me one right in the kidney. They don't fight fair in those parts."

Maybe that was it. Maybe it was just that Central Europeans were dreadfully in earnest. The one who'd plugged Henlein and touched off this mess—he must have known he wouldn't get away. He did it anyhow. A generation earlier, Gavrilo Princip and his Balkan buddies hadn't counted the cost, either.

"I wish they'd move us forward," Walsh said. "I don't give a shit about hanging out my washing on the Siegfried Line, but I'd like to *see* the goddamn thing."

"Careful what you wish for—you may get it," Collins said.

"Not here, by God." Alistair Walsh shook his head. "The Frenchies say they did their duty by Czecho when they stuck half of one toe into Germany. And we did ours by the Frenchies when we crossed over. Fight? Oh, no, dear!" His voice rose to a shrill, effeminate falsetto.

Joe Collins laughed. So did the Englishman behind the bar. The tapman could afford to. He'd done his bit the last time around, and paid enough so that nobody wanted anything else from him now. Walsh soaked up the beer. This was soft duty. He knew he shouldn't complain. Drinking pints in a Calais pub when he should have been in a trench brewing tea with hot water from the cooling jacket of his machine gun didn't feel right, though. Somebody in charge knew damn all about what was going on.

Or maybe that somebody knew entirely too well. There was a notion more frightening still.

PRAGUE DEAD AHEAD. LUDWIG ROTHE'S Panzer II approached the capital of Czechoslovakia from the east. Prague was surrounded, utterly cut off from any hope of relief. If the Czechs had any brains, they would surrender. If they had any brains, they would have surrendered a long time ago.

Luftwaffe planes dropped leaflets on the capital along with bombs. Winds swept some of the leaflets far from the target. Ludwig had seen a couple of them. They showed Prague in flames while Jewish-looking men labeled *FRANCE* and *ENGLAND* played the violin. The German caption beneath them read *Your allies fiddle while Prague burns;* Ludwig presumed the Czech forest of consonants meant the same thing.

Burn Prague did. The sour smell of smoke and damp clogged the panzer commander's nostrils. There was just enough drizzle to cut down visibility—not enough to do much against fires. Prague had been catching it since the war started. Not much of the place could still be standing. How many civilians and soldiers had died in the rain of high explosives? Ludwig could smell corpses, too.

But the Czechs fought on in the ruins, perhaps fueled by the courage of despair. *If you want us, come and get us. Come pay the butcher's bill for us,* they seemed to say. And they were making it as expensive as they could.

Fritz Bittenfeld drove the panzer past the burnt-out hulk of a Czech T-35, and then past a dead Panzer I that had had the turret blown clean off the chassis. Ludwig winced when he saw that. Nobody'd really intended the Panzer I for anything more than a training vehicle. It didn't have the firepower or the armor to fight other tanks.

If an emergency came along before your bigger machines were

ready, though . . . If that happened, you used what you had and hoped for the best. And sometimes you got it, and sometimes you bought the farm like the two sorry sons of bitches inside that baby panzer.

Ludwig knew too well his own Panzer II was only a small step up. Its main armament was a good deal better than the Panzer I's pair of rifle-caliber machine guns. It carried thicker armor, too. But the armor wasn't *that* much thicker. The cannon on Czech tanks had no trouble piercing it.

He looked this way, that way, the other way. While he was at it, he wished for eyes in the back of his head. Smashed buildings came closer and closer together as the *Wehrmacht* pushed into Prague's suburbs. Tanks and antitank guns and Czech soldiers with Molotov cocktails had all kinds of places to hide.

Landsers were supposed to root out such dangers. Panzers and foot soldiers worked best together. Each helped protect the other. Armor was great for disposing of machine-gun nests that could hang infantry up for days. Ground pounders returned the favor by spotting lurking soldiers or guns.

Broad-winged Heinkel 111s and slim Dornier bombers—Flying Pencils, people called them—gave Prague one more dose of modern war. Antiaircraft shells burst all around them. Not many Avias rose to challenge the bombers. The little biplanes sure looked as if they came out of the last war, but they'd given Germany's fancy new 109s all they wanted and then some. The Messerschmitts hadn't knocked them out of the sky. Bombers had finally plastered so many Czech airstrips that few Avias could get off the ground.

A Czech machine gun up ahead barked. Ludwig got ready to dive back into the turret. Anybody who talked about how the Slavs were a bunch of *Untermenschen* had never run into Czech engineering—or Czech infantry, for that matter. The guys in the brown uniforms knew what they were doing. They meant business, too.

Then, all of a sudden, the machine gun fell silent. So did all the guns on the Czech side. Little by little, German firing also wound down. Fritz's voice floated out of the speaking tube: "What's going on?"

"Beats me," Ludwig answered. "Stay ready for anything. It's liable to be some kind of trick."

"Don't worry. My asshole's puckered good and tight," the driver said. Ludwig laughed. Then he wondered why. If you hadn't shit yourself or come close, you hadn't really been in combat.

A Czech officer with a flag of truce came out from behind a battered house. He was an older man, old enough to have started out in the Austro-Hungarian army. He walked toward Ludwig's panzer, probably because it was the closest vehicle with a German cross on it. "Will you take me back to your commanders?" he called. Sure as hell, his German had a cloyingly sweet Vienna accent, with Slavic palatals under that.

"I will, sir, but what for?" Ludwig asked.

"I have come to arrange the surrender of Prague." No matter how sugary his accent, the Czech sounded infinitely bitter. "You've murdered enough innocent civilians. We can't stand it any more. I hope you're satisfied."

"I just want to get out of this in one piece," Ludwig said.

The Czech looked at him. "*Ja*, you go where they tell you and do what they tell you. You're nothing but a little cog in the machine— but it's a big machine, and it's slaughtered us. Will you give me a ride?"

"Of course, sir, if you can clamber on up. Not much room inside here, but you can ride on top of the turret. I'll take you back to Regimental HQ, and they'll know what to do with you. . . . Theo!"

"What is it?" the radioman asked.

"Get on the horn with the regiment. Tell 'em I'm bringing back a Czech colonel—I think he's a colonel—with a surrender offer for Prague. Tell 'em it looks like we've got a cease-fire up here for the time being, too."

"Nobody tells me anything," Theo grumbled. Sitting there at the back of the fighting compartment, he was the last to know, all right.

"I'm telling you now," Ludwig said.

He gave the Czech officer a hand. The man might not be young, but he was spry—he didn't really need the help. He might—he undoubtedly did—hate everything the German stood for, but he stayed polite about it. What did the diplomats call that? Correct—that was the word. Ludwig held out a pack of cigarettes. The Czech took one. "Thank you," he said again. "Have you also got a blindfold for me?"

The accent that made Ludwig think of strudel didn't go well with the cynical question. Trying to stay polite himself, the panzer commander said, "Your men fought well."

"We are still fighting well," the Czech said proudly. "This surrender offer is for Prague, perhaps for Bohemia, but not for all of Czechoslovakia. The war goes on in the east."

Ludwig didn't think his superiors would like that. He shrugged. He was only a sergeant. It wasn't his worry. From the bowels of the panzer, Theo said, "Regiment says to bring him in. And they say the truce here can hold, as far as they're concerned."

"In the last war, we did not have communications like these," the Czech officer said. "Do all of your panzers have radio sets?"

He sounded casual—so casual, he made Ludwig wary. "Sir, I'd better not talk about that. Security, you know," the German said. He spoke into the tube that let him talk to the driver: "Back to HQ, Fritz."

"Right, Sergeant." The Panzer II turned nimbly and headed back toward the east. The Czech officer seemed to be taking mental notes. If he was coming in to surrender, it might not matter. Ludwig sure hoped it wouldn't.

FIGHTERS DUELED OVER THE EBRO. Chaim Weinberg watched the new French machines mixing it up with the 109s. Now that France and Germany were at war, the supply spigot to Spain finally got turned on. The Republic had seen more new equipment the past two weeks than in the two years before.

Just because it was new didn't mean it was good. A French fighter spun out of control, trailing smoke. The Messerschmitt that downed it sought fresh prey.

Chaim wasn't the only guy from the International Brigades who swore. In how many tongues did those curses rise? He'd thought—everybody'd thought—enough stuff would come from France to let the Republic settle the Nationalists' hash in nothing flat. There was more, but there wasn't *that* much more. And Sanjurjo's bastards still seemed to be getting stuff from Germany and Italy. That shouldn't have happened, either.

England had the biggest navy in the world, didn't she? And the French had lots of ships, too. So why weren't they doing a better job of closing down Sanjurjo's supply lines? The only answer he could think of was that they didn't give a damn.

Then he stopped worrying about their strategic options. A couple of those Messerschmitts dove for the deck. They weren't running from the French planes. They were going to shoot up the Republican trenches.

Bullets kicked up spurts of dust, closer and closer. Chaim was too far from a dugout to dive into one. He folded himself into a ball to make as small a target as he could. The roar of the powerful engine and the hammering guns filled his world.

The 109 was overhead, so low that he imagined he felt the wind of its passage—or maybe it wasn't his imagination. Then the plane was gone. But even if the wind was imagination, he didn't want to unfold. He had to will himself into doing it.

Somebody not far away was groaning. That got him moving. You did for a buddy, because you wanted to be sure a buddy would do for you, too.

That big blond guy wasn't an American. Chaim thought Gyula was from Hungary. Gyula spoke several languages, including English. In every damn one of them, he sounded like the guy who played Dracula. What he said now wasn't in any language Chaim knew. It sounded impressive as hell, though.

"Wow," he said. "What's that mean?"

Gyula looked at him. The Hungarian had a mashed foot—no wonder he was groaning. He'd be lucky to keep it. "A horse's cock up your ass," he said in English.

For a second, Chaim thought the other guy was cussing at him. Then he realized Gyula was just answering his question. "Let me bandage you up," Chaim said. He yelled for stretcher-bearers in English and Spanish. His own accent was god-awful, but people would understand that.

"You better cut my shoe off," Gyula said. "Don't try to yank it over the wound. I kill you if you do that."

With that damn Bela Lugosi voice, he should have sounded silly. He should have—and no doubt he would have, if he didn't so obviously mean it. Clumsily, Chaim took the bayonet off his rifle. At least it had a blade; it wasn't one of the damn spears the French liked.

Gyula's boot was falling apart anyway. That made things easier. Chaim winced when he got a good look at the wound. The Hungarian's instep was smashed all to hell. Yeah, he'd lose most of the foot if not all of it.

He saw the same thing. As Chaim wrapped a puttee around the wound to slow the bleeding, he said, "I can go home now. Admiral Horthy won't draft me."

"*Mazel tov,*" Chaim said dryly. "He'll shoot you instead, and not in the foot." Gyula was close to forty. He'd fought in the last war, and for Bela Kun in Hungary's short-lived Communist revolution. If he went back to Budapest, he'd be about as welcome as the smallpox.

"Right now, I wouldn't mind. Hurts like a motherfucker," Gyula said. "Got any morphine?"

Chaim shook his head. "Sorry. Wish I did." He meant that. He could have got nailed as easily as Gyula. Dumb luck, one way or the other.

The stretcher-bearers showed up then. They were Internationals, too. That was good—or Chaim thought so. They'd be gentler with Gyula as they took him away. Spaniards faced their own pain with stolid indifference . . . and they were even more indifferent when somebody else got hurt.

Away they went. They wore Red Cross smocks and armbands. That might keep the Nationalists from shooting at them. On the other hand, it might not. This was a rough old war. You *really* didn't want to let the other side capture you, no matter which side you were on.

Cautiously, Chaim straightened up till he could peer over the lip of the trench. He wanted to make sure Sanjurjo's bastards weren't swarming forward. As soon as he did, he ducked down again. He wouldn't come up again in the same spot. He knew better than that. Why give the snipers a free shot at you? Guys who did that ended up with a new hole in the head.

He took a swig from his water bottle. It wasn't water, but sour white wine—horse piss, really. But it was less likely to give you the galloping shits than Ebro water was. He'd had dysentery once, and was glad he'd got over it. He sure as hell didn't want it again.

When he looked again, ten or fifteen yards down the trench from the place where he'd last popped up, he spied two or three Nationalists looking out of their trenches a couple of hundred yards away and toward him. As he ducked, he saw them ducking at the same time.

They're scared of me, he thought, not without pride. They even looked like Fascist assholes. Like most of Sanjurjo's better troops, they wore German-style helmets. But they were scared of a dumb Jew from New York City. If that wasn't a kick in the nuts, he didn't know what would be.

If you had a rifle in your hands, you were dangerous. It was as simple as that. The thing you had to remember, though, was that the other son of a bitch was dangerous as long as he had a rifle, too.

VACLAV JEZEK STUMBLED OVER THE border. Behind him, Slovakia was going to hell in a handbasket. The Germans were breaking in from the west. The Hungarians, not about to miss a chance to seize again what they'd ruled for centuries, were breaking in from the south. The Slovaks were up in arms—German-supplied arms—against what was left of Czechoslovakian authority. *Ingrate bastards,* Jezek thought, not that anybody gave a damn about his opinion.

He didn't know what the Poles would do with him—to him—either. Poland was also more or less at war with Czechoslovakia. By now, Tesin would be Cieszun, or however the hell the Poles spelled it. He doubted whether his own country tried very hard to defend the mining town. When a lion jumped you, you didn't worry about the jackals.

The country was rough and broken. Most of the leaves were off the trees, though, which made people easier to spot. And, being off the trees, the leaves lay underfoot. Every time Vaclav took a step, they crunched underfoot. They might as well have shouted *Here I am!*

But so what? He didn't want to sit around in a Nazi POW camp till the war ended. Whatever the Poles did to him had to be better than that . . . didn't it? Behind him, he could still hear bombs and shells bursting and machine guns going off. More Czech soldiers—the ones who could—were stumbling north, out of the fighting. They'd made the same calculation he had. Now . . . were the lot of them right?

Somebody up ahead shouted something. Vaclav *almost* understood it. Polish and Czech were closely related—not so closely as Czech and Slovak, but still. . . . A word here and there came through, even if each of them seemed to carry an extra syllable or two.

Vaclav stood still. He thought that was what the Pole was telling him to do. "I give up!" he shouted back. "You can intern me!"

The Pole came out from behind a tree. He wore a greenish uniform, not brown like Vaclav's (not filthy and tattered like Vaclav's, either) or German field-gray. The bayoneted rifle he carried looked extremely businesslike. Moving slowly and carefully, Vaclav unslung his own piece and laid it on the ground in front of his feet.

With a nod, the Pole advanced on him. They tried to talk. It was an exercise in near misses and frustration. Then the Pole—a big blond fellow—raised an ironic eyebrow and asked, *"Sprechen Sie Deutsch?"*

"Ja," Jezek said miserably. Two Slavs, having to go back and forth in German!

"Gut," the Pole said. *"Jetzt können wir wirklich einander verstehen."* And they *could* really understand each other now, no matter how much Vaclav loathed the idea. Still in German, the Pole went on, "Give me your name and rank and unit."

Dully, Vaclav did. "What will you do with me?" he asked.

"We have a camp a few kilometers to the north," the Polish soldier answered. "Did you say you wanted to be interned before?"

"Ja," Vaclav said again.

"I thought so, but I wasn't sure," the Pole said. "Well, you will be. You are not a prisoner of war, not here. Poland and Czechoslovakia are not formally at war."

"No. You just grabbed," Jezek said bitterly.

With a shrug, the big man in the green uniform answered, "So did you Czechs, after the last war. Otherwise, the coal mines down there would have been ours all along. And then you act like your shit doesn't stink."

"Oh, mine does. I know that," Vaclav said. "But if you are friends with Hitler, he will make you sorry."

"Better him than Stalin and the damned Reds," the Pole retorted.

"You find friends where you can. At least the Russians did something for us. More than France and England did," Vaclav said.

"What did you expect? They're full of Jews," the Pole said. No wonder he liked Hitler better than Stalin. He stooped, picked up Vaclav's rifle, and slung it over his own shoulder. Then he pointed north. "The camp is that way. Get moving, Corporal Jezek."

Shoulders slumped in despair, Vaclav got moving.

Chapter 5

The night was cool and damp. Most nights were, as October moved toward November. Willi Dernen peered at the Frenchmen who'd nipped off a few square kilometers of German soil.

They were warmer than he was. They'd started a fire and sat around it. From 300 meters, he could have potted them easily. Orders were not to piss them off, no matter what. If they wanted to sit on their asses as if they hadn't crossed the border, they were welcome to.

If they'd really come loaded for bear . . .

Willi's shiver had nothing to do with the weather. He was a blond, stolid watchmaker's son from Breslau, all the way over on the other side of the *Reich*. He could hardly follow the German they spoke here, and the locals had trouble with his accent, too. But he'd been on the Westwall since France and England declared war. He knew what would have happened had the French put some muscle into a push instead of tiptoeing over the border.

They would have smashed the Westwall as if they were made of cardboard. Not a *Landser* here thought any differently. The Westwall was Goebbels' joke on the democracies. On paper, and on the radio, it was as formidable as the Maginot Line. For real, construction gangs were still frantically building forts and obstructions. And the Westwall didn't have nearly enough troops to man what was already built.

Most of the *Wehrmacht* had gone off to kick Czechoslovakia's ass. What was left . . . the French outnumbered somewhere between three and five to one. That was the bad news. The good news was, they didn't seem to know it.

One of the Frenchmen pulled out a concertina and began to play. The thin, plaintive notes made Willi shake his head. How could the guys on the other side listen to crap like that? Horns, drums, fiddles—*that* was music.

Beside Dernen, Wolfgang Storch whispered, "We ought to plug him just so he'll shut up, you know?"

Trust Wolfgang to come up with something like that, Willi thought. He whispered back: "Damn you, you almost made me laugh out loud. That wouldn't be so good."

"Why not?" Storch said. "Probably make the Frenchmen piss themselves."

Willi did snort then, not because Wolfgang was wrong but because he was right. Willi had come *that* close to pissing *him*self when he was part of a firefight right after the French came over the border. The guy next to him took one right in the belly. The noises Klaus made . . . You didn't want to remember things like that, but you couldn't very well forget them. When Willi went to sleep, he heard Klaus shrieking in his nightmares. He smelled the other man's blood, like hot iron—and his shit, too.

One of the Frenchmen looked up. The guy with the concertina stopped playing. All of the men in khaki looked around. Willi pretended he wasn't there as hard as he could. It must have worked, because none of the enemy soldiers got to his feet or anything. Tiny in the distance, one of them shrugged a comically French shrug. The concertina player started up again.

"Let's head back and report in," Wolfgang said.

"Now you're talking. You and your stupid jokes." It was hard to stay really mad when you were whispering in a tiny voice, but Willi gave it his best shot. "We wouldn't've got in a jam if you weren't such a damn smartass."

"Your mother," Wolfgang answered sweetly.

Both Germans drew back as softly as they could. The French soldier with the concertina went on playing. Willi took that as a good sign. Maybe the Frenchmen were using the noise as cover. That would be a smart thing to do. It would also be an aggressive thing to do. The French might be smart. They'd shown no sign of aggressiveness.

All the same, Willi wanted no part of a nasty surprise. All it would take was a sergeant who'd been through the mill the last time around. Willi's father was a guy like that. When he and his buddies got together and drank some beer, they'd start telling stories. Like any kid, Willi listened. There probably weren't a lot of guys his age who hadn't heard stories like that. Some veterans, though, didn't care to talk. Willi hadn't understood that, not till Klaus got it. He did now.

They'd gone about half a kilometer when a no-doubt-about-it German voice challenged them: "Halt! Who goes there?"

"Two German soldiers: Dernen and Storch," Willi answered. He and Wolfgang were out in the middle of a field. The *Landser* who owned that voice might have been . . . anywhere.

"Give the password," the man said.

"*Sonnenschein,*" Willi and Wolfgang chorused. A Frenchman poking around could have picked it up from them, but the French didn't do much of that kind of poking.

"Pass on," the sentry said.

They did. The Germans were ready for anything. The French didn't seem to be. They didn't have to be, either—they had numbers, and the *Wehrmacht* didn't. But they acted as if that would go on forever. And it wouldn't.

Willi got a glimpse of just how true that was when he and Wolfgang finished making their report. They ducked out of Colonel Bauer's tent and found themselves in the middle of chaos. Soldiers were jumping down from trucks whose headlights were cut down to slits by masking tape. Some of the belching, farting monsters there weren't trucks at all. They were panzers.

Both Willi and Wolfgang gaped at them. Willi hadn't seen a panzer up till now in all the time he'd spent on the Western Front. He supposed there were a few, in case the French decided they were serious about attacking here. But he sure hadn't seen any.

"It must be all over in Czechoslovakia," he said.

"*Ja.*" Wolfgang nodded. "Took longer than it should have, too."

"Everything takes longer than it's supposed to," Willi said. "No matter how smart the generals are, the bastards on the other side have generals, too."

Wolfgang laughed at him. "Generals? Smart? What have you been drinking? Whatever it is, I want some, too."

"Oh, come on. You know what I mean. If the guys with the red stripes on their trousers"—Willi meant the General Staff—"don't end up smarter than the generals on the other side, we're in trouble."

"But everybody knows the generals on the other side are a bunch of jerks," Wolfgang said. "So how smart do our fellows need to be?"

Before Willi could answer, more panzers rumbled up. Shouting sergeants ordered them under such trees as there were. Not all of them would fit there. Soldiers spread camouflage netting over the ones that had to stay out in the open. Not many French reconnaissance planes came over, but the *Wehrmacht* didn't believe in taking chances when it didn't have to.

Wolfgang Storch pointed back toward the French soldiers they'd been watching. "Hope those assholes don't hear the racket and start wondering what's up."

"Don't worry about it," Willi told him. They laughed. Why not? Their side was doing things. The enemy was sitting around. If the French had no stomach for a fight but one came to them anyway . . .

"BURN EVERYTHING," SERGEANT DEMANGE SAID. "When we pull back into France, we want the Germans to remember we were here." The cigarette in the corner of his mouth jerked up and down as he spoke.

One of the guys in Luc Harcourt's squad splashed kerosene against the side of a barn. Luc grabbed a burning stick from the cookfire and touched it to a wet place. He had to jump back, or the flames might have got him. The barn sent a black plume of smoke into the leaden sky.

Other soldiers were torching the farmhouse near the barn. "Hey, Sergeant?" Luc called.

Demange eyed him as if he were a chancre on humanity's scrotum. But then, Demange looked at everybody and everything that way. "What do you want, kid?" he said. *Make it good, or else* lurked menacingly under the words.

"If we're doing everything we can to hurt the *Boches,* how come we're pulling out, not going forward?" As far as Luc could see, the whole halfhearted invasion was nothing but a sad, unfunny joke. Now it was ending without even a punch line.

"Well, we went in to give the Czechs a hand, *oui?*" the sergeant said.

"Sure," Harcourt answered. "So?"

"So now there's no more Czechoslovakia, so what's the point of hanging around any longer? That's how I heard it from the lieutenant, so that's what the brass is saying." Demange looked around to make sure no officers were in earshot. Satisfied, he went on, "You ask me what the real story is, we're scared green."

Maybe Demange would end up in trouble for defeatism if some-body reported him to the lieutenant. More likely, he'd eat the platoon commander without salt. And what he said made an unpleasant amount of sense. "We haven't fought enough to see how tough the Nazis really are," Luc said.

"You know that. I know that. You think the old men in the fancy kepis know that?" Demange made as if to wipe his ass, presumably with the collected wisdom of the French General Staff. "Come on, get mov-ing!" the underofficer added. "I think you just want to stand around and gab instead of working."

Luc liked work no better than anyone else in his right mind. Even standing around with thirty-odd kilos on his back wasn't his idea of fun. But the fire warmed the chilly morning. He sighed as he trudged away. Pretty soon, tramping along under all that weight would warm him up, too, but not so pleasantly.

Every once in a while, somebody off in the distance would fire a rifle or squeeze off a burst from a machine gun. For the most part, though, the Germans seemed content to let the French leave if they wanted to.

Here and there, the retreating French troops passed men warily waiting in foxholes and sandbagged machine-gun nests. The rear guard would give the *Boches* a hard time if they were inclined to get frisky. The soldiers Luc could see looked serious about their job. They probably thought they were saving the French army from destruction. And maybe they were right.

Maybe. But it didn't look that way now.

Luc's company marched out of Germany at almost exactly the place where they'd gone in a month earlier. Luc eyed the customs post, now wrecked, that marked the frontier. Men had suffered there. And for what? Maybe the important people, the people who ran things, under-stood. Luc had no idea.

"It's the capitalists who are making us pull out," Jacques Vallat said.

He'd been drafted out of an army factory in Lyon, and was as Red as Sergeant Demange's eyes. "The fools are more afraid of Stalin than they are of Hitler."

"Shut your yap, Vallat," the sergeant said without much heat. "Just keep picking 'em up and laying 'em down. When you get to be a general, then you can talk politics."

"If I get to be a general, France has more trouble than she knows what to do with," Vallat replied.

"You said it. I didn't." Demange might have come out of an auto factory in Lyon himself. He showed no weariness, or even strain. By the way he marched, he could have tramped across France with no more than some gasoline and an oil change or two.

Luc wished *he* had that endless, effortless endurance. He was a lot harder than he had been when he got drafted, but he knew he couldn't match the sergeant. Demange was a professional, a mercenary in the service of his own country. With a white kepi on his head, he wouldn't have been out of place in the Foreign Legion.

"Back in France," Paul Renouvin said. "Funny—it doesn't look any different. Doesn't feel any different, either."

"Oh, some, maybe," Luc said. "When I camp tonight, I won't have the feeling some bastard's watching me from the bushes."

"No, huh? You don't think the Germans'll sneak after us?" Paul said.

"*Merde!*" Luc hadn't thought of that. He'd figured that, once the French pulled back from Germany, the *Boches* would leave them alone. Why not? The Germans had pretty much left them alone while they were inside Germany.

"We're going to pay for this," Jacques Vallat predicted. "We had our chance, and we didn't grab it. Now they're done in Czechoslovakia. Where do they go next?"

"Didn't I tell you once to shut up?" Sergeant Demange's voice stayed flat, but now it held a certain edge. "You want to go pissing and moaning, go piss and moan to the captain."

"He'd throw me in the stockade," Vallat said with gloomy certainty.

"You'd deserve it, too," Demange said. "Running your mouth when you don't know shit . . . But if you're in the stockade, you can't do anything useful. Tonight, you fill up everybody's canteen."

Jacques' sigh was martyred. Everyone took turns at the different fatigue duties. That one was more fatiguing than most. And the men had already been marching all day. Not that the day was very long. Darkness came early, and with it rain. Luc's helmet kept the water off his head, and the greatcoat let him stay pretty dry, but marching through rain and deepening twilight wasn't his cup of tea.

But tents and hot food and strong coffee waited for the soldiers who'd withdrawn from Germany. It wasn't as good as ending up in bed with a pretty girl—but what was? Nobody was shooting at him. He had a full belly, and he was warm. When you were a soldier, that seemed better than good enough.

PEGGY DRUCE HAD HOT FOOD, even if most of it was boiled potatoes and turnips. She had coffee. The Germans insisted it was the same stuff they drank. If it was, she pitied them. Nobody was shooting at her. She'd never thought she would have to worry about that . . . till the day she did.

She was a neutral, which meant the Germans treated her better than the English and French they'd also caught at Marianske Lazne. She got plenty of potatoes and turnips and godawful coffee. They had enough to keep body and soul together, but not much more. And if she were a Jew . . .

Till the war started, she'd looked down her snub nose at Jews. If you weren't one, you did. She'd taken it for granted, the same way she'd taken for granted that nothing bad could ever happen to her. She was an American. She had money. She had looks.

Shells didn't care. Neither did machine-gun bullets. She'd seen things at Marianske Lazne she wouldn't forget as long as she lived. (And she wouldn't call the place Marienbad any more, even if that was easier to say. The Germans used the old name anew. If they did, she wouldn't.)

Not all of what she wished she could forget came during the bombardment, or when she was bandaging wounded afterwards.

Quite a few Jews had been stuck in the resort with everybody else. The ones who were foreign nationals aimed their passports at the Nazis the way you'd aim a crucifix at a vampire. Peggy had no idea whether crucifixes worked; in that part of Europe, some people might. But the passports did. By their growls, the German soldiers and the SS men who followed them into Marianske Lazne might have been Dobermans brought up short by their chains. However much they growled, though, they treated Jews who weren't from Czechoslovakia no worse than any other foreign nationals they'd nabbed.

Jews who *were* from Czechoslovakia . . . Peggy shuddered at the memories. Jews from Czechoslovakia were basically fair game. It wasn't so much that the Blackshirts kicked some of them around for the fun of it. It wasn't even that the soldiers set others to scrubbing sidewalks with toothbrushes.

No. It was the way the Germans grinned when they did it. Peggy had had the misfortune to watch several SS men surround a plump, dignified, bearded, middle-aged Jew. The Jew wore ghetto attire: black trousers, long black coat, broad-brimmed black hat. In color, his clothes matched the Nazis' uniforms.

Which did him less than no good at all. One of the Blackshirts grabbed his hat and scaled it. He might have been a nasty kid on a schoolyard flinging another boy's cap. He might have been, yes, if he and his buddies didn't carry pistols and have the might of a mechanized army behind them. A schoolboy could punch another schoolboy in the nose. The Jew would have been committing suicide if he tried.

He just stood there, hoping they'd go away now that they'd had their sport. No such luck. A different SS man pulled out a big pair of pinking shears. He went to work on the Jew's beard. If he got some cheek or nose or ear while he did his barbering, that was part of the fun.

And the Jew just went on standing there. The look in his eyes was a million years old. It said his ancestors had been through this before, again and again. It said he hadn't done anything to deserve it, but deserving had nothing to do with anything. It said . . . It said *Father, forgive them; for they know not what they do.* Yes, that was from the New Testament, but so what? After all, what was Jesus to the Romans? Just another goddamn Jew.

Later, Peggy wondered why she didn't charge the SS bastards. *I should have,* she thought bitterly. Most of the time, she was somebody who went ahead first and worried about it later. Here, she only stood and watched. Maybe horror froze her. Maybe it was sheer disbelief. Could this really be happening right here before her eyes, here in Europe, cradle and beacon of civilization, here near the middle of the twentieth century?

It could. It was.

The Jew didn't say a word as he was shorn. He didn't flinch—much—whenever the shears drew blood. He just . . . looked at the SS men with those ancient, pain-filled eyes. And that didn't do him any good, either. When the barber was satisfied with his handiwork, he hauled off and slapped the Jew, hard enough to turn his head around. Another Nazi kicked the man in the ass. That got a groan from him and doubled him over.

"Enough for now," said the SS noncom with the shears.

"*Ja.* Let's find a fresh kike," another Blackshirt replied.

Peggy didn't speak a lot of German—her French was much better. She understood them, though. Off they went, laughing and joking. The worst of it was, they didn't act like men who'd just done something evil and cruel. As far as they were concerned, this was what they'd come to Czechoslovakia to do, the same way she'd come here to take the waters.

God help them, she thought. *God help us all.* But God didn't seem to be listening. Maybe He was out taking the waters somewhere Himself, or maybe He was off playing golf in Florida. He could do whatever He pleased. His Chosen People didn't look to be so lucky.

Even after the SS men went away, Peggy'd needed all of her nerve to go up to the poor Jew they'd abused. "Can I help you?" she'd asked hesitantly—in French, thinking more German was the last thing the man would want to hear then.

He'd straightened when she spoke to him. She remembered that, and the way he'd reached up to touch the brim of his hat, only to discover it wasn't there. Where blood running down his face and dripping from one ear didn't, the missing hat made him grimace.

Sadly, he'd answered, "*Madame,* do you truly imagine anyone could help me now?" His French was gutturally accented, but at least as fluent as hers.

She hadn't answered him. What could she have said? *Yes* would have been a lie, *no* too bitter to bear. She'd turned away instead.

And then, poor devil, he'd tried to comfort *her.* "When you are of my folk, *Madame,* you learn to expect such things now and again," he'd said.

Again, she hadn't answered. If he was right, that only made things worse. If he was wrong . . . But he wasn't wrong, dammit. You didn't have to like Jews—and Peggy didn't, not especially—to know they'd been getting the shitty end of the stick for the past 2,000 years. Had they ever got so much of it as the Nazis seemed to want to dish out, though?

People here in this camp claimed the *Luftwaffe* made a point of pounding Jewish districts in Prague and Brno and other Czech cities. Others said that was a bunch of hooey—nothing but stale propaganda. Peggy didn't know for sure; she hadn't been in any of those places while German bombers flew overhead. But she had no doubts at all about which way she'd bet.

One day, a uniformed German official—was there any other kind these days?—assembled the interned neutrals and harangued them in his language. Even though Peggy spoke some German, she couldn't follow word one. The big, beefy fellow had an accent she'd never heard before and hoped she never heard again.

"He has to come from somewhere near the Swiss border," a man standing near Peggy said to his wife. Peggy had guessed they were Belgians, but maybe they were from the French-speaking part of Switzerland.

Then the official switched to French. He had a devil of an accent there, too, but Peggy could understand him: he slowed down to speak a language foreign to him. "Now that the fighting is over, we are arranging transport to neutral destinations for you all. There will be railroad service into Romania in the near future, as soon as lines through Slovakia are repaired."

Quite a few people looked happy: Romanians, Bulgarians, Yugoslavs, Greeks. A lot of wealthy Balkans types came up to Czechoslovakia for the waters. It was the kind of thing their parents would have done in 1914. Some of those parents would have been citizens of Austria-Hungary. Even the ones who weren't, even the ones who hated it, would have been cultural satellites of the Hapsburg empire. That ramshackle state was twenty years dead now, carved up like a Christmas goose. But its influence lingered even though it was gone.

The Nazi official started over one more time, in what he fondly imagined to be English. Peggy raised her hand, then waved it. "Question, please!" she called in French.

"Yes?" The German didn't looked pleased at being interrupted.

"Suppose we don't want to go to Romania?"

"It is being arranged that you should go there," he replied, as if her desires were as distant and unimportant as the canals of Mars.

"But I don't want to." Peggy never liked it when anybody tried to arrange her life for her. One reason she loved her husband was that he had sense enough to stay out of her way. She went on, "I'm an American. I want to go up to Poland or Sweden or Norway, where it's easier to find a ship for the United States."

"If the *Führer*'s government has arranged that you should go to Romania, to Romania you will go." The German official might have said, *Sunrise tomorrow is at half past seven.* He would have sounded no more certain about that.

Which only proved he'd never had anything to do with Peggy Druce. "No," she said.

Had he worn a monocle, it would have fallen out. His eyes opened that wide. "Who do you think you are, to challenge the carefully arranged"—he liked that word—"plans of the *Reich*?"

"I'm an American citizen," Peggy said. St. Paul could have sounded no prouder proclaiming that he was a citizen of Rome. If the Germans didn't worry about doughboys coming Over There—well, Over Here—they'd forgotten about 1918.

Maybe Mr. Beefy had. "You are not in America now," he reminded her. "We are obliged to repatriate you as we can. We are not obliged to be convenient for you." By the way he said it, he would drive fifty miles out of his way to be inconvenient for her.

"You won't even let me buy a train ticket for somewhere I want to go? You won't even let me spend my own money?" Peggy had trouble believing that. People always wanted you to spend your money. That had been her experience for as long as she'd had money to spend.

But the Nazi's nasty smile said he was going to tell her no. It also made Peggy give back an even nastier smile: the bastard had some of the worst teeth she'd ever seen. "You will go where we want you to go when we want you to go there. We will tell you how to go. This is to prevent espionage, you understand. We are at war."

"*Certainement,*" Peggy replied. "If I told you where to go and how to get there, you would need to pack for a mighty warm climate. You can count on that."

The German official looked puzzled. So did her fellow internees. None of the handful of other Americans seemed to speak French well enough to understand what she'd just told him. The Europeans, most of whom knew French at least as well as she did, didn't get the American idiom. Bound to be just as well.

Romania! She threw up her hands. If she'd wanted to visit Romania, she would have gone there. Or she'd thought so, anyhow. Now she looked to be on her way whether she wanted to go or not.

BACK IN THE USSR. SERGEI YAROSLAVSKY didn't realize how lucky he was to have got out of Czechoslovakia in one piece till he found out how many aircrews and bombers hadn't. The Nazis had far better planes, and far more of them, than they'd shown in Spain.

Even trying to learn what had happened to the fellows you didn't see at the airstrip near Kamenets-Podolsk was risky. Ask too many questions, or the wrong questions, or even the right questions of the wrong people, and you'd end up in a camp. Over the past couple of years, generals—marshals!—had disappeared or been shot for treason after show trials. The NKVD wouldn't blink at gobbling up a junior officer.

The Fascists could kill you. So could your own side. With the Fascists, it wasn't personal. You were just an enemy. To your own side, you were a traitor. They'd put you over a slow fire and make you suffer.

Most of what Sergei knew about the missing crews, he knew because of Anastas Mouradian. Sergei still didn't like people from the Caucasus for beans, but they had their uses. In a Soviet Union dominated by Russians (*and by Jews*, Yaroslavsky added to himself), the southern peoples had to stick together to survive, much less get ahead. They had their own built-in underground, so to speak.

And so the copilot knew to whom he could talk and how much he could say. He had reasonable confidence what he said wouldn't go past the person he said it to. And Armenians and Georgians and such folk were like Jews: they . . . knew things. You never could tell how they knew, but they did.

One bomber had crash-landed in Poland. The pilot saved his crew, though the Poles interned them. Had the story ended there, Sergei would have been glad to hear it. If your plane had battle damage or mechanical failure, you just hoped you could walk away from the landing. But things took an ugly turn.

In a low voice, Mouradian said, "The families . . ." and shook his head.

Sergei needed no more than that to understand what was going on. "Camps?" he asked, dismally sure he knew the answer.

"*Da.*" Anastas Mouradian looked faintly pained that the pilot even needed to say the word. To Russians, Armenians and Georgians seemed sneaky, subtle, devious bastards. You never could trust them. Till now, Sergei had never wondered how he might seem to Anastas. Like a dim backwoods bumpkin? He wouldn't have been surprised.

He wasn't surprised to hear the aircrew's families had been seized, either. If you didn't come back to the *Rodina*—the motherland—the NKVD would figure you didn't want to. Battle damage? Mechanical failure? The secret police wouldn't give a rat's ass about any of that. They'd scent treason whether it was there or not. And everybody knew treason was contagious. Whether the bomber crew caught it from their families or spread it to them, the families would have to be cauterized.

NKVD men got paid to think like that. Ordinary Soviet citizens had to, if they wanted to stay . . . well, not safe—nobody was safe—but somewhere close, anyhow.

"*Bozhemoi,*" Sergei muttered. "You're sure?"

Mouradian's dark, bushy eyebrows leapt reproachfully. "If I say something happened, it happened." His voice went hard and flat. "*Yob tvoyu mat',*" he added—literally, *I fuck your mother.* As always, tone and emphasis were everything when you said something like that. Said another way, it would have started a fight. But he meant something more like *I shit you not*.

"All right, all right. I believe you," Yaroslavsky said. "It just . . . gets to you sometimes, you know?"

"*Nichevo*," Anastas answered. Everybody in the USSR, Russian or not, used and understood that word. *What can you do?* or *It can't be helped* fit too many Soviet scenarios, as it had in the days of the Tsars. Somebody once said Russian peasants ran on cabbage, vodka, and *nichevo*.

At a pinch, Sergei supposed you could do without cabbage.

As he had before, Mouradian looked around again. His voice dropped again: "You don't want to tell this to the Chimp. He used to drink with the bombardier on the plane that went down."

"He drank with everybody," Sergei said. Sure as hell, Ivan Kuchkov ran on vodka.

"Just keep quiet. He may find out about it anyway, but better he doesn't find out from you," Anastas Mouradian said.

"Right." Sergei nodded. If Ivan found out his drinking buddy was interned and the man's family off to the gulag, he'd want to break something . . . or somebody. He'd get drunk, which wouldn't make him any cheerier. And he'd babble about where he got the news. All of that could easily add up to trouble. Maybe changing the subject was a good idea: "Hear anything about when we'll start flying again?"

"Not supposed to be too long," the copilot said. "But who knows what that means?"

"Right," Yaroslavsky repeated. Like old Russia, the new USSR always ran late. Five-Year Plans were trying to drag the Soviet Union into a consciousness of time like that in the West. Clocks sprouted everywhere, like toadstools. But with a language where the verb *to be* had no present tense, how far could the apparatchiks go with their changes?

Sergei thanked the God in Whom he wasn't supposed to believe that

that was somebody else's worry. He just had to follow orders and not think too much. He was sure he could manage that.

A corporal in the groundcrew came over to him. "Sir, Captain Kuznetsov wants to see you right away."

"I'm coming." Yaroslavsky couldn't suppress a nasty twinge of fear. "Did he say why?" he asked. Was he bound for Siberia? Did Kuznetsov get a command to take him out and shoot him? Sometimes following your own orders and not thinking too much wouldn't save you. Sometimes nothing would.

But the corporal shook his head. "No, sir. Only that he wants to see you."

"I serve the Soviet Union!" Sergei hurried off toward the captain's tent. Anastas Mouradian nodded to him as he went. Something glinted in the Armenian's dark eyes. Sympathy? Anastas was no fool. He knew all the things that could happen. He knew they could happen to him, too. The corporal, by contrast, was too dumb and too stolid ever to get in trouble.

When Sergei ducked into the tent, he was relieved to see no uniformed strangers standing next to Captain Kuznetsov, who sat at a rickety table doing paperwork by the light of a kerosene lamp. Kuznetsov looked up and set down his pen. "Ah. Yaroslavsky." His tone could have meant anything—or nothing.

Sergei saluted. "Reporting as ordered, sir." If he was going down, he'd go down with style. Not that that would do him any goddamn good, either.

"*Da*," Kuznetsov said, again with nothing special in his voice. Then he went on, "Make sure you and your airplane are ready to fly out of here first thing tomorrow morning."

"Yes, *sir!*" Sergei couldn't keep the relief from his voice. An order that was a real order! "Uh, sir . . . Where are we flying to?"

"To Drisa, northwest of Polotsk," Captain Kuznetsov answered. "It's right near the Polish and Lithuanian borders—and it's about as close to East Prussia as we can get while we stay in the *Rodina*."

"I see." Yaroslavsky wondered if he did. "Will we be flying against Germany again, then, sir?"

"We have no orders for that at the present time," his superior said. He didn't go on to say whether he thought it was likely or unlikely. Sergei didn't presume to press him, either. If you gave an opinion that turned out to be wrong, somebody would make you pay for it. If you kept your mouth shut, no one could pin anything on you.

Along with the rest of the SB-2s in the squadron (except for one grounded by bad hydraulics), Sergei's flew out at first light the next morning. Ivan Kuchkov was badly hung over. Yaroslavsky wouldn't have wanted to fly like that, not with the two big engines throbbing and growling away. Nothing the bombardier could do about it, though, not unless he wanted to try his luck with the stockade—or, more likely, the NKVD. If Kuchkov complained, the engines' thrum kept anybody else from hearing him.

Russia scrolled along below the bomber: farmland and forest and swamp, with here and there a town looking all but lost in the vastness of the landscape. Puddles in the Pripet Marshes reflected the gray sky. Mouradian minded the map and made sure the bomber didn't stray too far west and end up in Polish airspace. Sergei wasn't afraid of what the Poles would do to him. They flew nothing close to the deadly German Messerschmitts. But what his own superiors would do to him for screwing up didn't bear thinking about.

"Drisa's in Byelorussia, yes?" Mouradian asked.

"Yes," Sergei agreed.

The Armenian sighed. "They'll talk like the Devil's uncle, then."

Russians didn't have any trouble following Byelorussian. Russians could follow Ukrainian, which differed more from their language. And of course Byelorussians and Ukrainians had to understand Russian. But

Anastas Mouradian had learned it in school. He spoke well, and understood standard Russian well. Its cousins, though, weren't open books to him, the way they were to Sergei.

North of the Pripet Marshes, patches of snow started showing up on the ground. It would be colder here. Sergei suspected he would spend a lot of time in his flight suit. Leather and fleece that could keep out the cold at 8,000 meters could do the same against even the Russian winter.

He landed the SB-2 on a dirt strip outside of Drisa—an unprepossessing place if ever there was one. His teeth clicked together when the plane touched down. The runway was anything but smooth. He didn't bite his tongue, though. And the SB-2 was built to take it. As he brought the bomber to a stop, he wondered how much it would have to take, and how soon.

Chapter 6

Another gray, damp, chilly day in Münster. Sarah Goldman sat in the rickety bleachers at a soccer pitch and watched her brother break away from the back who was trying to guard him. Both teams were made up of nothing but Jews. Saul was so much better than anyone else on the field, it wasn't even funny.

The goalkeeper ran out to try to cut down his angle. Saul got his toe under the ball, lofted it just over the fellow's luckless, reaching hands, and watched it bounce once and roll into the net.

"Goal!" Sarah shouted exultantly. Her mother and father clapped their hands. That made it 5–2 with only about ten minutes left in the second half. Saul's team had the game in the bag.

But he only shrugged, as if embarrassed at what he'd done. He probably was. This was his second goal of the match, and he'd assisted on two others. The soccer couldn't be much fun when you outclassed friends and foes alike. Saul might have made a professional in another year or two. It didn't seem he'd ever get the chance now.

Sarah supposed she ought to count herself lucky the Jews got any chance to play at all. Yes, these bleachers might fall down in a stiff breeze. Yes, she was sitting on a blanket because she'd end up with splinters in her *tukhus* if she didn't. Yes, the pitch was bumpy and looked as if it were mown by goats. This had to be the most miserable place to play for kilometers around.

Which was, of course, the only reason the Jews got to use it. Sarah pictured a plump, blond, uniformed athletic commissioner laughing till his jowls wobbled as he gave the two Jewish teams permission to play here. Maybe he thought a match here would be worse than no match at all. Were the teams involved full of Aryans, he might have been right.

Ever since 1933, though, Jews had had to take whatever scraps of comfort and pleasure they could find. Even a soccer match on a horrible excuse for a pitch was better than none. It gave people an excuse to get out of the house, an excuse to get together and see one another and gab.

Yes, a couple of policemen were also watching the game and the little crowd in the stands. What could you do about that? Nothing, as Sarah knew too well. If you were a Jew in the *Reich,* somebody was going to keep an eye on you.

She leaned over to her father and asked, "What do they think we're going to do? Roll up the chalk lines and carry them home in our handbags and pockets?"

Samuel Goldman shrugged. "Maybe they do. Maybe they think we can turn the lines into bombs or something, and use them to blow up NSDAP headquarters."

"Would you blow up Nazi headquarters if you could?" Sarah asked.

"Of course not!" Father's reply was too loud and too quick. "The National Socialists have done wonderful things for the *Reich.* They've made Germany wake up." *Deutschland erwache!* was a favorite Nazi slogan.

As Father spoke, his eyes told Sarah she'd been foolish. After a moment's thought, she knew just how, too. Father couldn't hope to give her a straight answer, not where anyone else could hear him talking. Yes, the only people in earshot were other Jews. But did that mean they wouldn't betray one of their own? *Fat chance*, Sarah thought bitterly. If ratting on fellow Jews would give them a moment's advantage, plenty of people would do it in a heartbeat.

Sarah hoped she would never stoop to anything as vile as that. She hoped so, yes, but she admitted to herself that she wasn't sure. Times kept getting harder and harder. If not for Father's gentile friends who gave him articles to write, she didn't know what the family would have done.

Mercifully, the match ended. The teams lined up and shook hands with each other. Players tousled one another's sweaty hair. The goal keeper on the other side mimed chipping the ball the way Saul had, then threw up his hands in mock—or maybe not mock—despair.

The sparse crowd came down onto the pitch. Practically everybody there was related to one player or another. "You were great, Saul!" Sarah made herself sound enthusiastic, even if she knew her brother wouldn't be.

And he wasn't. "Big deal," he said. "These guys try, but I feel like a grown-up playing against kindergarten kids." He sighed. "Any soccer is better than none—I guess." He didn't sound sure; not even close.

"If the Foresters would let you come back—" Sarah began.

Saul cut her off with a sharp, chopping motion of his right hand. "The Foresters would. They'd take me back like *that*." He snapped his fingers. "But if the SS says no . . . What are you going to do?" His wave took in the sorry excuse for a pitch, the fumbling opponents, and the paltry crowd. "You're going to play in matches like this—for as long as they let you, anyhow."

"Why would they stop you?" Sarah asked.

"Why?" Her brother snorted. "I'll tell you why. They're liable to realize we're having fun in spite of everything, that's why. And if they do—" Saul made that chopping motion again.

"Oh." Sarah left it right there. Saul's words had a horrible feeling of probability to them. The Nazis ruined things for Jews just to be ruining them. That was how *they* had fun. And since they had the *Gestapo* and the ordinary police and the *Wehrmacht* on their side, they could have fun any way they wanted.

One of Saul's teammates called to him. The older man thumped the hero of the match on the back and handed him a bottle of beer. Saul swigged from it. He made a face. "Even the beer's gone downhill since the war started," he said. "It tastes like . . . lousy beer."

What did he almost say? Horse piss? Goebbels piss? Whatever it was, it didn't come out. As Father had driven home to them again and again, you couldn't get in trouble for what you didn't say. Nobody could inform on you for what you were thinking. That might save your life.

Or it might not. If the Nazis decided to do something to the Jews, or to a particular Jew, they'd just go ahead and do it. They didn't need any excuses, the way they would have in a country where laws counted for more than the *Führer*'s will. On the other hand, if a Jew was dumb enough to give them an excuse, they'd grab it in a heartbeat.

Sarah often wondered what she would do if Hitler or Himmler or Göring or Heydrich or one of those people came to Münster. If she had a chance . . . If she had a rifle . . . If she knew how to use a rifle . . . If pigs had wings . . .

Even if she did exactly what she dreamt of doing, what kind of revenge would the Nazis take? Would more than three or four Jews be left alive in the *Reich* a day after a Jewish girl shot somebody like that? Odds were against it. Too bad. The whole folk were a hostage.

In small groups, people started walking off toward their houses. No bus or trolley line ran close to this pitch—what a surprise! Buses had almost disappeared since the war started anyhow; whatever fuel Germany had went to the *Wehrmacht* and the *Luftwaffe* and the *Kriegsmarine*. The only private cars that still got gasoline belonged to doctors.

Well, walking a couple of kilometers was supposed to be good for you. Saul didn't seem to fret about it. But Sarah was tired by the time she got home. Put together more exercise than she was used to and tight wartime rations—all the tighter because she was a Jew—and she felt as if she were walking uphill both ways.

There wasn't much hot water, either. Saul complained loudest about that—after ninety minutes of running up and down the pitch, he needed hot water most. Or he thought he did, anyhow. Staring at his grass- and mud-stained soccer togs, Mother only sighed. Those wouldn't come clean in cold water, either.

Staring glumly at black bread and cabbage and potatoes on her supper plate, Sarah asked, "What are we going to do?"

"If we get through this alive, we're ahead of the game," her father said, eyeing his supper with similar distaste. Sarah started to cry. She'd wanted reassurance, but all she'd got was something she had no trouble seeing herself.

A RUNNER BROUGHT SERGEANT HIDEKI FUJITA'S squad the news: "Radio Berlin says Russia bombed East Prussia last night," the man reported. He stumbled a little over *Russia* and *Prussia*, but Fujita followed him. The sergeant had studied a map. East Prussia was the part of Germany the Reds could reach most easily.

Fujita glanced west, toward the Halha River and the high ground on the far side. He would have been happy had only Mongol troops prowled there. But, without a doubt, Russians were peering at the Japanese positions through field glasses and rangefinders. Were they listening to some incomprehensible Soviet broadcast telling them that, 10,000 kilometers off to the west, their vast country had just given another punch in the European war?

If they were, what did they propose to do about it? Would they send more men out to this distant frontier to strengthen their Mongolian puppets? Or would they think the fight against Germany—which was, after all, much closer to their heartland—counted for more than this distant skirmish?

"Any intercepts?" Fujita asked the runner. The Russians were tough bastards—at least for Westerners—but they had horrible radio security. Half the time, they'd send in plain language what they should have en-coded.

But this time the lance corporal shook his head. "Not that I heard about, anyhow," he answered.

"All right," Fujita said. "Any gossip about what *we'll* do on account of this news?"

"Not that I heard about, Sergeant-*san*," the runner repeated.

"Too bad." Fujita made himself shrug. "One way or another, we'll find out sooner or later."

Whatever Japan did, the sergeant suspected it wouldn't happen at once. Fall and winter weren't the best time for campaigning up here. As if to prove as much, the wind swung around to blow out of the west the next morning, and carried choking clouds of yellow-brown dust from the Mongolian heartland with it.

It blew hard for three days. Dust from Mongolia blew all the way down to Peking and beyond. So close to the source, the storm was ap-palling. When the sky finally cleared, when the sun no longer seemed to shine through billowing smoke, the whole landscape had changed. Dunes had shifted. Some had grown, others disappeared. Dust buried the scraggly patches of steppe grass.

Captain Hasegawa, the company commander, shook his head after coming by to survey the outpost. "Can you imagine living your whole life in country like this? Turn your back on it, and half of it blows away."

The mere thought was enough to make Sergeant Fujita shudder. "Sir, as far as I'm concerned, the Mongols are welcome to it." Then he corrected himself before Hasegawa could: "Well, they're welcome to all of it that doesn't belong to Manchukuo, anyhow."

"*Hai*. To that much and not a centimeter more," Captain Hasegawa said. Fujita let out a small sigh of relief—he wasn't in trouble, anyhow. Hasegawa looked out over the altered countryside. "At least the Russians will have as much trouble seeing what we're up to as we do with them."

"Yes, sir." Fujita didn't care to argue, even if he wasn't one hundred percent convinced. Oh, the captain was right—the Russians wouldn't be able to operate as usual during dust storms, either. But what about the Mongols themselves? The Japanese in this miserable place were probably lucky the natives hadn't sneaked through the dust and slit all their throats.

"You heard the Russians are really going after the Germans?" Captain Hasegawa asked.

"Oh, yes, sir," Fujita said. "The runner got here the day before the storm started."

"All right," the company commander said. "Well, you can bet we'll take advantage of that. We'd have to be idiots not to."

And so? Officers are idiots all the time. Fujita didn't say that. Sergeants might take it for granted, but somebody with more gold and less red on his collar tabs wouldn't. Fujita rubbed at his eyes, which still felt gritty. His teeth crunched every time he closed his mouth. He found something safe: "Whatever they want us to do, we'll do it. You know you can count on that, sir."

Of course we'll do it. If we disobey the orders, they'll kill us. And our families back in the Home Islands will be disgraced. Sergeant Fujita knew exactly how things worked. For common soldiers and noncommissioned officers, the army was a cruel, harsh, brutal place. Officers didn't have it so bad—but they necessarily looked the other way while noncoms kept privates in line.

Many Japanese soldiers began coming up toward the front a few days later. Sergeant Fujita would rather have seen them move up during the dust storm, too. Pointing in the direction of the high ground on the other side of the Halha, he complained, "The Russians can watch everything we do."

"For now," Captain Hasegawa said. "Once we get moving, we'll take their observation posts away from them, *neh?*"

"Yes, sir." Fujita said the only thing he could. He wished he were as confident as the company commander—and, presumably, the high command. But the Japanese and the Russians had been banging heads on the border between Manchukuo and Mongolia for a while now. The Red Army had more airplanes, more armor, and more artillery—and had had the better of the skirmishes. Why should anything change now?

As if plucking that thought out of his head, Captain Hasegawa said, "The round-eyed barbarians will worry more about the Germans than they do about us. This is our neighborhood. They look towards Europe. They can't help it."

Since Fujita had had pretty much the same notion—and since Hasegawa was his superior—he couldn't very well disagree. All he could do was hope it was true . . . and hope his own side brought in enough force to win once the serious fighting started.

Artillery did come forward along with the foot soldiers. So did sleek, modern monoplane fighters. Sitting on the ground, they looked as if they ought to sweep the Soviet biplanes from the sky.

Armored cars and a few tanks also rattled up to the front line. Fujita was glad to see them, and wished he were seeing more of them. This might be the back of beyond for the Russians, but they had plenty of tanks here.

"Don't worry about it," Captain Hasegawa told him when he cautiously expressed misgivings. "This isn't the only place where we'll be facing off against the Russians. We'll put our tanks where we need them most."

And where would that be? Fujita wondered. But a moment's thought gave him the answer. If Japanese armor would strike anywhere, it would strike at the Trans-Siberian Railroad. Back before the Russo-Japanese War, the Tsar had been able to ship troops down through Manchuria. The Soviets couldn't do that any more; Japan controlled the railroads in what was now Manchukuo. But, just on the other side of the border, the railroad was Stalin's key to defending Vladivostok and the rest of eastern Siberia. Break the line, take it away from the Reds, and the port and the whole vast country would fall into Japanese hands like a ripe persimmon.

The Russians weren't blind. They could see that, too. They would fight as hard as they could to protect the Trans-Siberian Railroad. But the Russian heartland lay thousands of kilometers off to the west. Japan lay right across the sea that bore her name. The Amur separated Manchukuo from the USSR, the Yalu divided Chosen—Korea, to old people—from Stalin's ramshackle Asiatic empire. Logistics, then, were all on Japan's side.

So the big fight would be there, along the border between Japan's mainland possessions and Soviet Siberia. This Mongol business was only a sideshow. It would never be anything but a sideshow—that was how it looked to Sergeant Fujita, anyhow.

He sighed. "We're stuck here, *neh?*"

"Yes, I think we are." Captain Hasegawa sent him a shrewd look. "Why? Would you rather be on the Amur?"

"Yes, sir, I would." Fujita didn't beat around the bush. "What happens there really means something. This . . . This is nothing but a bunch of crap. Please excuse me for saying so, sir, but it's true."

He waited for a reprimand, or maybe even a slap in the face. You weren't supposed to complain about your assignment. Oh, you could grouse with your buddies. But to a superior you were supposed to pretend everything was fine. Well, things weren't fine. And, dammit, the company commander asked. All Fujita did was tell the truth. Of course, sometimes that was the most dangerous thing you could do, even more dangerous than charging a Russian machine-gun nest.

"We do need men here. We can't let the Russians and Mongols steal what's ours," Hasegawa said. "But I admit, I wish I weren't one of them, too." He shrugged. "Somebody has to do it, though, and it looks like we're the ones."

Sergeant Fujita sighed one more time: a martyr's sigh. "Yes, sir."

JOAQUIN DELGADILLO WATCHED ITALIAN TANKS clank toward the front. The crews looked impressive in their black coveralls. Delgadillo didn't let the stylish uniforms fool him. The Italians looked much less impressive in full retreat, and he'd seen that move more often than he cared to remember.

Mussolini's soldiers didn't want to be in Spain. They cared nothing for Marshal Sanjurjo's war. And they fought like it, too. If the Reds who fought for the Republic didn't run away, the Italians would.

The Condor Legion, now . . . The Condor Legion was different. Joaquin Delgadillo didn't like Germans. He didn't see how you could. To him, as to any Spaniard with a working set of *cojones*, Germans were technicians, not warriors. They made no bones about why they'd come to Spain: to learn what they needed to know for the upcoming European war. Now that war wasn't upcoming. It was here.

But the armored forces and machine-gun units in the Condor Legion had never got a name for cutting and running, the way the Italians had. Maybe courage wasn't what kept them in the field. Maybe it was just professional self-respect. Whatever it was, you had to admire it. This might not have been the Germans' fight, but they performed as if it were.

Now the Germans in Spain had the same enemies as the ones back in Germany: Communists, freethinkers, republicans, liberals of every stripe. And they, and the Italians, and Marshal Sanjurjo, were doing everything they could to crush the enemy here before the aid flooding in from France and England let the Red Republic seize the initiative.

Those Italian tanks kept rattling forward. Vinaroz, on the eastern coast, lay a few kilometers to the north. Sanjurjo's men had already taken the town once, when they cut the Republic in half. Now an enemy drive down from Catalonia, one backed by French armor and aircraft, had recaptured it.

"What do you think?" Delgadillo asked his sergeant. "Can we get it back?"

Miguel Carrasquel shrugged. "That's what our orders are," he answered, which meant, *We'll keep trying till we're all dead, or till the orders change—and don't expect the orders to change.* Carrasquel had bad teeth and was missing half his left ear. His grin, then, looked most unpleasant. "What's the matter, Prettyboy? Don't want to get messed up?"

Joaquin didn't think he was especially handsome. But the sergeant called anybody who hadn't been wounded *Prettyboy*. You didn't want to get mad about it. Carrasquel was a good man with a knife.

Machine-gun bullets spanged off the Italian tanks and tankettes. The commanders in the impressive black coveralls ducked down behind the shelter of their armor. One or two of them waited too long, and got hit before they could. The armored fighting vehicles clattered forward anyhow. Joaquin nodded to himself. He didn't mind people ducking when the enemy shot at them. He did it himself—who didn't? As long as you carried on regardless, you earned your pay.

Tanks were magnets for machine-gun fire. He'd seen that before. Fewer bullets fought the Nationalist foot soldiers who loped along with the mechanical monsters. Since Joaquin was one of those soldiers, he approved of that. One bullet hitting you was one too many.

Most of the men up ahead didn't wear uniforms at all: not what he thought of as uniforms, anyhow. They had on overalls instead, as if they were factory workers. That made them Catalan Communists or anarchists. Up till the war started, they had been factory workers. The ones still alive after two and a half years of fighting knew their business as well as any other veterans.

Clang! That cry of metal against tortured metal wasn't a machine-gun bullet. That was an AP shell from a cannon striking home. Sure as the devil, a tankette came to an abrupt halt. Smoke and then fire poured from it. Ammunition inside started cooking off. Joaquin didn't think either Italian got out.

"Tanks!" Somebody pointed ahead. The man's voice wasn't panicked, but it wasn't far removed, either. More often than not, the Nationalists had had tanks and the Republicans hadn't. With aid flooding over the Pyrenees from France, the miserable Reds were getting more of their own.

These machines were French, all right. By the look of them, they'd been around since the last war. But they had turrets and treads and cannon and enough steel to keep out small-arms fire. If they weren't exactly swift . . . well, so what?

One of them fired at an Italian tank. *Clang!* There was that horrible bell-like sound again. The Italian machine's armor wasn't thick enough to hold out an armor-piercing round. Somebody got out of an escape hatch in the turret before the tank brewed up. It didn't do him much good—a burst from a machine gun cut him down before he'd run ten meters.

Tanks on both sides stopped to fire at foes, then got moving again to make themselves harder to hit. The Italian tankettes kept on moving and shooting. They mounted only machine guns, and weren't dangerous to real tanks. They could do horrible things to infantry, though.

As the tanks slowed, so did the rest of the Nationalist advance. Joaquin flopped onto his belly behind a pile of rubble that had been a stone barn. Every so often, he rose up enough to fire. Then he crawled somewhere else before squeezing off another round. No sniper would draw an easy bead on him. Veterans learned things like that. The guys who didn't . . . didn't get to be veterans.

Sergeant Carrasquel crouched behind a fence not far away. Delgadillo waited for the sergeant to order him forward again. But the squad leader stayed where he was, firing every now and then. He kept his mouth shut. Maybe he'd decided the attack wouldn't get much farther no matter what.

Joaquin Delgadillo sure felt that way. The Republicans had been tough even while outnumbered and outgunned. This push, plainly, aimed to take back as much as possible from them while they still were.

It also seemed designed to get a lot of Nationalist soldiers killed. Mortar bombs started whispering down around Joaquin and Sergeant Carrasquel. Both men dug like moles. Joaquin hated mortars. The Republicans had been using a Russian model for a long time. Now they also had French tubes, and those were just as good or maybe even better.

Somebody yowled like a wildcat, which meant a jagged steel fragment had bitten him. Joaquin hoped it was no one he knew. You always hated to hear a buddy get it. That reminded you how easily you might stop something yourself.

"*Ave Maria*," Joaquin whispered. As he went through the Hail Mary in Latin, his left hand found the rosary in his tunic pocket. *Keep me safe,* he thought. *Let Marshal Sanjurjo win, but please, God, keep me safe.*

THE NORTH SEA IN NOVEMBER was nowhere a skipper wanted to go. It was even less pleasant in a U-boat than it would have been in a larger surface warship. Lieutenant Julius Lemp guided U-30 north and east. He had to get around the British Isles to take up his assigned position in the mid-Atlantic.

He liked everything about his boat except the way it rolled and pitched in the heavy seas. Type VII U-boats made everything that had come before them seem like children's toys by comparison. They had outstanding range. They could make seventeen knots on the surface and eight submerged, and could go eighteen hours at four knots underwater.

During the last war, the British mined the northern reaches of the North Sea, trying to bottle up the U-boats. With hundreds and hundreds of kilometers between Scotland and Norway, they couldn't sew things up tight there the way they did in the Channel. But they could make life difficult, and they did.

They were supposed to be trying the same thing this time around. Lemp had orders to sink any minelayers he spotted. Odds against spying any were long: it was a big ocean, and he couldn't see very much of it, even with the Zeiss binoculars hanging around his neck. But his superiors were thorough. They wouldn't have got those wide gold stripes on their sleeves if they weren't.

Gray clouds scudded low overhead, driven by a strong west wind. In clear weather, Lemp would have scanned sky as well as sea with his binoculars. One thing had changed from the last war: airplanes were much more dangerous than they had been. They could carry bigger bombs, and carry them farther. And they all had radio sets, so they could guide enemy warships to a U-boat's path.

In this weather, though, a plane would have a devil of a time spotting the U-30. Lemp thought a pilot would have to be nuts even to take off, but he also thought pilots *were* nuts. Maybe it evened out.

About the most interesting thing he saw on his watch was a puffin that landed on the conning tower for a moment. With its plump, dignified body and the big beak in bright crayon colors, the bird looked as if a talented but strange child had drawn it. It also looked confused, as if wondering how this convenient little island had popped up in the middle of the sea. Then it noticed Julius Lemp—and then it was flying away again, as fast as it could.

"I don't like puffin stew," Lemp said. The wind blew his words away. Chances were the puffin wouldn't have believed him anyway. Birds didn't live to grow old by trusting people.

At 1400 on the dot, Ensign Klaus Hammerstein's shoes clanged on the iron rungs of the ladder leading up to the top of the conning tower. "I relieve you, sir," the youngster said formally, and then, "Anything I need to know?"

"Don't talk to puffins," Lemp replied, deadpan.

Hammerstein's left eyebrow—the sardonic one—rose a few millimeters. "Hadn't really planned to . . . sir." He took a deep breath, and his expression cleared. "Nice to get up here, isn't it?"

"Don't remind me. I'm going the other way." With a sigh, Lemp descended into the bowels of the U-30.

When the sun shone brightly, when the sky was blue, when the sea was smooth, you could easily think that coming off watch and going back into the iron coffin that let you do your job was like going from heaven to hell. With winter on its way in the North Sea, the change wasn't that bad, but it sure wasn't good.

Bowels . . . Julius Lemp wished he hadn't thought of that particular word, because it fit much too well. U-boats filled with every stench in the world; they might have been a distillery for bad smells. High on the list was the reek from the heads. Toilets that worked without putting the boat at risk of flooding were something German engineering was . . . almost up to. No U-boat had ever been lost because of a malfunctioning head—which didn't make the toilets a nice place to be around.

Unwashed bodies, musty clothes, and stale food added to the reek. U-boats carried enough drinking water. Water for washing was a luxury they didn't bother with. Seawater and saltwater soap were supposed to make up the lack. As with the heads, theory ran several lengths in front of performance.

Bilgewater added a swampy smell as old as the sea—as old as boats, anyhow. When you first came down into it, the combination was enough to knock you for a loop. After a while, you stopped smelling it—your brain blanked it out. But when you'd been breathing fresh salt air, the change was like getting a garbage can thrown in your face.

The sailors looked as if they might have been demons from hell, too. The orange light bulbs didn't help. More to it than those, though. A U-boat skipper couldn't insist on spit and polish the way officers in ordinary warships did. The men were too cramped together here—and U-boat crewmen were commonly harder cases than sailors in surface ships, too.

A lot of them started beards as soon as they left port. Shaving with saltwater soap was no fun. Even if it were, these guys were a raffish lot. They enjoyed flouting regulations. Lemp couldn't very well ream them out for it, not when he was sprouting strawberry-blond face fungus himself.

Off-duty men looked up from a game of skat. Nobody jumped to his feet and saluted. If you sprang to attention on a U-boat, you were liable to coldcock yourself on an overhead pipe. In that, U-boats were like panzers: being a shrimp helped.

He hadn't been below long when a shout floated down from the conning tower: "Ship ho! Ship off the starboard bow!"

That sent him scrambling up the ladder again. He wanted to see the ship for himself. No—he needed to see it for himself. If it was a warship, he would sink it if he could. No German surface units were in these waters. But if it was a freighter . . . Life got complicated then. Belgium and Holland, Norway and Denmark and Sweden were neutrals. Sinking a freighter bound for one of them could land the *Reich* in hot water. Freighters shaping a course for England, though, were fair game.

Up into the fresh air again. "Where away, Klaus?" he asked.

"There, sir." Hammerstein pointed. "A smoke smudge."

"*Ja.*" Lemp saw it, too. "We'll have to get closer, see what it is." They could do that. The U-30's diesel engines gave off less smoke than did ships burning fuel oil or coal. And the gray-painted U-boat sat low in the water, making it hard to spot. Julius Lemp called down the hatch: "Change course to 350. I say again—350."

"*Jawohl*. Changing course to 350," the helmsman answered, and the U-30 swung almost due north.

Lemp and Hammerstein both raised their binoculars, waiting for the ship to come up over the horizon. Lemp didn't forget the rest of the seascape and the sky. You could get caught with your pants down if you concentrated too much on your prey. That was how you turned into prey yourself. Every so often, when the skipper lowered his field glasses for a moment, he looked over at Ensign Hammerstein. The pup hadn't forgotten to look other places besides dead ahead, either. Good.

"That's no freighter, sir," Hammerstein said after a while.

"Damn right it isn't," Lemp agreed. The silhouette, while tiny, was too sleek, too well raked, to haul anything so mundane as barley or iron ore. Easier to mistake a thoroughbred for a cart horse than a freighter for a . . . "Destroyer, I think, or maybe a minelayer."

"I want one of those!" the ensign said. "The bastards are danger-ous."

"Too right they are," Lemp replied. Admirals sneered at mines—but admirals didn't have to face them. Sailors who did had a healthy respect for them. Mines were worse than a nuisance—they were a scourge. And they were an economical scourge, because they murdered ships without endangering the murderers . . . most of the time. But not today! Lemp set a hand on Hammerstein's shoulder. "Let's go below."

The U-30 stalked the enemy warship at periscope depth. That slowed the approach, but no help for it. If the ship spotted the U-boat, she could get away—or fight back. In a surface action, the U-30 was doomed. Her deck guns were for shooting up freighters and shooting down airplanes, not for taking on anything with real weaponry.

"It *is* a minelayer, by God!" Lemp said. The silhouette matched the one in *Jane's Fighting Ships.* How thoughtful of the English to help destroy themselves. The enemy vessel went about her business without the slightest suspicion the U-30 was anywhere in the neighborhood. That was just how Lemp liked it. It might as well have been a training run. He sneaked to within a kilometer.

At his orders, the torpedomen readied three fish in the forward tubes. The enemy ship filled the periscope's field of view. Fighter pilots from Spain said you had to get close to make sure of a hit. The same held true under the sea.

"First torpedo—*los!*" Lemp called. *Clang! Whoosh!* "Second torpedo—*los!*" *Clang! Whoosh* "Third torpedo—*los!*" *Clang! Whoosh!*

Under two minutes to the target. The minelayer showed sudden, urgent smoke—someone aboard her must have spotted the wakes. But you couldn't do much, not in that little bit of time. And Lemp had aimed one of the torpedoes on the assumption that the enemy vessel would speed up.

Boom! "Hit!" Lemp shouted exultantly. The U-30's crew cheered. Then a much bigger *Boom!* followed. The exploding torpedo must have touched off the mines the enemy ship carried. The minelayer went up in a fireball—and the U-boat might have been under the worst depth-charge attack in the world. It staggered in the water. Light bulbs blew from bow to stern, plunging the boat into darkness. Several leaks started.

With matter-of-fact competence, the crew went to work setting things to rights. Torches flashed on. Sailors began stopping the leaks. Lemp ordered U-30 to the surface. If there were survivors, he'd pick them up. He didn't expect trouble, anyhow.

And he didn't get any. Bodies floated in the chilly water. He saw no British sailors still alive. With that stunning blast, he was hardly surprised. A little disappointed, maybe, but not surprised. The minelayer had already gone to the bottom.

"Resume our previous course," he told the helmsman. "We'll celebrate properly when we're clear."

"Resuming previous course." The petty officer grinned. Schnapps was against regulations—which didn't mean people wouldn't get a knock after a triumph like this.

Chapter 7

These days, the British Expeditionary Force was mechanized. That meant Staff Sergeant Alistair Walsh got to ride a lorry from Calais to this piddlepot hole in the ground somewhere right next to the Belgian border. Then he jumped down out of the lorry . . . and he was back in the mud again. Twenty years unwound as if they had never been.

If anything, this was worse than what he'd known in 1918. He'd fought through the spring and summer then, and got wounded early in fall. Guys who'd been through the mill talked about how miserable trenches got when it was cold and wet. Guys who'd been through the mill always talked. This time, they were right.

He squelched when he walked. So did everybody else. People screamed "Keep your feet dry!" the same way they screamed "Always wear a rubber!" Not too many people listened—and wasn't that a surprise? The first cases of trench foot meant rockets went up from the people with red stripes on their caps.

Walsh remembered a trick he'd heard about in the last war. "Rub your feet with Vaseline, thick as you can," he told the men in his company. "Do your damnedest to keep your socks dry, but greasing's better than nothing."

Only one man came down with trench foot, and he didn't follow instructions. "Good job, Sergeant," said Captain Ted Peters.

"Thank you, sir," Walsh answered. He was old enough to be the company commander's father, but he would have had to start mighty young. "Some of these buggers haven't got the sense God gave a Frenchman."

"Or a Belgian." Peters scratched at his skinny little mustache. Walsh didn't think much of the modern fashion. If he was going to grow hair on his upper lip, he wanted a proper mustache, not one that looked put on with a burnt match. But he couldn't deny that the captain was a clever bloke. Peters went on, "You know why we haven't crossed the border and taken up positions where we might do some good?"

"Belgians haven't invited us in, like," Walsh answered.

"That's right. They're neutral, don't you know?" The way Captain Peters rolled his eyes told what he thought of that. "They think they'll offend the *Boches* if they get ready to defend themselves. Much good that kind of thing did them in 1914."

Maybe he'd been born in 1914. Maybe not, too. Either way, he was right. "The Germans jumped them then. They'll jump them again. Hitler's a bigger liar than the damned Kaiser ever was," Walsh said.

"Too bloody right he is," Captain Peters agreed. "You can see that. I can, too. So why can't King Leopold?"

"Because he's a bleeding idiot . . . sir?" Walsh suggested. "Like one of those ostriches, with its head in the sand?"

"He's got his head up his arse," Peters said. Walsh goggled; he hadn't thought the captain talked like that. "Thinks the French are as bad as the Germans. Thinks *we* are, for Christ's sake."

"What can you expect from a wog?" Walsh said. As far as he was concerned, wogs started on the far side of the Channel. The French were wogs on his side, which meant he cut them some slack. The Belgians weren't, and he didn't.

He had genuine respect for the bastards in the field-gray uniforms and the coal-scuttle helmets. The Germans fought hard, and in the last war they'd fought as clean as anyone else. What more could you want from the enemy?

Patiently, Captain Peters answered the question he'd meant as rhetorical: "I would expect an ounce of sense. If the balloon goes up—no, *when* it goes up—we're going to have to rush forward to reach the positions we should already have. So will the French. That will give the Germans extra time to advance and consolidate, time they simply shouldn't have."

"What can we do about it, sir?" Walsh said.

"Damn all," the company commander replied, which was about what the sergeant had expected. "Leopold won't listen to reason."

"Maybe something ought to happen to him—an accident, like," Walsh said. "Not cricket, I know, but . . . Got to be some Belgians what can add two and two, right?"

"You'd think so. But if we try something like that and muck it up, what happens then?" This time, Peters answered his own question: "We throw Leopold into Hitler's arms, that's what. If the Belgians line up with Germany, we're buggered for fair."

Sergeant Walsh only grunted. He didn't worry about Belgian soldiers. Who in his right mind would? But a Belgium leaning toward Hitler gave the Germans a red carpet for invading France. As soon as he called up a map in his mind, he saw as much. "We'd best not muck it up, then," he said.

Peters lit a cigarette. Then he offered Walsh the packet, which an officer didn't have to do. Walsh took a coffin nail and sketched a salute. Peters' cheeks hollowed as he sucked in smoke. "Don't get your hopes up for anything like that, Sergeant," he said. "Not bloody likely, no matter how much sense it makes. The Belgies like Leopold, same as we like our King. That's what he's there for—to be liked."

"Edward's gone," Walsh pointed out.

Now Captain Peters grunted. "You like to argue, don't you?" he said, but a chuckle told the sergeant he wasn't really angry. "If you could arrange for Leopold to fall in love with a popsy . . ."

"Could I have a couple of months' leave to set it up, sir?"

"Why would you need so bloody long?"

"Well, sir, I've got to try out the popsies, don't I, to see which one he'd like best," Walsh answered innocently.

That won him a snort from the company commander. "Sorry, Walsh." He looked east, across the Belgian frontier. "I'm not at all sure we've got two months."

ONCE UPON A TIME, U.S. MARINES swaggered through the streets of Peking. People got out of the way for them. They had to be careful nowadays, though. They still counted for more than the Chinese did. But when Japanese soldiers came through, the leathernecks had to be the ones who stepped aside. Orders said so.

Pete McGill hated the orders, even though he understood the need for them. One Marine could wipe the floor with one Japanese soldier. Four or five Marines could lick four or five Japanese soldiers. The little men were plenty tough, but they *were* little.

And a platoon of Japanese soldiers could beat and stomp four or five Marines if they found any excuse to do it. They had, once or twice. U.S. military authorities protested when it happened. The Japs ignored the protests. As far as they were concerned, Peking was theirs now. All the other foreign troops stayed there on sufferance.

So now the idea was not to give them any excuses. "Hell of a note," Corporal McGill complained. He and some of his buddies had just come out of the *Yü Hua T'ai*—the Restaurant of Rich and Fine Viands.

He was full of shrimp and scallops, the specialties of the house, or he would have complained more. But he was also full of *kao liang,* which was brewed from millet and strong as the devil (some people said the Chinese also threw in pigeon droppings to give it extra body).

"Damn straight." Herman Szulc knew what Pete was talking about. The big Polack had taken aboard even more *kao liang* than he had. Szulc got mean when he drank, too. "Ought to bust those little cocksucking monkeys right in the chops, just to show 'em they can't get away with shit like that."

"Ain't supposed to," Pooch Puccinelli said. He always did exactly what he was told, and worried about everything else later. That made him a damn good Marine. Had the orders been to jump on the Japs with both feet, he would have. Since they were to go easy, he obeyed again—and he would do his damnedest to make sure everybody else followed along.

Szulc scowled at him. "I don't got no orders not to bust *you* in the chops."

"Well, you can try," Pooch answered. Without orders, he didn't back away from anything or anybody.

"Cut the crap, both of you," McGill said. He didn't want to have to break up a brawl between his pals. He didn't want to get sucked into one, either. "What do you say we go get our ashes hauled?"

"Now you're talking!" Puccinelli was always ready for that. Herman Szulc didn't say no. What Marine would have? Peking was pussy paradise. There were lots of whorehouses, they were cheap, most of the girls were pretty, and all of them were versatile. The only drawback was, it was mighty easy to come down venereal. Flunk a shortarm inspection, and the Corps landed on you like a ton of bricks.

With money in his pocket and *kao liang* in his veins, Pete wasn't inclined to worry about that—not now, anyway. Even a Marine corporal was a rich man in Peking. He knew damn well the Restaurant of Rich and Fine Viands had overcharged him and his pals as much as the Chinamen thought they could get away with. He didn't care . . . too much. The chow was good, and it was still damn cheap. Whorehouses worked the same way. You could get whatever you wanted, and it wouldn't cost you half of what you'd pay in Honolulu or San Diego. The Chinese put down less? Well, so what?

The Marines came out of Hsi La Hutung—an alleyway wider than McGill's wingspan, but not by a whole lot—and out onto Morrison Street. Somebody'd told McGill that the Chinese name for the street was Main Street of the Well of the Prince's Palace, but it was Morrison Street to all the foreigners in Peking. Iron sheeting covered the well these days, but people still shoved it out of the way and drew up water every now and then. Some of the Royal Marines said Morrison had been a writer for the *Times* of London, and he'd lived at Number 98. Nowadays, an Italian firm occupied the building.

Chinese on foot, Chinese on bicycles, plump Chinese riding in rickshaws pulled by gaunt Chinese, older Chinese women hobbling along on what they called lotus feet, Chinese (inevitably) selling things, Chinese spitting and blowing their noses . . .

Chinese scrambling out of the way . . . Chinese leaping from the street onto the rickety sidewalks . . . Chinese bowing low . . .

"Oh, fuck," Puccinelli said. "Here come those goddamn slant-eyed mothers."

Chinese were slant-eyed, too, but Pooch wasn't talking about them. Up Morrison Street came a long column of Japanese soldiers. They marched in formation, a bayoneted rifle on each tough little man's right shoulder. When a noncom spotted a Chinaman who failed to show proper respect, four Japs jumped out of the line, grabbed the offender, and kicked him and beat him with rifle butts. They left him groaning and bloody and hustled back into place.

"Nod to the slanty bastards," McGill said. He met a Japanese sergeant's eye and nodded, equal to equal. The Jap gazed back. His gaze showed nothing for a moment. But then he nodded back. He'd won the exchange—Pete had acknowledged him first.

The other Marines also nodded to the Japanese troops. They got a few nods in return. Most of the Japs just ignored them. Nobody gave them a hard time. As far as Pete was concerned, that would do fine.

When the tail of the column got out of earshot, Szulc said, "Been a lot of the little monkeys going through town lately."

"Yeah." McGill nodded. "I hear they're mostly getting on trains and heading north."

"They gonna finally get off the pot with the Russians?" Szulc said. "Talk about deserving each other . . ." No Marine in Peking felt anything better than grudging respect for the Japanese, and Pete had never run into a Polack who had anything good to say about Russians.

"Who cares? That ain't our worry any which way. We were gonna get laid, remember?" Puccinelli kept his mind firmly on what mattered—or in the gutter, depending on how you looked at things.

NUMBER 1 GOOD TIME, the joyhouse said in English. It had a bigger sign in Chinese. Pete would have bet that was dirtier. The Chinese had no idea what shame was, as far as he could see.

"Marines!" the madam exclaimed. *Meal tickets!* was what it sounded like. Sure as hell, they would have to pay more for this than the locals did, too. "Make you happy!" the middle-aged woman went on. *Make me rich,* she probably meant. Her cut of the wages of sin looked pretty nice. She wore brocaded silk. Gold gleamed around her neck and on her fingers and ears; jewels sparkled in her hair.

"Show us the girls!" That was Szulc, who also didn't believe in dicking around when it came to dicking around.

"Yes, yes, yes!" The madam was all smiles. Pete McGill heard the ching of a cash register in her agreement. Well, what the hell did you expect when you went to a whorehouse? This gal had blond sisters back in the States. He'd dealt with his share of them. All the same, it did take a little of the edge off.

He got the edge back when he picked his girl. She reminded him of a Siamese cat, except her eyes weren't blue. He paid the madam and took the girl upstairs.

His being large and hairy didn't faze her. She wasn't just in from the countryside, then; she'd seen round-eyes before. She didn't know any English, though. *Oh, well,* McGill thought. He could show her what he wanted. He could—and he did.

The way she gasped and squeezed him inside at the end made him think he brought her off, too. Of course, whores were part actresses. If they made the john think he was a prize stud, he'd shell out more. And Pete did give her an extra dollar, saying, "Don't tell the old bitch downstairs."

She hugged him and kissed him and made the fat silver coin disappear even though she was naked. Pete didn't see exactly where it went. Into her lacquered hair? Or . . . ? He shrugged. It wasn't his worry.

Szulc was sitting in the waiting room when he got down there. Puccinelli took longer coming back. "Twice!" he said proudly.

"You went off in your pants the first time?" McGill gibed.

"Not likely!" Pooch said. "You shoulda heard that broad squeal!"

"Thank you! Thank you! Drink?" the madam said. Herman Szulc looked ready, but Pete shook his head and steered his buddies out.

"You don't wanna have any fun," Szulc complained.

"I don't wanna get drugged and rolled," McGill answered. "I may be dumb, but I ain't that dumb. If I was a regular there, I might chance it, but not when it's my first time in the joint."

"Let's go some place where they do know us and drink there," Pooch said.

"Now you're talking!" Szulc said. It sounded good to Pete, too.

When they got back to the barracks, they were drunk as lords. The next morning, McGill repented of his sins. Coffee and aspirins blunted down the whimwhams without stopping them.

Pete felt so rotten, he almost forgot about the long column of Japanese troops he'd seen the night before. Almost, but not quite. He reported to Captain Horner, his company commander.

Horner heard him out, then nodded. "Uh-*huh*," the officer said thoughtfully. "You think they were going to head north?"

"Well, I don't know for sure, sir," McGill replied. "If I was a betting man, though, that's how I'd lay my money."

"If you were a betting man . . ." Horner snorted. "You'd bet on how many raindrops landed in a pail in twenty minutes." He had a Tidewater accent thick enough to slice. A hell of a lot of Marines, and especially Marine officers, had a drawl. And Captain Horner knew him damn well.

"One good thing, sir," McGill said. The captain raised a blond eyebrow. Pete went on, "If the Japs *are* heading north like that, they ain't gonna jump on us right away."

"You hope," Horner said. Pete nodded. The company CO was right. He sure as hell *did* hope.

INTERNED. OFFICIALLY, VACLAV JEZEK WAS classed as a displaced person. It wasn't quite the same as being a POW. The Poles were treating all the Czechs who'd got over the border—soldiers and civilians, men, women, and children—the same way.

Yeah, they were treating them all the same way, all right. They were treating them all like dogs.

Barbed wire fenced off the Czechs' encampment from the rest of Poland. Poles with rifles and sandbagged machine-gun nests made sure the Czechs didn't come through the wire. The DPs lived under canvas despite rain and cold. They ate Polish army rations. That was what the Poles claimed, anyhow. If it was true, Vaclav pitied Polish soldiers.

Most of the Polish guards treated the Czech men—and especially the soldiers—like animals in the zoo. (Quite a few of them were friendly to the Czech women—what a surprise! And some of the women gave their all, too, for better food or more food or whatever else they happened to need.)

A few of the guards turned out to be human beings in spite of being Poles—that was how Jezek saw it, anyhow, though he wasn't an unbiased observer. He could talk to them in bits of Czech and Polish and in (dammit!) German. "We don't want you people here," one of the decent guards said. "You embarrass us."

"Why?" Vaclav said. "All we did was get out alive after the fucking Nazis went and jumped us."

"But Poland and Germany are friends," the Polish soldier said. "That's why we don't want you here."

"Friends with Germany? God help you!" Jezek said. "Is the pig friends with the farmer? Till he's a ham, he is."

The Pole—his name was Leszek—pointed east. "Germany keeps the Russians away. Better Hitler than Stalin any day."

"Better anybody than Hitler," Vaclav said stubbornly. "Anybody. Better the Devil than Hitler."

Leszek crossed himself. "Stalin is the Devil. He turns churches into stables and brothels. And half the Reds who run Russia are kikes. Hitler knows what to do about *them,* by God. We ought to give ours what-for, too. If we don't, they'll steal the country out from under us."

Vaclav didn't care about Jews one way or the other. He just said, "If you end up in bed with the Nazis, you'll get it as bad as the Jews do."

"You're only mad because the Germans beat you," Leszek said.

"Sure. And Poland never lost a war," the Czech retorted. Even if Leszek wasn't a bad guy, that reminder was more than he could stomach. He stomped off. Vaclav wondered if he'd come back with his buddies to do some real stomping. But Leszek didn't, which only proved he had an even temper.

A few days later, a Czech-speaking Polish officer addressed the displaced persons. He used Czech words, all right, but he pronounced them like a Pole: with the accent always on the next-to-last syllable, not at the beginning of a word, where to Czech ears it belonged. "A Czechoslovak government-in-exile has been formed in Paris," he said. "Its leaders say they will care for anyone who comes to them. I am looking for volunteers at the moment."

Never volunteer. Any soldier knew that ancient basic rule. Vaclav's hand shot up all the same. Anything had to be better than this. And what would the Poles do to Czech soldiers who didn't volunteer? Ship them back over the border into German hands? Then it *would* be a POW cage for the rest of the war—if it wasn't a bullet in the back of the neck.

Several other men also raised their hands, and a few women as well. The rest stood where they were without doing anything. The Polish officer's lips thinned. He must have expected a bigger response. When he saw he wouldn't get one, he said, "All right. Take whatever you have and meet me by the east gate in fifteen minutes." He strode away, his polished boots gleaming.

Vaclav didn't need fifteen minutes to gather his belongings. The Poles had relieved him of his rifle and ammunition and helmet and entrenching tool. He'd eaten the iron rations he'd carried. About all that was left in his pack were a blanket, a spare pair of socks, a housewife for quick repairs—he'd never make a tailor—some bandages, and his bayonet, which the Poles hadn't wanted. It made a perfectly good eating knife.

A couple of Czechs who hadn't raised a hand joined the men and women who had. They must have decided, as Vaclav had, that anything beat this.

The Polish officer led a squad of riflemen. "Come with me," he told the Czechs. "Make sure you come with me. If you try to run off, I promise you will never do another foolish thing again."

Off they went, at a brisk military march. Some of the Czechs weren't young, and couldn't keep up. Grudgingly, the Polish officer slowed down for them. He might have laid on a truck or two. He might have, but he hadn't.

They marched for eight or ten kilometers. It didn't faze Vaclav; he'd done far worse with far more on his back. Other interned soldiers also managed easily. But some of the civilians looked ready to fall over dead by the time they got to a shabby little railroad depot sitting there in the middle of nowhere.

Half an hour later, a train chugged up from out of the west. "Get aboard," the officer said.

"But—it's going east!" one of the women complained.

"*Ano.*" The Pole nodded. He said that in perfectly proper Czech; in his own language, *yes* was *tak.*

"Paris is that way!" The woman pointed in the direction from which the train had come.

"So is Germany," the officer reminded her. The woman's face fell. The Pole went on, "The train will take you to Romania. There are supposed to be arrangements to transport you from there to France. If there aren't . . ." He shrugged. Vaclav had no trouble understanding that. If there weren't, it was the Romanians' worry, and the Czechs'. It wouldn't be the Poles', not any more.

He wasn't the only one to figure that out. Three or four people balked and refused to get on the train. The woman who thought they would cross Germany to get to France was one of them. She wasn't bad-looking, but Vaclav felt better about boarding after she didn't want to. If someone stupid wanted to stay, leaving looked like a better plan.

The conductor spoke no Czech, only Polish and German. Those were enough. One car seemed reserved for the DPs. "No dining car for you," the conductor told them. "We bring you food." His scowl said they weren't paying customers, so they didn't deserve anything good. Jezek sighed. He didn't suppose they'd let him starve.

And they didn't. Cabbage and potatoes with little bits of sausage wasn't his idea of a feast, but it wasn't so bad as it might have been. It was better than he'd got in the displaced persons' camp.

Krakow. Tarnow. Przemysl. Lwow. Kolomyja. And then the Romanian border. Polish and Czech were close cousins. Most Czechs and a lot of Poles knew enough German to get by. Romanian was something else again. The Romanian customs men who knew another language spoke French. That must have made them very cultured. It didn't help Vaclav one damn bit.

An older man in his compartment translated for him—and for several other people. "I told them who we are and why we're going through their country," the Czech reported.

"What do they say?" Vaclav asked.

"They know about us. They know they're supposed to let us in," the older man replied. "I don't think they're very happy about it, though. They want to be rid of us."

"Everybody does," Vaclav said bitterly. The older man didn't contradict him. He wished the fellow would have.

Romanian stewards replaced the Poles. Romanian cooks must have done the same thing, because the next meal the DPs got was a bowl of cornmeal mush. "*Mamaliga,*" said the man who dished out the food. "*C'est bon.*"

"He says it's good," said the Czech who spoke French.

He could say whatever he wanted. That didn't make it true. The *mamaliga* did fill Vaclav's stomach, though; when he finished the bowl, he felt as if he'd swallowed a medicine ball.

Vaclav could look out the window as the train rolled through Romania. Neither he nor any other Czech was allowed to step out onto the platform at stops, though. Romanian soldiers with rifles made sure they stayed inside their car. Lenin could have been sealed in no tighter when he crossed Germany to join the Russian Revolution. "We're in quarantine," said the older man who spoke French.

"How come? What did we do?" Vaclav said.

"We loved our country. We still do," the other man answered. "The Poles and Romanians don't want to make Hitler angry—the Romanians worry about Hungary, too, because most of the people in northwestern Romania are Magyars. So they'll get rid of us, and they'll try to pretend we're not here while they're doing it."

He proved exactly right. Even when the train reached Constanta, the port on the Black Sea, Vaclav and his fellow DPs had precious little freedom. They were herded from their car to a waiting bus. No one was allowed close enough to speak to them; they might really have been diseased.

The corporal's first glimpse of the sea left him underwhelmed. It was flat and oily-looking. It didn't smell especially good, either. And the Greek freighter that would take them to France was a rust-streaked scow.

"Italy's in the war," Vaclav said as he clumped up the gangplank. "What if they bomb us?"

"Then we sink," the older man answered with a veteran's cynicism—he must have fought in the World War. He went on, "But I don't think they will. Greece is neutral. The Italians want Albania. They won't make her neighbor angry by going after Greek ships."

"You hope," Vaclav said, showing off his own cynicism.

"Don't you?" the other man returned. Vaclav could only nod.

Sailors shouted unintelligibly. The freighter's engine groaned to life. Coal smoke belched from her stacks. Longshoremen on the wharf cast off mooring lines. The ship shuddered as she backed clear.

A couple of Romanian officials stood there watching. To make sure none of the Czechs jumped overboard and tried to swim ashore? Maybe they thought the DPs would be so stupid. France was worth going to. Romania? Only a Romanian could want to live here.

Land receded. The ship rocked on the waves. The air smelled of salt and, faintly, of garbage. Vaclav didn't care. He was out of his cage. He was going toward something. It might be only a bullet in the ribs when he got back into action. He knew that. Next to God only knew how long inside the displaced-persons camp, even a bullet in the ribs didn't look so bad.

LUDWIG ROTHE ATTACKED HIS PANZER II'S Maybach engine with a wrench. As far as he was concerned, the engine could have been stronger. Could have been, hell—*should* have been: 135 horsepower just wasn't enough to shove nine tonnes of steel as fast as the panzer ought to go. Trying to do the job made the engine wear out faster than it would have otherwise.

Not far away, another panzer crew was working on a captured Czech LT-35. That was a tonne and a half heavier than a Panzer II, and had only a 120-horsepower motor. Its gun made it formidable, though. Rothe had seen that in Czechoslovakia. He wished the Germans could have taken the Skoda works undamaged instead of bombing them into rubble. But then he shrugged inside his black coveralls. What could you do?

Aschendorf was all the way on the other side of Germany from Czechoslovakia. The Dutch frontier lay only a few kilometers to the west. Camouflage netting hid both German and captured panzers from the air. They'd moved into position at night, with only blackout lights to keep them from running into one another or running off the road.

Nobody'd told Ludwig what the High Command had in mind. But nobody'd ever called *Frau* Rothe's boy a *Dummkopf*, either. He didn't figure the panzers were massing on the border with Holland to drive around looking at tulips.

He called over to the sergeant who commanded the LT-35: "Hey, Willi! Got a butt on you?"

"Oh, I might." Willi Maass patted his pockets and came up with a pack. Ludwig ambled over. Willi gave him a cigarette and then a light.

He lit one himself a moment later. He was a big brown bear of a man, dark and hairy, with some of a bear's stubborn ferocity, too. After he blew out smoke, he asked, "So when does the balloon go up?"

"Whenever the *Führer* wants," Ludwig answered. The cigarette was crappy. He didn't think it was all tobacco. Imports had gone down the toilet since the war started. During the last war, England had squeezed hard enough to make people starve. Things were nowhere near so bad now. Not yet, anyway.

The papers were full of stories about how good the war bread was, compared to what it was like the last time around. It was black and chewy, but it did still taste as if it was mostly made from grain. If it was a lot better than the last war's version, that must have been really dreadful.

"Well, sure," Willi said. "But when'll that be?"

Ludwig looked around. It was camouflage netting and dummy buildings as far as the eye could see. "Can't sit too long," he said. "We'll start feeling like moles in holes if they leave us here for weeks at a time. Besides, camouflage or no camouflage, pretty soon the French and the English will figure out something's going on. Or do you think I'm wrong?"

"Not me," the other sergeant said. "I think you hit the nail right on the head. I'd just as soon get going, too. I feel like moss'll start growing on my panzer if we wait around much longer."

"I'll tell you something else makes me think we're going to get rolling pretty damn quick," Ludwig said. Willi Maass made a questioning noise. Rothe explained: "I saw *Waffen*-SS units coming in yesterday. Those guys are like stormcrows—they don't show up till something's about to pop."

"Well, you've got that right," Willi said.

They both smoked for a while and let it rest right there. You never could tell who was listening. Ludwig didn't know what to think about the *Waffen*-SS. It looked like Himmler's effort to horn in on the

Wehrmacht. Not many men in the army liked that idea. Rothe knew damn well he didn't. On the other hand, the guys with the SS runes on their right collar tabs had fought like mad bastards in Czechoslovakia. If there was trouble, they were nice to have around.

"It'll be interesting," Maass offered.

"Interesting. Yeah." Ludwig stubbed out his cigarette under his boot. "I better get back to work."

Willi Maass laughed. "Nice to know you're eager about it."

"Ah, fuck you—and your shitty cigarette," Ludwig said. Laughing, he and Maass both headed back to their panzers.

Captain Gerhard Elsner came by a few minutes later. He eyed the exposed motor and Rothe's grubby hands. "Can you be ready to move tomorrow at 0600?" the company commander asked.

"Sir, I can be ready to move in twenty minutes," Ludwig answered proudly. "I've got ammo. I've got gas. My driver and radioman are here. Let me slap the louvers down, button her up, and we go."

"That's what I want to hear," Elsner said. He'd been a noncom in the last war, and wore the Iron Cross Second Class. "Unless it rains or snows between now and then, we're going to give them what for."

"At 0600? We'll be there," Ludwig promised. "It'll still be dark, or close."

"No darker for us than for them," Captain Elsner said. "We'll be ready. We'll know where we're going and what we're up to. They won't."

"*Ja.*" Ludwig hoped it would make a difference.

Everybody got a good supper: one more sign things would start any minute. The panzer commander stuffed himself. After this, it would be whatever he could get his hands on: iron rations and horsemeat and whatever he could steal from houses and shops. He shrugged. Holland was supposed to be rich. If he hadn't starved in Czechoslovakia, he wouldn't over there, either.

Nobody'd bothered to tell him why Germany needed to invade its smaller neighbor. He didn't worry about it. Why should he? He was just a sergeant. When the officers pointed him in some direction and said *Go,* he went. An attack dog would have done the same thing. That was what he was: the *Führer*'s attack dog.

He lay down to sleep by his panzer. So did Fritz Bittenfeld and Theo Hossbach. But Fritz wasn't all that interested in sleeping. He kept going on about what Dutch women would be like, and Belgian women, and French women. . . .

Theo didn't say anything. He hardly ever did, except when he had to. Fritz *wouldn't* shut up, though. Finally, Ludwig said, "You can't screw them all."

"I can try," the driver said valiantly.

Ludwig laughed. Next thing he knew, Captain Elsner was shaking him awake. What seemed like a million engines throbbed overhead: the *Luftwaffe,* flying west to soften up whatever the Dutchmen had set up to try to slow the attack.

He was gnawing on black bread and sausage when his panzer rolled out—at 0600 on the dot. Artillery thundered all around him. The noise was terrific. He wouldn't have wanted to be a green-uniformed Dutch soldier with all that coming down on his head. No, indeed. He was on the right side—the one giving the pounding, not the poor sons of bitches taking it.

Chapter 8

Two and a half weeks before Christmas. As Hans-Ulrich Rudel scrambled into the pilot's seat of his Ju-87, he was damn glad the campaign in the West was finally getting started. His squadron commander didn't like him. If the major had had the chance, he would have shipped Rudel off to operational reconnaissance training. But not even an officer with an ice cube for a heart like the squadron CO wanted to be a man short when the big fight started.

And so Hans-Ulrich, a milk drinker, a minister's son, a new-minted twenty-two-year-old second lieutenant, looked out through the Stuka's armored windshield. "You ready, Albert?" he asked the rear gunner and radioman.

"You bet, *Herr Leutnant*." Sergeant Albert Dieselhorst's voice came back tinnily through the speaking tube. Dieselhorst was at least ten years older than Rudel. He drank all kinds of things, but milk wasn't any of them.

Groundcrew men in khaki overalls fitted a crank into the socket on the port side of each Ju-87. They looked at their wristwatches. Either they'd synchronized them or someone gave an order Hans-Ulrich couldn't hear through the thick glass and metal shielding the cockpit. They all yanked the cranks at the same instant.

Hans-Ulrich stabbed the starter button with his forefinger at the same time. Thanks to one or the other or both, the big twelve-cylinder Junkers Jumo 211 engine thundered to life at once. It put out 1,100 horsepower. The squadron flew brand-new Ju-87Bs, which had almost twice the power of the older, slower A model a lot of units were still using.

Fuel . . . good. Oil pressure . . . good. Rudel methodically went down the list. He gave the groundcrew man a thumbs-up. The fellow grinned and returned it. Hans-Ulrich looked around. All the props were spinning.

Sergeant Dieselhorst said, "Everybody goes today, even the guys who have to flap their arms to take off."

"*Ja*," Rudel said, laughing. He was damned if he would have let any minor mechanical flaw ground him on this day of days.

One by one, the big monoplanes with the inverted gull wings taxied down the dirt runway and took off. Finding west was simple: all they had to do was fly away from the rising sun. Holland lay only a few minutes away. Hans-Ulrich had a 250kg bomb under the Stuka's belly and a pair of 50kg bombs on each wing. The squadron was supposed to go after concentrations of Dutch infantry and artillery. He thought they could do that.

"Orange triangle," he muttered to himself. That was the emblem Dutch fighters used on fuselage and wings. A lot of them painted the rudder orange, too. The Ju-87 wasn't the fastest or most graceful plane, especially when weighted down with almost half a tonne of bombs. He had to hope the Me-109s would keep most of the enemy aircraft away.

Boom! A black puff of smoke appeared in the sky below and in front of his plane. The Stuka staggered in the air, like a car driving over a fat pothole.

"They know we're here," Albert Dieselhorst said dryly.

"They only think they do," Hans-Ulrich said. "We haven't started showing them yet."

Looking down from 2,500 meters, he watched smoke rise from artillery bursts. He could see panzers moving forward. They were tiny, like tin toys. But when they fired their guns, fire belched out. No tin toy could match that.

No Dutch panzers met the German machines. Either the Dutch didn't have them or didn't know how to deploy them. Hans-Ulrich wondered why not. Holland was a rich country. It hadn't even had its economy wrecked in the last war. Why wouldn't it pony up the cash to defend itself properly?

Weak. Decadent. Probably full of Jews, Rudel thought. *Always trying to do things on the cheap. I'll bet they're sorry now, when it's too late.*

The Dutch did have some field guns—75s or 105s—close enough to the frontier to help their infantry resist the German onslaught. That was where the Stukas came in. The squadron leader put a wing over and dove on the gun positions. One after another, the rest of the Ju-87s followed.

Acceleration shoved Hans-Ulrich against the back of his armored seat. He hoped Sergeant Dieselhorst was well strapped in—that same acceleration would be trying to tear him out of his rear-facing seat.

Hans-Ulrich spotted three or four gun pits close together. He steered toward them as his altimeter unwound. You had to be careful to pull up. In Spain, a whole flight of Stukas had smashed into the ground because they didn't start to come out of their dives till too late.

There was an automatic gadget that was supposed to make you pull up. Hans-Ulrich had quietly disconnected it. He wanted to stay in control himself, not trust his life to a bunch of cams and cogs.

As he dove, the wind-driven sirens on his mainwheel legs screamed. Even inside the cockpit, the noise was unearthly. During training, he'd heard it from the ground. Coupled with the engine's roar, it sounded as if a pack of demons and the hounds of hell were stooping on the target.

He watched the Dutch artillerymen scatter like ants from a kicked anthill. They weren't cowards, not in any ordinary sense of the word. The poor bastards were just up against something they'd never known, never imagined, before. Rudel had wanted to run, too, that day on the training field.

And nobody had bombed him. He yanked the switch that loosed the bombs, then pulled back on the stick for all he was worth. The Stuka's airframe groaned as it went from dive to climb, but the plane was built to take it. His own vision went red for a few seconds. That was the danger point. The dive bomber could pull more g's than the pilot could.

But color came back to the world. Clarity came back to Hans-Ulrich's thoughts. For a little while there, all he'd remembered was that he had to hang on to the stick. He gathered himself. "You good back there, Albert?"

"Hell of a roller coaster, *Herr Leutnant*," Dieselhorst answered. "You blew that battery to kingdom come, too. I saw the bombs go off. Right on target."

"Good. Good," Rudel said. "I thought I aimed them right, but I'm pulling up by the time they go off."

"You'd better be," Sergeant Dieselhorst said. They both laughed. Why not? Laughing came easy when the war was going well.

And then tracers flamed past the cockpit. Dieselhorst's machine gun chattered. A Dutch Fokker fighter—like the Ju-87, a monoplane with landing wheels that didn't retract—zoomed past, much too close for comfort. The enemy pilot sent Rudel an obscene gesture as the Fokker flew off.

"*Gott im Himmel!*" Hans-Ulrich said. "Where the devil did he come from?"

"Beats me," the rear gunner answered. "I thought our fighter pilots were supposed to keep that kind of *Scheisse* from happening."

"Theory is wonderful," Rudel said. Sergeant Dieselhorst laughed again, but shakily.

The Stuka flew back toward the *Reich* for more fuel and more bombs. Hans-Ulrich spotted a column of trucks and buses heading east, toward the fighting. The trucks were painted the grayish green of Dutch army uniforms. A convoy bringing troops and supplies to the front—had to be.

Hans-Ulrich dove again, not so steeply this time. His thumb rested on the firing button atop the stick. He had two forward-firing machine guns mounted in his wings. The Ju-87 seemed to stagger in the air as his bullets stitched through the convoy.

A bus ran into a truck. The bus caught fire. Another bus rolled off the road and into a ditch. Soldiers bailed out of their vehicles and ran like hell. It was almost like going after partridges with a shotgun.

Almost. Some of the Dutch soldiers didn't run very far. They unslung their rifles and started shooting at the Stuka as it roared away. Infantrymen didn't have much of a chance against aircraft, but no denying the balls on these guys. And damned if a bullet from somewhere didn't clang through the Stuka's tail assembly. A few meters farther forward . . .

My armor would have stopped it, Hans-Ulrich thought. *That's what it's there for.* Reassuring to remember you had eight millimeters of steel at your back, five millimeters under you, and four millimeters to either side. It wouldn't keep everything out, but it beat the hell out of not having any.

Soldiers fired green flares. That was the German recognition signal. They didn't want their own Stukas shooting them up. Hans-Ulrich waggled his wings to show he'd seen.

He bounced in on a dirt strip a few kilometers inside the German border. Groundcrew men and armorers cared for the Stuka. Hans-Ulrich rolled back the canopy so he could stand up and stretch. "You've got a couple of bullet holes, sir," a groundcrew man reported.

"I know I got hit at least once," Rudel answered. "Anything leaking? All my gauges are good, and the controls answer."

"No leaks," the man assured him.

"Well, then, I'll worry about it later," he said. "*Mach schnell, bitte.* We've got a war to fight, and no time to waste."

Five minutes later, he was airborne again.

ONE OF THE THINGS ALISTAIR WALSH had forgotten about war was what a bloody balls-up it made of traffic. Or maybe things had been different in 1918. By the time he got to the front then, all the civilians had run off. Either that or they'd got killed. Anyhow, they weren't around to get in the way.

Things were different now. The Dutch and the Belgians hadn't expected the Nazis to jump on them. Sergeant Walsh didn't know why they hadn't—his opinion was that they were a pack of goddamn fools—but they hadn't. Now that the shells were bursting and the bombs came whistling down, half of the locals decided they really wanted to go to some place where things like that didn't happen.

And so they did. Whatever small respect Walsh had acquired for the Belgian army during the last go-round dissolved like his stomach lining in the presence of cheap whiskey. He didn't particularly expect the Brussels Sprouts to fight. (He knew damn well the Germans would fight, and hoped the French would, too. About all other foreigners he remained deeply pessimistic.) But couldn't they at least act like traffic police?

On the evidence, no. Now that the balloon had gone up, the Belgians weren't threatening to shoot at anybody who crossed their sacred border. The British Expeditionary Force, the French Seventh Army to its left, and the French First Army to its right were moving into Belgium to take up positions to throw back the Germans. They should have done that sooner, but King Leopold kept saying no. So they were doing it now.

Or they were trying to.

When lorries and tanks and long columns of khaki-clad men on foot headed east, and when mad swarms of autos and horsecarts and donkey carts and handcarts and terrified men, women, and children on foot headed west, and when they all ran headlong into one another . . .

Nobody went anywhere. The lorries and tanks tried to push forward. Drivers screamed in English, which mostly didn't help. Not many Englishmen knew enough French to do them any good—if French would have done them any good, which wasn't obvious. If Belgian troops had channeled the refugees down a few roads and left the rest open for the soldiers who were trying to save their miserable country for the second time in a generation . . .

Too much to hope for, plainly.

"We're not going to make our stage line today, are we, sir?" Walsh asked before the first day was very old.

"Too bloody right we're not," his company commander agreed.

Planes flew off toward the east. That, at least, was reassuring. Till now, the RAF had left the Germans alone. The *Luftwaffe* had also left the BEF alone, but Walsh didn't think about what that meant. He got his first lesson a little past noon.

The day was chilly, but only partly cloudy. The sun had risen late and would set early. It hung low in the sky, a bit west of south. The English soldiers were trying to fight their way through yet another clot of refugees. These people were gabbling in Flemish, or possibly Dutch. Whichever it was, it sounded enough like German to raise Sergeant Walsh's hackles.

"Don't they know we've got to get up there so we can fight?" he demanded of nobody in particular, or possibly of God.

His soldiers weren't listening. They were too busy yelling and swearing at the frightened people in front of them. As for God . . . When Walsh heard the rumble in the sky, he thought at first it was more RAF planes going over. The poor damn refugees knew better. That sound scattered them faster than all the yelling and swearing the British troops had done.

That timbre wasn't quite the same as the one Walsh had heard before. And those shark-nosed planes with the kinked wings had never come out of British factories. They dove almost vertically, like hawks after rabbits. And as they dove, they also screamed. The sound alone was plenty to make the sergeant want to piss himself.

"Get down!" he screamed. "Hit the dirt! Get—!" He followed his own order, just in the nick of time.

Blast picked him up and flung him around. He did piss himself then, but realized it only later. A lorry caught by a bomb turned into a fireball. Men and pieces of men flew through the air. A marching boot thudded down six inches in front of Walsh's nose. It still had a foot in it. He stared, then retched. He'd seen such things twenty years earlier, but he'd done his damnedest to block them out of his mind ever since.

More bombs went off among the refugees and the marching troops. Shrieks rang out through and even over the stunning *crump!*s of explosives. Wounded soldiers screamed for medics and stretcher-bearers. Wounded civilians simply screamed.

The nasty dive-bombers roared away toward the east, the direction from which they'd come. Alistair Walsh was just getting to his feet when more planes flew in from that direction. At first, he thought they were RAF fighters returning from strikes against the Nazis—their lines weren't so aggressively unfamiliar as those of the previous attackers. But then fire spurted from their wings and from their propeller hubs. They were shooting at—shooting up—the British column and the poor damned hapless refugees.

"Down!" Walsh yelled again, and fit action to word.

When a bullet struck flesh, it made a wet, slapping noise. He remembered that from the last time around, however much he wished he didn't. German airplanes had strafed trenches in 1918. It hadn't seemed nearly so horrid or dangerous then. For one thing, he'd been a fool of a kid twenty years earlier. For another, the German air force, like the Kaiser's army, had been on the ropes. And, for one more, he wasn't *in* a trench now.

More screaming engines made him grab his entrenching tool to see what he could do about digging in. Then a few people started cheering as if they'd lost their minds. Suspecting they had, he warily looked up. British Hurricane fighters were mixing it up with the bastards with the hooked crosses on their tails. Walsh started cheering, too.

A Hurricane went into a flat spin and slammed into the ground, maybe half a mile away. A black, greasy column of smoke marked the pilot's pyre. Then, trailing smoke and flames, one of the German fighters crashed into a stand of trees even closer to where Walsh lay.

He yelled like a man possessed. So the Germans *could* die. That cloud of smoke, broader and lower than the one rising from the Hurricane, was the first proof of it he'd seen in this war.

Another Hurricane, also smoking but not so badly, limped off to the west, out of the fight. Sergeant Walsh hoped the pilot managed to put it down safely, or at least to bail out if he couldn't land it. To his vast relief, the German fighters seemed to have had enough. Like the dive-bombers before them, they flew back toward the *Vaterland*.

He tried standing up again. As he did, he noticed he wasn't the only bloke emerging from a half-dug scrape. The other chaps in khaki weren't so bloody stupid. If the buggers on the other side started banging away at you, of course you'd do what you could to keep from getting ventilated.

But the advancing column had stuck its dick in the meat grinder.

One tank lay on its side, blown off its tracks by a bomb that burst right next to it. Several trucks burned. Others weren't going anywhere soon, not with from one to four flat tires or with bullets through the engine block . . . or with dead or wounded drivers. What bombs and machine-gun bullets had done to the foot soldiers was even worse. And as for that mob of refugees . . .

A woman who might have been pretty if she weren't dirty and exhausted and terrified screamed in Dutch or Flemish. She wasn't wounded—not as far as Walsh could see, anyhow. She was just half crazy, maybe more than half, because of everything that had happened to her.

Walsh had a devil of a time blaming her. A few days ago, she'd been a shopkeeper's wife or a secretary or something else safe and comfortable. Then the roof fell in on her life—literally, odds were. Now she had nothing but the clothes on her back and whatever was in the cute little handbag she carried. How long before she'd start selling herself for a chunk of black bread or a mess of fried potatoes?

How many more just like her were there? Thousands, tens of thousands, all over Holland and Belgium and Luxembourg and eastern France. And their husbands, and their brats, and . . . "Oh, bloody hell. *Bloody* hell," Walsh muttered under his breath.

Still, civilians *weren't* his worry, except when they got in the way and kept him from getting to where he needed to be to do his job. Sorting out his soldiers and keeping them moving damn well was.

Captain Ted Peters came over to him. The young officer looked as if he'd just walked into a haymaker. This was his introduction to combat, after all. *Combat, meet Captain Peters. Peters, this is combat.* Walsh shook his head. He had to be punchy himself, or his brain wouldn't be whirling like that.

"Well, Sergeant, I'm afraid you're the new platoon commander," Peters said. "Lieutenant Gunston stopped a large fragment of bomb casing with his belly. Gutted him like a sucking pig."

"Christ!" Walsh said.

"A bit of a rum go, I'm afraid," Peters said, which would do for an understatement till a bigger one came down the pike. He did his best to ignore the ammunition cooking off in burning vehicles, the cries of wounded men and women and kids and animals, and the stenches of burning paint and burning rubber and burning flesh and fear and shit.

When the company commander didn't say anything more, Walsh did: "I should say so! We've got ourselves all smashed up, and we haven't even set eyes on a goddamn German."

"I did," Captain Peters answered, not without pride. "One of those dive-bombers was so low when he pulled up that I could see him through the glass of his cockpit. And I got a *good* look at his rear gunner. The bastard almost punctured me after the plane pulled out of its dive."

"What are we going to do when we have to fight them face to face, sir?" Walsh asked. "How the devil can we, when it looks like they've got more airplanes than we do?"

"We shot down one of their fighters, after all," the officer said. "I'm sure we'll do better with practice, too."

"Right . . . sir," Sergeant Walsh said tightly. He wasn't sure of any such thing. England's chosen method of fighting seemed to be stumbling from one disaster to the next till she figured out how to beat the set of foes who had been beating her. It worked the last time around only because the USA stuck its oar in the water. Things were moving faster now, much faster. Would—could—muddling through work at all?

Captain Peters had no doubts. Or, if he did, he didn't let them show, which was the mark of a good officer. Walsh didn't let the privates and corporals he led see his doubts, either—or he hoped like hell he didn't, anyhow. "All we can do is go on," Peters said. "We have to clear these civilians out of the way and take up our assigned positions. We'll have the French and the Belgians fighting along with us. The *Boches* will end up sorry they ever started this war—you mark my words."

"Right . . . sir," Alistair Walsh said again. No, he didn't believe a word of it. But you also couldn't let your superiors see your doubts. You couldn't even—or maybe you especially couldn't—let yourself see them.

SERGEANT LUDWIG ROTHE SPOTTED A TRUCK out somewhere close to a kilometer away. He raised his field glasses to his eyes. The last thing he wanted to do was shoot up his own side by mistake. But the magnified image showed it was a French model, and bound to be full of Dutchmen.

"Panzer halt!" he yelled into the speaking tube.

"*Jawohl!* Halting," Fritz Bittenfeld answered. The Panzer II jerked to a stop.

Rothe peered through the TZF4 sighting telescope. It was only two and a half power—downright anemic after the binoculars. But it let him draw a bead with the 20mm cannon. He wouldn't have opened up on enemy armor from farther out than 600 meters. The panzer's main armament wouldn't penetrate serious protection from farther out than that. It would chew up soft-skinned vehicles as far as it could reach, though.

The trigger was on the elevating handwheel, to the left of the gun. Ludwig fired a three-round burst. The Dutch truck stopped as if it had run into a stone wall. Smoke poured out from under the hood. Rothe fired another burst, which emptied the magazine. He slapped in another ten-round clip. The other guys might—hell, they did—use bigger rounds in their main armament, but he could shoot a lot quicker than they could. Sometimes that made all the difference in the world.

Sometimes it didn't matter a pfennig's worth. Not far away, another

Panzer II burned like billy-be-damned. It had stopped a 105mm shell fired over open sights at point-blank range. None of the crew had got out. That was no surprise—hitting a Panzer II with a 105 was like swatting a mosquito with a table. The Dutch artillerymen who'd fought the gun were dead now, which didn't do that panzer crew one goddamn bit of good.

"Can we get going again, Sergeant?" Fritz asked pointedly. A halted panzer was a panzer waiting to stop something.

"Wait a second." Ludwig looked through the TZF4 again. Yes, the Dutch truck was definitely laid up. "Go ahead," he said.

As soon as he gave permission, the panzer seemed to bound forward. The flat Dutch plains made ideal panzer country. But the buildings and trees up ahead made equally ideal places to hide antitank guns. Even if the Dutch had taken a big punch at the start of the fight, they were still in there swinging.

Ludwig felt a tap on the back of his left leg. He ducked down into the turret. "*Was ist los?*" he asked the radio operator.

"Bridge up ahead," Theo Hossbach answered. "We've got paratroops holding it. The Dutchmen are giving them a hard time."

"I bet they are," Rothe said. They hadn't been ready for soldiers jumping out of Ju-52s and taking bridges and airports away from them. Well, who would have been? Nobody in the last war fought like that. Hell, in the last war even pilots didn't wear parachutes. As far as Ludwig was concerned, that meant everybody who'd got into an airplane during the last war was out of his goddamn mind. The panzer commander brought his mind back to the business at hand. "Up ahead, huh? Which map square?"

"C-9," Theo told him.

"C-9?" Ludwig repeated, and the radioman nodded. Rothe unfolded the map so he could see where he was—or where he thought he was, anyhow. Wrestling with the map inside the cramped turret made him feel like a one-armed paper hanger with the hives. At last, though, he got it open. "Well, Jesus Christ! We're in C-10 now. Tell 'em we're on our way."

"Will do." Theo shouted into the microphone that connected the panzer to the platoon, company, regiment, and division commanders. Everybody could tell Ludwig what to do. Half the time, everybody seemed to be trying to tell him at once. But all German panzers came with radios, so they could work together. That hadn't been true of the Czechs. The *Wehrmacht* was using captured Czech panzers—the more, the merrier. Before they went into German service, technicians installed radio sets in the machines that lacked them.

Machine-gun bullets clattered off the Panzer II's steel flank. Ludwig did some shouting of his own: to Fritz, through the speaking tube. "Got you, Sergeant!" the driver yelled back. The panzer swung a little south of west.

That damned Dutch machine gun kept banging away. Ludwig wondered why. A Panzer II had less armor than it should have—he'd seen as much. One hit with any kind of cannon shell and you bought yourself a plot. But, by God, the beast did carry enough steel to keep out machine-gun bullets. And every round the silly Dutchmen wasted on the Panzer II was a round they weren't shooting at the foot soldiers they could really hurt.

Most of the time, Rothe would have stuck his head out so he could see what was going on. Right this minute, that looked like a bad idea. *Yeah, just a little,* he thought with a wry chuckle. He had four vision ports in the turret: two on the left, one on the right, and one at the back. The bullets were spanging off the left side of the turret, so. . . .

There it was! The machine gun's muzzle spat flame from the front of an apple orchard. Ludwig traversed the turret. He fired back at the enemy gun. The Dutch crew manning it had run for cover by the time his weapons bore on it. They'd seen danger coming and got out of there. That meant they'd harass somebody else pretty soon, but he didn't know what he could do about it.

"That's got to be the bridge, Sergeant." Fritz's voice came back through the speaking tube.

"It does?" With the turret swung to the left, Rothe couldn't see much of what the driver was talking about. He brought it back to face straight ahead again. Sure enough, there was a bridge. And the people around it were shooting at the people on it and right by it. The soldiers hanging on to the bridge wore field-gray. The bastards attacking them were in Dutch gray-green. With leaves off the trees and grass going yellow, neither uniform offered a whole hell of a lot of camouflage.

The Dutch soldiers were too busy trying to drive the paratroopers off the bridge so they could blow it to pay much attention to advancing panzers—several other machines had come with Ludwig's. One of them was a great honking Panzer III—a fifteen-and-a-half-tonne monster with two machine guns and a 37mm cannon that could fire a useful high-explosive shell.

It could, and it did. Three or four rounds from that cannon put two Dutch guns out of action. "*Gott im Himmel,* I wish *we* had one of those!" Ludwig knew he sounded jealous. He didn't care. He wished the *Wehrmacht* had more of the big panzers, too. They could do things his lighter machine couldn't—and they could take punishment that would turn the Panzer II into scrap metal . . . or into a bonfire.

He opened up with his machine gun. The Dutch soldiers scattered. They hadn't looked for an attack from the rear. Well, too damn bad. They also seemed less willing than the Czechs had been to hold in place till they got killed. Say what you would about the Czechs, they had balls.

Three or four He-123s swooped down on the Dutch troops. Next to Ju-87s, the Henschel biplanes looked like last week's—hell, last war's—news. That didn't mean they couldn't do the job. They shot up the Dutchmen and dropped bombs on their heads. The bombs weren't big ones—Ju-87s could carry a lot more—but the Henschels put them right on the money.

Ju-87s had sirens to make them sound even scarier than they were. The He-123s didn't. But, when they dove, they might have been firing God's machine guns. Ludwig had heard that just the right engine RPMs on those babies could make them as demoralizing as all get-out. A lot of what you heard was bullshit. Not this. He forgot who'd told him, but the guy had the straight goods.

He stood up in the turret to get a better look around. A Dutchman fired a couple of wild rifle shots at him. He gunned the enemy soldier down with his MG34. Two more Dutch soldiers dropped their weapons and raised their hands.

Ludwig almost killed them in cold blood. At the last second, he caught himself. He pointed brusquely toward the rear. Keeping their hands high over their heads, they stumbled off into captivity . . . if they didn't run into some other trigger-happy German soldier before anybody took charge of them.

Not my worry, Rothe thought. He was glad he hadn't squeezed the trigger. They'd fought fair, and so had he. Sometimes, in the heat of battle, you did things you wished you hadn't later. This time, Ludwig didn't—quite.

His panzer stopped at the eastern end of the bridge. A paratrooper waved to him. "Good to see you, by God," the fellow called. "It was getting a little hairy here." His helmet fit his head more closely than the standard *Wehrmacht* model. He wore a coverall over his tunic, along with rubber knee and elbow pads.

And he wasn't kidding. Several of his buddies lay sprawled or twisted in death. A medic tended to a wounded trooper. Other groaning men waited for whatever he could do for them.

"Can we cross the bridge?" Ludwig asked.

"*Ja,*" the paratrooper answered. "We pulled the wires on the demolition charges before the Dutchmen could set them off. And we've cleared the mines on the roadway and chucked them in the river. I *think* we got 'em all."

"Thanks a bunch." Ludwig wished the paratrooper hadn't added the last few words. The son of a bitch only laughed at him. He bent down and shouted into the speaking tube: "Take us across, Fritz."

"Will do," the driver said. "What's on the other side?"

"More Dutchmen with guns," Ludwig told him. "What the hell do you expect?"

"How about some gals with big tits?"

"Yeah, how about that?" Rothe said dryly. He wished he had a control that would let him pour ice water on Fritz. The driver was the horniest guy he'd ever run into. The worst part was, he did get laid a lot. Ludwig knew that if *he* used a no-holds-barred approach like that, all he'd get was his face slapped.

The Panzer II rumbled forward. Fritz did have the sense to take the bridge slowly. If the paratroopers had missed a surprise or two, he'd have a chance to stop or to go around it. Ludwig gave the roadway a once-over, too. They didn't blow up, so he and Fritz didn't miss anything important.

They went past not only dead German paratroopers but also quite a few dead Dutchmen. Some of them were in what looked like police uniforms. No, they hadn't looked for soldiers to fall out of the sky so far behind their front. These must have been second-, or maybe third-, line defenders. Whoever they were, they'd fought hard. It hadn't done them any good, though.

As soon as Ludwig heard a machine gun rattle to malignant life, he ducked down into the turret again. But the Dutch had put up a better fight on the east side of the bridge than they did here. Maybe losing it had broken their spirit. Or maybe they simply didn't have what they needed for a proper defense here.

A car with half a dozen Dutch officers screamed up the road toward the bridge—and toward the panzer. "Aren't you going to blast those shitheads?" Fritz demanded.

"Let's see what they do first," Ludwig answered.

They stopped right in front of the panzer. One of the officers started shouting at Ludwig in Dutch. He understood maybe one word in five. He thought they were telling him to turn around and drive the Nazis away. That was pretty goddamn funny.

"Sorry, friend," he said. "We *are* the Nazis. And you're prisoners, as of now."

He might not have known Dutch, but the Dutch officers understood German. The looks on their faces when they realized that panzer wasn't theirs . . . "You should let us go," said the one who'd yelled in Dutch before—he spoke good German, too. "We made an honest mistake."

"In your dreams, pal," Ludwig said sweetly. The panzer's machine gun and cannon were mighty persuasive.

"YOU! DERNEN!" ARNO BAATZ HAD a voice as effortlessly penetrating as a dentist's drill.

"Yes, Corporal?" Willi Dernen did his best to sound meek and mild. He didn't want trouble from a lousy *Unteroffizier,* not now, not when they were about to give the *poilus* the big one right in the teeth. Guys promoted to noncom went off to a special school for a while. Willi didn't *know* what went on there, but he figured it was where they turned you into a son of a bitch if you weren't one already.

Baatz glared at him, there in the gloom of earliest dawn. "Have you got your full ammunition supply?"

"Yes, Corporal," Willi repeated—truthfully. Only a dope didn't bring along as many rounds and as many rations as he could, and *Frau* Dernen hadn't raised any dopes.

Had he been lying, Baatz would have had to feel him up to prove it. You still couldn't see anything more than ten centimeters from the end of your nose. That didn't bother Willi. A Frenchman who could see you was a Frenchman who could blow your brains out.

Muttering, the corporal stomped off to harass somebody else. Beside Willi, Wolfgang Storch chuckled almost silently. "Awful Arno's on the rag early today, isn't he?"

"What was that, Storch?" Baatz snapped. His ears stuck out like jug handles. Maybe that was what made them so sharp.

"Nothing, Corporal," Wolfgang said. Baatz went right on muttering, but he didn't come back. He might have heard, but he hadn't understood. *Just like a corporal,* Willi thought.

Before Willi could say that out loud and get a laugh from Storch, hundreds—no, thousands—of German guns opened up. Everywhere from the North Sea to the Swiss border, they hurled death and devastation at the enemies of the *Reich.* Through the thunder, Willi heard the steadier rumble of aircraft engines overhead. Their takeoffs must have been timed so they'd cross the border just when the artillery bombardment opened. Right now, the damned Frenchies would be thinking hell had opened up on earth. And they wouldn't be so far wrong.

Lieutenant Neustadt blew his whistle. He looked so young, it almost seemed a boy's plaything when he did. But his voice, more bass than baritone, gave that the lie: "Forward! Now we get to see France for ourselves!"

The French had seen little bits of Germany. Willi aimed to do more than that. He wanted to goose-step through Paris in a victory parade. His great-grandfather had done it after the Franco-Prussian War. His father never stopped complaining that *he* hadn't got the chance. Willi wanted it.

There was the place just on the German side of the border where the French troops had camped when he and Wolfgang spied on them. There was the crossing point the Germans had booby-trapped when they pulled back after the real war against Czechoslovakia started. Now Willi needed to look back over his shoulder to see it. That meant, that had to mean, he was in France.

If you stood on the other guy's soil, you were winning. The last time around, the Allies never did drive Germany all the way out of France and Belgium. Things fell apart on the home front before they could. And here the *Wehrmacht* was again.

A rifle boomed up ahead. A French machine gun opened up, its fire noticeably slower than a German MG-34's. Somebody not too far from Willi fell over and grabbed at his leg. He yelped and ki-yied like a dog hit by a car. "Medic!" The shout went up from half a dozen throats.

"Keep moving!" Arno Baatz yelled. "Even if they've mined the fields, keep moving!"

Even if they've mined the fields? Willi thought. He suddenly didn't want to move at all. Corporal Baatz had a way of encouraging his men, all right. Lieutenant Neustadt's whistle shrilled. "We need to go forward!" he called. "Victory lies ahead! Paris, too!" That made a pretty good antidote to Baatz's minefields.

French shells screamed in—not many, but enough to send men and pieces of men flying. Willi's father had talked about the goddamn French 75s in the last war. Here *they* were again, and just as horrific if you were on the receiving end.

In the last war, Germany couldn't do much about them. Now Stukas swooped down on the French batteries, underwing sirens wailing like damned souls. Bombs going off were much louder than shells. The French artillery quieted down in a hurry. Willi trotted past a gun pit a few minutes later. He looked at what was left of the 75 and its crew. Gulping, he wished he hadn't.

More rifle fire came from behind a stone fence. The *Landsers* moved to outflank the defenders even before Corporal Baatz started yelling commands. Willi plopped down in a shell hole and banged away at the *poilus* by the fence. After a few minutes, one of them waved something white.

Neustadt shouted to them in French. Willi didn't speak a word of it. The French soldiers stood up with their hands high. In their long greatcoats and crested helmets, they looked as if they'd come from the last war. The lieutenant jerked his thumb toward the east. Nodding, babbling with gratitude for not getting shot out of hand, the *poilus* stumbled away into captivity.

"They'll have watches. They'll have cash," Wolfgang said discontentedly. "Now the rear-echelon assholes'll clean 'em out."

"Don't get your bowels in an uproar," Willi said—he was less inclined to grumble than his friend. "You think they're the only froggies we'll catch?"

"Well . . . no," Storch admitted. "But maybe they had extra-good stuff. We'll never find out."

Up ahead, a Panzer I was burning. Something heavier than a machine gun had hit the little panzer and knocked it out. One crewman in black coveralls lay dead a few meters away. The other—the driver—hadn't made it all the way out. He was on fire, too. Willi gulped again. The stink reminded him of a pork roast forgotten in the oven.

But other panzers kept pushing forward. They shot up or ran over French machine-gun nests. That made life a lot easier for the foot soldiers who followed in their wake. Willi didn't mind not facing machine guns, not even a little bit.

More Frenchmen surrendered. As he'd predicted, Willi got himself a small wad of francs and a watch with a case that looked like gold. There were corpses to plunder, too, if you had the stomach for it. Dead men and pieces of dead men . . . Willi was astonished at how fast he got used to them or developed a knack for not thinking about them. Definitely better not to wonder whether this crumpled chunk of shredded meat had played the concertina or that one always puked when he got plowed.

Some people didn't care. He went past one body that had a finger on the left hand neatly sliced off, presumably so the slicer could get at a ring. Willi hoped he wouldn't do anything like that. He also hoped he wouldn't end up a body lying there for someone else to frisk.

It could happen. Not all the *poilus* were ready to give up. The French fought from foxholes and trenches. They fought from behind fences, and from farmhouses. They didn't fight with the coordination of the German war machine, but they fought. They reminded Willi of a guy who got staggered in a barroom brawl but swung back instead of falling over.

Why *didn't* they fall over, dammit? Life would have been so much simpler—to say nothing of easier—if they had.

More 75s screamed in. The *Wehrmacht* troops did some screaming of their own. One of the first things you learned in training was to flatten out when you got shelled. Willi tried to get flatter than a hedgehog squashed on the *Autobahn*.

"The lieutenant's down!" somebody yelled. Willi looked around without raising his head. Sure as hell, there was Lieutenant Neustadt, both hands clapped to his belly and a godawful shriek coming out of his mouth. Stretcher-bearers ran up and lugged him away. Willi swore under his breath. That didn't look good.

"We have to keep going!" Sandwiched between Neustadt and Corporal Baatz, Sergeant Lutz Pieck hadn't shown much personality up till now. All of a sudden, the platoon was his, personality or not.

Keep going they did—till they ran up against four French machine guns with interlocking fields of fire. You couldn't advance against those, not unless you'd written your suicide note. Willi took his entrenching tool and started digging a hole.

Sergeant Pieck sent a runner back. Before long, a mortar team came up. The men started dropping bombs on the machine gun nests. They silenced three of them. The soldiers stalked the fourth and put it out of action with grenades. One machine gunner came out with his hands up. Corporal Baatz shot him in the face. He fell over and never twitched again. Willi knew he might have done the same thing. You couldn't use one of those murder mills and then expect to give up as if you'd got caught playing bridge.

Pieck looked as if he wanted to say something about it, but what could he say? Only the Last Trump would bring the Frenchman back to life. And Arno Baatz was a mean bastard who didn't listen to anybody. Pieck pointed west instead. "Forward!" he commanded, and forward they went.

Chapter 9

Luc Harcourt had thought he knew what war was all about. He'd been in some skirmishes. He'd fired his rifle, and he'd come under fire. Artillery had gone off not too far from him. He'd had to worry about mines.

Now he discovered he'd been a virgin trying to figure out how to play with himself. He'd played at war. So had the Germans. Well, playtime was over. The bastards on the other side meant it. If he wanted to go on breathing, he had to mean it, too.

Shells bursting all around him had announced the new dispensation. This wasn't just a little harassing fire. This was a storm of steel, the kind of thing men his father's age talked about. The noise alone was enough to make you shriek—not only the thunderous bursts, but also the horrible screams and wails of fragments knifing through the air. Before long, the screams and wails of the wounded added to the chaos.

And he had to deal with things his old man'd never needed to worry about. Dive-bombers howled down out of the sky. If bursting artillery shells were terrifying, bombs were ten times worse. Shells could carry only so much explosive. Otherwise, they'd blow up before they got out of the gun barrel. Artillerymen disliked such misfortunes. The only limit to a bomb's size, though, was whether a plane could get off the ground carrying it.

German fighters strafed French positions as soon as the bombers went away. Luc wondered where the devil the French fighters were. He didn't see any.

Before long, he realized he'd shat himself somewhere during the bombardment. He tore off his drawers and threw them away. He wondered if he would ever be able to face his buddies. Then he wondered how many of them had fouled themselves, too.

He didn't have long to worry about it. Somebody yelled, "Tanks!" If that wasn't panic in the other soldier's voice . . . well, why not?

He'd never seen a German tank—or, for that matter, a French one—in the earlier skirmishes. He'd never seen dive-bombers then, either. He hadn't missed the dive-bombers one bit. He didn't miss the tanks, either.

Better to hope they would miss him. Here they came, all right: snorting black monsters spitting fire from the guns in their turrets. German soldiers in field-gray loped along between them.

A shell from a French field gun hit a German tank. It spun sideways and stopped. Flame and greasy black smoke burst from it. A soldier scrambled out of an escape hatch, his black coveralls on fire. A burst of machine-gun fire cut him down before he could find somewhere to hide.

But the rest of the tanks kept coming. The machine gun fired at one of them. Bullets struck sparks from its armor, but that was all. Then the tank fired at the French machine gun. It fell silent.

Luc drew a bead on one of the German foot soldiers. He fired. The man went down. Dead? Wounded? Just scared shitless? (Luc knew too well how easy that was.) He never found out.

He did realize he'd have to fall back if he wanted to stay alive. The Nazis were going to overrun this forward position no matter what. Back in the last war, he would have had trenches to retreat through. They'd made positions kilometers deep. This one wasn't. No one had taken the war, or the Germans, seriously enough to set up defenses in depth.

Oh, farther back, well out of artillery range, the Maginot Line was there to make sure no German advance got too far. That might end up making France happy. It didn't do a goddamn thing for Luc.

Almost the first thing he saw when he scrambled out of the trench and fell back to the southwest was somebody else's wadded-up underwear. Just for a minute, that made him feel much better. Then a tank's machine gun stitched up the grass all around his feet. None of the bullets bit him, but he damn near—*damn* near—crapped himself again.

"Over here!" Sergeant Demange shouted. "We can still hold them off!"

Hold them off? Whatever the noncom was smoking, Luc didn't think it came in Gauloises or Gitanes. But staying with somebody who had an idea about what to do next seemed better than running at random. Luc trotted toward Demange, who seemed in charge of a solid position anchored by a farmhouse.

"Jesus!" Luc said, huddling in the kitchen. None of the windows had any glass in them. He didn't know why bombs and shells hadn't flattened the farmhouse. Luck—had to be.

"Fuck Jesus," Sergeant Demange said. "Fuck the *Boches*. Fuck everybody, especially our dumbshit generals."

"What did the generals do?" Luc asked, trying to catch his breath.

"*Rien*," Demange snarled with savage scorn. "Not a goddamn fucking thing. They let us sit here with our thumbs up our asses till the Germans were ready to hit us. And now the Germans are. And we're ready, too—ready to take it on the chin."

"We've got to fight hard for the sake of the international working class." That was Valentin Laclos, one of the several Communists in the company.

Sergeant Demange withered him with a glare. "Fuck the international working class. And fuck you, too, Laclos. If Stalin was on Hitler's side, you'd screech that we ought to lay down and open our legs for the *Boches*. You can't even fart till Moscow tells you it's okay."

Luc admired the noncom's seamless contempt for the world. Demange despised everything and everybody. Chances were he even hated himself. If you had to ride herd on a bunch of snot-nosed soldiers, how could you do anything else?

More German artillery started landing around the farmhouse. As Luc had seen, the windows had already blown out, or rather, in; broken glass glinted on the floor. A shell fragment struck a stone wall and whined away.

"What do we do, Sergeant?" Luc asked.

"Fight, dammit," Demange answered. "Not for the international whatever the hell. Fight because they'll kill you for sure if you don't."

Not necessarily, Luc thought. If he threw down his rifle and threw up his hands, maybe he could sit out the rest of the war in a POW camp. Plenty of Frenchmen had done it the last time around. They'd had a thin time, though—literally. Black bread and turnips and cabbage and not enough of any of them . . . The Germans themselves were starving. They had precious little to spare for prisoners.

And there was no guarantee that surrendering meant becoming a POW. He'd heard French veterans talk about that. If you had the time, if you had the men, maybe you'd take captives back for interrogation. If you didn't? It was their hard luck, that was all. He had no reason to believe the *Boches* acted any differently. He'd already seen you could kill somebody without hating him in the least.

One of the other guys in the farmhouse looked out a window. "Our side's falling back again, Sergeant," he reported.

Sergeant Demange muttered to himself. "We'd better do the same," he said unhappily. "If we get surrounded and cut off, we're liable to have to see if those Nazi cocksuckers'll let us give up. I don't like the odds."

His thoughts came uncomfortably close to Luc's. Once the sergeant made up his mind, he wasted no time. He divided the soldiers crowding the farmhouse into two groups. One he sent out. The other stayed behind in the strongpoint to give covering fire.

Luc got put in the second group. He couldn't even complain, because Sergeant Demange headed it. While their buddies got away, they fired out the windows. A few bullets came back, but only a few.

"Germans aren't here in numbers. That's something, anyhow," Demange said, slapping a new clip onto his Fusil MAS36 and lighting a fresh Gitane from the one that had burnt down almost to his lips. He spat out the tiny butt and stuck the new smoke in his mouth. Then he pointed to the west-facing doorway. "All right. Let's get out of here."

They trotted away. Out in the open, Luc felt horribly naked. A shell could slice him to dogmeat out here. Somebody yelled. He almost shat himself one more time. Then he realized the shout came in French, not German. His asshole unpuckered. His heart came down out of his throat.

"Our guys," Demange said laconically.

The soldier who'd shouted stood in a halfway decent trench line. He and his pals had a couple of Hotchkiss machine guns and, better yet, a 37mm antitank gun in a sandbagged revetment. The gun had two rings painted on the barrel. Kill brags? Luc hoped so.

"As long as the dive-bombers don't come, we're fine," somebody said.

"Where are *our* dive-bombers?" Luc asked plaintively. Nobody answered him.

That cannon did knock out a German tank at better than 300 meters. The machine guns settled the poor bastards who tried to bail out of it. Even so, Luc wondered again where the French panzers were. The next one he saw in this whole war would be the first.

And he wondered if blasting the one tank would bring a storm of vengeance down on everybody here. To his vast relief, it didn't. Night came early. That would slow down the Germans . . . he hoped.

After dark, a runner jumped down into the trench. The French soldiers nearly killed him before they realized he was on their side. He brought orders: fall back once more.

"Why?" Sergeant Demange growled. "We've got 'em stopped here."

"Yes, but they've broken through on both sides of us. If we don't retreat now, we won't get the chance later," the runner replied.

"*Merde,*" said the sergeant. Then he said something so foul, it made *shit* sound like an endearment. And then he said something he must have thought filthier yet: "All right, God damn it to hell and gone. We *will* retreat."

THE ENGINE THUNDERED TO LIFE. The big prop spun, then blurred into invisibility. The Ju-87 throbbed. *"Alles gut?"* Sergeant Dieselhorst shouted through the speaking tube.

"*Alles gut,* Albert," Hans-Ulrich Rudel said after studying the gauges. You couldn't trust them with everything. The way the plane sounded, the way it felt—those counted, too. They could warn of trouble the gauges didn't know about yet. But everything did seem good this morning.

Groundcrew men pulled the chocks away from his wheels. A sergeant waved that he was cleared to take off. He pulled back on the stick. The dive-bomber sprang forward over the yellow, dying grass. The field was almost as smooth as concrete. The Dutchmen had done a devil of a job of keeping everything neat. Now Germany could take advantage of it.

Up went the Stuka's sharklike nose. Rudel climbed as fast as he could. The sooner everybody got into formation, the sooner everybody could go do his job.

"Target—Rotterdam." The squadron commander's voice crackled in his earphones. "The Dutch there think they can go on eating herring and drinking beer while the war stays at the front. They've got the wrong idea, though. In this war, the front is everywhere."

Hans-Ulrich grinned. "You hear that, Dieselhorst?"

"No, sir. What did he say?"

" 'In this war, the front is everywhere.' " The pilot quoted the squadron CO with savage relish.

His number-two wasn't so impressed. "Not everywhere. Do they think the Tommies and the Ivans are going to bomb Berlin?"

"Don't be silly," Rudel said, though a tiny icicle of doubt slithered up his back. The Czechs had, there just before they quit. But that was only a last thumb of the nose, a defiant fleabite. It wasn't as if they did any real damage.

One Stuka had to pull out of the formation with engine trouble. The rest droned on. The vibration filled every particle of Hans-Ulrich's being, everything from his skin to his teeth to his spine to his balls. It wasn't as much fun as getting laid, but it was as compelling.

Bf-109s loped along with the bombers to hold enemy fighters at bay. Four days into the assault on Holland, the air opposition wasn't what it had been. The Dutch didn't have many planes left, while English and French fighters didn't seem to be operating this far forward.

Hans-Ulrich didn't miss them a bit. The Ju-87 was terrific at smashing up ground targets. But even the Czech Avia biplanes had shot down too many dive bombers. For faster, more heavily armed fighters, Stukas were sitting ducks.

He could see where the front lay by the artillery bursts and by where the smoke was rising. General Staff officers with red *Lampassen* down the outside seams of their trousers scribed neat lines on maps and imagined they knew what war was all about. Even up here, buzzing along at 2,500 meters, Rudel could see and smell what war was doing to Holland. *Better to Holland than to the* Reich, he thought.

As soon as they crossed the front, Dutch AA opened up on them. All the Stuka pilots started jinking without waiting for orders. A little faster, a little slower, a little to the left or right, up a little, down a little—anything to keep from giving the gunners an easy target. The neat formation suffered. With luck, the planes wouldn't.

But one of them, trailing smoke, turned back toward the east. That didn't look good. Hans-Ulrich hoped the pilot and rear gunner came through all right. Next to that, getting the Ju-87 down in one piece was small potatoes.

A near miss made his own bus stagger in the sky like a man missing the last step on a flight of stairs. Shrapnel clanged against the left wing. Everything went on working. *"Danke, Gott,"* Rudel murmured. His father the minister would have come up with a fancy prayer, but that did the job.

"Alles gut?" Dieselhorst asked again.

"Alles gut," Hans-Ulrich said firmly.

Holland wasn't a big country. There lay Rotterdam, on both banks of the New Maas. It was a big shipping town, with the most important quays on the north side of the river. Most of the city, including the central square, was on the north bank, too.

"There's the square we're supposed to hit," the squadron leader said. "Follow me down." The underside of his wings flashed in the sun as he aimed his Ju-87 at Rotterdam's heart like an arrow. One after another, the planes he led peeled off after him.

Acceleration shoved Hans-Ulrich against the back of his armored seat. Facing the other way, Albert Dieselhorst experienced dives very differently. He always thought the Stuka was trying to tear the straps off him and pitch him out over his machine gun and through the window behind him.

No antiaircraft fire here. The Dutch must not have thought Germany would attack the towns. Didn't they pay attention to what happened in Czechoslovakia? If they didn't, too bad for them.

Rudel yanked the bomb release lever. Suddenly, the Ju-87 was lighter and more aerodynamic. He pulled back on the stick to come out of the dive. The Stukas, he saw, weren't the only planes working Rotterdam over. High above them, Do-17s—Flying Pencils to friend and foe alike—and He-111s sent bombs raining down on the port. They couldn't put them just where they wanted them, the way a Ju-87 could. But all that high explosive was bound to blow *somebody* to hell and gone.

"*Alles gut?*" Dieselhorst asked one more time. "Sure looks good," he added—he was the one who could see what the bombs had done.

"Couldn't be better," Hans-Ulrich answered, and flew back toward the airstrip from which he'd taken off.

SERGEANT ALISTAIR WALSH WAS WHERE HE was supposed to be: on the Dyle, in central Belgium. The whole BEF was on the line of the Dyle—the whole BEF, less what the Germans had blown sky-high. If what had happened to the rest of the force was anything like what had happened to Walsh's unit, the BEF was missing more than it should have been.

One of the soldiers in Walsh's platoon waved to him. "What's up, Puffin?" Walsh asked. Everybody hung that name on Charlie Casper—he was short and round and had a big red nose.

He also had news: "Bloody goddamn Dutchmen just tossed in the sponge."

"Where'd you hear that?" Walsh demanded in angry disbelief.

"Bloody goddamn wireless."

"But they can't," Walsh said, though he knew too well that they could. He went on protesting: "They just started fighting—what?—five days ago. We all just started five days ago." Except for a few useless rounds aimed at German planes, he had yet to fire a shot.

"And now they've bloody well stopped," Puffin Casper said. "Bunch of damn rotters. Said the Germans bombed the hell out of that damn Rotter place, and they couldn't take any more of that, so they went belly-up."

Something seemed to have gone missing there. Whatever Puffin had heard, he hadn't got it straight. But if the big news was right—and Walsh had no reason to doubt it was—what difference did the details make? Not bloody much, as Casper would have said.

Walsh looked north. "So they'll hit us from that way *and* from the east," he said. "Just what we need."

"Frenchies'll help us," Puffin said.

"Well, maybe." Walsh didn't argue, not right out loud. Casper was only a kid. If he had confidence in the French army, more power to him. He might even end up right. The French Seventh Army, which was in place north of the BEF—on the far side of the Scheldt—was supposed to be big and strong. Maybe it was. Or maybe the BEF would have to go it alone. Back in 1918, British forces seemed to have done that when the Kaiser's army hit them with one haymaker after another.

(That the French would have said the same about the British had never come to Walsh's notice. If it had, he would have called the man bold—or rash—enough to give him such news a goddamn liar.)

Artillery rumbled, off to the east. Some of those were Belgian guns, firing at the advancing Germans. And some of them were German, making sure the bastards in field-gray kept on advancing. The gunfire was getting louder, which meant it was getting closer to the Dyle. Sooner or later—probably sooner—Walsh figured he would make the Germans' acquaintance again.

An officer came up to him. For a second, he thought the man was British. Then he saw the funny rank badges. *A Belgian,* he realized. Ordinary Belgian soldiers looked like Frenchmen, mostly because of the Adrian helmets they wore. But officers had British-style uniforms.

"Where is your command post?" the Belgian asked in accented but understandable English.

"Why do you want to know . . . sir?" The British sergeant knew he sounded suspicious, but he couldn't help himself. The Dutch had just thrown in the towel. What if the bloody Belgies were about to do the same thing? Their king hadn't wanted to let any Allies in till the very last instant—which was liable to be too late.

But this fellow said, "The better to arrange cooperation between your forces and mine. You are a sergeant, is it not so?"

What do you think you're doing, asking me questions? was what he meant. Walsh didn't think he could get in much trouble for slowing up a wog, but he didn't want to find out the hard way he was wrong. He pointed north. "Go that way, oh, three hundred yards, and you'll see the regimental tent."

"Yards?" The Belgian officer scratched his head.

"Yes, sir." Alistair Walsh felt like scratching his, too. Then he figured out what had to be wrong. Stupid foreigners with their idiot measures. "Uh, three hundred meters." Close enough.

The Belgian nodded. "Ah. Thank you." Off he went, happy as a ram in clover.

"What do you want to bet they're the next ones out?" Puffin Casper said dolefully.

"Wouldn't be surprised," Walsh agreed. "They'll tear a nasty hole in our lines if they do bugger off, though."

"They'll care a lot about that, they will," Puffin said.

More Belgian soldiers came back over the Dyle. Some of them still looked ready to fight. They were just blokes doing their jobs. Others had done all the work they aimed to do for a while. They slipped back toward the rear first chance they saw. Still others were walking wounded. Some of them seemed angry. Others seemed weary and in pain, as they no doubt were. Still others might have been relieved. They'd fought, they'd got hurt, and they were still alive. Nobody could expect them to do anything more.

Englishmen would have reacted the same way. The idea that foreigners could act just like ordinary people never failed to surprise Walsh.

And then, with the throb of airplane engines overhead, the only foreigners he cared about were the Germans. He ran for the closest trench and jumped in.

These weren't dive-bombers, anyway. They stayed high overhead and let their bombs rain down on the general area of their targets. The whistles as the bombs fell weren't quite so bad as the screaming sirens on those vulture-winged diving bastards. They sure as hell weren't good, though.

When the bombs burst, it seemed as if a million of them were going off at once. Blast threw Walsh around. Blast could kill all by itself without fragments. It could tear lungs to shreds without leaving a mark on a body. Walsh had already seen that. He wished he hadn't chosen this exact moment to remember it.

Engines of a different note made him look up. Fighters were tearing into the bomber formations. He let out a whoop. Somebody else sprawled in the trench said, "Blimey, there really is an RAF!" The soldier sounded astonished.

Walsh didn't blame him. He hadn't seen many British planes himself. But they were there now. Two broad-winged bombers tumbled out of the air, wrapped in smoke and fire. Parachutes sprouted in the sky. Walsh waited for the British pilots—he assumed they were his countrymen, though they might have been French—to machine-gun the descending German airmen. But they didn't. He wondered why not. Not sporting? Were he hanging helpless from a silk half-bubble, he didn't suppose he would have wanted a German blazing away at him.

"Blimey!" the other soldier said again. "That bugger's going to come down right on our 'eads, 'e is."

He didn't quite. But he landed no more than fifty yards away. Walsh aimed his rifle at him. "Give up right now, you fucking bastard!" he bawled.

The German paid no attention to him. The fellow sprawled on the ground, clutching his ankle and howling like a dog with its tail caught under a rocking chair. The parachute flapped and billowed like a live thing, threatening to drag him away.

"Easiest prisoner I ever took," Walsh said. "If he hasn't broken that, I'm a Belgian myself."

"But do you want to go out there and get 'im?" the other British soldier asked. "What if more bombers come over?"

"Urr," said Walsh, who hadn't thought of that. Letting the German flyer's countrymen blow him to pieces was a distinctly unattractive notion. But so was listening to him.

When Walsh said so, the other man replied, "Then shoot 'im. Or if you don't care to, I will."

"No," Walsh said. If he were lying there with a broken ankle, he would want a German to take him prisoner. And he thought there was a pretty good chance some German would. The bastards in field-gray fought hard. They'd fought hard even when they knew the game was up in 1918. They mostly fought fair, though. Of what army could you say more?

That made up his mind for him. He scrambled out of his hole and trotted toward the downed *Luftwaffe* man. The German saw his rifle and held up his hands. He gabbled something in his own language. If that wasn't *I give up!*, Walsh really was a Belgian.

He pointed to the pistol on the flyer's belt. "Throw that damn thing away, and make it snappy!" he said.

"*Ja! Ja!*" Maybe the German understood a little English, even if he didn't seem to speak any. Or maybe the sergeant's gestures made sense to him. Walsh kept his finger on the trigger while the man disarmed himself. If he turned out to be a fanatic, he'd be a dead fanatic pretty damn quick. But he didn't. He tossed the little automatic—smaller and neater than the Enfield .38 revolver that was the British standard in this war, to say nothing of the last go-round's man-killing brute of a Webley and Scott .455—into the bushes.

"All right." Walsh knelt beside him and pointed to the trench from which he'd come. "I'm going to take you back there." He got the German's arm around his shoulder. Grunting as he rose, he went on, "This may hurt a bit."

The airman hopped awkwardly on one leg. He tried not to let his other foot touch the ground at all. Sure as the devil, that ankle was ruined. Well, he'd done worse to plenty of Dutchmen and Belgians and Englishmen.

"Give me a hand with this bugger," Walsh called. Unenthusiastically, the other British soldier did.

Once in the hole, the flyer reached inside his coverall. He came closer to dying than he probably realized. But he came out with . . . *"Zigaretten?"* he said, proffering the packet.

"Thanks." Walsh took one. So did the other soldier, who gave him a light. They both took a drag. "Bloody hell!" Walsh said. "Tastes like hay and barge scrapings." If this was what the Germans were smoking, no wonder the bastards acted mean.

He gave the *Luftwaffe* man a Navy Cut. People said they were strong. God only knew they were cheap. But the new prisoner's eyes went wide when he puffed on it. *"Danke schön! Sehr gut!"* he said. He reverently smoked it all the way down to the end. It probably had more real tobacco in it than he usually got in a week.

Stretcher-bearers took him off to the rear. If he got more proper cigarettes, odds were he was glad enough to go.

CHRISTMAS WAS RIGHT AROUND THE CORNER, but Peggy Druce found Berlin a singularly joyless place. She supposed she should count her blessings. If she weren't from the neutral USA, she would have been interned, not just inconvenienced. All the same . . .

So many shops were empty. Hardly any cars rolled down the street. Even the trolleys operated on a wartime schedule, which meant you took a long time to get anywhere. The city was blacked out at night. As far as Peggy could tell, the whole damn country was blacked out at night.

Maybe all of Europe was blacked out. Peggy tried to imagine Paris dark at night. The picture didn't want to form. The City of Light was bound to be as shrouded as any other European capital. After what the Germans did to Prague and Marianske Lazne and the rest of Czechoslovakia, they wouldn't leave Paris alone. She supposed it was a genuine military target. But the idea of bombs falling on it made her almost physically ill.

She walked past a restaurant not far from the hotel where they'd put her up. She hadn't the slightest desire to go inside. Like everyone else in Germany, she had a ration card. Even in a restaurant, she had to spend points on what she ate. Whatever she got, most of it would be cabbage and potatoes and black bread. Fats of any sort—butter, cheese, lard—were hard to come by. Milk and cod-liver oil were reserved almost exclusively for children and nursing and pregnant women.

A man with a white mustache walked past her. He tipped his hat as he went by. His wool suit had seen better years, but he couldn't do much about that. The Germans had ration points for clothes, too. If you bought a topcoat, that was about it for the year. Peggy didn't have all the clothes she wanted, either; most of what she'd brought to Czechoslovakia was still there. Or, maybe more likely, it was on some German woman's back these days.

A team of horses drew an antiaircraft gun down the street. The horses might have come straight out of the Civil War. The field-gray uniforms on the soldiers were modern, though. As for the gun, it might have appeared from the future. She didn't think she'd ever seen a piece of hardware that looked more lethal.

Newsboys held up papers full of headlines about German triumphs. People walked past without buying. If the Berliners were enthusiastic about the war, they hid it well.

"English and French air pirates bombard German towns!" a boy shouted. "Many innocent women and children murdered! Read about the latest enemy atrocities!"

Peggy almost stopped at the street corner to argue with him. Only the thought that her husband would have told her she was crazy made her keep her mouth shut. She admired Herb's common sense, most of the time without wanting to imitate it. And she'd seen the fun the Nazis had knocking Czechoslovakia flat. If they were on the receiving end for a change, if this wasn't all just propaganda and nonsense, boy, did they ever deserve it!

But the kid wasn't to blame for that. He was only doing his job. The ones who were to blame were Hitler and Goebbels and Göring and Himmler, and she couldn't very well tell them where to head in. If she took it out on the newsboy, what would happen to her? Neutral or not, American or not, she didn't want a visit from the *Gestapo.*

Because she looked as shabby as everybody else, the Berliners assumed she was a German, too. They'd nod and say, *"Guten Morgen."* She could manage that. She understood German tolerably well, but she spoke French much better. When people here expected much more than *Good morning* from her, she stumbled badly.

She hated that. She also hated being so dowdy. She'd made a life of standing out from the crowd. No one would ever have noticed her if she didn't make a point of getting noticed. If she disliked anything, it was invisibility.

A few minutes later, ambling along on a day as gray and gloomy as her mood, she found a way to get noticed. She walked past a place whose window said ROTHSTEIN'S BUTCHER'S SHOP. It wasn't bigger or fancier or more run down than the shops to either side: a secondhand bookstore to the left, a place that sold wickerwork purses and baskets to the right. The wickerwork place was busy—wicker, unlike leather, didn't eat up ration points.

Rothstein's, however, had a large sign taped in the window: GERMAN PEOPLE! DON'T BUY FROM DIRTY JEWS!

Next thing Peggy knew, she was walking through the door. Maybe a demon took hold of her. Only when the bell over the door jangled did she realize what she'd done. And she'd been so proud of herself for wanting to steer clear of the *Gestapo*! Well, so much for that.

Behind the counter, Rothstein looked astonished. "You aren't one of my regulars!" he blurted. "You aren't even—" He stopped, but *Jewish* hung in the air anyway.

"You're right. I'm not. Give me a chicken leg, please." Peggy had enough German for that. She could boil the leg on the hot plate in her room. It would make a better lunch—maybe lunch and supper—than she was likely to get in the hotel restaurant or a café. Not much good food left for civilians in Berlin.

Moving like a man in a dream, Rothstein weighed the leg. *He* was unmistakably a Jew, with a long nose and dark, curly hair. "It comes to 420 grams—almost a week's ration for meat," he said. "If you like, I will bone it, so it costs you fewer points."

"*Bitte*," Peggy said.

Deftly, he did. "Now it is only 290 grams. I need coupons for so much, and two Reichsmarks fifty." As he spoke, he wrapped the chicken in—what else?—butcher paper.

Sixty cents American money, more or less. That was a hell of a lot for a leg. Peggy paid without blinking. She also handed over the swastika-marked ration coupons. Those were part of the game, too.

Rothstein gave her a meticulously written receipt. "*Danke schön*," he told her. "You are very brave. You are also very foolish."

"I hope not," Peggy said. "*Auf wiedersehen*." *Till I see you again*, it meant literally. She wondered if she was brave enough—or foolish enough—to come back.

She got out fast, but not fast enough. Somebody'd squealed on her.

Two blackshirts were trotting up the street toward Rothstein's. "What kind of *Dummkopf* do you think you are?" one of them roared. "How dare you go into that damned Jew's place?"

"Let me see your papers," the other one yelled. "Immediately!"

"Sure." Peggy took out her American passport and brandished it like a priest turning a crucifix on a couple of vampires.

The SS men recoiled almost the way vampires would have, too. "Oh," one of them said disgustedly. "All right. We can't give you what you deserve for buying there. But we can make the Jew sorry for selling to you."

"And we will," the other added, gloating anticipation in his voice.

"He didn't know I was an American." If Peggy sounded appalled, it was because she was.

"He knew you weren't one of his regular kikes. He'll pay, all right." The SS men stormed into the butcher's shop. A moment later, Rothstein cried out in pain. Peggy burst into tears. Dammit, you couldn't win here.

Chapter 10

People were saying the Maginot Line would save France. People were saying it would have to save France. Luc Harcourt didn't give a damn about what people were saying. All he knew was, he was getting sick of being marched backward and forward and inside out.

He'd been bombed and shelled and shot at in the retreat from the German frontier. He'd been bombed in the encampment behind the Maginot Line where raw reinforcements filled out the regiment. Fortunately, those little *billets-doux* had fallen from planes flying high above, not from the *Boches'* nasty dive-bombers. They landed all around the camp, but hardly any on it.

Now he and his surviving buddies and the strangers in their clean uniforms who'd just joined them were moving up toward the front again. This time, from what Sergeant Demange said, they'd end up in southern Belgium. *If we get there in one piece,* Luc thought.

That wasn't obvious. Hell, whether they'd get there at all wasn't obvious. They'd started out from the transit camp in trucks. Luc hadn't much cared for that—as if his opinion mattered a sou's worth. But if

German planes shot up your truck, wouldn't you roast like a pork loin in the oven? Of course you would—and your meat would end up smelling like burnt pork, too.

No German planes harried the trucks. That didn't mean they carried Luc and his comrades very far toward the front. German bombers had done their worst to the roads leading north and east. If a truck couldn't get through, if it sank to the axles when it tried to use the muddy fields instead of the cratered roads . . .

If all that happened—and it did—you got out and you damn well walked. "Here we are, back in 1918," Sergeant Demange said, the cigarette in the corner of his mouth twitching as he talked.

"This isn't so bad, Sarge," Luc said. "Back then, you wore horizon-blue. Now you're in khaki."

"Oh, shut up, smartass. Once they get muddy, all uniforms are the same color," Demange said. "The only thing you know about a guy in clean new clothes is that he doesn't come up to the front much, so you can't trust him."

Ahead, the rumble of artillery got steadily louder. The Frenchmen were heading its way—and it was heading theirs. And behind them came a rumble of engines—*something* had got past the unholy mess the Nazis had made of the roads. "Move to one side, damn you!" someone yelled.

When Luc saw French tanks, he was only too glad to stand aside and let them go by. The officer who'd shouted, a tall colonel with a small mustache and a big nose, stood very straight in the cupola of the lead machine. The French tanks were larger and had smoother lines than the German machines Luc had already seen too closely. By the determined look on the colonel's face, he didn't want to stop till he got to Berlin.

"He's a fishing pole, isn't he?" Luc remarked.

"Two fishing poles," Sergeant Demange answered. That was what Luc thought he heard, anyway: *deux galles.* But Demange went on,

"Colonel de Gaulle knows more about tanks than anybody else on our side, I think."

"Is that who he is?" Luc had heard of de Gaulle, though he hadn't known him by sight. The tall officer did indeed advocate tanks so tirelessly—and tiresomely—that he infuriated his superiors. "Did you serve under him last time?"

"Nah. Wish I would have." Sergeant Demange spat out a tiny butt and ground it into the mud with his boot. He lit another Gitane, then continued, "If I remember straight, he got wounded and captured early on last time around, and sat out most of the war in a POW camp."

"Lucky stiff," muttered somebody in back of Luc. He almost turned around to find out who let his mouth run ahead of his brain like that. A tiny bit louder, and Sergeant Demange would have heard it, in which case God help whoever it was. On second thought, Luc didn't want to know. If he didn't, the ferocious little sergeant couldn't squeeze it out of him.

The last tank growled past. None of the other commanders looked to be within ten centimeters of Colonel de Gaulle. Maybe that was just as well for them. They couldn't have much room inside the turret when they needed to duck down and fight.

Luc's company stopped at a field kitchen as daylight leached from the sky. A cook with a double chin—cooks never went hungry—shoveled potatoes and cabbage and stewed pork into his mess tin. He stared at his supper with resigned dismay. "Which side are we on, anyway?"

"Funny guy," the cook said. "I've only heard that one five times in the past half-hour. You don't want it, you can go hungry. You think I give a rat's ass?"

Luc prodded a pale piece of pork with a forefinger. "I thought that's what this was." The cook swore at him in earnest then.

Washed down with *vin* extremely *ordinaire*, the stew wasn't bad. Luc smoked a cigarette, then wrapped himself in a blanket inside what had been somebody's house till a bomb blew out most of one wall. His buddies had a makeshift brazier going: a bucket half full of hot coals hung from a scrap-metal tripod so it didn't set the floor on fire. It gave off less heat than Luc wished it would, but it was better than nothing.

He slept like a hibernating animal. Not only were nights endlessly long, but he'd never been so worn in his life. Some of the guys in his company fell asleep while they marched—and they kept going, too. He envied them—he didn't seem able to do that himself.

Some time in the middle of the night, a hard hand shook him awake. He groped for his belt knife. Sergeant Demange's low-voiced chuckle stopped him. "Take it easy," the noncom said. "If I wanted you dead, you'd be holding a lily by now. But no. Go out and stand watch for a couple of hours."

"Do I have to?" Luc asked around a yawn.

"Damn right you do. Suppose German parachutists came down out of the sky? What would we do without a warning?"

"At night?" Luc didn't believe it. But the Fritzes had done all kinds of nasty things with parachutists. Maybe they'd make a night attack behind the French line. And no maybe about what Sergeant Demange would do if Luc gave him any more lip. With a martyred sigh, Luc got out of the blanket and put on his boots and his helmet. He was already wearing everything else, including his greatcoat.

His breath smoked inside the battered house. It smoked more when he stepped outside. The night was mostly clear. Stars glittered frigidly in a sky blacker than dried blood. Carolers would have loved a night like this. Right now, Luc would have bet nobody in Europe loved anybody else.

The war hadn't gone to bed. Off to the northeast, the thunder of artillery went on. He could see flashes against the horizon. *Ours or theirs?* he wondered. After a moment, he decided it was probably both.

Just ahead lay towns whose names brought back thunderous memories of the last war's early days: Charleroi and, a little farther east, Namur. The Germans were swarming this way again, like field-gray ants towards an enticing picnic feast. They'd fallen short of Paris the last time around. Either they would again or . . .

Luc didn't want to think about *or.* He didn't want to think about anything. He wanted to go back to sleep, or to fall asleep out here. Fear of the *Boches* didn't hold him back. Fear of Sergeant Demange did.

After what seemed like forever but probably wasn't, another soldier stumbled out of the house. "Go back to sleep," he said. "I've got it." A moment later, he added, "Damn Sergeant Demange anyway," under his breath.

"Sure," Luc said. He went back inside, wondering whether Demange ever slept. On all the evidence, he seemed a piece of well-made machinery rather than a man. Maybe he ran on cigarette smoke and coffee.

Come to think of it, maybe I do, too. Luc found the blanket he'd so sorrowfully abandoned. He took off boots and helmet and lay down again. The blanket didn't seem to do a thing to get him any warmer. He wondered if he'd lie there till dawn finally came. Next thing he knew, he was asleep.

"Wake up, you bum. You snore."

"I do not," Luc answered automatically, even before his eyes opened. Twenty minutes later, with some kind of mush and strong coffee inside him, he was marching again.

Refugees from Namur and Charleroi crowded the road. Some of them cheered the soldiers in their odd Walloon French. Others swore at them: "If we weren't in the way between the Germans and your damned country, they'd leave *us* alone!"

"As far as I'm concerned, Hitler's welcome to Belgium," Sergeant Demange retorted. "And you cocksuckers deserve him, too. Now get the hell out of our way before we open up on you!"

He would have done it. Not only that, he would have laughed while he did it. The Belgians must have figured that out, because they tumbled off the road with haste that would have been funny if this were a film and not the ruination of their lives.

Then more Belgian soldiers started falling back past the oncoming French. "*You* can have a taste of those bastards," a Walloon said. A couple of Flemings added something to that, but Luc didn't know what it was. If they hadn't worn Belgian uniform, he would have shot them. Their language sounded too goddamn much like German.

Charleroi had got the bejesus knocked out of it in the first war. Luc supposed it must have been rebuilt since, but it had got pounded again. Some of the wrecked buildings were still smoking. The Nazis had just worked it over, then. Half a rag doll lay in the gutter. At another time, it might have been poignant enough to move Luc to tears. But he'd seen men who looked like that. He glanced at the doll and marched on.

Out beyond Charleroi, some of Colonel de Gaulle's tanks were firing at the enemy. German shells landed around them. Without waiting for orders, Luc yanked the entrenching tool off his belt and started digging in. If Sergeant Demange didn't like it, he'd say so. A look out of the corner of Luc's eyes told him the noncom was digging, too. Nodding to himself, Luc made the dirt fly.

SOME FRENCH KING A LONG TIME ago said, "Paris is worth a Mass." Vaclav Jezek had learned that in history class. As far as he was concerned, Paris was mostly a mess. By steamer from Constanta to Marseille, dodging Italian subs and seaplanes. By train from Marseille to Paris. By taxicab to the Czech embassy, which served as headquarters for the government in exile.

By taxi again to a camp outside Paris. The camp held about a regiment's worth of Czechoslovakian soldiers: mostly Czechs, with a sprinkling of antifascist Slovaks and Ruthenians. Hardly anyone had his own weapon. The French wasted little time passing out rifles. They were eager to get all their friends into the fight against Hitler's legions.

Next to none of them spoke any Czech, though. They did the same thing as the Pole who'd interned Vaclav: they used German. It worked—most Czechs knew at least some, and could translate for the ones who didn't. But speaking the enemy's language with your friends was humiliating and infuriating.

The Germans seemed to know where the camp was. Their bombers visited it every so often. This wasn't the first time Vaclav had had to sprint for a trench—far from it. The bombers also visited Paris. On the radio, the Germans claimed to be hitting only military targets. That would have been funny if it didn't make Jezek want to cry.

Three days before Christmas, his platoon jammed itself into a bus. A generation earlier, buses had hauled French troops from Paris to the war-saving Battle of the Marne. Some of the machines the Czechoslovak regiment used looked to be of vintage close to 1914.

It was cold outside. It didn't stay cold inside the bus for long, not when it was full of twice as many men as it was supposed to carry. Everybody lit a cigarette. Inside of seconds, the smoke made Vaclav's eyes sting. He didn't care. He was smoking furiously himself. Gauloises packed a heftier jolt than the miserable excuses for tobacco he'd got since he was interned.

The driver, a middle-aged Frenchman, chain-smoked with his passengers. A patch covered his left eye but didn't hide all the damage a bullet or shell fragment had done to his face. He seemed to manage all right with one eye, at least as far as driving went.

Whatever springs the bus might have had once upon a time had long since gone to the big coachwork shop in the sky. Vaclav felt every pothole, every rock. "I wonder if we'll have any kidneys left by the time we get wherever we're going," he said to the soldier sitting next to—half on top of—him.

"Why worry?" the other man replied. His dark, curly hair and hooked nose said he was a Jew. Vaclav normally had little use for Jews, but he supposed you could count on them to fight the Nazis. This fellow went on, "If we've still got 'em when we get there, the Germans'll blow 'em out of us, right?"

Vaclav eyed him. Maybe you weren't so smart if you supposed something like that. "If you don't think we can beat them, why did you sign up for this?"

"You gotta try." The Jewish soldier paused to light a Gitane. He spoke Czech like a big-city man; if he wasn't from Prague, Vaclav didn't know anything. After sucking in smoke, he added, "Damn Poles don't like Jews any better than the Germans do."

"I guess not." Vaclav hadn't thought of that; it was nothing he'd ever needed to worry about.

"So how about you, *goy*?" That wasn't Czech or German, but Vaclav had no trouble working out what it meant. "How come you're here? How come you aren't yelling, '*Heil Hitler!*'?"

Who do you think you are, asking me *questions like that?* After a moment, Vaclav tried to shrug. Inside the crowded bus, it wasn't easy. "Fuck Hitler," he said simply.

"That'll do." The Jew nodded. "I'm David. Who the hell are you?"

"Vaclav." Jezek laughed. "Like everybody else, almost."

David started singing the Christmas song about Good King Wenceslaus. He knew all the words. Vaclav must have looked flabbergasted, because the Jew started to laugh. "I've been hearing it ever since I was born," David said. "Hell, I must have heard it while I was still inside my mom. I'd better know it."

"I guess." Vaclav hadn't thought about that, either. If you were a Jew, you had your own stuff. But everybody else's stuff had to land on you, too, whether you wanted it or not. If that wasn't weird, what was?

After a few seconds, somebody else started singing about Good King Wenceslaus. It was that season of the year. A moment later, the Czech carol filled the bus like cigarette smoke. "Well, I see what you mean," Vaclav said.

David nodded again. "Bet your ass. It's always like this."

The driver didn't speak any Czech. To him, the carol was just noise. He didn't need long to get sick of it. He yelled something in French. Not enough of the Czech soldiers spoke enough French for it to do any good. Then the driver screamed, "Shut up, you fucking pigdogs!" *auf Deutsch.* Maybe he'd learned it in a prison camp or something. That got people's attention—maybe not in a good way, but it did.

"Ah, your mother," David said, first in Czech, then in Yiddish.

Vaclav realized things were starting to go wrong when a gendarme—or maybe he was a military policeman—waved the bus onto a detour. The new road was narrow and twisty. The driver started swearing. So did the Czech soldiers as they slid from side to side.

Then the side road petered out—or maybe there was a crater up ahead. *"Heraus!"* the driver said as the bus' door wheezed open.

"What do we do now?" Vaclav asked.

"What else?" David said. "We walk."

Walk they did. Vaclav had lost his conditioning after getting interned. Tramping along with a forty-kilo pack on his back wasn't his idea of a good time. The road seemed uphill both ways. Despite spatters of sleet, he soon started sweating. He threw down a cigarette butt and heard it hiss to extinction in an icy puddle.

That sparked a thought: "They say smoking is bad for your wind."

"Screw 'em," David replied. He had another cigarette in his mouth.

Airplane motors droned high overhead. Bombs whistled down out of the clouds. They fell at random across the French countryside. The low ceiling grounded the German Stukas. Vaclav didn't miss them—those bastards could put one right on top of an outhouse if they saw you walk in there to take a crap.

His platoon, of course, wasn't the only unit on the march. He sometimes wondered if there was anybody in France who wasn't. They went past a bunch of Frenchmen who'd got hit by one of those randomly falling bombs—a 250-kilo job, or maybe a 500. It wasn't pretty. If the swine that went through a meat-packing plant wore uniforms, they would have looked a lot like this about halfway through.

Czech medics did what they could to help their French counterparts. You had to hope the French would have done the same for a Czech outfit. The rest of the platoon went around the blood and the moans and the shattered bodies. Vaclav didn't look closely at them. He'd already seen more death and devastation than he ever wanted to remember.

And now you're volunteering to be part of it again? he asked himself. *You could have sat tight in that internment camp. It wasn't exciting, but nobody was out to blow your balls off, either.*

His shrug made the straps on that heavy pack dig into his shoulders. Too late to worry about it now. He'd been bored in the camp. Maybe he'd been stupid to leave. But if everybody sat tight, if nobody tried to stop Hitler, wouldn't the little bastard with the ugly mustache end up telling the world what to do?

It looked that way to Vaclav. He glanced over at David, slogging along beside him. David had his own reasons to hate the Nazis, all right. Most of the time, Czech and Jew would have been wary around each other. Not here. The Germans had brought them together. A miracle of sorts, or maybe just proof of the old saying, *The enemy of my enemy is my friend.*

Bombs turned a roadside meadow into a lunar landscape. Cattle lay sprawled like soldiers. They weren't bloated and stinking. Some of them still moved and lowed piteously, so they'd gone down in this latest bombardment. Part of the weight Vaclav carried was rations. All the same . . .

"Fresh meat!" David got the words out before he could.

The platoon commander was a fresh-faced lieutenant named Svabinsky. Maybe he could have kept the soldiers from running into the field, maybe not. But he didn't even try. "Beefsteaks!" he said happily, and pulled the bayonet off his belt.

They weren't exactly beefsteaks. No butcher worth half his pay would have given them such a fancy name. They were chunks of meat haggled off the carcasses by hungrily enthusiastic amateurs. Toasted over a roaring fire, Vaclav's had a charred crust and a bloody interior. He didn't care. The gobbet was big enough to make his belly shut up. What else mattered in the field?

He rolled himself in a blanket and lay down by the fire. Lieutenant Svabinsky made sure people fed it through the night. Some time in the middle of the long, cold darkness, the blaring of car horns woke Vaclav. People shouted in French and French-accented German and even, once or twice, in Czech. Road damage might have stopped the buses, but the French army had cobbled together this swarm of automobiles to bring the Czechoslovakian soldiers up to the front.

As Vaclav stumbled towards one of them—they showed no lights, of course—he laughed through a yawn. The French were in a fix, the same way his own country had been. But they were trying to muddle through. He couldn't imagine the efficient Germans coming up with a mad arrangement like this.

He piled into a car. As soon as it was packed, the driver took off. Vaclav hoped the fellow knew where he was going. He must have. Even staying on the road couldn't have been easy, but the Frenchman did it. Vaclav dozed off again, jerking awake whenever the car hit a pothole.

Somebody outside said something in a language that sounded like German. Vaclav's eyes flew open. Morning twilight let him see a soldier in a French-looking uniform. What came out of the man's mouth still sounded like German. *A Belgian,* Vaclav realized. *Are we in Belgium already?*

The soldier turned out to speak French, too. That helped the driver, though not Vaclav. The Czech was glad to have a little light. The road was worse than ever, and wound through rugged, heavily wooded country. "What is this place?" Vaclav asked in German.

"They call it the Ardennes," the driver answered in the same tongue.

"Why do they want us here?" Vaclav said. "You'd have to be crazy to try and push an attack through terrain like this."

With a magnificent Gallic shrug, the driver said, "With people like the Germans, who can tell?" Somebody yelled and waved. The Frenchman hit the brakes. The car—a battered old Citroën—lurched to a stop. "You get out here."

Getting out was harder than squeezing in had been. Vaclav stretched and twisted to work the kinks out of his back. He wished he had some coffee.

"Youse is the Czechs?" What the French officer spoke sounded more like bad Polish than Czech, but Vaclav could—barely—follow it. The Frenchman went on, "Come these ways—I will shove you into positions." He was trying, anyhow.

And maybe the Czechs did need to be shoved into positions. Artillery growled up ahead. It wasn't too close, but it was there. Maybe the Germans *were* crazy. Or maybe this was a feint, with the main force up in the north, the way it looked.

His shrug wasn't so fancy as the driver's but it would do. He didn't have to decide whether the Nazis were making a big push here or a little one. All he had to do was go where people told him and shoot at anybody and anything decked out in German field-gray.

He wasn't the only Czech soldier yawning as a ragged column formed. He figured he could just about manage what they needed from him.

"STILLE NACHT! HEILIGE NACHT!" Hans-Ulrich Rudel sang, along with the rest of the flyers and groundcrew men at the forward base in Hol-

land. They had a tree, brought west from Germany and decorated with gingerbread men and candles and tinsel and ornaments made from scrap metal by mechanics in between patch jobs and other repairs on the Stukas.

Hans-Ulrich had heard that carol and all the others since before the day he first knew what the words meant. With his father a churchman, it couldn't very well have been any different. But at his father's house, and at his father's church, the songs hadn't seemed to mean so much. People sang them because they'd always sung them, sang them without thinking about what the words really said.

Things were different here. *You don't know what life is worth till you lay it on the line,* Rudel thought. Everybody here knew this Christmas might be his last. That made it count for ever so much more than it had back in peacetime.

One of the other pilots raised a glass of schnapps. "Absent friends," he said, and knocked back the shot.

"Absent friends," the *Luftwaffe* men chorused. Most of them had something strong to hand, too.

Hans-Ulrich didn't. A groundcrew man clucked at him. "Shouldn't drink toasts in water. It's unlucky."

"Not water," Rudel replied with dignity. But his eggnog *was* unfortified.

"Close enough. Too damn close." The other pilot raised his glass again. "And here's to close enough and too damn close, as long as the bastards miss."

"Amen!" Hans-Ulrich drank to that, too, even if it was with plain eggnog.

Off in the distance, guns boomed. The ceiling was too low to let planes take off and land, but the war went on. One of the groundcrew men, a graying, wrinkled fellow with only three fingers on his left hand, said, "Wasn't like this the first Christmas in the last war."

"I've heard about the truce, Franz," Hans-Ulrich said. "Was it really as big a thing as people say—our *Landsers* playing football with the Tommies, and all that?"

"I know people who watched the games," Franz answered. "I know one guy who played. I didn't see 'em myself—my regiment was opposite the Frenchmen. We didn't play football with them. But we did come up out of the trenches and meet in no-man's-land, damned if we didn't. We traded cigarettes and rations and stuff you could drink, and we all said what a bunch of assholes our officers were. . . . No offense, sir."

Everybody laughed. Rudel made sure his laughter was louder than anyone else's. You couldn't let the men think you were a stuffed shirt, even if you were—maybe especially if you were. Hans-Ulrich knew he was, at least by most people's standards.

He shrugged. He had his father's stern Lutheran God, and he had the *Führer* (whom he saw as God's instrument on earth), and he had his Stuka (which was his own instrument on earth). As long as he had them, he didn't need to worry about anything else.

Or so he thought, till bombs started walking toward the hut where he and his countrymen were celebrating Christmas. The weather might be lousy here, but it was good enough farther west to let planes take off, and the English or French were paying a call.

They were bombing blind, of course, up there above the clouds. *Let it fall, and it's bound to come down on somebody's head.* That had to be what they were thinking, and they were right. The *Luftwaffe* did the same thing when the weather was bad, as it so often was at this season.

Hans-Ulrich didn't want to be the first one running for a trench. He also didn't want to wait too long and go sky-high in case the bombardiers got lucky. The line between courage and foolhardiness could be a fine one.

Franz took the bull by the horns. "I'm never going to go up for the goddamn *Ritterkreuz*," he said, and dashed out the door.

Where one man went, others could follow without losing pride. A zigzag trench ran only a few meters outside the hut for such occasions as these. As Hans-Ulrich jumped down into it—his boots squelched in mud—he tried to imagine winning the Knight's Cross to the Iron Cross himself. He'd got an Iron Cross Second Class a week before: an early Christmas present, his CO called it. But you could win an Iron Cross Second Class just by staying alive at the front for a couple of weeks—oh, not quite, but it seemed that way.

Franz had the ribbon for one, no doubt from the last war. Back then, the Iron Cross Second Class was almost the only medal an enlisted man could win. Hitler had an Iron Cross First Class, which made him an exceptional hero, because he'd never even reached sergeant.

And then Hans-Ulrich stopped worrying about Hitler's Iron Cross or anything else but living through the next few minutes. The enemy planes up there were bombing blind, but they couldn't have done better on a sunny, clear summer's day. They might not have done so well, because high-altitude bombing was turning out to be one of the big disappointments of the war. It was neither as accurate nor as terrifying and intimidating as the experts had claimed it would be.

Which didn't mean winding up on the wrong end of it was any fun. Now Rudel got a taste of what he gave the foe. The earth shook under him like a blancmange. The noise was impossible, overwhelming. Blast did its best to tear his lungs out from the inside.

After the longest six or eight minutes of Hans-Ulrich's life, the bombers droned away. *"Der Herr Gott im Himmel!"* he said. Then he said it again, louder, because he couldn't hear himself the first time. He stuck his head up and looked over the lip of the trench.

The hut still stood, but it leaned drunkenly. Its windows were blown out—or, more likely, in. Bomb craters turned the landscape into a miniature Verdun. Something a few hundred meters away was burning enthusiastically—a truck, Hans-Ulrich saw.

Sergeant Dieselhorst stuck his head up a few meters from Hans-Ulrich. "I wouldn't mind not doing that again," the rear gunner remarked, and then, apropos of nothing that presently surrounded him, "Merry Christmas."

"Merry Christmas," Rudel echoed automatically. "Where were you? You weren't singing carols—I know that."

"I should hope not," the noncom said. "If you want to waste your time that way, go ahead, but I was doing something more important: I was sleeping, by God." He pointed to some trees not far away. "I was happy as a clam under there, but then the goddamn bombs started coming down."

He sounded irate in a particular way. Hans-Ulrich nodded, because he felt that same indignation. When he went out and dropped a fat one on a French truck column, that was business. But when the sons of bitches on the other side tried to blow *him* to the moon, it felt like dirty pool. How *dare* they do such a thing? Didn't they know the *Führer* and the *Reich* were going to win any which way? Why were they working so hard in what was bound to be a forlorn hope?

And why were they coming so close to killing him? That was the real question.

"I wonder if we've got any fighters up there," somebody said. "If we do, those Allied shitheads'll be sorry in a hurry."

Hans-Ulrich nodded. He'd listened to Me-109 pilots going on about what sitting ducks British and French bombers were. They couldn't run, they couldn't hide, and they couldn't fight back. He would have liked that better if his Stuka weren't in the same boat. No matter how scary it seemed to the troops on the ground, it couldn't get out of its own way. If the Messerschmitts didn't keep enemy fighters away from them, Ju-87s would tumble out of the sky as often as the Western Allies' bombers did.

"We ought to pay those damned sky pirates back," someone else said, lifting a phrase popular in German papers.

Dieselhorst's snort put paid to that. In case it hadn't, the sergeant went on, "How? We can't take off. Even if the weather didn't stink, some of that load came down on the airstrip. They're going to have to flatten it out again before we can use it. We might as well drink and play skat, because we aren't flying for a while."

A sergeant feeling his oats could sound more authoritative than any major ever hatched. Sergeants mysteriously, mystically *knew* things. Officers could command, but they didn't have that amazing certainty.

"Anybody think more of those fuckers are coming?" asked a ground-crew man in greasy, muddy coveralls. By his tone, he wanted somebody like Dieselhorst to pat him on the head and say something like, *No, don't worry about it. You're safe now.*

But no one said anything of the kind. Hans-Ulrich realized he wouldn't have minded some reassurance, either. When the silence had stretched for a bit, the groundcrew man swore again. Maybe that made him feel a little better, anyhow. Rudel didn't usually grant himself even that safety valve, though some of the close calls he'd had on missions made him slip every now and then. He always felt bad about it afterwards, but coming out with something ripe made him feel better when he did it.

He climbed out of the trench and brushed mud and dirt off of himself. "We might as well go back," he said. "The best way to get even with the enemy is to have a good time."

When the *Luftwaffe* men went back inside their shelter, they found that blast and wind had blown out most of the candles on the Christmas tree. A pilot with a cigarette lighter got them going again. He flicked the lighter closed and put it in his pocket. "God only knows how long I'll be able to get fuel for it," he said. "Then it's back to matches—as long as we have matches."

He wore an Iron Cross First Class. Nobody could accuse him of being a coward or a defeatist . . . but he sounded like one. Hans-Ulrich wanted to take him aside and talk some sense into him. But when he tried to do that, the people he was talking to had a way of getting angry instead of appreciating his advice. He didn't like it, which didn't mean he hadn't noticed it. He kept his mouth shut.

Caroling some more would have been nice, but nobody seemed to want to. That made a certain amount of sense: if you were listening for airplane engines, you didn't want to be noisy yourself. Rudel missed the music all the same.

Sergeant Dieselhorst had come in with the rest of them. He was drinking schnapps. Soon enough, he was laughing and joking with the rest of the men. Hans-Ulrich wished *he* could fit in so easily—or at all.

Chapter 11

A chilly wind whipped snow through the air almost horizontally. A good coal stove heated the officers' barracks outside of Drisa. All the same, Anastas Mouradian shivered. "I'll never be warm again," he said in his deliberate Russian. "Never, not till July and the five minutes of summer they have here."

Sergei Yaroslavsky and the other men in the barracks were all Russians. They hooted at the effete southerner. They'd all seen plenty of weather worse than this. "Hell, we could fly in this if we had to," Sergei said.

"And we might, too," somebody else added. "Is it five o'clock yet?"

After a glance at his watch, Sergei said, "A couple of minutes till."

"Good," the other flyer said. "Turn on the radio. Let's hear the news."

Mouradian was closest to the set. He clicked it on. It made scratchy, flatulent noises as it warmed up. There were better radios—Yaroslavsky had seen, and heard, that in Czechoslovakia. He didn't say anything about it. Things weren't so bad as they had been during the purges the year before, but a careless word could still make you disappear.

Or you could disappear for no reason. Plenty of people had.

"Comrades! The news!" the announcer said. "In the West, the capitalists and Fascists continue to murder one another." He gave a summary of the day's fighting—or rather, the claims and counterclaims about the day's fighting, finishing, "Plainly, by the lies and contradictions on display, neither side in this struggle of reactionary decadence is to be believed."

"May the Devil's grandmother eat them all up," another pilot said. The sentiment was unexceptionable. The way the man put it wasn't. Russians talked about the Devil and his relations all the time. When the Soviet Union was aggressively atheist, though . . . Such talk could land you in trouble if someone who didn't like you reported it.

Anything could land you in trouble. Sergei'd just been thinking about that.

"In the Far East, Japanese imperialists continue to encroach on the territory of the fraternal socialist Mongolian People's Republic," the announcer said. "The Foreign Commissar, Comrade Litvinov, has stated that such incursions cannot and will not be tolerated indefinitely."

"Wonder if that's where we go next," Mouradian said. Sergei had wondered the same thing when he was ordered to fly their SB-2 out of the Ukraine. But they'd ended up at the other end of the USSR instead, about as far from the trouble in Mongolia as they could get.

And there might have been reasons for that, because the next words out of the newsreader's mouth were, "The semifascist Smigly-Ridz regime in Poland has once more rejected the Soviet Union's just and equitable demands for an adjustment of the border in the northeast. The Poles still cling to their ill-gotten and illegal gains from the war they waged against the USSR in the early 1920s."

Everybody leaned toward the radio. In portentous tones, the announcer went on, "Comrade Stalin has spoken with grave concern of the way the Polish regime mistreats the ethnic Byelorussians in the area in question. How long the peace-loving Soviet people can tolerate these continued provocations, only time will tell."

He went on to talk about the overfulfillment of the norms for the current Five-Year Plan. Yaroslavsky listened to all that with half an ear; it didn't directly affect him. The other did. When Stalin said he didn't like the way somebody did something, that somebody was commonly very sorry very soon. And hardly anything could make a country sorrier faster than flight after flight of SB-2 bombers.

"I didn't think we'd go," Sergei said. "If the Poles yelled to the Nazis for help, that would put German troops right on our border, and—" He didn't say *and that wouldn't be so good.* Most of the men in the barracks had served in Czechoslovakia. They knew what rough customers the Hitlerites were.

Anastas Mouradian picked up where he left off: "If the Nazis get bogged down against England and France, they'll be too busy to do anything about what goes on here."

Several flyers nodded. Sergei was one of them; it looked that way to him, too. He would have said it if his crewmate hadn't. "Soldiers are moving up toward the border. So . . ." The pilot who said that let his voice trail off. He wasn't a general, and he wasn't a prophet. You didn't want to come out with anything that might be remembered too well.

"We aren't going to fly right this minute," another officer said, and produced a bottle of vodka. Despite what Sergei had said before, he was obviously right. The bottle went round. Pretty soon, another one followed it. One more after that and they wouldn't have been able to walk or see, let alone fly. The Red Air Force ran on vodka as surely as it ran on aviation gasoline.

They got their orders the next day. Sergei still felt the drinking bout. Like the other flyers Lieutenant Colonel Borisov summoned to his office, he did his best not to show it. "We are going to liberate our Byelorussian brethren from the yoke of the Polish semifascist regime," the squadron commander declared. "Marshal Smigly-Ridz has refused to be reasonable and democratic, and so we must persuade him."

He's refused to do what we want, and so we must pound the shit out of him. Sergei had no trouble translating Communist jargon into what went on in the real world. By the knowing grunts that came from several other men, neither did anyone else.

"Red Army units will enter the territory to be liberated at 0700 tomorrow morning," Borisov declared. His eyes were cat-green but set on a slant; like so many Russians, he likely had some Tatar in the woodpile. "Your assignment will be to strike at Polish troops, and to bomb the rail junction at Glubookoje to prevent the Smigly-Ridz regime from bringing up reinforcements. Questions?"

"What if the weather doesn't let us fly, Comrade Lieutenant Colonel?" Sergei asked.

"Then we will stay on the ground," Borisov answered. "But our superiors do not believe that is likely."

What exactly did he mean there? Did higher-ups in the Red Army and Red Air Force have reliable forecasts of good weather? Or would the SB-2s take off no matter how rotten the weather was? Yaroslavsky suspected the latter. With air-cooled engines, the bombers wouldn't freeze up the way they might with liquid cooling. And they'd had skis installed instead of landing wheels, so they could deal with snow pretty well. Even so . . .

Sergei suspected a plan somewhere said, *Air support will be laid on at such and such a time in such and such places with so many bombers and so many escorting fighters.* Bad weather? Plans like that didn't worry about such mundane details. Come what might, the air support *would* be laid on.

"Other questions?" Borisov asked.

His tone said he didn't really want any more, but Anastas Mouradian raised his hand anyway. Frowning, Borisov nodded at him. "What do we do if the Nazis come in on the Poles' side, Comrade Lieutenant Colonel?" Mouradian asked.

Several people inhaled sharply. That was a question with teeth, all right. Borisov didn't look happy. "The hope and expectation are that this will not occur."

"Yes, sir," Mouradian said, and he waited.

The contest of wills was silent. The squadron commander didn't want to say anything else. Mouradian didn't want to come right out and ask, *But what if it does?* That silence stretched tighter and tighter. Finally, it snapped. So did Borisov: "We are at war with Germany. If German troops or aircraft operate against us, we are to prosecute the war against them. Is that clear?"

"Yes, sir. Thank you, sir," Mouradian said.

It was clear to Sergei, too. He didn't like it. Poland and Romania had been the USSR's shield against Fascist Germany. If the Poles scream for help to their Western neighbor, that shield was gone. Stalin never would have made demands on Poland if the Germans weren't up to their eyebrows in war on their other frontier. But if they weren't quite up to their eyebrows . . .

Sergei had faced Messerschmitts and German antiaircraft guns in Czechoslovakia. He didn't relish doing it again. Of course, the next time anyone set over him gave a damn about his opinion would be the first.

Maybe the high command *did* know something. Sergei was sure stranger things had happened, though he couldn't think of one offhand. The day was cold, but it was bright and sunny. The SB-2 was fueled up and bombed up and ready to go. Sergei and Mouradian and Ivan Kuchkov climbed in.

Groundcrew men spun the bomber's props. The engines roared to life. Sergei ran his checks. All the instruments looked good. The SB-2 slid down the snow airstrip. Sergei pulled back on the stick. The nose went up. The airplane left the ground. Anastas Mouradian cranked up the landing gear. The skis retracted almost as neatly as wheels.

Snow down below made navigation a challenge. It would have been harder yet if artillery bursts hadn't shown the way. Tanks and soldiers were swathed in white, but cast long shadows across the even whiter snow. There was the border, and there were the Soviet troops crossing it to liberate the fraternal, peace-loving people who lived just to the west.

And there were the Polish oppressors: more soldiers in white with shadows stretching over the snow. Antiaircraft guns opened up on the SB-2s. After facing German fire, Sergei didn't think much of this.

He saw a good concentration of troops and trucks ahead. There was the railroad line, too. If he plastered the neighborhood, he could do what Lieutenant Colonel Borisov wanted done. "Ready, Ivan?" he bawled into the speaking tube.

"Ready, sir!" the noncom answered.

"*Khorosho.* Mouradian will tell you when to drop," Sergei said. Anastas was down in the bottom front of the SB-2's glasshouse cockpit, peering through the bombsight.

"Now!" he shouted, and the stick of bombs tumbled from the plane's belly. As always, the SB-2 immediately got peppier and more maneuverable. Yaroslavsky took advantage of that by getting out of there as fast as he could. He'd seen a couple of gull-winged PZL fighters in the neighborhood. They weren't supposed to be anywhere near as dangerous as Me-109s, but any fighter was dangerous if you happened to be a bomber.

Other SB-2s were also hitting that concentration. The Poles down there had to be catching hell. Well, if they wouldn't give the Soviet Union what it was rightfully entitled to, this was what they got.

Back to the airstrip he flew. He found it, much to his relief. The ski-carrying landing gear descended. Getting down was an adventure, but at last the SB-2 slid to a stop. Groundcrew men wearing white snow smocks over greatcoats rushed forward to refuel the plane and bomb it up again. "How'd it go?" one of them called, his breath smoking in the frosty air.

"Routine," Sergei answered. "Just routine."

"HAPPY NEW YEAR!" PEGGY DRUCE said as the clock struck twelve. "It's 1939. Oh, boy!" She raised a glass of what was supposed to be scotch. The stuff tasted more like oven cleaner. In wartime Berlin, you took what you could get and you were damn glad you got anything.

A handful of other people sat drinking in the hotel restaurant. They were split about fifty-fifty between neutrals stuck in Berlin and Germans who felt like tying one on even if the world seemed to be going to hell in a handbasket. Some of the Germans were civilians, others in uniform. The other way to tell them apart was that the military men were drinking harder.

The radio blared out war news. Everything was going well in the West—if you believed the announcer, anyhow. "Soon a battle of annihilation will sweep the French and English out of Belgium, which they invaded with flagrant disregard for international law!" the fellow declared. He had a high, shrill, unpleasant voice. Peggy thought so, anyhow; it put her in mind of screechy chalk on a blackboard.

Then he started screaming about what the evil Communists in Russia were doing to Poland. "It is a Jewish-Bolshevist conspiracy to terrorize small nations!" he said.

What about Czechoslovakia? Peggy wondered. *What about Holland? What about Luxembourg? What about Belgium?* Asking questions like that was pointless here. Even if the *Gestapo* didn't haul you away and start pulling out your toenails, the Germans wouldn't get it. They thought anything they did was okay because they did it. If the other guy did the same thing, he was a dirty, rotten nogoodnik.

And then the newsman came out with something Peggy hadn't

heard before: "Because of the magnitude of the unprovoked invasion, Marshal Smigly-Ridz has asked the *Führer* for aid against the Bolsheviks. Foreign Minister von Ribbentrop has stated that that aid will be forthcoming. We are already at war with the Soviet Union. Now we have the chance to teach the Reds and the Jews the lesson they deserve."

Peggy looked around. Nobody she could see looked excited about teaching the Russians a lesson. One of the soldiers, a major old enough to have fought in the last war, knocked back half a tumbler's worth of something, put his head on his folded arms, and fell asleep at his table. The good-time girl who'd been with him stalked away in disgust.

Another soldier stood up and raised a glass on high. "Here's to the two-front war!" he yelled.

His buddies dragged him down. They spoke in low, urgent voices. He didn't want to listen. When they couldn't make him shut up, they hauled him out into the cold, pitch-black blackout night. Peggy wondered if it was already too late for him. Was somebody in there taking notes? She wouldn't have been surprised. People said there was at least one informer in every crowd. Peggy didn't always believe what people said, but it seemed likely here.

Music started coming out of the radio. Saccharine-sweet, it was as annoying as the newscaster. Jazz was one more thing the Nazis wouldn't put up with. Degenerate Negro music, they called it. No matter what they called it, what they made themselves was sappy and boring.

A naval officer came up to the table where Peggy was drinking by herself. "May I join you?" he asked.

"Sure." Peggy held up her left hand so the diamonds in her wedding ring sparkled. "Don't expect too much, that's all."

He smiled. His long, weathered face didn't seem to have room for amusement, but it turned out to. "Thank you for the warning. I may need it less than you think, though." He set down his drink and showed off the thin gold band on the fourth finger of his own left hand. "If I ask your name, will you think I am trying to seduce you?"

"Probably," Peggy answered, which startled a laugh out of him. She gave him her name even so, and asked his.

"I am Friedrich Reinberger—a *Korvettenkapitän,* as you see." He brushed the three gold stripes on one cuff with the other hand. Then he switched languages: "Lieutenant commander, you would say in English."

"Okay." Peggy was feeling ornery, so she asked, "Where's your wife, Lieutenant Commander?"

"In Dachau, not far from Munich, with the *Kinder,*" Reinberger nodded. Peggy nodded—he sounded like a Bavarian. "I was called here to report on . . . certain things when my destroyer came into port. Maria, I think, believes yet I am at sea."

He finished his drink and waved for another one. The blond girl who came over to get his glass wore a black gown cut down to there in front and even lower in back, and slit up to there down below. Reinberger followed her with his eyes as she sashayed back to the bar. He didn't slobber or anything, but he did watch. Peggy couldn't very well blame him; it was a hell of a dress. If she were ten years younger—hell, five years younger—she would have wanted it herself.

The girl brought back a new drink. By then Peggy was ready for a refill, too. That gave the German naval officer another chance to eye the girl's strut. He made the most of it. When Peggy got the fresh drink, Reinberger raised his glass. "To 1939," he said.

"To 1939," Peggy echoed, and drank with him. If he'd said something like *to our victory in 1939,* she wouldn't have. She was damned if she wanted to see the Nazis win. But toasting the year was harmless enough.

"What is an American doing in Germany in the middle of a war?" Reinberger asked.

Peggy looked him in the eye. She was tempted to spit in his eye, but he didn't seem like a bad guy. Still, she didn't sugarcoat the truth: "I was in Czechoslovakia when you people invaded it."

"Oh." He shrugged. "If the Czechs were more, ah, reasonable, it might not have come to that. But they thought England and France would save them, and so. . . ." Another shrug.

"Dachau." Peggy wasn't drunk, but she felt a buzz. Her wits worked slower than she wished they did. It wasn't a big city or anything, but she'd heard of it before. How come? After a moment, she remembered. "Dachau! Isn't that where they—?" She didn't know how to go on.

"Yes, that is where they—" *Korvettenkapitän* Reinberger didn't finish it, either. He did say, "Every nation has in it people who are not trusted by the government. We keep them there."

From some of the whispers Peggy had heard, the SS did more to people in Dachau than just keep them there. But she couldn't prove that. Probably the only way to prove it was to end up on the inside. She had a magpie curiosity, but she didn't want to know *that* badly.

"Where in the United States do you live?" Reinberger asked. It wasn't the smoothest change of subject Peggy had ever seen, but it also could have been worse.

"Philadelphia," she answered. Homesickness rose up inside her like a great choking cloud. She had to look down at the tabletop and blink several times while tears stung her eyes.

"I know something of the port—I visited before the last war, and again three, no, four years ago now. But all I know of the city is that it is large."

"Third biggest in the country," Peggy agreed, not without pride. *And we don't lock people up there even if they aren't trusted by the govern-ment. And we never would, not unless they were niggers or Japs or some-thing.*

The music on the radio got a little less syrupy than it had been. "Do you care to dance?" Reinberger asked.

She gave him a crooked grin. "Sure you wouldn't rather ask the bar-girl? You've got a better chance with her."

"I be not"—he shook his head—"I am not looking for that, not now. How do I expect Maria to stay for me if I do not stay for her?"

A lot of Germans had trouble with *Sauce for the goose is sauce for the gander*. Meeting one who didn't made up Peggy's mind for her. "Okay," she said.

He danced well enough. He stayed with the beat, and he led firmly. If he lacked the inspiration, the sense of fun, that separated really good dancers from people who were just all right—then he did, that was all. He held Peggy tight without trying to mash himself against her or grope her. He was . . . correct, a diplomat would have called it.

"Thank you," she said when the music stopped. "That was nice."

"*Ja.*" He nodded. "And thank you also." As they went back to the table, he added, "Much better than shooting up Russian ships in the Baltic."

"Well, gee! There's a compliment!" Peggy exclaimed. Lieutenant Commander Reinberger laughed. He waved for another drink. Peggy nodded to show she wanted one, too. The barmaid in the startling out-fit fluttered her fingers to show she saw. Peggy asked, "That's what you were doing before you got leave? Shooting up Russian ships?"

"*Ja,*" Reinberger said. "The Baltic in winter is perfectly filthy, too. Storms, fog, waves, ice . . . and always maybe a U-boat waits to give you a present. Anyone who enjoys combat a *Dummkopf* is."

"Hitler did," Peggy said incautiously. She wondered if she would find out more about what went on in Dachau than she ever wanted to know. *Your big mouth,* she told herself, not for the first time.

The barmaid came back with the fresh drinks then. She almost fell out of that dress as she bent over to give Reinberger his. He noticed. She wanted him to notice. But he didn't do anything or say anything about it. She looked annoyed as she walked away.

"From everything I know, the *Führer* is braver than most men,"

Reinberger said. That was the straight Nazi line. From everything Peggy'd heard, it also happened to be true, which was discouraging.

"Did the Russians shoot back?" she asked.

"They tried. Wallowing freighters with popguns have not much chance against warships," Reinberger answered. "They are brave enough themselves, no matter what the radio says." So he didn't think much of Dr. Goebbels' endless propaganda barrage. That was interesting. "No matter how brave you are, though, you must have the tools to do the job."

No sooner were the words out of his mouth than air-raid sirens started wailing. The headwaiter shouted, "The basement is our bomb shelter. Everyone go to the basement at once."

"Have the English and French begun to bomb Berlin, then?" Reinberger asked as people headed for the door.

"Not even once, not since I've been here," Peggy answered. "Do you suppose it's the Russians?"

The German naval officer looked almost comically surprised. "I never dreamt they could," he answered, starting down the stairs. "Not impossible, I suppose, but it didn't once cross my mind." Somewhere not far away, bombs *crump!*ed outside. Peggy knew that hateful, terrifying sound much too well.

Even though it was New Year's Eve—no, New Year's Day now—some people hadn't gone dancing into 1939. Grumpy, sleepy-looking men in bathrobes over pajamas and women in housecoats over nightgowns joined the more alert crowd from the party. A mustachioed man who spoke German with a Bela Lugosi accent said, "They told me this could not happen." Whoever they were, more bomb bursts said they didn't know what they were talking about.

A woman added, "Göring said you could call him Meyer if the enemy ever bombed Berlin."

Crump! Crump! Boom! As far as Peggy could see, the fat *Luftwaffe* boss had just saddled himself with a Jewish-sounding name. As far as she could see, he deserved it. He deserved worse, but he wasn't likely to get it. People didn't get what they deserved often enough.

Boom! That one sounded as if it came down right on top of the hotel. The lights in the cellar flickered and went out. People screamed on notes ranging from bass to shrill soprano. The Germans and their friends sounded an awful lot like the international crowd at Marianske Lazne. When you dropped bombs on them, people were all pretty much alike. Peggy would have been perfectly happy never to have learned that lesson.

Everyone cheered when, after about half a minute, the lights came on again. A few minutes later, sirens shrilled the all-clear. "Happy New Year," Lieutenant Commander Reinberger said dryly.

"Hey, we're alive," Peggy answered. "Anybody wants to know what I think, that makes it happy enough."

WHEN JOAQUIN DELGADILLO JOINED THE Nationalist army in Spain, he didn't do it to meet General Sanjurjo. He did it because he couldn't stand the Spanish Republic. He probably would have done it even if someone as dull and cautious as General Franco commanded his side.

That didn't mean he wasn't delighted to get a glimpse of Sanjurjo. The story was that the general's airplane had almost crashed coming from Portugal to Spain when the revolt against the Republic broke out. People said Sanjurjo didn't want to leave all his fancy clothes behind. So what if they would have weighed down the plane? A real man, a real Spaniard, didn't worry about things like that.

Still, Joaquin was willing to admit it was probably good that the pilot *had* worried about them. The youngster had seen too many men on both sides throw away their lives for no good reason. The Republicans were bastards, but no denying they were brave bastards. And his own side didn't put up with cowards, not even for a minute.

Now General Sanjurjo stood on a low swell of ground and pointed south. He wasn't any too impressive to look at. He was old and short and squat and dumpy. But he had a good voice. And he had some of the same gifts Germans said Hitler did: while he was talking, you believed him.

"More than two hundred years ago, Britain stole part of our fatherland from us," Sanjurjo said. "Ever since, Gibraltar has been a thorn in Spain's side. Now it is full of Communists and fellow travelers, people who ran away there so they wouldn't get what was coming to them."

General Sanjurjo laughed a very unpleasant laugh. "Well, they're going to get it whether they want it or not. And you, *soldados de España,* you're going to give it to them. Will you stop before you reach complete victory?"

"No!" Joaquin shouted with everyone else in the detachment.

"Will you teach England a lesson the likes of which she hasn't had for hundreds of years?"

"Yes!" the men yelled.

"With Italy and Germany and God on our side, can anyone hold us back?"

"No!" Joaquin shouted once more.

"Then strike!" General Sanjurjo cried. "Strike hard for Spain!"

As if on cue—and it probably was—Spanish guns opened up on Gibraltar's border defenses. Motors thrummed overhead as German and Italian bombers flew off to pound what the British insisted was one of their crown colonies.

Down inside Gibraltar, antiaircraft guns filled the air with puffs of black smoke. Other guns fired back at the Spanish artillery. How many ships did the Royal Navy have inside the harbor? They were vulnerable to air attack—no doubt about it. But they could put out impressive firepower till the bombers silenced them.

Joaquin knew what shells screaming in meant. He didn't wait for orders before he hit the dirt and started digging. The British shells landed several hundred meters away, but why take chances? He wasn't the only guy who started scraping a foxhole out of the hard, grayish-brown ground, either. Anyone who'd ever seen any action knew what to do.

"Come on! Get up! Get moving!" Sergeant Carrasquel shouted. Plenty of people did, without even thinking. A good sergeant was one you feared worse than enemy fire. Joaquin stayed right where he was. Then Carrasquel kicked him in the ass. "You, too, Delgadillo? You think the Pope gave you a dispensation?"

However much Joaquin wished his Holiness would do exactly that, he couldn't very well claim it was true. Running all hunched over—as if that did a peseta's worth of good—he hurried toward the border. Along with Spaniards in mustard-yellow khaki, he also saw other troops wearing gray uniforms.

Germans! Maybe they were from the Condor Legion, the force of "volunteers" doing what they could for the Spanish Nationalists. Or maybe they were *Wehrmacht* regulars. The Nazis and the Nationalists had the same enemies these days, after all. Putting Gibraltar out of action would hurt England all over the Mediterranean.

But that wasn't why seeing those big, fair men in field-gray so heartened Joaquin Delgadillo—and, no doubt, most of the other Nationalist troopers who recognized them. Spaniards on both sides were amateurs at war. The honest ones on both sides knew and admitted as much. Left to their own devices, they probably would have made a hash of the attack on Gibraltar. The British, whatever else you could say about them, weren't amateurs.

And neither were the Germans. If they were involved in this, it would go the way it was supposed to. That didn't mean Joaquin couldn't get blown to cat's-meat. He knew as much. But he could hope he wouldn't get blown to cat's-meat for no reason at all, the way he might with only Spaniards running the show.

Shells made freight-train noises overhead. Some of the trains sounded enormous. And some of the shells, when they burst, *were* enormous. The ground shook under Joaquin's feet. Great gouts of earth fountained skyward. And not just of earth: he saw a man, legs pumping as if he were still running, rise fifty or a hundred meters into the air and then plunge earthward again.

"Naval guns!" somebody shouted, as if explaining a thing somehow made it less fearful.

Did the British have battleships tied up at Gibraltar? Were the guns now firing on the advancing Spaniards and Germans designed to fight off battleships trying to batter their way into the harbor? Joaquin neither knew nor cared. He knew only that, whether designed for the job or not, those guns were terrifyingly good at murdering infantrymen.

Up ahead, machine guns started their deadly chatter. Joaquin dove for cover and started digging in again. If you wanted to stay alive in the vicinity of machine guns, you had to do that. Artillery was supposed to have taken out the British murder mills. Joaquin laughed bitterly. They told you that before every attack. They lied every goddamn time. And you were supposed to go on believing them? Sure you were!

Rumble of engines, rattle of tracks . . . The Condor Legion and the Italians had tanks. These were German machines, even if they carried Spanish markings. *Good,* Joaquin thought. The Germans handled their tanks as if they were fighting for their own country. The Italians handled theirs as if they'd been given a job they didn't want to do. The least sign of trouble and they found an excuse for not going forward.

Clang . . . Boom! That was the sound of an antitank round slaughtering a tank. Joaquin raised his head a few centimeters. Sure as hell, one of the German machines was ablaze, sending up orange flames and a tall column of greasy black smoke. If God was kind, the British round had killed the men in the tank right away. If He wasn't, they'd burned like a roast when the slut who was supposed to be watching it got drunk and forgot it was on the fire.

Another tank hit a mine. This one didn't catch fire, but it did throw a track, slewing sideways and stopping in a horribly vulnerable position. If the attack suppressed the guns that could reach it, the men inside might yet live. Joaquin liked those odds . . . about as little as he liked his own.

"Forward!" an officer shouted. His whistle squealed. Delgadillo looked around again. He didn't see the man giving the orders. If the bastard didn't have the guts to stand up himself, who would stand up for him?

Then Sergeant Carrasquel rasped, "Come on, you lazy *puto*! You think I'm going to do this all by myself?"

He ran forward. The British machine guns didn't cut him down right away. Joaquin knew why, too: only the good died young. Joaquin thought of himself as good. But he knew the sergeant wouldn't agree. He also knew Carrasquel would hound him if alive and haunt him if dead. So he got up and loped after the noncom.

Crack! Crack! Any bullet you heard like that came much too close to your one and only irreplaceable carcass. When you heard a bunch of them, you were mighty damn lucky if you didn't get ventilated.

Tanks were good for taking out machine-gun nests, even the concrete positions the British had built near the border. Gibraltar wasn't very big. If you could get past the frontier defenses, you could go ahead and overrun the place . . . couldn't you?

Down by the harbor, or maybe in it, something blew up with a full-throated roar that staggered Joaquin. Maybe it was an ammunition dump, or maybe a cruiser. Whatever it was, it wouldn't trouble the Spaniards any more.

More guns poured deadly fire down on them. Joaquin hit the dirt again. He didn't care if Sergeant Carrasquel pitched a fit. What kind of defenses did England have here, anyway? A cannon or machine gun on every square centimeter of ground, and more buried to pop up and spew death? He wouldn't have been surprised. This had to be more than General Sanjurjo expected.

Stukas peeled off one by one and bombed enemy positions. One of the dive-bombers didn't rise into the sky again. It added its funeral pyre to the rest of the stinking, choking smoke in the air. Nobody was using gas, but sometimes it hardly seemed to matter.

Someone not far from Joaquin started shrieking for his mother. That only made him dig harder. More bullets snarled past him. The English seemed to have all the ammunition in the world. As he dug, he realized he had yet to see his first British soldier.

Chapter 12

Alistair Walsh was alive and breathing and somewhere in France. He heartily approved of the first two. The last wasn't so good. He couldn't remember just when the BEF got driven back over the border. They gabbled away in French in the western part of Belgium, so he couldn't tell by any shift in language. But this was France, all right, and the Germans were still doing their damnedest to break through.

They hadn't managed yet. Walsh remembered the black days in the spring and early summer of 1918, when whole British regiments—Christ, divisions!—got swallowed up in the Kaiser's last offensive. This was worse. Then storm troops with submachine guns had spearheaded the German attacks. They were right bastards, but they went at the speed of shank's mare, like everybody else in the Great War.

Nowadays, the Nazis had tanks. They sliced through infantry like a hot knife through lard. The BEF and the French had tanks, too. Officers swore on a stack of Bibles—and swore profanely—that they had as many tanks as the Germans, maybe more. They sounded as if they knew what they were talking about. But whether they did or not, they never seemed to have enough of them at the places were it counted.

And so the bastards in field-gray—funny how the mere sight of that color, and the beetling shape of that helmet, could put your wind up— kept carving slices out of the Allies, forcing them to retreat if they didn't want to get cut off and surrounded. The Nazis made it over the Dyle in rubber boats. Machine guns knocked out the first boats, but German tanks and antiaircraft guns on the far side of the river silenced the machine guns. As soon as the Germans won a bridgehead, they ran pontoon bridges over the Dyle and got their tanks across. Things went downhill from there.

"Hey, Puffin!" Walsh said. "Got a fag on you?"

"Sure, Sergeant." Puffin Casper looked like hell. His greatcoat was filthy and torn. His tin hat sat at an anything but jaunty angle on his head. He hadn't shaved since God only knew when, and he hadn't bathed since a while before that. Walsh couldn't very well gig him—he was no lovelier, and no cleaner, himself. And he'd smoked his last cigarette an hour earlier.

He took a couple from the packet Puffin held out. "Thanks," he said, and cupped his hands in front of his mouth to get one lit in spite of the cold, nasty wind. It wasn't raining right this minute, and it wasn't snowing, either. Dirty gray clouds clotted the sky. Before long, it would be doing one or the other. Or maybe it would split the difference with sleet, which was worse than rain or snow.

Somebody not far away started cussing. The vile words held no special heat, as they might have if the swearer had mashed his thumb with a spanner. No, his fury was cold and disgusted. Walsh knew what that meant: he'd just heard bad news. If everyone around him was lucky, he'd found out his fiancée was having it on with the corner greengrocer. If not . . .

"What's buggered up now?" Walsh asked. Knowing was better than not knowing—he supposed.

"Bloody Belgies have packed it in," came the reply. "King Leopold's asking Hitler for an armistice."

"What? They can't do that!" Under other circumstances, the outrage in Walsh's voice would have set him laughing. True, the Allies had agreements not to seek separate peaces. But it wasn't as if the Dutch hadn't already done it. And it wasn't as if everybody didn't already know Leopold was a weak reed and halfway toward liking the Germans, either.

All the same, the news was a jolt. A corner of Belgium had stayed free all through the last war. The Belgian army had stayed in the field all through the last war, too. Now the whole country was spreading its legs for the Germans after three weeks.

"I know they can't," said the soldier with the news. "Sods are doing it anyway. And wherever they're holding the line, the Nazis can pour right on through."

"Christ!" Walsh hadn't thought of that. "Sweet suffering Jesus Christ!" Sweet suffering Jesus Christ had had a birthday not long before, not that anyone let it get in the way of the serious business of slaughter. Walsh found a real question to ask: "What are we doing about it?"

"Chamberlain's deplored it, the wireless said," the other soldier answered.

"Oh, *that'll* set Adolf's mustache quivering, that will. Deplored it, has he? Bleeding hell!" Walsh could have gone on for some time, but what was the point? Chamberlain had survived two votes of confidence since the war broke out, by a diminishing margin. One more might sink him. That wouldn't have broken Walsh's heart. He also feared it wouldn't have much effect on the way the BEF was fighting.

A British machine gun up ahead started barking. A moment later, another joined in. "Oh, bleeding hell," Walsh muttered again. He'd hoped things would stay quiet for a while. The weather was bad enough to have made any push in the last war bog down in mud and slush. But there were many more paved roads for wheels to use now, while tracks could force a way where even men on foot had trouble going.

To his glad surprise, he heard engines coming up from the south-west. "Matildas!" somebody yelled. The British tanks waltzed up to the line a few minutes later. Waltz was about all they could do; they made eight miles an hour on roads, and were slower off. They had thick armor—German antitank shells mostly bounced off of them. But they carried only a single rifle-caliber machine gun. Walsh would have wished for French machines that had some hope of keeping up with German panzers . . . and of knocking them out in a stand-up fight.

Still and all, any tanks were better than none. If panzers came after you and you couldn't hope to fight them, what choice did you have but to fall back? Walsh waved to the tank commanders, who rode head and shoulders out of their cramped turrets. "Give 'em hell!" he shouted.

"That's what we're here for," a tank commander answered in elegant Oxbridgian tones. Walsh's own accent was decidedly below the salt. After mixing with men of every class in the last war and since, he could make sense of all kinds of accents, from Received Pronunciation to Cockney to broad Yorkshire to Scots burr. They reminded him the whole country was in the fight.

The Matilda's rattled forward. Walsh dug his foxhole deeper and wider, and built up the earthwork in front of it. He also looked around to decide where he'd go if he had to get out in a hurry. You didn't want to have to worry about that at the last minute. He who hesitated then *was* lost.

A cannon barked—one of the Germans' 37mm antitank guns. They were small and light enough to keep up with advancing troops. A split second later, the shell whanged off a Matilda. The British tank's machine gun never hesitated. Walsh grinned. Sure as hell, Matildas were tough old gals.

But then a bigger gun boomed. This time, the noise of the impact was *Whang! Blam!* That Matilda brewed up. So did another one a moment later. Hitler's boys had an 88mm antiaircraft gun. In their thoroughness, they'd also seen fit to stock it with armor-piercing ammunition. Walsh didn't think a tank in the world could keep out an 88mm shell.

Puffin knew that report for what it was, too. "Bad luck they've got an 88 here," he said.

"Too fucking right it is," Walsh agreed. He wondered if the German monster had taken out the tank commander with the posh accent. He hoped not, for whatever that was worth.

Another Matilda went up in flames. The rest of them started pulling back. They couldn't even escape in a hurry. *Whang! Blam!* Another gout of flame, another column of smoke—another pyre.

And here came the German infantry. They loped forward in loose order, diving for cover whenever somebody fired at them. They shot back from their bellies. They had machine guns. Their air-cooled models were lighter and easier to lug along than most of the weapons the British used.

"Panzers!" The shout rang out from half a dozen throats at once.

The German machines were a hell of a lot faster than the poor Matildas. Most of their commanders also drove standing up in the turret. Walsh drew a bead on one. He pressed the trigger. The rifle bucked against his shoulder. The German threw up his hands, then slumped over sideways. It was a Panzer I—if the commander was wounded or dead, the driver couldn't man the guns. (Well, he could, but then he couldn't drive.) The machine turned around almost in its own length and got out of there.

Others came on. So did the foot soldiers they shepherded. Bullets thudded into the mud in front of Walsh. None got through. All the same, the neighborhood wasn't healthy any more.

Walsh scrambled out of his hole and ran for the stone fence he'd spotted not far away. Out in the open, he felt worse than naked—he felt like a snail with its shell pulled off. Bullets cracked past him and stitched the mud near his feet.

With a gasp not far from a wail, he threw himself down behind the fence. Then he popped up and fired at the Germans. Four men threw themselves flat because of one bullet. They were out in the open, too, and knew how vulnerable they were. Walsh shot at one of them. The man twisted, grabbing his leg.

"Sorry, pal," Walsh said. Most of the time, you didn't see the enemy you hit. Here he'd done it twice in a few minutes. Instead of making him proud, it just made him hope the Germans wouldn't do the same thing to him.

HUDDLING IN A SLIT TRENCH with half-frozen mud on the bottom wasn't what Hans-Ulrich Rudel had had in mind when the war started. That didn't mean he wasn't doing it. His squadron's latest airstrip lay a few kilometers west of Oostende, on the Strait of Dover. You could damn near spit from Belgium to England here.

And you could damn near spit from England to Belgium. The RAF had come over every night since Belgium threw in the towel. Night bombing wasn't very accurate, but you didn't want to stay in your nice, cozy sleeping bag when the bombs whistled down. A couple of intrepid souls had tried it. One of them was in the hospital, the other dead.

Fragments from a big one that hit much too close whined past overhead. "Those miserable pigdogs!" Hans-Ulrich said around a yawn. He was amazed at how little sleep he could get by with. "We ought to bomb them for a change, keep them up all night."

"How do you know we aren't?" somebody else said. There in the chilly darkness, Rudel couldn't tell who it was.

"We'd hear about it on the radio if we were," he answered. "They wouldn't keep something like that quiet—they'd brag about it."

"*Er hat Recht,*" another *Luftwaffe* man said. The rest of the shivering Germans must have thought Hans-Ulrich was right, too, because nobody contradicted him. The *Reich* boasted about what it did to its enemies. And why not? They deserved what they got for presuming to oppose it.

"And here, we really could do it," Hans-Ulrich said musingly. He'd spent the war plastering positions on the Continent. That needed doing, of course, but if the English thought they could send bombers out from their island without getting any attention in return they had to be out of their minds.

Another big bomb burst nearby. The English were either good or lucky. "It'll be a mess come morning," someone said dolefully.

That proved all too true. The runways were cratered. One Ju-87 was a write-off in spite of the revetments in which the bombers hid. Another had taken enough damage to keep it out of the air for a while. A snorting steamroller and a pick-and-shovel crew started setting the strip to rights. Hans-Ulrich fumed. The day was bright and clear—perfect flying weather, no matter how cold it was—but here he sat, stuck on the ground.

Damn the English anyway!

Without the steamroller, setting things straight would have taken even longer than it did. Three days went by before the strip was flyable again. The British bombers came over by night twice more, but their aim wasn't so good. The airstrip came away unscathed.

When the fourth morning also promised good weather, the squadron commander summoned his pilots and said, "*Wir fahren gegen England.*" He paused for a moment, then went on, "No, I'm not throwing a song title at you. We are going to go against England." He eyed Rudel. "Maybe someone from the High Command was in the trench with you a few nights ago, because I got the order yesterday."

"Yes, sir," Hans-Ulrich said. He hoped the tune from "*Wir fahren gegen England*" wouldn't get stuck in his head. It was catchy.

"There are airfields near Ramsgate," Major Bleyle continued. "We are to hit them and the aircraft that use them. The English need to learn they can't play these games with us. And with our Stukas, we can put our bombs where they do the most good."

The pilots nodded. A dive-bomber was ever so much more precise than some machine flying five kilometers up in the middle of the night. On the other hand, a bomber five kilometers up was almost impossible to find and even harder to shoot down once found. A Ju-87, by contrast, was a low-flying, lumbering brute. The only way to make it more visible would be to paint it bright red.

"Will we have escorts?" Hans-Ulrich asked.

"*Ja,*" Bleyle said. "We'll have some 109s with us. They should hold off the English fighters." Hans-Ulrich nodded, satisfied. The Messerschmitts had done the job on the Continent. Why wouldn't they over England, too?

An hour and a half later, he was in the air. Sergeant Dieselhorst sat in the rear-facing seat behind him. If the 109s failed, the sergeant's machine gun could help keep the RAF away.

As usual, the 109s put Hans-Ulrich in mind of sharks. They were made for one purpose and one only: to go out and kill things. Their leader waggled his wings at the Ju-87s. The Messerschmitts formed up around the dive-bombers. They droned on toward the English coast, plainly visible through the Stuka's armor-glass windshield.

A short flight: less than half an hour, even cruising. Rudel watched his instruments. Everything was green. The maintenance men did a hell of a job. His thoughts leaped ahead to what needed doing when he reached the target.

He could see Ramsgate not far ahead. The airstrips the Stukas were supposed to hit lay a little west and south of the town. The German air fleet would swing in that direction, and . . .

And British fighters jumped them. Hurricanes with red-white-and-blue roundels mixed it up with the Messerschmitts. The *Luftwaffe* had already seen that Hurricanes were at least as good as anything the

French flew. Were they as good as 109s? If they weren't, they came unpleasantly close.

While some of them engaged the German fighters, others bored in on the Ju-87s. One dive-bomber after another fell out of the sky. Hoarse shouts of fear and alarm dinned in Hans-Ulrich's earphones. So did the shrieks of the dying. "Mother!" someone wailed. "I'm burning, Mother!" Rudel switched frequencies in a hurry. It didn't help much.

Sergeant Dieselhorst fired at something. A couple of bullets had hit Hans-Ulrich's Stuka, but only a couple. He feared that was nothing but luck.

He also feared the Germans had made a mistake with this attack. On the Continent, bombing targets close to their own lines, they could generally count on an advantage in numbers. Damaged planes didn't have far to go to get back to friendly territory. Here, the deep blue sea lay between the raiders and friends. Only it wasn't blue. It was grayish green, and looked cold.

"Drop your bombs anywhere!" The squadron commander's voice cut through the din on the radio. "Drop them and get away! This is too hot for us!"

Hans-Ulrich wouldn't have argued with that. He pulled the bomb-release lever. Ramsgate lay below. If hundreds of kilos of explosives came down on civilians' heads instead of on the airstrip for which they were intended—well, too bad. Wasn't it the RAF's fault for interfering with the planned operation?

A British fighter flew right in front of him: a biplane, a Gloster Gladiator. It looked outdated, but the Czech Avias had proved even planes like that could be dangerous. He fired at it. The Gladiator, far more agile than his Stuka, spun away when the pilot saw his tracers.

Even though Rudel mashed the throttle against the instrument panel, he knew he wasn't home free—nowhere near. A Hurricane could still catch him from behind. For that matter, so could a Gladiator. The

Ju-87 was built for muscle, not for speed. He'd never felt the lack so much before.

"Anything on our tail, Albert?" he called through the speaking tube.

"Not right now, thank God," Dieselhorst answered, which also summed up the way Hans-Ulrich felt.

He looked around for more Stukas and for Messerschmitts. Of course they wouldn't go back in the neat formation they'd used to approach England. They'd be all over the sky. All the same, he saw far fewer German planes than he should have. When fighters came after them in swarms, Ju-87s were alarmingly vulnerable.

The 109s had held their own against the Hurricanes. He was sure they'd more than held their own against the Gladiators. Even that came with a price, though. If a Hurricane fighter bailed out of a shot-up fighter, he landed among friends. He could fly again as soon as he got another plane. A Messerschmitt pilot who bailed out over England was out of the war for good even if he came down unhurt.

There was the Belgian coast ahead. The RAF seemed content to have broken things up on their own ground. They weren't pursuing hard. Hans-Ulrich eased back on the throttle. He'd never dreamt he could be so proud of nothing more than making it home from a mission in one piece.

AIR-RAID SIRENS WOKE SARAH GOLDMAN out of a sound sleep. She needed a moment, or more than a moment, to realize what they were. Münster had tested them a few times before the war started, and a few more afterwards. But the luminous hands on the clock by her bed said it was two in the morning. Only a maniac would test the sirens at a time like this.

Sarah didn't doubt that a lot of the Nazis running Münster were maniacs. But they weren't the kind of maniacs who'd do something like this. Which meant . . .

Ice ran through her when she realized what it meant. This wasn't a drill. This was a real air raid!

She threw off the covers, which made her realize how cold it was inside the house. Throwing a robe over her flannel nightgown, she ran for the stairs.

She bumped into somebody in the dark. The grunt made her realize it was her brother. "Where do we go, Saul? What do we do?"

"Find someplace low, I guess," he answered. "What else can we do? We're Jews. We can't go to any of the regular shelters—they won't let us in."

Somehow, Sarah had forgotten that. She couldn't imagine why. It wasn't as if regulations didn't spell it out. The Aryans in charge of things in the *Reich* made no bones about how they felt. If they saved their own kind and watched Jews get blown to ground round, they would go out and have a beer afterwards to celebrate.

Sarah didn't think all the *goyim* in Münster felt that way. Life would have been impossible in that case. It wasn't now—it was just difficult. As she hurried down the stairs, she realized she might have to change her mind about that. If a bomb hit them and they weren't in a proper shelter, life *would* be impossible.

"Come on!" Saul said. "Under the dining-room table!"

"Will it hold up if the house comes down on it?" Sarah asked doubtfully.

"No, but it's the best chance we've got," he said. She decided he was right.

Their mother and father crowded under there with them. Samuel and Hanna Goldman took the outside places. When Saul tried to protest, his father spoke two harsh words: "Shut up!" The gentle classical scholar never talked like that. The front-line soldier of half a lifetime ago might have, though. And Saul *did* shut up, which would do for a miracle till a bigger one came along.

Airplane engines droned overhead. Antiaircraft guns began to thunder. "Will they shoot them down?" Sarah said.

"They'll try," her father answered: not a vote of confidence.

Through the roar of the guns, Sarah heard other noises—high, shrill, swelling whistles. The flat, harsh *crump!*s that followed made the guns seem whispers beside them. The windows rattled. The whole house shook. *Is this what an earthquake feels like?* she wondered. But how could she tell? She'd never been in an earthquake.

"We need to put masking-tape squares on our windows," Samuel Goldman said, his voice eerily calm.

"Will that keep them from breaking?" Hanna asked.

"No. But it will help keep them from spraying glass all over the inside of the house if something comes down close to us—I hope," he said.

After what might have been twenty minutes or twenty years, the bombs stopped falling. The airplane engines went away. The guns kept banging for several minutes more. Shrapnel pattered down on the roof like hail. At last, silence fell.

"Well, that wasn't *too* bad," Sarah said. She was so glad to be alive, so glad it was over, she straightened up too fast and banged her head on the bottom of the table. That was the only hurt any of the Goldmans took.

"It wasn't too good, either," her father said. "I don't remember any raids that bad in the last war."

"Neither do I," her mother said.

A siren screamed—that was a fire engine, heading somewhere. The Goldmans made their slow, careful way to the front door and looked out. Münster was black as a tomb . . . except for two or three orange glows on the skyline, one of them only a few blocks away. By the sound, the fire engine was going there. It couldn't go very fast, not unless it wanted to plow into something.

"This is terrible," Sarah said. "The enemy never did anything like this before. Why would they start now?"

Saul nudged her. "The enemy is running Germany," he whispered.

"So why did you try to join the *Wehrmacht*, then?" she whispered back. He turned away without answering. She knew what the answer was: her brother and her father still wanted to be Germans, but the Nazis wouldn't let them.

If her father heard the whispers, he didn't show it. "Let's go back to bed," he said. "We might as well try, anyhow. We can't do anything else here."

"Except thank God we came through in one piece," her mother said.

Her father didn't answer. He'd always been less religious than her mother—and even Sarah wondered whether God had His eyes on the Jews in Germany these days. She went upstairs doubting she'd be able to fall asleep again. But she did.

She came down to breakfast: black bread and ersatz coffee that tasted like and probably was burnt barley. Her father was reading the newspaper. AIR PIRATES SLAUGHTER INNOCENT CIVILIANS! the headline screamed.

"The British claim it's retaliation for something our planes did over there," her father said. "Dr. Goebbels says that's a bunch of filthy lies, of course."

"Of course," Sarah echoed. In both what they said and how they said it, they sounded perfectly loyal. A message got passed even so. Just for a moment, Samuel Goldman's eyes glinted behind his spectacles. Then he raised the newspaper, hiding his face.

Sarah felt herself smiling. She was still cold. She'd just discovered she was in danger of getting blasted off the face of the earth. In spite of everything, though, she was happy. She wondered why.

LUDWIG ROTHE SWORE AS HE guddled around, deep in the bowels of his Panzer II's engine. "Hold that flashlight higher, Theo," he said. "I can't see what the hell I'm doing here."

"Carburetor again, Sergeant?" Hossbach asked, moving the flashlight not quite enough.

"No, it's the damn fuel pump. I'm sure of it. We've boiled the carb out so often, we could boil coffee in it." If Rothe sounded disgusted, it was only because he was. "Damned engine still keeps missing. I'm going to fix that pump or steal a new one somewhere or go back to the May-bach works and bend a wrench on somebody's head."

"Sounds good to me, Sergeant," Fritz Bittenfeld said. After pausing to light a cigarette, the driver went on, "Why the devil can't they make an engine that does what it's supposed to, for God's sake?"

Part of the reason was overstrain. The engine only put out 135 horsepower. That wasn't much when it was trying to haul nine tonnes around. Rothe was not inclined to feel charitable, especially not right after he cut his hand on a sharp metal edge in the engine compartment. "Why? I'll tell you why. Because they're back there and safe, that's why," he snarled. "They don't have to worry about what happens when things go wrong. *We* do. Hold that goddamn light higher, Theo!"

"Sorry," Theo said, and still didn't move the light enough. He made a good radioman. Radio waves suited him—they were out there in the ether, and you couldn't see them. When it came to things more closely connected to planet earth, he wasn't so great.

Somehow, Ludwig got the fuel pump out anyway. Six or eight panz-ers had halted here, somewhere near the border between Belgium and France. Their crews worked on them, aided by a couple of mechanics. A few hundred meters away, two batteries of 105s sent death and destruc-tion across kilometers toward the British and French troops battling to slow the Germans down.

As he tore the fuel pump apart, he wished his panzer could carry a gun like the ones artillerymen used. A gun like that and you'd have yourself a land dreadnought. The 20mm on the Panzer II was a door-knocker by comparison, and not much of a door-knocker at that. Even Panzer IIIs carried only a 37mm piece—and they were still rare birds.

Enemy panzers didn't have much more. Some of the French ma-chines mounted 47mm guns. But the French and the British didn't seem to know how to make a fist. They used their panzers in penny packets. Individually, their machines were at least a match for anything the *Reich* made. But if Germany had swarms of panzers at the *Schwerpunkt* and the enemy didn't, the German drive *would* go forward. And so matters had proved up till now. Would the Low Countries have fallen in less than a month otherwise?

Foot soldiers came forward through the little motor park. At first, Ludwig paid little attention. Then his eyes snapped from the legend on their cuff bands—*Leibstandarte Adolf Hitler*—to the SS runes on their collar tabs. Here was something out of the ordinary! He'd heard that some SS men were going to the front alongside *Wehrmacht* troops, but he'd never seen any before. And wasn't the LAH . . . ?

These fellows, all of them big and fair, carried submachine guns and looked either nervous or extremely alert. They were almost out of artillery range of the enemy, so Rothe thought they were being silly . . . till he saw the middle-aged man in their midst.

He kicked Theo in the ankle. "*Achtung!*" he hissed, and stiffened to attention himself.

"Are you out of your mind?" the radioman said—nobody paid attention to parade-ground formalities in the field.

"*Achtung!*" Ludwig repeated. He jerked his chin toward the gaggle of SS men and their charge.

Hossbach's eyes followed that gesture. At attention or not, Rothe almost burst out laughing at the way they nearly bugged out of Theo's head. Fritz was gaping, too. Well, hell—who wouldn't?

Hitler came over to the Panzer II. Automatically, Ludwig saluted. The other crewmen echoed the gesture a beat later. The *Führer* returned the salutes. "Is everything all right here?" he asked. Up close, his voice was even more resonant, even larger than life, than it was over a microphone in a stadium or on the radio.

"Y-Yes, sir," Ludwig managed. "Just routine repairs. We'll be at 'em again soon." He felt dizzy, half drunk. Talking to Adolf Hitler! He would remember this day for the rest of his life, even if he lived to 112. (Having seen what happened to front-line fighters here and in Czechoslovakia, he knew how unlikely that was. He knew, but he didn't dwell on it. He tried not to, anyhow.)

"Your fuel pump giving you trouble?" the *Führer* asked.

Theo's eyes bugged out all over again. Ludwig Rothe's did the same thing this time. "How the devil did you know *that,* sir?" he blurted.

One of the big SS men guarding Hitler growled like an angry Rottweiler. But the *Führer* only chuckled. "I get reports. I read them. I remember them," he answered. "That's the most common failing on the Panzer II. I have had a few things to say to the Maybach people about it. An improved model is now in production."

"Good. Very good." Ludwig wondered what had happened to the people responsible for the current piece of junk. Maybe he was better off not knowing.

"We will use it to go on to victory," Hitler continued. A lock of hair flopped down over his forehead. He brushed it back with a gesture so automatic, he must have used it thousands of times. "We will!" he insisted. "Victory may be coming a little more slowly than some of the poison dwarfs back in Berlin believe, but it is no less sure on account of that."

Several of the LAH bodyguards growled this time. *Wehrmacht* men called the *Waffen*-SS asphalt soldiers, but Ludwig wouldn't have wanted to mess with any of these guys. "I'm sure of it, *mein Führer,*" he said, not because that was the thing to say but because he really believed it.

Maybe Hitler sensed as much. Or maybe, once the *Führer* got rolling, he was no easier to stop than a river. "Victory *is* sure!" he thundered, as he might have on the radio. "And the mad mongrels and traitors who tried to stop the *Reich* from gaining it have got what they deserved. Oh, yes! That they have!" His eyes blazed.

The only trouble was, Ludwig didn't know what he was talking about. "Sir?" the sergeant said.

One of the *Leibstandarte* men murmured warningly. The fellow wore what would have been a major's shoulder straps if he were in the *Wehrmacht,* but the SS had its own weird set of ranks. Major or whatever the hell he was, the *Führer* ignored him. "Some of those pigdogs—fancy aristocrats and even a few military men, I'm sorry to say—thought they could run the country better than I am doing it. Well, the ones who are left alive are seeing how they like the arrangements at Dachau."

"*Mein Führer*—" the SS officer said urgently.

"*Ja,* Jens, *ja.*" Hitler sounded—indulgent? He turned back to the panzer crew. "Do not gossip about this, *bitte.* We have not said anything in the papers or on the radio. We do not want the enemy to know there is even so much as a mustard seed's worth of dissension in the *Reich.* You are good fellows—I can see that. I'm sure you won't blab."

"Of course not, *mein Führer,*" Ludwig said quickly. Fritz and Theo also stammered out reassurances. Rothe had never imagined he would end up knowing a state secret. By the way that officer was looking at him, the *Waffen*-SS man thought he would be better off dead.

"That's what I thought," Hitler said. He caught the officer's eye again. "Don't give them any trouble—you hear me? They said they'd keep quiet, and I expect they meant it. Unless you're sure—and I mean sure—they didn't, leave them alone."

"*Jawohl, mein Führer,*" the LAH man said. The look he gave Rothe and the other panzer men shouted that he still wanted to dispose of them. But he didn't look as if he had the nerve to go against Hitler's direct order. Who in his right mind would?

"All right." Hitler nodded to Ludwig, then to his driver and radioman. "I hope you stay safe, my friends. I know it's warm work, but it needs doing. Fight hard!" He nodded again, then stumped away, his retinue all around him.

"*Der Herr Gott im Himmel!*" Fritz whispered.

"Somebody pinch me. I think I'm dreaming," Theo said, also in a low voice. That amounted to about the same thing.

"He's . . . something." Ludwig heard the awe in his own voice. He tried to imagine why anyone would move against the *Führer*. True, the war wasn't won yet, but Germany was still moving forward, and a lot faster than she had the last time around. What was wrong with that?

Plainly, the traitors had paid for their folly. Dachau . . . Rothe's shiver had nothing to do with the weather. If half what he'd heard was true, the plotters who'd got killed outright might have been the lucky ones.

Chapter 13

Luc Harcourt was alive. That was all he knew, all he cared about. He'd seen more war than he ever wanted to meet. He'd smelled blood and pus and death and his own shit in his pants. Nobody'd ever ragged him about that. He knew damn well he wasn't the only one.

This ruined barn was a good place to grab a cigarette. What was left of the walls kept a German sniper from drawing a bead on him and punching his ticket. He sucked in harsh smoke, held it as long as he could, and finally let it out again.

"Man," he said, and paused for another drag. "I never wanted a smoke this much when I was a civilian."

"Not even after a fuck?" Sergeant Demange had a cigarette between his lips, too, but then he always did.

"Not even then," Luc said. "Then I like it. Yeah, sure—but of course. But there's a difference between liking a smoke and really needing one, you know what I mean? When the bastards are trying to kill you, a cigarette's all you've got."

"Well, not quite," Demange shook his canteen so it sloshed. "What do you have in here?"

"*Pinard*," Luc answered. The cheap, nasty red wine was nonregulation, but it was also less likely than water from God knew where to give you the runs. You couldn't very well get lit on a liter of *pinard*, either. "How about you, Sergeant? What do you have?"

"Calvados," Demange said proudly. "That'll put hair on your balls, by God."

"Boy, will it ever," Luc said. The apple brandy of northern France was liquid dynamite. He hoped the sergeant would offer to share, but Demange didn't. Demange was for Demange, first, last, and always. Luc didn't resent it the way he might have from someone more hypocritical about it.

Paul Renouvin said, "Calvados? *C'est rien*." He didn't look like a college man any more. He was as scrawny and filthy and ragged and unshaven as any of the other soldiers in the barn.

But he still knew how to get under Demange's skin. The sergeant jerked as if all of his lice had bitten him at once. "Nothing, is it, asshole? Well, what the devil have you got that's better? Whatever it is, it better be good, or I'll whale the living shit out of you." Renouvin was ten centimeters taller and a good bit heavier. Luc would have bet on Demange every time.

Paul caressed his canteen as if it were a beautiful woman's bare tit. "Me? I've got scotch," he murmured.

"Why, you lying prick!" Demange said. "Scotch, my left one! Where would a no-account cocksucker like you get scotch?"

"Off a dead Tommy officer," Renouvin answered calmly. "Good stuff, too."

"Tell me another one. You think I was born yesterday? You think I fell off the turnip truck?" The sergeant pointed to the canteen. "Give me a taste of that. Right now, too. If it isn't scotch, I'll tear your ears off and shove 'em down your throat."

"But what if it is?" Renouvin asked.

Rage made Demange reckless. "If it is—fat chance!—you can have all my applejack."

"You heard him, boys," Paul said. Luc and the other *poilus* nodded. Why not? This was the best sport they'd had in a while. Luc forgot about the cold and the dirt and the fear. He forgot about the battery of 75s banging away not far from the barn, even if they were liable to bring German artillery down on everybody's head before too long. He watched Renouvin open the canteen and pour a little of the contents into the screw-on cap. With elaborate ceremony, Renouvin passed the cap to Demange. "Here you go, Sergeant. *Salut.*"

"If you're trying to get me to drink piss, you'll fucking die— I promise you that," Demange said suspiciously. He sniffed at the cap before he drank from it. Luc watched his face, but those ratlike features gave nothing away. Like a man moving in a dream, the sergeant sipped.

He didn't say anything for more than a minute. He just sat there motionless, even the perpetual cigarette in the corner of his mouth forgotten. Then, without any particular rancor, he said, "You *son* of a bitch." He flipped the cap to Renouvin, who put it back on the canteen. And Demange handed him his own canteen. "Here. Choke on it."

"We'll all choke on it—and then on the scotch. How's that?" Paul said. He swigged from the Calvados, then passed it along.

Luc thought that was mighty smart—not university-smart, maybe, but soldier-smart for sure. A man who had both scotch and applejack was a man who made his buddies jealous. A man who shared them made friends for life—or at least till one of the other guys got his hands on something nice.

Two big knocks of good, strong booze. Shelter from the winter weather. A soldier's life could be simple sometimes. A few tiny pleasures, and everything seemed wonderful.

The next morning, replacements came up to the front. Luc eyed them with mingled suspicion and contempt. They were too pale, too neat, too plump. They carried too much equipment. Their uniforms weren't dirty and torn. Their noncoms hardly knew how to swear.

"Poor darlings!" someone jeered. "Someone forgot to lock the nursery, and look where they ended up."

A shell burst half a kilometer away. Some of the new fish flinched. That made Luc want to start laughing. "They have to come closer than that to hurt you," he said. "Don't worry—they will."

A lieutenant as young and unweathered as his troops pointed an angry finger at him. "Where is your superior, soldier?" he snapped.

"I guess I'm him . . . sir," Sergeant Demange said, the usual Gitane bobbing in the corner of his mouth as he spoke. "What do you need?"

He was grimy and unshaven. He looked as if he'd killed better men than that baby lieutenant—and he had. The officer had the rank, but Demange had the presence. Luc watched the lieutenant's bravado leak out through the soles of his boots. "Tell that man to be more respectful," he managed, but his voice lacked conviction.

"Sure," Demange said, and then, to Luc, "Be more respectful, you hear?"

"Sorry, Sergeant." Luc went along with the charade.

"There you go, sir," Demange said to the lieutenant. "You happy now?"

Plainly, the lieutenant wasn't. Just as plainly, being unhappy wouldn't do him one goddamn bit of good. Demange's attitude and graying stubble said he'd fought in the first war, while the lieutenant hadn't done much fighting in this one yet. His tongue slid across the hairline mustache that darkened the skin just above his upper lip, but he didn't say anything more. He just kept on walking.

More German shells came in. Maybe the *Boches* were probing for that battery of 75s. Whatever they were doing, those rising screams in the air said this salvo was trouble. "Hit the dirt!" Luc yelled. He was already flat by the time the words came out. Several other veterans shouted the same thing—also from their bellies.

Bam! He felt as if a squad of Paris *flics* were beating on him with their nightsticks. Blast picked him up and slammed him back down again. "Oof!" he said—he came down on a rock that would bruise his belly and just missed knocking the wind out of him. Jagged fragments whined overhead. Several of them spanged off the barn's stone wall. One drew a bloody line across the back of Luc's hand. What he said then was worse than *Oof!*

More shells landed a couple of hundred meters away, and then more farther off still. Luc opened and closed his hands a couple of times. All his fingers worked—no tendons cut. Only a scratch, as these things went. It still hurt like blazes, though.

Cautiously, he raised his head. When he did, he forgot about his own little wound. One or two of the German shells had come down right by—maybe even among—the raw troops. They didn't know anything about flattening out. You could scream at them, but they needed a few seconds to get what you were saying and a few more to figure out what they should do.

All of which added up to a few fatal seconds too long.

Some of the soldiers were still standing. More were on the ground now—men and pieces of men. The air was thick with the stink of blood, as it might have been after explosions in a slaughterhouse. This wasn't quite that. This was explosions that produced a slaughterhouse.

A soldier stared stupidly at the spouting stump of his arm. Not three meters from him, the kid lieutenant stood there with his face white and twisted into a rictus of horror. *"Merde,"* Luc muttered. He scrambled to his feet and ran over to the maimed kid. A leather bootlace did duty for a tourniquet. The spout became a tiny trickle.

And the soldier came out of shock and started to shriek. Luc dug the morphine syrette out of the fellow's wound kit and jabbed him with it. The drug hit hard and fast. The soldier's eyes closed and he passed out. Luc thought he would live if he hadn't bled too much. Unlike most battlefield wounds, the amputation was almost as neat as if a surgeon had done it.

The poor lieutenant still hadn't unfrozen. Some of his men were helping the veterans help their buddies, but he stood rooted to the spot. "You all right, sir?" Luc heard the rough sympathy in his own voice. This wasn't the first freeze-up he'd seen. It was a bad one, though. He tried again, louder this time: "You all right?"

"I—" The officer shook himself like a dog coming out of cold water. Then, violently, he crossed himself. And then he bent over and was sick. Spitting and coughing, he choked out, "I regret to say I am not all right at all."

"Well, this is pretty bad." Luc held out his canteen. "Here. Rinse your mouth. Get rid of the taste."

"*Merci.*" The lieutenant did. As he handed the canteen back to Luc, he suddenly looked horrified and took off for the closest bushes at a dead run.

"He just realize he shat himself?" Sergeant Demange asked dryly.

"That's my guess," Luc said.

"He's not the first. He won't be the last, either," Demange said. "I've done it in both wars, Christ knows. You?"

"*Oui.*" If the sergeant hadn't admitted it, Luc wouldn't have, either. But since he had . . . Luc knew that was a big brotherhood, sure as hell. It probably included more than half the people who'd ever come under machine-gun or artillery fire. More than half the people who'd ever been up to the front, in other words. "War's a bitch."

"And a poxed bitch to boot," Demange agreed. Luc found himself nodding.

SNOW FLEW AS NEAR HORIZONTALLY as made no difference. The wind howled out of the north. Anastas Mouradian looked out the window of the flimsy hut by the airstrip and shuddered. "I wish I were back in Armenia," he said in his accented Russian. "We have civilized weather down there."

Another officer swigged from a bottle of vodka and then set it down. They weren't going to fly today—why not drink? "Shit, this isn't so bad."

That was too much for Sergei Yaroslavsky. "The Devil's grandmother, it's not! *Bozhemoi,* man! Where d'you come from?"

"Strelka-Chunya," the other man answered.

"Where the hell is that?"

"About a thousand kilometers north of Irkutsk."

"A thousand kilometers . . . north of Irkutsk?" Sergei echoed. Then he said, *"Bozehmoi!"* again. Irkutsk lay next to Lake Baikal, in the heart of Siberia. Go north from there and you'd just get colder. He hadn't imagined such a thing was possible, which only went to show your imagination reached so far and no further. He made as if to doff his fur cap. "All right, pal. If you come from there, this *isn't* so bad—for you."

"But why would anybody want to go there in the first place?" Mouradian asked. That struck Sergei as a damn good question, too.

And the Siberian flyer—his name was Bogdan Koroteyev—had an answer for it: "My people are trappers. If you're going to do that, you have to go where the animals live."

Through the roaring wind, Sergei heard, or thought he heard, a low rumble in the distance. "Is that guns?" he asked.

"Or bombs going off." The Siberian had put away enough vodka so he didn't much care. "Damn Poles are stubborn bastards." He shoved the bottle across the rickety table. "Want a slug?"

"Sure." Sergei poured some liquid fire down his throat. "Damn Poles."

Things in northeastern Poland weren't going as well as they might have. The radio and the newspapers didn't say that, but anyone with a gram of sense could read between the lines. The Red Army kept attacking the same places over and over again. Every attack sounded like a victory. If they were victories, though, why weren't the glorious and peace-loving soldiers of the Soviet Union advancing instead of spinning their wheels?

Not that wheels wanted to spin in weather like this. Supplies moved forward on sledges—when they moved forward at all. Bombers and fighters had long since traded conventional landing gear for ski undercarriages. Men wore skis or snowshoes whenever they went outside.

One of the flyers wound up a phonograph and put on a record. It was Debussy. Sergei relaxed. Nobody listened to Chopin or Mozart or Beethoven any more. Nobody dared. Listening to music by a composer from a country at war with the USSR might be enough to make the NKVD question your loyalty. Who could say for sure why people disappeared? Who wanted to take a chance and find out? But Debussy, a Frenchman, was safe enough.

More explosions, these not so distant. The windows in the hut rattled. "Those *are* bombs," Mouradian said. "The weather somewhere off to the west is good enough to let airplanes get up."

"Fuck 'em," Koroteyev said. "They're trying to rattle our cage, that's all. They can't find anything to hit, so they drop things anywhere and hope they'll do some good. Fat chance!" He belched and lit a cigarette.

"Even when you can see it, hitting what you aim at isn't easy," Sergei said.

"Turn on the radio, somebody," Mouradian said. "It's just about time for the news."

The flyer closest to the set clicked on the knob. The dial lit up. Half a minute later—once the tubes warmed up—music started blaring out of the speaker. It wasn't quite the top of the hour. The march wasn't to Sergei's taste, but you could put up with anything for a couple of minutes.

"Here is the news," the announcer said.

"Moo," Koroteyev added irreverently. Chuckles ran through the hut. The announcer's accent said he came from the middle reaches of the Volga: he turned a lot of *a* sounds into *o*'s. It really did make him sound as if he ought to be out in a field chewing his cud.

But what he had to say grabbed everybody's attention: "Spreading their vicious campaign of terror ever more widely, the reactionary Polish junta under the thuggish leadership of Marshal Smigly-Ridz bombed both Minsk and Zhitomir yesterday. Casualties are reported heavy, because neither city was prepared for such treachery and murder. Numbers of innocent schoolchildren are among the slain."

One of the pilots swore violently. He spoke Russian with a Ukrainian accent, so that some of his *g*'s turned into *h*'s. Sergei wondered if he was from Zhitomir or had family there.

"General Secretary Stalin has vowed vengeance against the evil Polish regime," the announcer went on. "Our bombers have targeted Warsaw for retaliation."

Our bombers taking off from where? Sergei wondered. He would have bet piles of rubles that nobody could fly from anywhere near Minsk. Maybe things were better farther south, down toward the Ukraine. He supposed they must have been, or the Poles couldn't have struck at it. In this blizzard, they must have been bombing by dead reckoning—and damned lucky to boot—to hit Minsk at all.

Then the man reading the news said, "Observers in Minsk report that some of the planes striking the capital of the Byelorussian Soviet Socialist Republic were German Heinkels and Dorniers. And so we see that the Hitlerites are indeed supporting their semifascist stooges in Warsaw. They too shall suffer the righteous wrath of the workers and people of the Soviet Union."

Several flyers sitting around the table nodded. Sergei started to do the same thing. Then he caught himself. How the devil could observers in Minsk identify the bombers overhead? Minsk wasn't far from here. It had to be as socked in as this miserable airstrip was.

Sergei opened his mouth to say something about that. Before he could, Anastas Mouradian caught his eye. Ever so slightly—Sergei didn't think any of the other flyers noticed it—his copilot shook his head.

The newsman continued, giving more reports of the Poles' atrocities and then going on to talk about the war news from Western Europe. Sergei ended up keeping quiet. Mouradian was bound to be right. If the authorities told lies and you pointed it out, who would get in trouble? The authorities? Or you?

Asking the question was the same as answering it.

Did the rest of the flyers see that the newsman was full of crap when he talked about Minsk? Or didn't they even notice? Were they so used to believing everything they heard on the radio that they couldn't do anything else?

Then something else occurred to Sergei. He grabbed the vodka bottle and took a good swig from it. But not even vodka could drown the subversive thought. If that newsman was lying about the weather in Minsk, what else was he lying about? Had the Poles really bombed the city at all? Had the Germans joined them? How much of what he said about the war in the West was true?

Was anything he said true? Anything at all?

How could you know? How could you even begin to guess? Oh, some things were bound to be true, because what point would there be to lying about them? But others? Had the top ranks of the Soviet military really been as full of traitors and wreckers as the recent purges left people believing? If they hadn't . . .

Even with the fresh slug of vodka coursing through him on top of everything else he'd drunk, Sergei recognized a dangerous thought when he tripped over one. You couldn't say anything like that, not unless you wanted to find out exactly what kind of weather Siberia had.

Or would they just shoot you if they realized you realized they didn't always tell the truth? He wouldn't have been surprised. What could be more dangerous to the people who ran things?

Anastas watched him from across the table. Did the Armenian know what he was thinking? Did Mouradian think the same things, too? Then Sergei stopped worrying about himself, because the Russian newsman went on, "Since German planes were used in the terror bombings of peaceful Soviet cities, justice demands that we also retaliate against the Fascist Hitlerite swine. This being so, Red Air Force bombers have struck at the Prussian city of Königsberg. Damage to the enemies of the people is reported to be extremely heavy. They richly deserve the devastation visited upon them!"

"*Bozhemoi*," whispered somebody down the table from Sergei. It sounded too reverent to be conventional cursing. Nobody reprimanded the flyer, though—not after that news!

No matter what Sergei had been thinking, he didn't doubt this for a moment. The USSR wouldn't claim to have bombed Germany if it hadn't really done it. And if the USSR bombed Germany . . . In that case, the war against Hitler had just gone from the back burner to the front.

Maybe those *were* Heinkels and Dorniers up there, inaccurately bombing the airstrip. Maybe Germans in field-gray would join Poles in greenish brown (although the Poles, like the Soviets, had the sense to wear white camouflage smocks in the wintertime). Maybe Hitler and Smigly-Ridz would show the world what the USSR already knew: they'd been in bed with each other all along.

A different announcer exhorted his listeners to buy war bonds. "Help make farmers and workers safe from the threat of Fascism!" he boomed. "Subscribe to the latest war bond program!"

Sergei already bought war bonds. So did everyone else in the Red Air Force and Army and Navy. Contributions came out of their pay before they ever set eyes on it. Losing the money didn't hurt nearly so much that way as it would have if Sergei'd had to dig into his own pockets.

"As long as the Nazis stay busy in the West, we'll do fine against them," Koroteyev said.

Several men nodded. Sergei was one of them. Then Anastas Mouradian said, "Sure we will—just like we did in the last war."

Silence slammed down around the table. Germany had been busy against France and England and Belgium in 1914—everybody knew that. And everybody also knew the Kaiser's armies had smashed the Tsar's again and again. If not for one disaster after another on the front, the Revolution might never have started, much less succeeded.

The Siberian looked at Anastas. "One of these days, you'll open your mouth so wide, you'll fall right in."

"No doubt, Comrade," Mouradian replied. "If it can happen to the whole country, why can't it happen to me?"

That only brought more silence. People stared at the Armenian, then quickly looked away. They might have been gaping at a car wreck. "*How* much have you drunk?" Sergei asked. Sometimes you could get out of trouble by blaming it all on the vodka. He'd done that himself a time or three.

His copilot gave the question his usual serious—if not sober— consideration. "Either too much or not enough," Mouradian said at last. "And it's not too much, so. . . ." He grabbed the vodka bottle, raised it, and tilted his head back.

Sergei reached out and grabbed it away from him. "To each according to his needs," he said, and got rid of what was left. With the air of a man performing a conjuring trick, the Siberian produced another bottle. Loud applause greeted it. The drinking went on. With any luck at all, by this time tomorrow nobody would remember what one mouthy Armenian was going on about.

SOME OF THE MEN IN Hideki Fujita's squad were from Hokkaido. The northern island was notorious for winter weather that blew straight down from Siberia. Fujita had been through some rotten winters himself before they shipped him off to the border between Manchukuo and Mongolia.

Or he thought he had, anyhow.

Now he had to admit that what he'd known about winter was about the same as what an eleven-year-old knew about love. The kid could imagine he understood what was what. And a jackass could suppose it was a nightingale, too. That didn't make it sound like one when it opened its mouth, though.

Fujita wore a fur cap—the earflaps, at the moment, down. He wore a thick, heavily lined, fur-collared greatcoat. It was double-breasted, to make it harder for drafts to sneak in. He had stout gray felt mittens and knee-high felt boots with leather uppers. He had on two pairs of wool socks and two pairs of long woolen underwear.

He was freezing his ass off just the same. You had to go out on patrol, freezing or not. If you didn't, the Russians or the Mongols would make you sorry. The Russians were used to cold weather—like what Hokkaido got, this stuff blew down from Siberia. The Mongols were used to it, too. And the Mongols were as sneaky, and as dangerous, as so many poisonous snakes. They could slither through openings where you didn't think there were any.

Sergeant Fujita looked at his watch. If it hadn't frozen and quit moving, he still had more than an hour out here before his relief came. "Zakennayo!" he muttered. That felt like forever.

At last, though, a superior private named Suzuki found him out in the middle of the blowing snow. Suzuki wore as much winter gear as Fujita, and a white camouflage smock on top of it all. He looked miserably cold just the same. But, cold or not, he said the magic words: "I relieve you, Sergeant."

"Good," Fujita said. The howling wind grabbed the world and tried to swirl it away. "What's going on back at the camp?"

"Somebody from regimental headquarters is there," Suzuki said.

"Oh, yeah?" Automatic suspicion filled Fujita's voice. Like any veteran noncom, he distrusted any break with routine. He had his reasons, too. "What does the guy want? Are we going to have to try and attack the Mongols and the Russians again? They've got more tanks and better artillery than we do. *And* they hold the high ground."

None of that would matter a sen's worth if the powers that be in Mukden or in Tokyo decided to send the guys at the pointy end of the bayonet into action once more. Fujita knew it only too well. And Superior Private Suzuki only shrugged. "I can't tell you anything about that, Sergeant," he answered. "The guy got there just when I was starting out here."

"I'd better go find out, then," Fujita said. "Try to stay warm. If you want to build up a wall of snow to keep the wind from blowing straight through you, nobody will say boo."

"Maybe I will," Suzuki said. "It's pretty bad."

"Is it ever!" Fujita headed back toward the tents that housed his company. Halfway there, he tried to get a cigarette going. He soon gave it up as a bad job. He had plenty of practice lighting up in a strong wind, but this one defeated him.

Getting under canvas did let him light a match. He gratefully sucked in smoke. Then he said, "Suzuki was going on that somebody from regimental HQ showed up here."

"That's right, Sergeant-*san*," one of the privates in the tent said. "People say we're pulling out of here."

"What, the company?" Fujita asked. "I won't be sorry—I'll say that. We've been bumping noses with the Mongols and the Russians too damn long."

"Not just the company—the whole regiment. Maybe everybody on this whole front," the private answered. "That's what people are saying, anyhow." The disclaimer let him off the hook in case the rumors he dished out proved nothing but a bunch of moonshine.

"The regiment? The whole front?" That was so much more than Sergeant Fujita had expected, he needed a minute to take it all in. "If we leave, where do we go next? Back to Japan?" *If you're going to wish, wish for the moon,* he thought.

"I'm very sorry, Sergeant-*san,* but I don't know." The private—Nakayama, his name was—sounded not only sorry but apprehensive. Privates got knocked around when sergeants wanted to know things and they didn't have the answers handy.

Had Fujita been in a bad mood, he might have hit Nakayama a couple of times to make himself feel better. But the sheer scope of what was going on left him more awed than angry. And walloping a private because of rumors wasn't exactly fair—which wouldn't have stopped Fujita if he really felt like doing it.

"I'm sure the captain will tell me in the morning," he said.

"Yes, Sergeant-*san.* Of course he will," Nakayama said quickly. He and the other privates in the tent let out almost identical sighs of relief. Sergeant Fujita affected not to notice them. He'd been a private himself once upon a time. He remembered what looking up at a sergeant-ogre was like. Discipline would suffer if this bunch of conscripts realized that, though. In the gloom, none of them could see him smile.

Sure enough, Captain Hasegawa summoned Fujita and the company's other senior noncoms first thing in the morning. Without preamble, the company commander said, "We are leaving the Mongolian frontier region and redeploying to eastern Manchukuo."

"Where will the redeployment take us, sir?" Sergeant Fujita asked. If it was to Mukden—the capital—or Harbin or some other big city, that wasn't so bad. It was a lot better than staying stuck on the edge of Mongolia. *And what isn't?* Fujita thought. Unfortunately, that had an answer.

If the regiment got shipped up to the Amur frontier with Russia, it just traded one miserable spot for another.

"I'm afraid I don't know the answer to that," the company commander said. "No one has told me, not yet. Even if I did know, I wouldn't tell you till we were well away from the border. The same reason applies in both cases: security. We don't want to take the chance that the Mongols or the Russians would seize you and squeeze you. No matter how honorable you wanted to be, you might not manage to kill yourself in time."

"I understand, sir. Please excuse my stupidity." Fujita bowed his head in embarrassment not far from shame.

Captain Hasegawa didn't come down on him as hard as he expected. "It's all right, Sergeant," the officer said. "The courier who brought me the news also had to explain the facts of life to me, you might say. Make sure you have your men ready to move out when I give the word, that's all."

"Yes, sir. I will, sir. Thank you, sir." Fujita bowed again, this time gratefully. The company commander hadn't made him lose face—had, in fact, gone out of his way to let Fujita keep it. You had to repay that kind of consideration with loyalty.

The order to abandon the position they'd defended for so long came that afternoon. Retreat often meant a loss of face, too. Not for Fujita, not this time: he was only obeying the orders he got from his superiors. But wouldn't Japan itself be embarrassed if it abandoned land to which it had asserted a claim?

"They'll probably say it was Manchukuo's claim, not ours," Superior Private Hayashi predicted as the company marched through the drifted snow toward regimental headquarters. "That way, we aren't responsible for it."

"Makes sense," Fujita said. Having an educated man in the squad came in handy now and then. Of course, without Japan there would have been no such country as Manchukuo. But that didn't have much to do with anything. Blaming the hapless Chinese and Manchus was much easier than blaming the mother country. And if the Emperor of Manchukuo didn't like it, too bad.

Trucks waited at the headquarters. Seeing them made Sergeant Fujita realize how serious Japan was about getting its men away from this stretch of the border. Japan wasn't a motorized country like Germany or the United States. It had to save its vehicles for really important things. If getting out of western Manchuria was this important . . .

Away rumbled the trucks, north and a little east. "Hailar," Fujita said even before his own machine set out. "We've got to be going to Hailar." That miserable Mongolian town was one of the two railheads closest to the disputed areas. The other, Arshaan, lay to the southeast.

Maps showed roads across this endless steppe. They were at best dirt tracks. At this time of year, with snow deep on the ground, whether you were on the road was often a matter of opinion. The truck carrying Fujita and his squad rumbled past another one that had overturned. Maybe the driver had tried to corner too fast. Maybe he'd run into a ditch. He would end up in trouble any which way.

Much the biggest and most modern building in Hailar was the railway depot. A few natives in sheepskin coats stared at the trucks that could go almost anywhere far faster than any horse ever foaled. What did they think, watching the modern world roll through their ancient town? Actually, what they thought hardly mattered. The modern world was here whether they liked it or not.

A train that would go east stopped at the depot—stopped a little past it, in fact, because snow and ice on the rails meant the brakes didn't grab as well as they would have most of the time. Some soldiers were already aboard, and had come this far west before starting east again. Fujita's unit left the cars packed as tight as tinned fish—the only way the Army seemed to know how to travel.

Well, the sergeant thought, *we won't be cold any more.* Each car had its own stove. And so many men stuffed the cars, the stoves might prove afterthoughts. Body heat would be plenty to keep everybody warm.

Slowly, the train started to roll again. Fujita still didn't know where he was going. He shrugged—being a sergeant, he had room to do that. What difference did it make. He'd get there whether he knew or not. Then he'd do . . . whatever needed doing.

Chapter 14

Chaim Weinberg shivered in a trench. The war on the Ebro seemed to have frozen solid. The whole Spanish Civil War seemed to have frozen solid. The Soviet Union wasn't sending aid to the Republic any more—Stalin was using the planes and tanks and guns himself. After the broader war broke out, a surge of aid had come from France and England, who'd ignored the Republican cause before. Now, with the Low Countries conquered and France herself invaded, they were ignoring it again.

The only good news was, Hitler and Mussolini were also ignoring General Sanjurjo's Spanish Fascists. With the Royal Navy and the French actually paying attention to the Mediterranean, the reactionaries would have had a devil of a time getting anything through anyway.

And so both sides were running on momentum, using—and using up—what they'd had before the great powers forgot about them. Before long, one side or the other would run out. The side that still had something would win—unless seeing their proxies in trouble prodded rich sponsors into action again.

Meanwhile . . . Meanwhile, Weinberg lit a cigarette. It was a Gitane, part of the bounty that had flowed in from France. It was a damn sight better than native Spanish smokes, which tasted of straw and lots of other things besides tobacco. Chaim still longed for an American cigarette. With a Lucky or a Chesterfield, you didn't feel as if you'd swallowed a welder's torch every time you inhaled.

He smoked the Gitane down to a tiny butt, then stuck that in a leather pouch he wore on his belt next to his wound dressing. He'd got used to saving dog-ends when tobacco was even scarcer than it was now. Wrap half a dozen of them and you had yourself another cigarette. He would never have stooped so low in the States, but things were different here.

Nobody'd been trying to kill him in the States, for instance. He'd made a crude periscope: two hand-sized chunks from a broken mirror mounted on opposite ends of a stick. (Seven years of bad luck? Getting shot was bad luck. He hadn't broken this mirror himself, but he would have without even blinking if he'd needed to.) He stuck it up over the lip of the trench to see what the enemy was up to.

Smoke rose here and there from the Fascists' trenches. Nobody was shelling them; the artillery on both sides stayed quiet. But cold struck impartially. There were fires in the International Brigades' position, too.

A khaki-clad Fascist soldier came head and shoulders out of his hole for a moment. He wasn't a sniper—he was dumping a honey bucket. One good thing about the cold: no flies right now. The Spaniard ducked down again before a Republican sharpshooter could fire at him.

Chaim didn't think it was sporting to shoot a man who was easing himself or getting rid of slops. But bastards on both sides had rifles with telescopic sights. They thought they weren't earning their pay if they didn't use them. And so, every now and then, men got shot at their most defenseless.

Not far away, Mike Carroll was cleaning his rifle. The French had used Lebels by the million in the last war. They'd been old-fashioned then, and they were obsolete now . . . which didn't mean you still couldn't kill people with them. How many different kinds of rifles, how many different kinds of ammunition, did the Republicans use? Too goddamn many—Chaim knew that.

Carroll paused. "Spot anything interesting?" he asked.

"Sure," Weinberg answered. "Naked blond broad taking a sun-bath out in front of the Fascist line. Big tits, pretty face—what more could you want? Natural blonde, too. Either that or she peroxides her bush."

The other American started to put down the rifle and grab for the periscope. Just too late, he caught himself. "Fuck you, you lying ass-hole," he said. "You had me going."

"Yeah, well, she's a hell of a lot better than what's really there." Wein-berg told him about the guy with the bucket.

"Whole war's full of shit," Carroll said. "Sanjurjo's guys, you . . . Everything. And nobody gives a shit about us."

"You just notice?" Chaim lit another Gitane. Mike Carroll looked like a puppy hoping for table scraps. Chaim handed him the pack. He took one with a nod of thanks and lit it with a Zippo. He fueled the lighter with kerosene—regular lighter fluid was impossible to come by on either side of the line here.

"Maybe we ought to go up to France," Carroll said moodily. "More Fascists—worse Fascists—to kill there."

"Good luck," Chaim said. Mike winced. He had about as much chance of getting up to France without authorization as he did of sprouting wings and flying there. Political officers behind the Interna-tional Brigades' lines checked everybody's papers. If you didn't have or-ders to pull you out, you were in trouble.

Even if you got past the commissars, plenty of other Republican of-ficials in towns and on trains would want to know where you were going and who said you were supposed to go there. If they didn't like your answers, they would either shoot you or chuck you into a Spanish jail. Not many things were worse than front-line combat, but a Spanish jail was one of them.

"All of a sudden, the States don't look so bad, you know?" Mike said with a grin that was supposed to mean he was half kidding, anyway.

"Maybe they'll let you repatriate," Chaim said. Sometimes the Internationals wanted nothing but willing fighters. Sometimes they figured you had to be willing or you wouldn't have volunteered. It all depended on the officer, on how the fighting was going—sometimes, people said, on the phases of the moon.

"Ah, fuck it," Mike said: the usual comment of every line soldier in every war since the beginning of time. "I'm just blowing off steam, you know what I mean?"

"Sure," Chaim said. And he did, too. It wasn't as if he'd never pissed and moaned since he got here. "All I wish is, people would remember us. We were a big deal till the rest of Europe blew up. Who gives a shit about Spain now? Stalin's forgotten all about it." That was a dangerous thing to say; the International Brigades toed Moscow's line. But a love of truth was part of what had led Chaim to Spain. He wouldn't give it up even here.

Mike Carroll had a tobacco pouch on his belt, too. He stuck the remains of the Gitane into it. "Well, so has Hitler," he answered. "That's not so bad."

"You know who remembers?" Chaim said. He waited till Carroll raised a questioning eyebrow. "Us and the Spaniards, that's who. It's not just fucking politics and games and shit for us. It really matters. Do you want that fat prick over there"—Chaim pointed toward the Fascists' lines—"running this whole goddamn country?"

He'd never talked that way in New York City. Back home, he'd always had the feeling his mother was listening and would wash his mouth out with soap. But everybody swore on the battlefield. By now, Chaim could cuss in English, Yiddish, Spanish, Catalan, German, French, and Russian. Talk without swear words seemed as bland as food without salt and pepper.

"If I wanted that, I'd be over there myself," Mike Carroll said. The Italians and Germans who fought on Sanjurjo's side had no choice. But for them, only a handful of foreigners—mostly English and Irishmen— had joined the enemy. Men from all over the world opposed the Fascists. If that didn't say something . . .

Before Chaim could decide what would be true if that didn't say something, a rifle bullet cracked between him and Carroll. Both of them hit the dirt. "We've been standing up and waving our arms too damn much," Mike said ruefully. "They got a sniper to take a shot at us."

"Yeah." Chaim hadn't quite pissed himself, but he'd come mighty close. Well, so had the bullet. "Good thing he's a shitty sniper." A good marksman would have hit one of them. Maybe this guy couldn't decide which one to aim at.

"Spaniards." Mike Carroll's shrug punctuated that—but didn't expose him to any more rifle fire. "They're brave as all get-out—the guys on both sides. But . . ." His voice trailed away.

Chaim knew what he was talking about. "Yeah. But," he said, making the word sound like a complete sentence. It might as well have been. Spaniards didn't keep proper lookout. They didn't like digging trenches. They didn't bother cleaning their weapons unless somebody screamed at them—and a lot of the time not then, either. Their logistics were a joke. Food and ammunition came to the front when they felt like it. That was how things looked, anyhow. Their hospitals were almost as bad as their jails.

But they *were* brave. Point them at an objective and they'd take it or die trying. Tell them they had to hold a strongpoint and it was ¡No pasaran! You were embarrassed to falter or fall back, because you knew they wouldn't. If only they would pull themselves together . . .

"Don't hold your breath," Mike said when Chaim suggested that. Then the other American asked, "Do you think we can nail that sniper?"

There was a serious suggestion. "Worth a try," Chaim said. "He'll make this whole stretch of trench dangerous unless we do get rid of him. How do you want to work it?"

"We ought to call a sharpshooter of our own," Carroll said. Chaim gave him the horse laugh. Republican snipers were few, far between, and none too good. The other American's ears turned red. "Okay, okay. Which of us do you think is a better shot?"

"I am," Chaim answered without false modesty. "Let me find a position where I can look out without getting drilled. Then you hold up a cap on a stick, and I'll see what I can see."

"I'll do it. Wave when you're ready," Mike said.

"Yeah." Chaim worked his way fifty yards down the trench. Some bushes—brown and leafless in the winter cold—offered cover there. Cautiously, he peered out through them. Nobody fired at him. He brought his rifle up over the top and rested it on the dirt. Then, carefully keeping his hand below the level of the parapet, he signaled to his buddy.

Up went the cap. A shot rang out. Mike not only jerked the cap down but also let out a scream. Chaim saw where the sniper fired from, but the Fascist ducked away before he could plug him. Now . . . Was the *maricón* dumb enough to shoot from the same position twice in a row? Everybody knew you shouldn't, but some boys did anyhow. Only one way to find out . . .

"Move a little and pop up again," Chaim called, as softly as he could.

Mike did. He even put the cap on the stick sideways this time, so it would look different. Chaim peered down his rifle barrel. He had the range, he had windage. . . .

He had a target. Yeah, the guy on the other side was greedy and stupid, all right. He showed one shoulder and his head, and that was all Chaim needed. He pressed the trigger, not too hard. Red mist exploded from the enemy sniper as he slumped back into his trench.

"You get him?" Carroll asked.

"Uh-huh. Don't have to worry about that for a while, anyway." Chaim might have been talking about delousing or killing a rat. He'd got rid of a nuisance—that was all. Well, now the nuisance wouldn't get rid of him. Nothing else counted. He lit another Gitane.

IT WAS A FINE, BRIGHT MORNING in western Belgium—colder than an outhouse in East Prussia in February, but sunny and clear. The sun came up a little earlier than it had a month earlier, at the end of December. Chances were spring would get here eventually: no time real soon, but eventually.

Breath smoking in the chilly sunrise air, Hans-Ulrich Rudel walked to the squadron commander's hut to see what was up. Something would be. He was sure of that. This time of year, days with decent flying weather were too few and far between to waste.

Other Stuka pilots nodded to him. He nodded back. He didn't have a lot of buddies here. Not likely a milk drinker would, not when most of the flyers preferred brandy and loose women. But he kept going out and doing his job and coming back. That won him respect, if no great liking.

Cigarette smoke blued the air inside the hut. Hans-Ulrich didn't like that, either, but complaining was hopeless. He tried not to breathe deeply.

"We're going to bomb England again," Major Bleyle announced. That got everyone's attention, as he must have known it would. He went on, "They've been hitting our cities—miserable air pirates. What can we do but pay them back? We will strike at Dover and Folkestone and Canterbury, just on the other side of the Channel. Questions?"

Hands flew up, Rudel's among them. The squadron commander pointed to somebody else—he didn't much like Hans-Ulrich, either. But the other pilot said about what Rudel would have: "How are we going to come back in one piece? Stukas are sitting ducks for English fighters."

"We'll have an escort," Bleyle said.

"We had an escort the last time, too," the pilot pointed out. "Some of the enemy planes kept the 109s busy, and the rest came after us."

"We'll have a better escort this time," the squadron commander answered. "Not just 109s, but 110s, too."

The pilots all paused thoughtfully. Bf-110s were brand new. If half what people said was so, they were formidable, no doubt about it. The big, two-engined fighters mounted two 20mm cannon and four machine guns in the nose, plus another, rear-facing machine gun on a mount like the one in the Stuka. If all that firepower hit an enemy aircraft, the poor devil would go down.

"And there'll be Heinkels and Dorniers overhead," Major Bleyle added. "The enemy won't be able to concentrate on us the way he did before. We're going to knock eastern England flat. Let's see how they like it."

One by one, the Stuka pilots nodded. Most of them had seen enough to know war wasn't always as easy as they wished it would be. They'd signed up to take whatever happened, the bad along with the good. Hans-Ulrich suspected things would turn out to be harder than the squadron CO made them sound. By the thoughtful looks on the other men's faces, so did they. But if the people set over you told you to try, what else could you do?

He took the word to Sergeant Dieselhorst. The gunner and radioman shrugged. "Oh, well," he said. "Maybe she'll have engine trouble. We can hope, anyway."

"It won't be that bad," Rudel said.

"No, I suppose not . . . sir." Dieselhorst spoiled it by adding, "It'll be worse."

The Stuka had no engine trouble. Some groundcrew man's head would have rolled if it did. The mechanics and armorers gassed it up and bombed it up. It roared down the runway and lumbered into the air with the others.

Bf-109s and 110s took station around the dive-bombers. The 110s—*Zerstörers*, they called them: destroyers—certainly *looked* formidable. With all that firepower in the nose, they packed a mean punch. Idly, Hans-Ulrich wondered how maneuverable they were. He laughed. His own Ju-87 dodged like a rock.

There was the North Sea. There ahead lay England. The popular song dinned in his head. He *was* going up against England. If the enemy bombed the *Reich*, the *Luftwaffe* would repay blood with blood, murder with murder.

He saw ships—boats—whatever they were—on the sea. Did they belong to the *Kriegsmarine* or the Royal Navy? Were they radioing a warning to the English mainland now? Was that how the RAF had been so quick to attack the Stukas the last time they raided southeastern England? Rudel shrugged. Not his worry, though he did think he'd mention it if he happened to remember after he got back to Belgium.

If I get back to Belgium. He did his best to stifle that thought. You didn't want to go into battle with your head full of doubts and worries. He was no more eager to go into *this* battle than any of his squadron mates. The Ju-87 was terrific when it enjoyed air superiority. When it didn't . . .

Several 109s seemed to leap out ahead of the pack. Following their path with his eyes, Hans-Ulrich spied another plane out ahead of the oncoming German air armada. Tracers from the Messerschmitts blazed toward the stranger, which dove and spun down toward the ocean. It wasn't a fighter. They charged after it and sent it smoking into the water.

Someone in the squadron voiced on the radio what Hans-Ulrich was thinking: "Now—did he get word out before we shot him down?"

"We'll find out," somebody else said in sepulchral tones.

And they did. English fighter planes rose to meet them: biplane Gladiators, monoplane Hurricanes, and a handful of new, sleek Spitfires. The RAF fighters bored in on the *Luftwaffe* bombers. They wanted no more to do with the escorts than they had to. The 109s and 110s couldn't hurt their country. Bombers could.

What was going on higher in the sky, where the Heinkels and Dorniers had escorts of their own? Rudel couldn't check. He was too busy trying to stay alive. Even a Gladiator could be dangerous.

Sergeant Dieselhorst fired a burst. "Get anything?" Hans-Ulrich asked.

"Nah," the rear gunner answered. "He'll bother somebody else, though." That suited the pilot fine.

Cannon fire from a nearby Me-110 knocked down a Hurricane. A moment later, another Hurricane bored in on the two-engined German fighter. That combat didn't last long. The Hurricane easily outturned the 110, got on its tail, shot it up, and shot it down.

Hans-Ulrich saw he was over some kind of city. He thought it was Dover, but it might have been Folkestone or any other English port. It lay by the sea—he could tell that much. And he could tell it was time to unload the frightfulness he'd brought across the ocean. He yanked the bomb-release lever. The Stuka suddenly felt lighter and nimbler.

"Now we get the devil out of here?" Dieselhorst's voice came brassy through the speaking tube.

"Now we get out of here," Hans-Ulrich agreed. No point in lingering. The Stuka sure wasn't agile enough to dogfight against a British fighter.

A broad-winged He-111, afire from the nose back, plunged into the North Sea just off the coast from the town that was probably Dover. An enormous cloud of steam and smoke rose: a couple of thousand kilos' worth of bombs going off when the Spade hit. Hans-Ulrich hadn't seen any parachutes. Four men dead, then.

"You know what happens next, don't you?" Dieselhorst said.

"What's that?" Rudel asked. He looked every which way. He didn't see any Indians, which was what *Luftwaffe* pilots called enemy planes. That let him ease back on the throttle a little. The Continent loomed ahead. He'd probably make it to the airstrip.

"They come over tonight or tomorrow night and bomb the crap out of some of our towns," Dieselhorst said. "Where does it end? With our last two guys coming out of the ruins and going after their last guy with a club?"

"That's not for us to worry about. That's for the *Führer*." But Hans-Ulrich couldn't leave it there. "As long as we've got two guys and they've got one, as long as our two get their one, we win. And we're going to. Right?"

"Oh, yes, sir," the gunner answered. Nobody could or wanted to imagine Germany losing two wars in a row. Losing one had been bad enough.

But when Hans-Ulrich put down at the Belgian airstrip, he waited and waited, hoping against hope that more Stukas would come home safe. A few had returned before him. A few more straggled in afterwards. But so many were lost over England or the North Sea. . . . The squadron would need a new CO, among other reinforcements. Hans-Ulrich hoped the *Reich* would have two men with clubs coming out of the ruins, not just one.

EVERY NIGHT, THE PANZERS IN Sergeant Ludwig Rothe's platoon reassembled—or they tried to, anyhow. By now, Rothe's crew was the most experienced one left in the platoon. Neither he nor his driver nor his radioman had got badly hurt. Given how thin-skinned Panzer IIs were, that was something close to miraculous.

Rothe had commanded the platoon on and off on the drive across the Low Countries and into France. Lieutenants and their panzers were no more invulnerable to flying shells than anybody else. But the platoon had an officer in charge of it again: a second lieutenant named Maximilian Priller.

He was dark and curly-haired. He had a whipped-cream-in-your-coffee, strudel-on-the-side Viennese accent. Before the *Anschluss,* he'd served in the Austrian Army. Like a lot of German soldiers, Rothe looked down his nose at Austrians as fighting men. He had nothing bad to say about Lieutenant Priller, though. No matter how Priller talked, he knew what to do with panzers.

"Our next stop is Coucy-le-Château." Priller pointed the place out on a map he unfolded on his knees. His German sounded funny in Ludwig's ears, but he spoke fluent French. "Well, not our next stop—where we go through next. It's only about five kilometers ahead. We ought to drive the enemy out by the middle of the morning. Questions, anybody?"

"Do we soften them up with artillery first, or do we break through with the panzers?" another sergeant asked.

"With the panzers. That way, we've got surprise working for us." Priller cocked an eyebrow. "We see who gets the surprise—us or them."

The four sergeants who commanded the other panzers in the platoon all chuckled, Ludwig among them. It was laugh or scream, one. Maybe the French troops in front of the Germans would panic and flee. On the other hand, maybe they'd be waiting with panzers of their own, minefields, antitank guns: all the things that made life in the panzer force so . . . interesting.

"We've bent them back a long way," Max Priller said. "If we break through here, we drive the sword into their heart. We want them all disordered. Then we can race them to Paris. Better than even money we win."

"Paris . . ." Ludwig and a couple of the other sergeants said together. Back in the Middle Ages, knights went on quests for the Holy Grail. In the twentieth century, Paris was the Holy Grail for Germany. The Kaiser's army had come so close. Armchair generals kept talking about von Kluck's turn. If he hadn't made it, or if the Russians hadn't caused so much trouble off in the East . . .

Russia was making trouble again. The *Wehrmacht* had done well here, or Ludwig thought it had. In a month, it had knocked Holland, Belgium, and Luxembourg out of the fight. The radio said German bombers were giving England hell to pay back the British terror raids on German cities. Maybe this attack would have gone smoother in better weather. Only God could know something like that, though.

"Tell your men," Priller said. "We go at 0600."

It would still be dark. Somebody'd get a surprise, all right. Well, what could you do? Rothe went back to his panzer. Fritz was toasting some bacon he'd liberated from a farmhouse. Theo was swapping tubes in and out of the radio, trying to figure out which one was bad.

Fritz looked up from the little cookfire. "It's going to be bad," he said. "I can see it on your face. How bad is it?"

"We hit the town up ahead at 0600," Ludwig answered bluntly.

Theo paused with a tube in each hand. He looked down at them, muttering; Rothe guessed he was remembering which one he'd just pulled and which was about to go in. Fritz stared up from the sizzling slab of bacon. "Fuck," he said.

"I know," Ludwig said. "What can you do, though?" He pointed to the bacon. "Is that done? Let me have some if it is."

Off in the distance, some guns opened up. *French 75s*, Ludwig thought, recognizing the reports. The damned things dated back to before the turn of the century. They'd been the great workhorses of the French artillery during the last war; Ludwig's father swore whenever he talked about them. They could fire obscenely fast. This time around, German 105s outranged them. That did you no good if you ended up on the wrong end of things, though.

These shells came down a good distance away. Fritz cut the bacon into three pieces. "Well, maybe we'll surprise them," he said. "They don't seem to know where we're at. . . . Here you go, Sergeant."

"*Danke.*" Ludwig blew on his share, then took a bite. It tasted about the same as bacon would have back home. He might have had it boiled there, but he might not, too. He gulped. "Yeah, maybe we will," he said, and bit into the bacon again.

Theo stared at the orange glow inside the tube he'd just swapped in. "That does it," he said. "Now we'll be able to hear all the stupid orders we'll get from the shitheads back of the lines—and from Lieutenant Priller, too." His faith in those set over him had, well, limits. Ludwig suspected Theo didn't have much use for him, either. He also suspected— no, he was sure—he wouldn't lose any sleep about it.

The French 75s quieted down. Had somebody given them a target, or were they shooting at some jumpy officer's imagination? Ludwig laughed. He had no use for French higher-ups. Why did he think the men who ran the *Wehrmacht* had a better handle on what they were doing?

Because we're in France, and the damned Frenchmen aren't in Germany, he answered himself. And maybe that meant something and maybe it didn't. They'd all find out some time not long after 0600.

He slept by the Panzer II. So did the driver and the radioman. If shelling came close, they could dive under the panzer. The treads and the armored body would keep out anything this side of a direct hit.

Lieutenant Priller came along at half past four to make sure they were alert and ready to go. "We can do it," he said. "We're going to do it, too."

"Have we got any coffee?" Ludwig asked plaintively. And damned if they didn't. It wasn't the ersatz that came with army rations, mixed with burnt barley and chicory. It came from the real bean, no doubt taken from the French. It was dark and mean and strong. Ludwig dumped sugar into it so he could choke it down. Sure as hell, it pried his eyelids open.

As they had in the runup to the strike against Czechoslovakia, engineers had set out white tapes here to guide the panzers forward without showing a light. Rothe cupped a hand behind his ear, trying to hear if the French up ahead had any idea they were coming. He couldn't tell. Fritz had the engine throttled back, but its low rumble still drowned out the little sounds he was looking for. Nobody was shooting at the Germans as they moved up to the start line, anyhow.

Ludwig glanced down at the radium-glowing dial on his watch. 0530. A couple of hours later, he checked again. 0550. He laughed at himself. Time stretched like a rubber band when you were waiting for the balloon to go up.

When it did go up, it went all at once. One second, quiet above the engine noise. The next, German artillery crashed behind the panzers. German machine guns stuttered to life, spitting fire to either side. "Let's go!" Rothe yelled through the din. The engine grew deeper and louder. It had to work like a bastard to shove all that armored weight around.

A couple of French Hotchkiss machine guns returned fire, but not for long. The panzers and assault teams with submachine guns and grenades silenced them. Standing head and shoulders out of the turret, Ludwig whooped. The last thing he wanted was tracers probing toward him.

The Germans had jumped off just before earliest dawn. As day broke, the French landscape seemed to stretch out ever farther before them. Rothe fired a few machine-gun bursts at soldiers in khaki. If they were here, they were bound to be enemies. He was at the spearpoint of the field-gray forces pressing down from the northeast.

Bam! A French antitank gun belched flame. The 37mm round missed the Panzer II. A good thing—a hit would have turned it into blazing scrap metal. Rothe almost shit himself even so.

More to the point, he traversed the turret and fired several short bursts at the gun. Seeing bullets spark off its steel shielding, he gave it a few rounds from the 20mm cannon. Those got through. French artillerymen tumbled like ninepins. "There you go!" Fritz shouted. Theo, tending to his radio in the bowels of the Panzer II, couldn't see a damned thing.

But one stubborn Frenchman fired the gun again. The 37mm shot snarled past, a few meters over Ludwig's head. He shot back with the panzer's main armament. And he gave an order you didn't hear every day in armored warfare: "Charge! Run that gun down!"

"*Jawohl!*" Fritz said. The Panzer II's engine snarled. The stubborn French soldier was still alive behind the riddled shield, trying to serve the gun by himself. Seeing the panzer bearing down on him, he finally turned and fled. Ludwig shot him in the back with the machine gun. A guy like that was too dangerous to leave alive.

Crunch! The panzer clattered over the antitank gun. For a nasty moment, Ludwig feared the panzer would flip over, but it didn't. When he looked back over his shoulder, he saw the new kink in the gun's barrel. Nobody would use that one against the *Reich* any more, which was the point.

Here and there, infantrymen with rifles fired at the panzers, trying to pick off their commanders. Every once in a while, they managed to do it, too. But the panzers had a whole slew of advantages. They were on the move. Their commanders could duck behind armor. And they carried a machine gun and a light cannon against a bolt-action rifle.

Staying on the move was the biggest edge. Even if you didn't take out an infantryman, you left him behind in a matter of seconds. Sooner or later, your own foot soldiers could deal with him. In the meanwhile, the panzers charged ahead, flowing around enemy strongpoints and raising hell in the rear.

But Coucy-le-Château was too big and too strong to go around. Some of the soldiers Ludwig shot at in the outskirts wore lighter khaki and steel derbies in place of darker uniforms and domed helms with vestigial crests. Englishmen! They didn't like machine-gun bursts any better than the French (or Ludwig, come to that).

A machine gun chattered from the middle of an apple orchard. The gun moved. Ludwig realized it was mounted on some sort of tank. He gulped, wondering if the enemy machine's cannon was taking dead aim at his panzer. Not nearly enough steel separated him from the slings and arrows of outrageous gunners.

But he realized little by little that the other panzer didn't carry a cannon. All it had was that machine gun—it might as well have been a German Panzer I.

It waddled out of the apple grove. It didn't seem able to do anything but waddle—a man running fast would have had no trouble outdistancing it. He fired three quick rounds from the 20mm gun. Two of them hit the turret, but they didn't come close to punching through. The Matilda might be slow. It might have a laughable armament—even a Panzer I sported a pair of machine guns, not a singleton. But it was damned hard to wreck.

It was if you tried to kill the crew, anyway. If you crippled it, though . . . Ludwig fired the 20mm at the Matilda's tracks and road wheels. Before long, the ungainly thing slewed sideways and stopped. Ludwig's panzer clanked past it. Now it was nothing but a well-armored machine-gun position. The infantry could deal with that.

Medieval-looking ramparts surrounded Coucy-le-Château. The hilltop château that gave the town its name had had chunks bitten out of it, probably in the last war. Mortar bombs from the château started falling among the German panzers. Half wrecked or not, the place had *poilus* or Tommies in it.

"Theo!" Ludwig said. "Let the artillery know they're firing from the ruin."

"Right," the radioman answered, which might have meant anything.

He—or somebody—must have done it, because 105s started knocking more pieces off the château. Then a flight of Stukas screamed down on it. Their bombs did what guns could only dream about. The enemy mortars fell silent.

More Stukas worked over Coucy-le-Château. One of them got shot down and crashed into the town, turning itself into a bomb. The rest roared away. The onslaught stunned the defenders. With narrow, winding streets, Coucy-le-Château might have been a nasty place to try to take. But some of the garrison fled west and south, while the rest couldn't surrender fast enough.

Breakthrough? Ludwig didn't know, but he had hopes.

Chapter 15

January. The North Atlantic. A U-boat. The combination was not made in heaven, as Lieutenant Julius Lemp knew only too well.

Oh, he could take the U-30 down below periscope depth, and she'd escape the fearsome waves topside. The only trouble was, down below periscope depth she'd be about as useful to the war effort as if she were a five-year-old's toy in a Berlin bathtub.

A five-year-old splashing around couldn't whip up a worse storm in that tiny tub than God was kicking up out here on the broad ocean. One ten-meter wave after another rolled down on the U-30. Because she was so much smaller and had so much less freeboard than a surface warship, it was like taking one soggy right to the chin after another.

Lemp tied himself to the rail atop the conning tower so an extra-big wave wouldn't sweep him out to sea. He wore oilskins, of course. He knew he'd get soaked anyhow. This way, it would take a little longer, though.

He wondered why he'd bothered bringing the binoculars with him. So much spray and stray water splashed the lenses, he might as well have peered through a couple of full beer steins. You had to try all the same. Why else did they send you out in filthy weather like this?

Another wave smashed over the bow. It splashed past the 88mm deck gun and crashed into the conning tower. Lemp got himself a faceful of ocean. "Fuck," he said, spitting salt water. He would have made a bigger fuss had it been the first time, or even the fifth.

He looked at the binoculars. They were good and wet now. Ironically, that might make them easier to look through than when they'd just been spray-splashed. He raised them to his eyes and swept the horizon with a hunter's intent patience.

He or one of the other watchstanders did this as long as there was enough daylight to see by. At night, he did take the boat down twenty-five or thirty meters so the men could cook a little and could rest without getting pitched out of their cramped bunks and hammocks.

Something glided past him on the wind: a petrel, on the prowl for fish, not ships. Stormy weather didn't bother the bird. Lemp wished he could say the same.

The U-boat's bow sank down into a trough. That meant the following wave would be worse than usual. And it was. If not for the fastening—and for his holding on to the rail for dear life—it would have swept him into the Atlantic. Would he have drowned before he froze? That was the only question there.

He wanted to ride on top of a crest, not get buried by one. Eventually, the U-30 did. That gave him those extra ten meters from which to look around. He didn't expect to see anything but the scudding gray clouds that had kept him company ever since leaving Germany. His watch would be up pretty soon. Then he could descend into the U-boat's crowded, stinking pressure hull, dry off, and change into his other, slightly less soaked, uniform.

When you didn't expect to see something, you probably wouldn't, even if it was there. Lemp almost missed the smoke trail to the northwest. His hands were smarter than his head. They snapped back of themselves and gave him another look at it. Without even noticing he'd done it, he stopped shivering. He stopped caring he was wet clean through.

He pulled out the plug on the speaking tube that let him talk to the helmsman and the engine room. "Change course to 310," he ordered. "All ahead full."

Hollow and brassy, the answer came back: "Changing course to 310, skipper. You found something?"

"I sure did," Lemp said as the diesels' building throb told him their crew had got the command, too. "Now we have to see what it is and whether we can run it down."

He thought they had a decent chance. Not many freighters could match the U-30's surface speed. And he could get mighty close before the ship spotted *his* exhaust: diesel fuel burned much cleaner than heavy oil, to say nothing of coal. The U-boat's low, sharkish silhouette shouldn't be easy to pick up, either.

The other side of the coin was, he couldn't make seventeen knots in seas like this. Now that the U-30 had turned away from taking the swells bow-on, she got slapped in the port side instead. British corvettes—U-boat hunters—were said to roll on wet grass. The U-30 was doing the same thing. As long as she straightened up every time, Lemp couldn't complain.

His stomach could, and did. He was a good sailor, but he seldom faced a challenge like this. He gulped, hoping lunch would stay down. If he was going to sink that ship, he had to get ahead of her before submerging to wait for her to reach him where he lay in wait. A U-boat's greatest weakness was that it was slower submerged than its quarry was on the surface.

He ordered another course change, swinging closer to due north. The ship was making a very respectable turn of speed. In turn, that argued she was big and important: a ship England particularly wouldn't want to see lost.

When the U-boat rose to the crest of another wave, Lemp got a good look at the enemy vessel. He whistled softly, though he couldn't even hear himself through the howling wind. She had to be 15,000 tons if she was a gram!

"A Q-ship," he muttered under his breath. In the last war, England had put disguised guns on several merchantmen. They looked like ordinary freighters . . . till an unwary U-boat skipper approached them on the surface, confident of an easy kill. Several such skippers had paid with their boats—and with their lives. Lemp shook his head. "Not me, by God! Not me."

The enemy wasn't zigzagging. She didn't know he was around, then. *Good*, he thought, imagining what 15cm guns could do to his hull. And the U-30 *was* overhauling her. He smiled wolfishly. Yes, she'd get a nasty surprise before long.

He went below. No time to change now. After the hunt would have to do. He'd kept his sausage and noodles down on the conning tower. He almost lost them for a second time leaving the cold, pure ocean air for the stinks and smokes of the pressure hull. His eyes also needed a moment to adjust from gray daylight to the dim orange lamps the U-boat used.

"Take her down to periscope depth, Peter," he said.

"Periscope depth. Aye aye, skipper," the helmsman said. Dive warnings hooted. Air hissed out of buoyancy tanks; water gurgled in to take its place. The U-30 could dive like an otter when she had to. The crew practiced all the time. If a destroyer or an airplane came after you, you had to disappear in a hurry or you'd disappear forever.

Lemp raised the periscope. The instrument wasn't perfect. It got out of alignment, and the upper lens took even more splashes and spray than his binoculars did. But the periscope didn't need to be perfect this time. Here came the merchant cruiser, fat and happy as if she had the world by the tail.

"Course 190. All ahead one third," Lemp ordered, and the batteries that powered the U-30 underwater sent her toward her prey.

The target was making about ten knots. The torpedoes could do better than thirty. If the range was down to . . . he peered through the periscope again . . . 900 meters, he needed to launch . . . now!

"Fire one!" he snapped, and then, "Fire two!" and then, "Fire three!"

Wham! . . . Whoosh! One after another, the fish leaped away from the U-boat. "All three gone, skipper," the torpedomen reported.

"*Ja*," Lemp agreed absently. In these waves, he couldn't watch the wakes as well as he would have liked. On the other hand, the merchant cruiser would have a harder time seeing them coming, too.

At the very last moment, she started to turn away. The very last moment proved much too late. The first torpedo caught her up near the bow. The dull *Boom!* filled the U-30. The soldiers whooped and cheered. Somebody pounded Lemp on the back. Discipline on a submarine wasn't the same as it was on a surface ship—nowhere close. The skipper kept his eyes on the periscope, so he never knew who it was.

A few seconds later, another, bigger, *Boom!* echoed through the water. The second torpedo hit the enemy ship just aft of amidships. "That does it." Lemp spoke with quiet satisfaction. "We broke her back. She's going down fast."

He waited for the impact of the third torpedo, but it didn't come. That one must have missed. He was annoyed. He hated to miss. But the two hits were plenty to sink the merchant cruiser. And that, after all, was the point of the exercise. He wouldn't be too hard on himself.

A lot of boats out. A lot of heads bobbing in the water as the ship slid under. The survivors wouldn't last long, not in seas like this. Lemp wondered if he'd sunk a troopship bringing soldiers from Canada to England. That would be an even stronger blow against the enemy than he'd thought he struck.

He also wondered if she'd got out an SOS. If destroyers, say, were hurrying this way on a rescue mission, he didn't want to hang around any longer than he had to. "Surface," he said. "Let's skedaddle. We've done our job here."

PEGGY DRUCE FINALLY HAD HER bags packed. In a couple of hours, she would head for the train station. The train would take her out of Germany and into neutral Denmark. In Copenhagen, she would get on a lovely American liner, the *Athenia*. Before too long, she'd be in New York. Two hours by train from Philadelphia. A million billion miles from a Europe that had lost its mind.

Somebody knocked on the door.

A hotel flunky, she thought. As soon as she saw the uniform, she realized the man wasn't from the hotel. It wasn't a military uniform, but civilians in the Third *Reich* liked playing dress-up, too. This guy, unless she was wrong, came from the Foreign Ministry.

And this guy, unless she was very, very wrong, was Trouble. With a capital T.

"You are Miss, uh, Margaret Druce?" he asked in pretty good English.

"Missus," Peggy corrected automatically. Just as automatically, she flashed her ring.

"Please to excuse me. And please to let me introduce myself. I am Konrad Hoppe, of the Sub-bureau for the Supervision of Interned Neutrals." He didn't click his heels, but he gave her a stiff little bow, something you'd never see in the States. As he straightened, he went on, "You were formerly scheduled to leave Germany today and to return to America in the near future."

Amazing how something as simple as an adverb could be scarier than the bombs that had rained down on Berlin at New Year's. "What do you mean, formerly?" Peggy demanded, doing her goddamnedest not to show how frightened she was.

"Ah." *Herr* Hoppe nodded, more to himself than to her. "Then you will not have heard any news this morning."

"What's that got to do with anything? Don't play riddles, if you don't mind. If you've got something to say, come out and say it, already."

"Very well, Mrs. Druce." This time, Hoppe got it right. And, this time, he really did click his heels. "I regret that I must be the one to inform you that the *Athenia* went down in the North Atlantic yesterday, bound for Copenhagen from New York City. Loss of life is reported to be heavy."

"Went down." Numbly, Peggy entered the words. They sounded innocuous, almost antiseptic. Little by little, her wits started working. "What do you mean, 'went down'? Went down how? Did a U-boat torpedo her?" That was the likeliest way she could think of for a ship to go down in the middle of the North Atlantic in wartime. "They can't do that! She's a neutral! She's an American!"

They *could* do that. They could do anything they damn well pleased. Sometimes, as an American herself, she had trouble remembering that in spite of all the horrors she'd seen. Maybe that made her a fool. Maybe it left her one of the last sane people on this poor, benighted continent.

Konrad Hoppe, dutiful employee of the Sub-bureau for the Supervision of Interned Neutrals, looked pained. "So the BBC claims. But this is one more lie from a nation of liars. The government of the *Reich* has denied any involvement in the sinking of the *Athenia*. If it was not an accident, the British torpedoed or bombed it themselves, to stir up hatred against Germany in America."

"That's the nuttiest thing I ever heard in my life!" Peggy exclaimed.

"It is not," Hoppe insisted. "For the British, it would make perfect sense. But why would the *Reich* sink an American ocean liner? Do you not think we learned our lessons on the folly of this in the last war?"

Peggy opened her mouth. Then she closed it again. She didn't know what to say. She couldn't imagine England doing anything so filthy. But she also had trouble believing Hitler wanted to antagonize the

USA. Wouldn't he be cutting his own throat if he did? He might be nuts, but he wasn't stupid. He wasn't *that* stupid, anyhow, or Peggy didn't think so.

"Maybe your guy just made a mistake," she said after a few seconds of thought. "Have you ever crossed the Atlantic in January? *I* have, and it's rough seas and nasty weather all the way."

"Our submarine captains do not make such errors," the Foreign Ministry official said stiffly. "It is impossible. And if you find the Atlantic in January so unappetizing, why did you book passage on the *Athenia*?"

To get the hell out of your stinking country. But if Peggy said something like that, some guys who wore different uniforms—those of the SS, say—were liable to have some sharp questions for her. Or pointed ones. Or hot ones. "To get away from the war," she did say, a couple of heartbeats slower than she might have.

"I am afraid this is not possible for you at the moment," Hoppe said.

"Can't I go to Denmark anyway?" Peggy yelped. The lights were on in neutral Denmark. Denmark had never heard of rationing, except as something other people suffered. Much more to the point, Denmark was a civilized country. Once upon a time, Peggy would have said the same thing about Germany. No more. No more.

"I am very sorry." Konrad Hoppe didn't sound sorry. If anything, he sounded coldly amused. He got to tell foreigners no, and the Foreign Ministry paid him to do it. If that wasn't heaven for the nasty little man, Peggy would have been amazed. A small, chilly smile on his lips, Hoppe went on, "That also for you is not possible."

"How come?" She wouldn't give up without a fight. "I've got the train ticket. I've got the Danish visa. Why can't I use 'em?"

"It is not the policy of the *Reich* to permit departures unless the return journey to the foreigner's home may be completed without delay," Hoppe droned.

"Why the—dickens not?" She wanted to say something hotter than that, but feared it would do her more harm than good.

"I am not obligated to discuss the *Reich*'s policies with those affected by them. I am obliged only to communicate them to you," Hoppe said primly.

Fuck you, Charlie. Peggy didn't say that, either. A few years earlier, she would have. Maybe she was finally growing up. She rolled her eyes. She didn't think Herb would believe it. That made her roll them again. God only knew when—or if—she'd see her husband again.

She tried a different tack: "Okay, you're not obligated. Could you do it because you want to, or because it'd be a civilized kind of thing to do?"

Yes, she'd throw that in Hoppe's face. And his sallow cheeks did turn red. Russians got ticked off if you called them uncultured. Germans were almost as bad. A lot of them had an inferiority complex about France and England. And, oddly, that had got worse since Hitler took over. It was as if the Nazis were uneasily aware of what a bunch of bastards they were, and embarrassed when somebody called them on it.

"I believe . . ." Hoppe's voice trailed away. A little muscle under one eye twitched, the only visible sign of what had to be a struggle inside him. Human being against Nazi functionary? Peggy knew which way she would have bet. But she would have lost, because the Foreign Ministry official went on, "I believe it is to keep people from blaming the *Reich* for disrupted schedules when those are not of our making."

Who sank the Athenia? Peggy wondered again. But Hoppe would only deny it one more time if she threw it in his face. If Goebbels was saying the British had done it, that was Holy Writ inside the Third *Reich*. Hoppe probably believed it himself, even if it seemed like obvious horse manure to Peggy.

"Well, suppose I sign a pledge that says I won't be offended?" Peggy proposed. "If I badmouth you in the papers or anything, you can haul it out and tell people what a liar I am."

He shook his head. "No. That is not good. You would claim you signed the document under duress. We have experience with others who prove ungrateful after going beyond our borders."

And why do you suppose that is? Peggy knew goddamn well why it was. Konrad Hoppe seemed not to have the faintest idea. That he didn't—that so many like him didn't—was one measure of modern-day Germany's damnation.

"I really wouldn't," Peggy said. *Honest! Cross my heart and hope to die!* She would have promised anything and done damn near anything to escape the *Reich*. If he'd propositioned her, she wouldn't have loosened his teeth for him. She wouldn't have come across, but still. . . .

"I am sorry. I have not the discretion to permit this." Now Hoppe did sound as if he might mean it, anyhow.

"Who does?" Peggy asked. "Ribbentrop?"

"*Herr von* Ribbentrop may have the authority." Konrad Hoppe stressed the aristocratic *von,* which the Nazi Foreign Minister, as Peggy understood it, had bought. "He may, I say."

"He's the head of the Foreign Ministry, right?" Peggy said. "If he doesn't, who does, for crying out loud?"

"Above the Foreign Minister—above everyone—is always the *Führer.*" Hoppe pointed out the obvious.

"Oh, my aching back!" Peggy burst out. "How am I supposed to get Hitler to pay attention to my case? There's a war on."

"I am afraid I can offer on that score no suggestions," the Nazi bureaucrat answered. "If you will excuse me . . ." He bowed once more and walked out without waiting to see whether Peggy would excuse him or not.

She thought about getting on the train for Denmark even if the Foreign Ministry said she couldn't. She not only thought about it, she headed for the station.

She presented her ticket. Then she had to present her passport. The conductor—he wasn't quite a conductor, but a more prominent kind of official, with a uniform a U.S. major general would have envied—checked her name against a list. As soon as he did that, she knew her goose was cooked. Damn Teutonic thoroughness anyway!

His Toploftiness looked up from the sheet of paper. "I am sorry, but for you travel is *verboten*," he said.

"It's not fair! It's not right!" she squawked.

The railroad official shrugged. "I am sorry. I can about that nothing do. I do not the orders give. I only carry them out."

"Right," Peggy said tightly. "What am I supposed to do now?"

"Go back to your hotel," the man replied. "Wait for German victory. It will soon come. Then, I have no doubt, you will be able where you please to travel. Although, since you are here in the *Reich* at this world-historical time, why would you anywhere else care to go?"

Peggy could have told him. She came that close—*that* close—to doing it. In the end, she held her tongue. Yeah, maybe she really and truly was growing up. Or maybe—and more likely—the *Gestapo* could scare the bejesus out of an immature person, too.

VACLAV JEZEK LOVED HIS NEW antitank rifle. The damn thing was long and heavy. It kicked like a mule. The round it fired was as big as his thumb. Despite that, it wouldn't penetrate all the armor on a first-rate German panzer. But against side or rear panels, it had a good chance of punching through. Then it would do something nasty to the men inside the metal monster, or maybe to the engine.

He didn't like the way he'd got his hands on the antitank rifle. The Frenchman who had lugged it around lost the top of his head to a bullet or shell fragment. He wasn't pretty when Vaclav found him. He'd bled all over the weapon, too. Now, though, you could hardly see the stains.

Somebody moved in the bushes a few hundred meters ahead. Jezek swung the rifle in that direction. It shot nice and flat out to a kilometer and more. What you could see, you could hit, and what you could hit. . . . Using the antitank rifle against a mere soldier was like killing a flea by dropping a house on it. Vaclav didn't care. He wanted Germans dead, and he wasn't fussy about how they got that way.

Czechs and Frenchmen and a few Englishmen were all intermingled here. They shouldn't have been, but the latest German drive had thrown the defenders in the Ardennes into confusion. Jezek had seen that in Czechoslovakia, to his sorrow. After a panzer thrust pierced the line you were trying to hold, you had to scramble like a madman to piece together a new one farther back. And the Germans were still pushing forward, and shelling you, and bombing you. . . .

"Anybody have more clips for the antitank rifle?" he called in Czech. He could have said the same thing in German, but it probably would have got him shot. He didn't speak French or English.

But one of the French noncoms assigned as liaison to the Czechs translated for Vaclav. The man's Czech was none too good, but he spoke French fine. And a couple of soldiers coughed up the fat clips Vaclav needed.

"Thanks," he said as he stowed them in a sack on his belt—they were too big for standard ammunition pouches.

"Any time, pal. I bet I've hated the Nazis longer than you have," the sergeant said. He had a slight guttural accent, curly auburn hair, and a formidable plow of a nose.

Another Jew. They're fucking everywhere, Jezek thought. The guy named David was back of the lines with a bullet through his leg right now. He'd get better. Whether the line would wasn't so obvious.

"I wouldn't be surprised," Vaclav said aloud. This fellow wouldn't duck out of the fight the way the damned Slovaks did, anyhow.

German 105s started tearing up the landscape a few hundred meters off to the south. Nobody in Vaclav's bunch even flinched. That wasn't close enough to worry about. The noncom said, "Maybe there'll be some cows down, and we can get ourselves fresh beef."

"Or pork." The words came out of Vaclav's mouth before he thought about them.

He didn't faze the noncom in French uniform. "I've eaten it," the guy said. "Beats the crap out of going hungry."

"Yeah, well, what doesn't?" Jezek replied.

They never got the chance to see if the Germans had done some worthwhile butchery for a change. Stukas screamed down from a treacherously clear sky. "Down!" Several soldiers yelled the same thing at the same time. Vaclav and the Jewish sergeant were two of them. They both fit action to word. Vaclav was already tearing at the muddy ground with his entrenching tool when the first bombs hit nearby.

Blast jumped on him with hobnailed boots. Fragments of bomb casing screeched malevolently through the air. He kept on impersonating a mole. Stukas came in bigger waves than this.

Sure as hell, more of them wailed down on him and his buddies. He'd heard they had sirens mounted on their landing gear to make them sound even scarier than they would have otherwise. As far as he was concerned, that was overdoing it. The damn things were scary enough anyhow.

The sergeant lay on his back, firing up at them with his rifle. That took guts, but it was bound to be a waste of ammo. How could you hit something that was going 500 kilometers an hour?

People were shrieking and wailing in a godawful Babel of languages. Medics ran here and there, slapping on bandages and lugging wounded soldiers away on stretchers. The medics wore Red Cross armbands and smocks. Some of them had painted Red Crosses in white circles on either side of their helmets. Every so often, they got shot anyway. German medics wore the same kind of outfits. Vaclav had never aimed at one of them on purpose. Still, he was sure they stopped bullets, too.

A French officer shouted something. It might as well have been in

Japanese for all the sense it made to Vaclav. The redheaded Jew—*just like Judas,* Jezek thought—translated: "We've got to get back over the Semoy. They're going to blow the bridges pretty soon, he says, to help stop the Germans."

"They think that will?" Vaclav didn't believe it for a minute. The Nazis were too good with pontoon bridges and rubber boats and parachutists and what have you.

"That's what he says." After a moment, the sergeant added, "Do you want to get stuck here?"

"Well—no," Vaclav admitted—the only answer that question could have.

A crackle of machine-gun fire made him hit the dirt again. Here came an obsolete but nasty little Panzer I, spitting bullets from both guns in the turret. No French tanks anywhere close by, of course. They were like policemen—never around when you needed them.

But a Panzer I wasn't so goddamn tough. Vaclav had heard they were originally intended as nothing more than training vehicles. They got thrown into combat when Hitler jumped Czechoslovakia. Even their frontal armor was only thirteen millimeters thick. That kept out small-arms fire. Anything more . . .

He worked the bolt and chambered a round. He wasn't shooting at a Stuka; the little German tank made a fine target. The tank commander, who was also the gunner, sat right between the machine guns. As always, the antitank rifle kicked like a son of a bitch. He'd have a nasty bruise on his shoulder. He didn't care, though, not when the Panzer I's machine guns suddenly fell silent.

"Good shot!" the Jewish sergeant yelled. The tank drove on, but so what? The driver couldn't shoot while he was driving.

And the Allied soldiers on this side of the Semoy couldn't stop the Nazis. Vaclav thanked God no German bombers struck while he was tramping over the bridge. He would have thanked God a lot more had

He done worse to the enemy sooner. In a world where you didn't get many big favors, you needed to be properly grateful for the small ones.

"COME ON! THIS WAY!" THE engineer called in a low, urgent voice. Willi Dernen assumed he was an engineer, anyhow. It was the middle of the night, and as black as the Jew Süss' heart outside. The man went on, "The pontoon bridge is right here. It has rope rails, so hang on to those. And so help me God, you assholes, we'll drown the first fucking *Dummkopf* who lights a cigarette before he's half a kilometer away from it!"

Who would be that stupid? Willi wondered. But the question answered itself. A *Dummkopf* would, that was who. Like every other outfit in the world, the *Wehrmacht* had its share and then some. A jerk who decided he needed a smoke right now would damn well light up, and so what if he gave the game away to some watching Frenchman?

Willi's feet thudded on planks. He reached out and found the rope. It guided him across the Semoy. The bridge swayed under his weight and that of his comrades, almost as if he were on the deck of a boat.

"You heard the man," Corporal Baatz said loudly. "No smoking!"

The engineer spoke in a deadly whisper: "Whoever you are, big-mouth, shut the fuck up!"

Snickers ran through Baatz's squad. One of them was Willi's. He was only an ordinary *Landser;* he didn't have the rank to tell Awful Arno where to head in. The engineer sure did—or acted as if he did, which was every bit as good. Baatz didn't let out another peep, even to protest.

Somebody up ahead said, "Careful. You're coming to the end of the bridge." Maybe fifteen seconds later, he said it again, and then again, to let the troops gauge where he was. Willi almost tripped anyhow, when the planking gave way to mud.

"Second platoon, form up on me!" That was Lieutenant Georg

Gross, who'd taken Neustadt's place after the former platoon commander bought his plot. Gross seemed like a pretty good guy, even if he
didn't ride herd on Arno Baatz hard enough to suit Willi. To an officer,
Baatz probably looked like a pretty good noncom. That only showed officers weren't as smart as they thought they were.

Somebody stepped on Willi's foot. "Ouch!" he said—quietly. "Watch
it," he added.

"Sorry," the other soldier said, and then, "Willi?"

"Wolfgang?" Willi chuckled. "Well, that's one way to find each other
in the dark."

"Listen to me, men," Lieutenant Gross said. "*Listen* to me, dammit!
The objective is Charleville-Mézières, southwest of here." The way he
pronounced the town's name said he spoke French, as Neustadt had before him. Much good it had done the other platoon leader. Gross went
on, "We've got about ten kilometers of marching to do before we get
there, maybe twelve. We'll go through the Bois des Hazelles—the Hazelwood—for part of the way. It should give us some cover."

"Depends," Wolfgang Storch muttered. "How many goddamn
Frenchies are in it now?"

"Questions?" Gross asked. Nobody said anything loud enough for
him to hear it. Wolfgang's question was a good one, but the lieutenant
wouldn't be able to answer it. They'd have to find out: the hard way,
odds were.

Southwest . . . Willi looked up into the sky, but clouds covered it and
told him nothing. He hoped it didn't start to snow while they were
marching. That would be all they needed, wouldn't it?

Willi might not know southwest from artichokes, but a soft click
and a slight rasp said Lieutenant Gross was opening his pocket com-
pass. "This way," he said confidently. "Follow me."

Like the fellow at the end of the pontoon bridge, he spoke up every
so often to let his men know where he was. Willi tramped along, trying
not to think. He wished he were back in Breslau and home in bed, or

even wrapped in a blanket in some shell hole. It was cold, and getting colder. Marching warmed, but only so much.

Some people did light up once they got far enough away from the bridge. The smell of harsh French tobacco filled the frosty air. Almost everybody smoked looted Gauloises or Gitanes in preference to the Junos and Privats and other German brands that came up along with the rations. The cigarettes the *Wehrmacht* got were supposed to be better than what civilians smoked back home. That only went to show better wasn't the same as good.

Ten or twelve kilometers. A couple of easy hours in the daylight. In black night, feeling his way along, stumbling or falling every so often, getting thwacked by branches that he couldn't see in the Hazelwood, Willi didn't have much fun. He also didn't go very fast. Neither did anyone else.

And there *were* Frenchmen in the Bois des Hazelles. Willi and his pals had to be coming to the end of it—the sky was starting to go from black to charcoal gray in the southeast—when someone called out, *"Qui va?"*

"Un ami," Lieutenant Gross said. *Ami* meant *friend;* Willi had picked that up from surrendering Frenchmen. Now—would it do the trick?

It didn't. The *poilu* gave forth with a fresh challenge, one Willi didn't get. Maybe he wanted a password. Whatever he wanted, Gross didn't have it. The shooting started a moment later.

The froggies, damn them, had a machine gun right there. It spat fire in the darkness. Tracers stabbed out at the oncoming Germans. They were scary as hell. Willi flopped down on his belly and crawled forward like a slug. He didn't want to get a centimeter higher off the ground than he had to.

As he crawled, he realized that those tracers weren't doing the guys at the Hotchkiss gun any favors. Every time the machine gunners opened up, they guided their enemies toward them. And it wasn't really light enough for them to see what they were aiming at. So . . .

Willi yanked the fuse cord on a potato-masher grenade. He flung it toward the machine gunners, who had no idea he was there. But the grenade hit a branch or something, because it didn't burst where he wanted it to. The Frenchmen serving the gun yelled, but they didn't scream. He froze. If they spotted him, he was sausage meat—and it was getting lighter.

Something off to one side distracted them. They turned the Hotchkiss in that direction and started banging away. They nailed somebody, too. That shriek sounded bad. But, while they were busy over there, Willi slithered behind a—hazel?—tree.

He pulled another grenade off his belt. He threw this one sidearm: not the way they taught you in basic, but he wanted to keep it low so it didn't bounce off anything. Then he flattened out again. If this one didn't do the job, though, he had the bad feeling flattening out wouldn't be enough to save his young ass.

Bang! He got screams this time. Then it was forward, as fast as he could scramble. He had no idea how badly hurt the Frenchmen were. He had to finish them before they or their buddies got that machine gun going again.

They were down. They were thrashing, not worried about the Hotchkiss at all. He shot them to make sure they didn't worry about anything else again. He was putting a fresh clip on his Mauser when a shape loomed up out of the morning twilight. He started to give it the bayonet, but checked himself when he recognized the familiar shape of a *Stahlhelm.*

With a dry chuckle, Corporal Baatz said, "I would've plugged you before you could drive that home."

"Let's go after the Frenchmen," Willi answered, and left it right there. He didn't think Baatz could have got him if he'd followed through, and he was half sorry he hadn't. Maybe more than half sorry.

More machine guns—and *poilus* with rifles, grenades, mortars, and all the other usual nastiness—crowded the Hazelwood. Methodically, the Germans cleaned them out and pressed on toward Charleville-Mézières. Panzers drew tracks across the snow on the flat, open country south and east of the woods. Pillars of smoke rising to the cloudy sky marked the pyres of a couple that would go no farther. But the runners were the ones that mattered. The French tried to make a stand in front of the town. Cannon and machine-gun fire from the German army sent them tumbling back in retreat.

Willi looked around. There was Wolfgang. His bayonet had blood on it—not Arno Baatz's, but somebody's, all right. "Where's the lieutenant?" Willi asked him.

"Down. I bet he loses his arm," Wolfgang answered. "The fucking Hotchkiss got him just before somebody did for it."

"That was me," Willi said.

"Yeah? Well, it needed doing." Storch paused to light up. Then he said, "Sergeant Pieck caught one right through the foot, too. That means Awful Arno's got a section—maybe the platoon, till they give us a new officer."

"Jesus Christ! I knew I should have stuck him!" Willi explained how he'd almost bayoneted Baatz by the French machine gun. His buddy was good for even more reasons why he should have than he'd thought of for himself. Willi pulled a pack of Gauloises out of his pocket, but the familiar winged helmet shielded no more cigarettes. "Let me bum a butt off you."

"What a useless creature you are! First you didn't scrag the corporal, and now you steal my smokes." Wolfgang gave him his own pack. Willi did have a match. He got the cigarette going. The two *Landsers* tramped on.

THE POLES HAD A GOOD medium bomber. The PZL P-37 could carry more than twice the bomb load of a Tupolev SB-2. Fortunately for the Red Army and Air Force, the Poles didn't have a hell of a lot of them.

Whenever the enemy found a chance, he did his best to strike at the airstrips the Red Air Force used.

Sergei Yaroslavsky took those raids for granted. The Poles made them at high altitude, and they got out of Soviet airspace in a hurry. An occasional bomb gave the groundcrew some work to do repairing a runway. More often than not, the bombs missed by hundreds of meters or even by kilometers. Nothing to get excited about.

Then things changed. Sergei was barely awake when antiaircraft guns around the airstrip started banging away at sunrise. He tumbled out of his cot, wondering if the gunners had the galloping jimjams.

They didn't. Bombs crashed down on the runways and on the bombers near them. Not all the bombers were in revetments, the way they should have been. It hadn't seemed worth the trouble.

"Those aren't Elks!" somebody yelled—that was the P-37's nickname. "Those are motherfucking Stukas!"

"*Bozhemoi!*" Yaroslavsky shouted. A bombardier said something electric about the way the Devil's grandmother had buggered up the antiaircraft guns. Satan and his relatives might be as out of fashion as God, but people hadn't forgotten about them, either.

Sergei threw himself flat in the snow. That was all he could do now. One after another, the Fascist dive-bombers stooped on the airstrip like falcons after pigeons.

Pigeons could at least try to get away. To mix the metaphor, the bombers on the ground were sitting ducks. And, while the pilots of those Ju-87s might be goddamn Nazi bastards, they were also more than competent professionals. One after another, they released their bombs, fired a burst from their forward machine guns, pulled out of their dives, and zoomed off to the northwest. They might almost have performed an aerial ballet.

The Germans had a word for that kind of ballet (they would): a *Totentanz,* a dance of death. Here, they were dishing it out. The Soviets had no choice but to take it.

Machine-gun bullets thudded into the snowbank, much too close to Sergei. Little white powdery puffs shot up into the air at the impacts. If a round hit him, a little red fountain might join the white. He burrowed into the drift. Burrowing wouldn't do him a kopek's worth of good, but he did it anyway. Fear and instinct drove harder than reason.

Not all the explosions came from German bombs. The SB-2s had been gassed up and bombed up. Before long, they would have taken off and punished the semifascist Poles. Well, behind the semifascist Poles loomed the Fascist Germans. And, no matter how virtuous the Soviets might be, they were getting hammered this morning.

Ever so cautiously, Sergei stuck up his head. The Stukas were gone, which didn't make the airstrip a safe place. An SB-2 a couple of hundred meters away was burning like the inside of a blast furnace. Ammunition for the plane's guns cooked off with a cheerful popping noise, spraying bullets every which way. And then one of the bombs—or maybe all of the bombs—blew.

What had been a fire turned into a fireball. Stunned, half deafened, Sergei burrowed into the snow again. Something large and hot smashed down well behind him—the explosion had thrown it a long, long way. He could tell it was hot because even his afflicted ears made out the hiss of steam coming off it as the snow put it out.

Another Tupolev bomber blew up, not quite so spectacularly—or maybe it was just farther away. Several more were on fire. One hadn't burned, but was broken in half behind the bomb bay. Intact SB-2s were the exception, not the rule. Whatever punishment the Poles were going to get would have to come from some other airstrip today.

Sergei made himself stand up. He looked around to see what he could do that might help. Other dazed survivors were also emerging from the snow like hares coming out of their burrows. Steaming patches here and there marked big chunks of wreckage.

And bloody patches here and there marked dead and wounded men. What looked like a chunk of aileron had decapitated the best mechanic at the airstrip. Sergei swore, but nobody could do anything for that poor son of a bitch now. The fellows who thrashed and writhed still had hope. Some of them did, anyhow.

Stooping beside a groundcrew man who groaned as he clutched a shattered ankle, Sergei wondered what kind of hope the man had. If he didn't bleed to death or die of gangrene or septicemia, he'd survive. The bomber pilot was no doctor, but he didn't see how the groundcrew man would keep that foot. What kind of life did a cripple have?

You should have wondered about that sooner, he thought. But pilots seldom got crippled. If anything went wrong in the air, or if your plane got shot down, you were likely to buy the whole plot, not part of one. Nobody in the USSR bought or sold or owned land, but Soviet flyers talked the same way as their Western counterparts.

After doing what he could to bandage the groundcrew man and telling a few reassuring lies, Sergei looked northwest once more: after the long-gone Stukas. In Czechoslovakia, he'd seen the Germans were good. Now he saw how good they could be with the advantage of surprise. *How smart were we to get into a war with people like this?* he wondered.

Chapter 16

Samuel Goldman passed several sheets of closely written paper to the visitor. "Here you are, Friedrich," he said, his tone an odd mixture of cringing and pride. "Everything that can be known about Xenophanes is here."

Sarah Goldman listened from the kitchen as her father and the other professor of ancient history talked. Friedrich Lauterbach had studied under her father. He still felt kindly toward him—this article for Pauly-Wissowa was a case in point. When it saw print, it would go under Lauterbach's name: he, after all, was an Aryan. But he paid Samuel Goldman for the work, and the family badly needed the money.

Now he said, "Thank you very much. I will type it myself tonight, so no secretary finds out about our . . . arrangement."

"Whatever you need to be safe," Sarah's father said. "Take a look at it now, if you care to. I have been very thorough." He was proud of that, too. Yes, he really might as well have been a German—except the damned Germans wouldn't let him.

"I'm sure it's fine, Samuel. Who knows your work better than I do, after all?" Lauterbach paused for a moment. "Here—let me give you this." As he always did, he sounded embarrassed about having to do business this way.

Another pause followed, a longer one. Sarah had to strain to hear her father's next words, for his voice dropped almost to a whisper: "But this is too much. This is much too much, twice as much as I could have expected for—"

"I'm giving you what I can," Lauterbach said. "There won't be any more, I'm afraid, not from me. I got my call-up papers yesterday. That's why I have to do my typing in a hurry."

"Oh," Samuel Goldman said, and then, "Stay safe. I would be with you if I could."

"You did what you had to do the last time around," the younger man said. "I know that—you could hardly walk when I studied with you."

"That isn't what's keeping me out now," Sarah's father said pointedly.

"And I know that," Lauterbach answered. "I think it's . . . unfortunate. But what can I do about it? I am only one man, and not a very brave one."

"As long as you don't tell the Tommies and the *poilus,* they won't know," Sarah's father said with a wry chuckle. "If I could fool them, so can you. You'll do fine. I'm sure of it."

"That makes one of us," Lauterbach said with a dry laugh of his own. "I'd better go, I'm afraid."

"True," Sarah's father agreed. "If they can prove you're friends with a Jew, that may be more dangerous than going up to the front."

"If things were different . . ." Lauterbach sighed. "But they aren't, and they aren't likely to be. Still, you've got a pretty daughter." Three or four footsteps took him to the door. It closed behind him.

He was, Sarah remembered, single. Did he mean . . . ? She shrugged. What he meant didn't matter, because things weren't different, and they sure weren't likely to be. He was dead right about that.

She went out into the front room. Her father stood there, holding the banknotes with the eagles and swastikas. Even the money proclaimed that things weren't going to be different. Samuel Goldman looked up. "You were listening?" he asked.

"*Ja.*" Sarah nodded. "Wasn't I supposed to?"

"It's all right." He grimaced. "I don't know what we'll do for cash when this runs out, though."

"Isn't there anyone else who will let you write for him?" Sarah asked.

"Maybe." Her father looked—and sounded—dubious. "The others have always been more nervous about it than Friedrich . . . and who can blame them?" His mouth twisted. "They never paid as well, either. But we do what we can, not what we want to, eh?"

"*Ja,*" Sarah said again. What else was there to say? She did her best to find something: "Saul brings in a little money."

"As a laborer." It wasn't quite as if her father said, *As a pimp,* but it was close. He went on, "He has a brain. He should use it. He should have the chance to use it. Or he should be a soldier. He'd make a better one than Friedrich Lauterbach, and you can bet on that."

"He doesn't mind so much. Honest, Papa, he doesn't." Sarah knew she was right about that. Her big brother had always exulted in his strength on the soccer pitch. Working with his body instead of his brain didn't humiliate him the way it would have their father.

"Why God decided to give me a water buffalo for a son, only He knows," Samuel Goldman said, and let it go at that.

The other worry was that, even though the Goldmans had money, they couldn't buy much. Nobody in wartime Germany could buy a great deal, but Jews suffered worse than ordinary Germans. They could buy only from shops run by their fellow Jews, and those shops always had less to sell than others. Food got worse and worse. Sarah's mother was a good cook, but disguise could go only so far.

Noodles flavored with nasty cheese didn't make much of a supper. Sarah picked at hers. So did her father. Saul shoveled in everything in front of him and looked around to see what else he could get.

"You can have mine if you want," Sarah said. "I'm not really hungry." The last part of that wasn't true, but she didn't feel like eating the mess in front of her.

"Thanks!" Saul said. As Sarah passed him her plate, her mother gave her a dirty look. Hanna Goldman wanted everybody to eat a lot all the time. Maybe the noodles and cheese could have been worse, but they could have been a lot better, too. As far as Sarah was concerned, Saul was welcome to them if he wanted them so much.

And he did. By the way he glanced up after he made them disappear, he could have put away another couple of helpings. But there were no more. He sighed and said, "The coffee will be ersatz, won't it?"

"*Aber natürlich*," Mother answered. "Burnt barley, with a little chicory if we're lucky."

"Some luck," Father said.

"Oh, well." Saul shrugged his broad shoulders. "The Army isn't getting much better?"

"How do you know that?" Samuel Goldman always looked for evidence. In better times, Sarah had admired that. Now she wondered whether it made any difference at all. Evidence? What did the Nazis care about that? But they had the guns and the goons. With those, they made evidence of their own.

What could you do if you'd lived by reason your whole life long but reason suddenly didn't count any more? Could you do anything at all, or were you just supposed to lie down and die?

That was what the Nazis wanted German Jews to do. That the Nazis wanted it was the best reason not to do it, as far as Sarah was concerned.

She wished her family had got out of Germany while escape was still possible. But her father clung too fiercely to his Germanness to see the need. He could see it now. Easy enough, when it was too late.

Instead of explaining how he knew, Saul said, "Maybe the British will send planes over tonight."

"How can you sound so cheerful about it?" Sarah asked him. "They're liable to blow us up." With Jews having to shelter in their homes, enemy bombers were more likely to blow them up than anybody else.

Her brother only shrugged again. "They haven't yet. And the more Nazis they send to the Devil, the better I'll like it. If I had a gun . . ."

"Saul," Samuel Goldman said sharply. "That will be enough of that."

"Should I turn the other cheek?" Saul retorted. "I don't see what for. I'm no Christian. They keep reminding me of that, in case I'm not smart enough to figure it out for myself."

"They're no Christians, either," Father said. "Pagans. Barbarians." He looked disgusted. "And they're proud of it, too." A Roman noble talking about wandering Ostrogoths could have packed no more scorn into his voice.

He would have silenced Sarah. Saul still felt like locking horns. "What about the German Christians?" he said. "Their preachers wear Nazi uniforms. Even the Catholics have swastikas in their churches. The students at their universities give the Nazi salute." His right arm shot out.

"They can call themselves whatever they want. The name is not the thing," Father insisted. "Trying to make you believe it is—that's only one more lie."

"Maybe so," Saul said. "But we both tried to join the *Wehrmacht* anyway, didn't we? And if they'd only let us, we'd be braying '*Heil* Hitler!' like all the other donkeys in the *Reich*, wouldn't we?"

Samuel Goldman opened his mouth, then closed it again. At last, he said, "I have no answer for that, because we would. If they'd let us be Germans, Germans we would have been. Since they make us into something else . . ." He left the table sooner than he might have.

No one else had much to say after that, either.

British bombers didn't visit Münster. They didn't drop anything close by, either. Especially in nighttime quiet, the sound of bombs going off carried a long, long way.

Saul went off to work early the next morning. Father looked lost, bewildered. He had nothing to do—nothing that would yield a Reichsmark, anyway. He started to fill his pipe, then thought better of it. The tobacco ration was miserably small. What he got smelled like burning overshoes, too.

Sarah went out shopping with her mother. When she was small, she remembered, she'd really enjoyed that. When she was small, they could walk into any shop in Münster and buy whatever they wanted. Shopkeepers fawned on them, as they fawned on any other customers.

Everything changed after the Nazis took over. Brownshirts stuck big signs—GERMANS! DON'T BUY FROM JEWS!—on the windows of Jewish-owned stores. And Jews were no longer welcome in shops run by Aryans. Some of the German shopkeepers seemed embarrassed about it. They did what they had to do to get along, no more. Others, though . . . Others gloated. Those were the scary ones.

Only a handful of shops Jews could go into were left now. The war'd just made things worse—not only for Jews, but for everybody. And the British air raids added to the burden of fear. The people across the street—Aryans—never stopped complaining about how their favorite bakery was gone. "Like someone yanked a tooth. It's not there any more," Frau Breisach would grumble.

She didn't know when she was well off. Of course she doesn't— she's an Aryan, Sarah thought. The one bakery in Münster that Jews could still use was way over on the far side of town. It wasn't open very

often, and didn't have much when it was. But when the choice lay between not much and nothing at all . . . you went over to the far side of
town.

They had a little wire basket with wheels. Sarah pulled it along behind her. It felt like nothing now. On the way back, it would be heavier.
She hoped it would, anyhow. Sometimes the bakery didn't open, or it
was sold out, or . . . *I won't think about any of that,* Sarah told herself
fiercely.

A gang of laborers was repairing a bomb crater in the middle of the
street. And there was Saul, as deft with a shovel as Father was with Greek
irregular verbs. He turned the Nazi slogan on its head: he drew joy
through strength.

The gang overseer was a wizened little man in his forties. The left
sleeve of his shirt was pinned-up and empty. *Maimed in the war,* Sarah
thought. *Maimed in the last war,* she amended. How many would get
maimed in this one? Too many—that seemed sure.

Maimed or not, he carried a swagger stick in his right hand. He also
had a foul mouth, and didn't care if women heard him use it. "Work
harder, you lazy prick!" he yelled, and lightly swatted a laborer on the
behind.

"*Ja, ja,*" the fellow muttered, and went on working the same way he
had before.

That didn't make the overseer any happier. "And you, too, you fucking kike!" he bellowed. When he hit Saul in the back with the swagger
stick, it was no tap. The whack echoed like a gunshot. Sarah thought it
would have knocked her over.

It barely staggered her big brother. Saul Goldman responded with
what had to be instinct, as he might have on the soccer pitch. He'd been
hit. He had a weapon in his hands. He used it. The flat of the shovel
blade crashed into the side of the overseer's head.

The man went down as if he'd stopped an artillery shell. His skull was all caved in and bloody. Sarah and her mother let out identical shrieks of horror—anyone could see that the overseer would never get up again.

Saul stared at the man he'd killed. He stared at his mother and his sister—all that in maybe a second and a half. Then he threw down the gore-spattered shovel. It clattered on the cobbles. He turned and ran as if a million demons were at his heels.

"After him!" one of the other laborers shouted. Chasing a Jew was more fun than fixing a bomb crater any day of the week. The gang pounded after Saul, some of them still brandishing their spades.

Sarah and her mother looked at each other, each mirroring the other's anguish. As if on cue, they both burst into tears.

A FRENCH PRIVATE FIRST CLASS wore a little brown hash mark on his sleeve to distinguish him from an ordinary private. Luc Harcourt was less than delighted when the indestructible Sergeant Demange told him he'd been promoted. "I'd've had more fun getting the clap," he said.

Demange's Gitane twitched as he chuckled. "Think of it as congratulations for living this long," he said.

Luc did. Suddenly, being a private first class looked a lot better. He said so, adding, "After all the shit I've gone through to get this, I'll be a general by the time the war finally ends."

"France is in trouble, yes. I hope to Christ France isn't in that much trouble," Demange said.

"Kiss my ass," Luc said. The sergeant only laughed. Luc had earned the right to swear at him. He did remember that he had to pick his spots with care.

"Anyway, sew that stupid thing on," Sergeant Demange told him. "You could be leading a squad at five minutes' notice. Hell, a couple of lucky German shell bursts and you could be leading a platoon."

He wasn't kidding. Luc had seen how fast casualties could chew a unit to pieces. He and Demange were two of not very many men who'd been with the company since before the German blow fell on the Low Countries. The rest were replacements, or replacements of replacements, or sometimes. . . .

Luc didn't want to command a squad, much less a platoon. All he wanted to do was hunker down tight, live through the war, and get on with his life. Not that anyone from Sergeant Demange on up cared what he wanted, of course.

"See? I told you France was in trouble," the veteran underofficer said. "And you will be, too, if you don't get cracking."

"Right." Luc knew better than to argue. Somewhere in his pack he had a little housewife with needle and thread. He dug it out and sewed on the hash mark. He would never put a seamstress out of business. He'd sewn up a couple of rips in his uniform. His stitches were large and dark and ugly, like the ones that held together the pieces of the Frankenstein monster in the American film.

French 75s threw shells at the Germans on the other side of the Aisne. Luc's company was dug in a couple of kilometers west of Soissons. The town had taken a beating in the Franco-Prussian War and again in the Great War. Now it was catching hell one more time. Luc had come through it on the way to this position. Bombs and shells had wrecked the cathedral; bits of thirteenth-century stained glass lay shattered in the streets. A priest stood by the ruins with tears running down his face. Luc had no tears left for people, let alone things.

Machine guns started stuttering up by the river. *French or German?* Luc wondered, cocking his head to one side to hear better. *Both,* he thought. That wasn't so good.

Sergeant Demange must have decided the same thing. "Are those shitheads trying to force a crossing?" he growled. "They'd better not get over, that's all I've got to say."

"Let's move!" Luc grabbed his rifle. He liked the idea of Germans on the south bank of the Aisne no better than Demange.

As they hurried up toward the riverbank, they gathered as many other soldiers as they could. Damned if that hash mark on Luc's sleeve didn't make ordinary privates follow him without arguing or asking a lot of questions. *I could get used to this,* he thought.

There was smoke on the river: not the ordinary war smoke of burning houses and vehicles, but a thick chemical haze the Germans used to mask what they were doing on the other side. Out of the smoke came black rubber boats paddled by field-gray soldiers in coal-scuttle helmets. Sure as the devil, the *Boches* were trying to get over.

French machine guns stammered out death again. A German dropped his paddle and slumped down in his raft. Then another one got hit, and another. The raft slewed sideways. It was probably leaking, too. German machine guns across the Aisne shot back, trying to silence the French fire. They put out more rounds per minute than the ones the French used, but they couldn't knock them out of action.

Luc flopped down behind some bushes and started shooting at the Germans in their rafts. It wasn't fair—they couldn't shoot back. That bothered him till a couple of machine-gun bullets cracked past maybe half a meter above his head. They cured any chivalrous notions he might have had.

Two or three rubber rafts actually made it to the south bank of the Aisne. The unhurt Germans in them jumped up and tried to set up some kind of bridgehead. With all that French firepower concentrated on them, they never had a chance. Inside of a few minutes, they were all dead or wounded.

"Assholes'll have to do better than *that,*" Sergeant Demange said, a fresh cigarette in his mouth and a fresh clip on his rifle.

"What else have they got behind that smoke?" Luc asked.

"We'll know in a few minutes," Demange answered, sending up

smoke signals of his own. "Looks like it's blowing away." He and Luc and the rest of the French defenders waited. Then he said one thing more: "Fuck me."

The Germans had lined up a couple of dozen tanks—Panzer IIs and captured Czech machines—on the north bank of the Aisne. Their cannon all pointed toward the French positions across the river from them. To Luc's frightened eyes, it seemed as if every single one of those cannon pointed straight at him.

Every single one of them seemed to open up at the same time, too, pouring shells and more machine-gun bullets down on the French defenders. Luc hugged the ground. His rifle was useless against those steel monsters. The machine gunners fired back at the German armor. He watched tracers fly across the Aisne and ricochets harmlessly spark off the tanks' armored carapaces.

One by one, the French machine guns fell silent. Luc didn't think the gunners were lying low, waiting to massacre the next wave of German rubber boats. He thought they were dead. Those cannon weren't all pointing at him after all. They were pointing at the guns that could do the German assault troops the most harm.

That second wave of boats splashed into the river even while the cannonading went on. The *Boches* hadn't silenced everything on the south bank: here and there, riflemen and even a machine gun or two opened up on the soldiers who paddled like men possessed.

But now the French didn't have enough firepower to keep the rubber boats from beaching on the near bank. Luc raised up a little to shoot at the men leaping out of the boats. As soon as he did, a machine gun from one of the tanks on the far bank started banging away at him. He had to flatten out again if he wanted to stay alive.

Some of the German assault troops carried submachine guns with big drum magazines. French doctrine scorned submachine guns. They fired pistol ammunition, and they were worthless out past a couple of hundred meters. Inside that range, though, they were uncommonly murderous. They threw around a hell of a lot of lead. Even if they didn't get you, they made you stay down so you couldn't shoot back.

And the damned *Boches* had brought along real machine guns, too. Hearing that malevolent crackle at such close range made Luc's asshole pucker. He had to bear down tight on his bladder to keep from wetting himself.

"Back!" Sergeant Demange's raspy voice penetrated the din. "We've got to get out of here, form a line somewhere else!"

"How?" Luc asked, which seemed to him the very best of good questions.

Even through the rattle of the German machine guns, he heard the underofficer laugh. "Carefully, sonny, carefully, unless you aim to get your dick shot off."

Even thinking of that made Luc want to clutch at himself. He crawled away from the riverbank, doing his best to keep the bushes between himself and the *Boches*. Only a few random bullets came his way. The Germans didn't seem to know he was there: news good enough to make an atheist thank God.

He flopped down again behind the crest of a small swell of ground that shielded him from the enemy. Sergeant Demange lay a few meters away, still puffing on a cigarette butt. "What do we do?" Luc said. "How do we throw them back into the river?"

"If we can bring a lot of tanks forward in a hurry, that might turn the trick." Demange stubbed out the cigarette in the dirt. "But what are the odds, eh?"

Luc mournfully considered them. "Not good," he said. "The Germans always have plenty of tanks where they need them the most. How come we can't do the same thing?"

"Because their High Command doesn't fight with its head up its ass," Demange answered. He rose up to shoot at somebody heading up-slope toward them. A wild scream said he'd hit what he aimed at, too.

Chambering a new round, he went on, "They know it's the twentieth century, damn them. How come we don't have any dive-bombers plastering the shit out of them right now?"

Having cowered under more Stukas than he cared to remember, Luc said, "I don't know, and I wish I did. How come we don't?"

"If we were fighting the Kaiser's army, we'd wallop the snot out of it," Demange replied. "It's the curse of winning—you get ready to do the same damn thing over again. The Germans lost, so they figured they'd better try something new. Now we're on the receiving end."

"Lucky us," Luc said in hollow tones. Ever so cautiously, he too peered back the way he'd come. The lines on that dark helmet moving through dead grass were unmistakable. He fired. The *Boche* scrambled for cover. Luc fired again. The German went down with a howl. He wasn't dead, but he wasn't dangerous any more, either. That would do.

"Good job," Demange said. "But we won't stop them all by ourselves. I wonder if anybody will, this side of Paris."

PEKING IN SUMMER WAS HOT and dusty. During the winter, it was colder than a witch's tit. How cold was that? Marines who'd been in Chicago said it was that cold. Pete McGill could compare it to his native New York City. He'd known some cold weather there, but Peking bottomed out worse.

And Peking would have felt cold even if it were in the nineties. As long as the Marines stayed close to the American legation, they were okay. But if they strayed very far into the city, Japanese soldiers were much too likely to whale the crap out of them.

Like any other Marine, McGill was convinced he was a better fighting man than some little, scrawny, buck-toothed, bowlegged Jap. He was convinced he could take two or three Japs, come to that. But when the odds got steeper still, even John Henry the Steel-Driving Man would have found himself in deep water.

The odds did get steeper, too. Peking was crawling with Japs these days. Some of them kept order in the city. The Japanese way to keep order was to shoot first and not ask questions later. Since Nationalist and Communist guerrillas and freelance bandits all afflicted Peking and the surrounding area, that Wild Wild East style had its points.

But even more Japanese soldiers were getting leave in Peking and then climbing onto trains and heading out of town. Pete would have liked it if the bastards never came back, but that was bound to be too much to hope for. They weren't going back to Japan—at least, they weren't heading southeast toward Tangku or Tsingtao, the ports from which they sailed for home.

No, most of them were going northeast on some of the new lines their people had built: up into Manchukuo. That made McGill gloat. "I wouldn't have believed it," he said one day in the NCOs' club, "but the sorry sons of bitches are heading somewhere colder'n this."

"Serves 'em right, sure as hell," another corporal agreed.

Pete emptied his glass. "Hey, Danny!" he called. "Bring me another beer, chop-chop!"

"Right, boss," the Chinese bartender said. The beer came from Tsingtao. It was pretty damn good. The Germans had run the place before the Great War, and they'd built a brewery there. Hitler was a bastard, yeah, but the squareheads knew what was what with beer. The brewery was under new management these days, of course, but some of the old magic remained.

When the beer came, Pete tipped Danny a nickel. To a Chinaman, a nickel was a big deal. Danny bowed almost double. He folded one palm over the other fist, which was what the Chinese did instead of saluting.

A sergeant named Larry Koenig came and sat down with Pete. He ordered a beer, too. Danny brought it over to him. Koenig lit a cigarette and offered Pete the pack—he was a good guy. "Thanks," McGill said. He took one and leaned close for a light.

Raising his mug, Koenig said, "Mud in your eye."

"Same to you." Pete answered the salute with one of his own. They both drank. After sucking foam off his upper lip, Pete lifted his mug again and said, "Here's to all the Japs getting the hell out of Peking."

"Hey, I'll drink to that, but you'll be bluer'n your dress uniform if you hold your breath and wait for it to happen," Koenig said.

"Yeah, I know. It'd be nice, though, wouldn't it?" Pete said. "They sure are moving a lot of guys through here—moving a lot of guys out of here."

"They'll keep Peking garrisoned, though, you bet. Hell, I would in their shoes." Koenig looked at his mug in mild surprise, as if wondering how it had emptied without his noticing. He waved to Danny for a re-fill. As he waited, he went on, "They hang on here, what are the Chinese gonna do about it? Not much, not so I can see."

"Yeah, man, yeah. Looks the same way to me," Pete said. With Peking in their hands, the Japanese could spill south and west all over the place. They'd done that for a while after overrunning the place. Now the flow was going in the other direction. "What do they need so many troops up in Manchukuo for?"

"Beats me." Koenig paused while Danny set the beer on the table in front of him. A lot of Marines didn't like to talk with Chinamen hover-ing around them. Pete didn't know whether Danny was a spy or not. He didn't much care, either. He didn't know enough himself to make what he said worth anything to anybody. But if the sergeant wanted to be tight-assed about it, he could. After Danny hustled back behind the bar to build somebody a highball, Koenig resumed: "Gotta be the Russians. I've figured it every different way I could, and that's what it comes out to every goddamn time."

"You really think so?" Pete said. "That'd be one hell of a scrap."

"Damn Russians have shit closer to home than Siberia to worry about," Koenig said. "If it was me, I wouldn't have started fucking with the Polacks when they knew that was liable to bring Hitler down on their necks."

"Yeah, old Adolf's bad news, all right," Pete agreed. "Me, I wonder how much the Russians really do know these days. They've been killing off generals like it's going out of style."

"Maybe we ought to try that. I don't know about the Corps, but it'd sure as hell work wonders for the Army and the Navy," Koenig said.

Pete snorted. Then he giggled. Then he guffawed. He wasn't sure it was a good idea, but he was damn sure it was funny. "I can see the FBI guys coming up to their desks. 'You—come with us!' And out they'd go, and—*bang!*"

"Plenty of 'em nobody'd miss," Koenig said.

"Ain't it the truth!" Pete nodded. "And you know what else? I bet there hasn't been an army since Julius Caesar's day where the noncoms didn't think it'd go better if some officers got it in the neck."

"Most of the time we'd be right, too." Like any sergeant worth his salt, Koenig was sure he knew better than the guys set over him. Since Pete McGill felt the same way, he didn't argue. Koenig waved for a fresh beer before continuing, "So if the Japs and the Reds bang heads, which way do you bet? My money's on the white men."

"Yeah, everybody said the same thing about the time you were born, too, and look how that turned out," McGill said. Anybody who came to Peking got his nose rubbed in that lesson. You couldn't come here without paying attention to what had happened in the Russo-Japanese War.

Sergeant Koenig turned red. He waited till Danny gave him his new seidel, then said, "You think the little yellow bastards can take 'em?" He paid no more attention to the barman than Pete would have.

"I dunno. They've sure got more combat experience than the Russians do. Hell, they've got more combat experience than just about anybody," McGill answered. "And it's way past the back of beyond for the Russians, *and* they're fighting somewhere else, *and* their army's fucked up. So yeah, I guess maybe I figure the Japs'll win."

"I got a sawbuck says you're full of it," Koenig declared.

As far as Pete was concerned, the problems with the Marine Corps started with sergeants, not officers. That attitude would probably change the day he got his own third stripe, but he had it now. Taking a sergeant down a peg would be a pleasure—and so would winning ten bucks. "You're on," he said.

Koenig stuck out his hand. Pete took it. The clasp turned into a trial of strength that ended up a push. They both opened and closed their hands several times after they let go.

Pete started to laugh. "What's so funny?" Sergeant Koenig asked.

"We just made a bet on who's gonna win a war that hasn't started yet," McGill answered. "How dumb will we look if it turns out the Japs're up to something else instead?"

"Dumb enough, I guess," Koenig said. "What? You never looked dumb before?"

"Not the past ten minutes, anyway," Pete said, which drew a laugh from the other noncom. He went on, "I tell you, I wish the Japs *would* get the hell out of Peking and stay out. Town was a lot more fun when the Chinamen were still hanging on to it."

"You got that right." Koenig nodded in what might have been approval. "See? You ain't as dumb as you look."

"Heh! I'm not as dumb as you look, either," Pete retorted. They were off duty. He could sass a sergeant if he felt like it. And he did—it wasn't a pleasure he got often enough.

"Wise guy," Koenig said, and then something in Chinese that sounded like a cat with its tail caught under a rocking chair. Behind the bar, Danny jumped a foot.

"Wow! What's that mean?" Pete asked, impressed in spite of himself.

"Can't tell you," Koenig answered. "If I said it in English, you'd have to try and murder me."

"Give it to me again," Pete urged. "Sounds like it's worth knowing."

Koenig repeated it. Pete tried to echo him. He got the tones wrong the first couple of times. He could hear that, but he had trouble fixing it. Danny held his head in his hands. Pete finally said it the right way, which made the bartender even more unhappy.

"What's it mean, Danny?" Pete called. Danny wouldn't tell him, either. That made him like his new toy even better.

Chapter 17

When Alistair Walsh saw a road sign saying how many kilometers it was to Paris, he knew things weren't in good shape. The whole point to the war was keeping the Nazis away from Paris, the same as it had been with the Kaiser's army the last time around.

They'd done it the last time—done it twice, in fact, in 1914 and then again in 1918. He wasn't so sure they could now. The BEF stumbled back and stumbled back. People were starting to talk about the Miracle on the Marne in 1914. Well, they were getting too damn close to the Marne again, and they sure could use another miracle.

He yawned. What he could use was sleep. One of the things nobody talked about was how wearing modern war was. You were fighting or you were marching or they were shelling you or bombing you or you were trying to promote something to eat. What you weren't doing was resting.

He wasn't the only one frazzled almost to death. Even though February remained chilly, exhausted soldiers curled up like animals by the side of the road. Some slept in greatcoats, some wrapped in blankets, some as they were regardless of the cold. You had to look closely to see their chests rising and falling to make sure they weren't corpses.

Exhausted civilians also slept by the roadside, singly and in family groups. They hadn't done any shooting; other than that, they had as much right to be weary as the soldiers. One poor woman must have been a restless sleeper. She'd kicked off her blanket and thrashed around so her legs and backside were out in the biting breeze. Walsh got an eyeful as he trudged along.

One of the Tommies with him chuckled. "What we're fighting for, right?" the fellow said.

"I've seen plenty worse," Walsh allowed. "If I lay down beside her, though, I bet I'd cork off before I could try getting her knickers down."

"Blimey! Me, too." The other soldier's face split in an enormous yawn. "Don't know how I put one foot in front of the other any more."

Behind them, German artillery thundered to life. Walsh jerked a thumb over his shoulder. "That's how."

"Too right it is. Got a fag on you, Sarge?"

Walsh listened for screams in the air that would warn of incoming shells aimed their way. Hearing none, he reached into a tunic pocket and pulled out a packet of Gitanes. "Here. Got these off a dead Frenchman. Nasty things, but better than nothing."

"I'd smoke whatever you've got and thank you for it. I'm plumb out, and I'm all—" The Tommy held out his arm in front of him and made his hand tremble.

"Know what you mean. I've run dry myself a couple of times." Walsh proffered the French cigarettes. "Take two or three, then."

"I'd be much obliged, if you don't mind." The soldier stuck one in his mouth and stashed the other two in a breast pocket of his grimy battledress. He struck a match and inhaled. "Cor!" he said in tones of deep respect. "Like smoking a bleeding blowtorch, ain't it?"

Walsh had also lit a Gitane. After blowing out smoke, he coughed like a man in the last stages of consumption. "What's that you say?" he inquired.

The other soldier laughed. He took a second, more cautious, drag. "Damn froggies like 'em this way, don't they?"

"I expect so. They'd make 'em different if they didn't," Walsh said.

"Fuck." The Tommy shook his head. "We ought to be on Adolf's side."

"Bugger that, mate," Walsh said. "Germans shot me once, and it's not for lack of trying they haven't done it again. Yeah, the French are a bad lot, but those bastards in field-gray are worse."

"Take an even strain, Sergeant. I was only joking, like." But then the soldier added, "They make damn good soldiers, though."

"They make damn good dead soldiers," Walsh said. He also had a healthy regard for German military talent. He'd never met an English soldier who'd fought the squareheads who didn't. To him, that only made Germans more dangerous. It didn't mean he wanted to switch sides. He pointed to the town ahead. "Is that Senlis?" He probably butchered the pronunciation, but he didn't care.

"I think so." The soldier to whom he'd given a smoke also seemed glad to change the subject.

At its core, Senlis had what looked like really ancient walls with towers. The spires of a cathedral poked up from inside them. Walsh remembered that the Germans had burned the town and shot the mayor and several leading citizens in 1914. The damage had been made good in the quarter-century since. All the same, he didn't want to fight alongside people who did things like that.

He also wasn't eager to fight against them. Willing, yes, but not eager. They were too bloody good at what they did.

In front of those old, old walls—would they go back to Roman days?—an English captain with half a company's worth of men was nabbing stragglers. "You and you!" he called to Walsh and the Tommy to whom he'd given some Gitanes. "You think we can hold this town, eh?"

The other soldier didn't say anything. It wasn't quite what the Articles of War called mute insolence, but it wasn't far removed, either. Sergeant Walsh said, "We can try, sir." He didn't agree with the officer, but he did admit the possibility.

That was plenty. "Fall in with me, then, the both of you," the captain said. "If the Hun tries to take this place, we'll give him what he deserves and send him off with his tail between his legs, what?"

How many years had it been since Walsh heard anybody call Germans Huns? More than he could remember. The captain was about his age, so he'd probably done time here in the last war.

Most of the civilians had cleared out of Senlis, which meant they were causing traffic headaches somewhere south and west of here. Soldiers could pick and choose the empty houses they tried to defend. Walsh went through his, but didn't find anything worth eating or drinking. *Too bad,* he thought.

He had three privates with him. They were all Yorkshire farm boys, and spoke with an accent he had to work to follow. His might have sounded just as strange to them, but that was their lookout. They understood him well enough to keep watch at all the windows—and to give him a tin of M & V. He felt better after wolfing down the meat-and-vegetable stew.

Senlis got a couple of hours' respite before the Germans turned their attention to it. Then artillery walked up to the town. Walsh crouched down with the three privates: they were Jim and Jock and, improbably, Alonzo. The house they'd taken over was made of stone. It would stop fragments unless it was unlucky enough to take a direct hit.

"Where's our guns?" Alonzo complained. *Goons,* it came out when he said it. However it came out, it was a damn good question. The Germans always seemed to put their guns where they needed them. The Allies . . . sometimes did.

Stukas screamed down out of the sky, one after another. Crouching huddled under the kitchen table, Walsh cursed the vulture-winged monsters and their sirens. He also cursed the RAF, both for not shooting them down and for not having anything like them.

Several windows in the French house were already broken. The ones that weren't blew in now, leaving small snowdrifts of glass spears on the floor. Walsh swore some more, resignedly. Sure as hell, he'd end up cutting his hand or his leg on them.

Somebody was yelling for a medic. Somebody else was screaming for his mother. One of the Yorkshire lads crossed himself. Alistair Walsh was no Catholic, but he understood the gesture. Nobody but a desperately hurt man made noises like that.

Before long, the screaming stopped. Walsh hoped the wounded man got morphine. More likely, the poor bugger passed out or just died. "Up, lads," the sergeant told the privates. "I expect we'll have company before long."

"Won't get no clotted cream from me," Jock said, chambering a round in his Enfield with a *snick!* of the bolt.

Sure enough, here came the Germans. They moved up in little stuttering runs from one bit of cover to the next. Some of them had leaves and branches fixed to their helmets with bands cut from old inner tubes. No, no one could say they weren't skilled at their murderous trade.

A Bren gun opened up a couple of houses away from Walsh's. He liked the British army's new light machine gun a lot. It really *was* light— you could pick it up and shoot from the hip if you had to. And it was air-cooled: no need to worry about pouring water (or, that failing, piss) into the metal cooling jacket around the barrel. Best of all, it worked reliably. What more could you want?

It made the Germans hit the deck. They started shooting at the house where it lurked. When they did, the muzzle flashes from their Mausers gave the British infantrymen good targets. Walsh fired and reloaded, then ducked down and crawled to another window to fire again.

Something bit him through the knee of his battledress. "Bloody glass," he muttered.

The Bren gun barked again. German medics in Red Cross smocks ran up to recover casualties. Walsh didn't shoot at them. Fair was fair. The Germans mostly didn't shoot at British medics.

A lull followed. The Germans seemed surprised anyone was fighting hard to save Senlis. Since Walsh had been surprised when the captain made a fight for the place, how could he blame them?

"What happens now, Sergeant?" Alonzo asked.

"They could shell us some more. They could call in the Stukas again, or the tanks," Walsh said. None of the three Yorkshiremen seemed to want to hear that. Walsh went on, "Or they could decide we're a tough nut and try to go around us instead of pushing through."

"That'd be good," Alonzo said. Jack and Jock both nodded. After a moment, so did Alistair Walsh.

AFTER SARAH GOLDMAN'S FATHER TIED his necktie every morning, he pinned his Iron Cross Second Class onto the breast pocket of his jacket. Samuel Goldman wanted to remind the Nazi thugs and *Gestapo* goons who came to scream at him that he'd done his duty for the *Vaterland* in the last war and would have done it again this time if only they'd let him.

Maybe the *Eisenkreuz* did some good. The Goldmans remained in their home. The Nazis hadn't hauled the rest of them off to Dachau or Buchenwald even if Saul had killed a member of the Master Race.

The Nazis hadn't caught Sarah's big brother, either. Saul had fled the labor gang . . . and, after that, he might have fallen off the face of the earth. Sarah had no idea what he'd done. Whatever it was, she admired it tremendously. The policemen with the swastika armbands also had no idea what he'd done. It drove them crazy.

"No, sir," Samuel Goldman told a foul-mouthed *Gestapo* officer. "He has not telephoned us. You would know if he had, *nicht wahr?* You must be tapping our telephone line."

"You bet your scrawny ass we are, Jew," the secret policeman said. "But he could be talking to some other lousy kike who's passing you coded messages."

"It is not so, sir." Sarah's father kept his temper better than she dreamt of being able to do. Maybe he had a deeper understanding of what was at stake in this game. Or maybe he was just blessed with a disposition more even than hers.

"Ought to take you all out and give you a noodle," the officer growled.

"I beg your pardon?" Somehow, Samuel Goldman still managed to keep the dignity a professor of ancient history and classics should have.

The *Gestapo* officer jumped up and walked around behind him. He put the tip of his outthrust index finger against the back of Samuel Goldman's neck. "*Bang!*" he said, and then, "A noodle."

"I see," Sarah's father replied, as coolly as if the man had explained how a new phonograph operated.

"Think you've got nerve, do you?" the *Gestapo* man growled. "You know what happens to assholes with nerve? They scream as loud as anybody else once we get to work on 'em. Maybe louder, on account of we don't fuckin' like tough guys."

Sarah and her mother listened from the kitchen, doing their best to keep quiet so they didn't remind the goon they were there. Her mother's face went pale as skimmed milk. Sarah's own face was probably the same color, but she couldn't see herself.

Out in the front room, her father stayed calm. "Nerve? Not a bit of it," he answered. "It's slang we didn't use in the trenches, that's all. You'll know that's true—you're the right age."

"*Ja, ja,*" the officer said impatiently. "You were in France. I fought in the East, against the Russians."

"*Ach so,*" Samuel Goldman said. "Well, that was no fun, either. I had two friends who went to the Eastern Front and didn't come back."

"Kaupisch and Briesen," the *Gestapo* man said. It wasn't a question—he *knew.* Sarah asked her mother with her eyes how the officer knew something like that. Hanna Goldman shrugged helplessly.

"That's right," Sarah's father said, his voice soft and sad.

"Both Aryans," the officer said. "Not *good* Aryans, or they wouldn't have made friends with a goddamn sheeny. Besides, I'm not here to talk about them. I'm here to talk about your stinking, murdering turd of a son."

If he'd said anything like that to Sarah, she thought she would have tried to brain him with an ashtray. Her father only sighed and said, "I don't know any more than you do. I probably know less than you do, because you've been chasing him ever since the tragedy took place."

"Why shouldn't we just kill you or take you off to a camp because of what that little cocksucker did?" the *Gestapo* man snarled.

Had he seen Saul? Sarah had her doubts. He wouldn't have called him *little* if he had. Saul was one meter eighty-eight centimeters tall; he weighed ninety kilos. You could say a lot of things about him, but not *little,* not if you wanted to stay within shouting distance of the truth.

As if the *Gestapo* cared! Or had to care.

Samuel Goldman sighed. "Because we had nothing to do with anything Saul may have done?" he suggested. Saul had done it, all right. Sarah would never forget the sound that shovel blade made smashing into the side of the work-gang boss' head. Saul had had plenty of provocation, but he'd done it.

The *Gestapo* man snorted. "You aren't even citizens of the *Reich,* only residents. I can do whatever I want with you. To you."

"Yes, sir. I know you can," Father said mournfully. "You asked why you shouldn't. I gave you the best answer I could."

"Are you playing games with me, Jewboy?" demanded the officer in the black uniform with the shiny metal buttons.

Sarah would have killed him for that, too, if she could. Her father didn't even flinch. "Games? No, sir," he replied. "All I'm doing is the best I can for my family and me. Wouldn't you do the same in my place?"

"Like you'd catch me in a kike's place! Fat chance!" the *Gestapo* man said. Sarah might have guessed he'd have no fellow-feeling. If you did, how could you do a job like his? Then he added, "If you see him, if you hear anything from him, you are to report it to us immediately. If you don't, you'll pay for it. Understand me?"

"Yes, sir," Samuel Goldman said. "I understand."

The *Gestapo* man stormed into the kitchen. "You're in there listening!" he yelled. "Think I don't know? You understand me, too?" He glared at them till they both nodded, too. Then he stomped out of the house. He might have suddenly remembered he had other Jews in Münster to terrorize. Chances were he did.

"As if we'd really tell on Saul!" Sarah exclaimed as soon as he slammed the door. "I don't think so!"

"But we will," her father said. She stared at him, wondering if her ears were working right. He nodded. "*Ja.* We will."

"But—why? How?" That wasn't Sarah. It was her mother, who sounded as bewildered as she felt.

"I'll tell you why." And Samuel Goldman did: "They're liable to cook something up and send it to us, that's why. Then, if we don't report it, they can arrest us for protecting a fugitive. So chances are we have to play the game by their rules—and we have to hope Saul has the good sense to know we might be under this kind of pressure."

Sarah was sure Saul would. Her father sounded anything but. She knew why, too. Devoted to the life of the mind, Samuel Goldman had never known what to make of his big, muscular son. Saul hadn't done badly in school, but it wasn't what he cared about. Father had to wonder whether somebody like that had any brains at all.

"Saul will do fine." Mother had confidence in him, too, which made Sarah feel better. Hanna Goldman went on, "And if they didn't catch him right away, they'll have a harder time of it now. Harder and harder the longer he stays free."

"I hope so," Father said, but, again, he sounded far from certain.

This time, Sarah was inclined to agree with him, however little she wanted to. Germany was a land that ran on forms and papers. Food was rationed. So was clothing. Everyone had an identity card and had to show it a dozen times a day. How could a Jew on the run *not* get caught in the spiderweb of officialdom and bureaucracy? Sarah couldn't imagine.

But so far Saul hadn't. And if he hadn't so far, maybe he could keep on doing whatever he was doing and stay free. Maybe. Sarah could hope so, anyhow. She could even pray, and she did, though she didn't think she was very good at it. Maybe God valued sincerity over style. She could hope that was true, too—and she did.

A FEW KILOMETERS UP AHEAD lay a railway-junction town called Hirson. Willi Dernen did his best not to care. Northeastern France had winters almost as beastly as the ones he'd grown up with in eastern Germany. Willi was holed up in a village called Watigny, east of the place that mattered to the fellows with the fancy shoulder straps.

One of these days, they'd order him to go forward. And he would. He wasn't thrilled about it, but he would. What they'd do to him if he didn't was certain, and dreadful. What the Frenchmen would do to him after he did might not be so bad. If he was lucky.

For the moment, even the generals could see that advancing through waist-deep snowdrifts was asking to get your dick shot off. German guns pounded Hirson. The French replied, but not many shells came down on Watigny. There were German batteries north and south of the village, but none close by.

About half the people who'd lived here fled before the *Wehrmacht* arrived. Not all those houses were vacant. French refugees from farther north and east—to say nothing of Belgians and even Dutchmen— squatted in some of them. The Germans took the rest. Before long, they'd probably throw out the squatters, too. For the time being, the officers in charge of security were still sorting out who was who.

People from the older generation remembered the last time soldiers in *Feldgrau* came through these parts. Some of them were among the folks who'd run away. Others seemed gruffly tolerant of the occupiers. Their attitude said this was nothing new to them. They'd done it once, and they could do it again.

By order of the divisional commander, the local tavern stayed open. The exchange rate was pegged at ten francs to the mark. That made even privates like Willi rich men—or as rich as they could be in a place like Watigny, where getting by was as much as anyone could hope for.

The tavern still had beer and wine, as well as brandy that came in china crocks and was probably homemade. It got you crocked, all right. Willi had found that out by experience. It also left you with a mother of a hangover. Strong French coffee and strong German aspirins blunted a *Katzenjammer,* though.

Willi and Wolfgang Storch slogged through the snow toward the oasis. Orders were that no German soldier could go in alone. Nobody'd got knocked over the head here. Maybe it had happened somewhere else. Or maybe the High Command was scared of its own shadow. That was how it looked to Willi.

He opened the door. Both he and Wolfgang hurried inside. Then he closed the door again to block the cold wind whining through the streets.

It was gloomy inside, but the fire gave some warmth. Frenchmen sat at a couple of tables, drinking, smoking, murmuring in the language

Willi didn't speak. Corporal Baatz and a couple of other noncoms occupied another. They didn't try to keep their voices down—they were the winners, after all.

Winners or not, Willi wanted nothing to do with them. A glance from Wolfgang said he didn't, either. They walked past the underofficers and up to the bar. The man behind it was big, broad-shouldered, and fair. He looked much more like a German than a Frenchman. But a photo on the wall behind him showed him in the uniform of a French soldier in the last war. The patch he wore over one eye didn't hide all the scarring around the socket. It did explain why he hadn't got mobilized this time around.

"*Guten Tag,* Claude," Willi said, more respectfully than not.

"*Guten Tag,*" the tapman answered. After he got wounded, he'd spent two years in a POW camp. He'd picked up some German there, and hadn't forgotten all of it. Other people of his generation had learned it from the Kaiser's soldiers who'd occupied the area. They still knew bits and pieces, too. "What you want, eh?" Claude went on.

"Beer, *bitte,*" Willi said.

"Brandy for me, please," Wolfgang added. They both laid money— German money—on the zinc bar.

Claude sighed, but he took it. What choice did he have? "Go and sit," he said, pointing to an empty table—shrewdly, the one farthest from where Baatz and his buddies were. "Michelle, she bring."

"Now you're talking!" Wolfgang radiated enthusiasm . . . or something related to it, anyhow. A grin also stretched across Willi's face. Claude's daughter was about their age. Like her father, she was large and solid and fair. On her, it looked good.

She came out from a back room. Claude gave her the drinks. She carried them over to the soldiers. "Thank you, dear," Willi said *auf Deutsch.* He trotted out one of his handful of recently acquired French words: "*Merci.*"

"*Pas de quoi,*" she answered gravely, and went away. As far as anybody knew, she didn't sleep with soldiers. Everybody thought that was too damn bad.

Arno Baatz waved his mug. "Fill me up over here!" he called. Claude brought a pitcher of beer to his table and poured the mug full. That didn't satisfy Baatz. "How come those no-account lugs get the pretty girl and I get you?" he demanded.

Claude's one eye skewered him like a lepidopterist's collecting pin. "Because they is—are—polite," the tapman answered, and he walked back to the bar.

"What? I'm not?" Corporal Baatz yelled, beer-fueled outrage making him even shriller than usual. "You take that back!"

"*Nein,*" Claude said with dignity.

Baatz jumped to his feet. "I'll show you, then, you stinking pigdog! Come fight like a man!"

Claude turned around and took one step back toward him: giving himself room to maneuver. Baatz rushed him. Willi wanted to avert his eyes. He couldn't stand the *Unteroffizier,* but no denying he was a rough man in a rough trade. He gave Claude one that should have dented a Panzer II. The barman blinked his good eye. Then he swung. His fist caught Arno Baatz right on the button with a noise like a cleaver smacking into a frozen side of beef. Baatz went straight over backwards. The back of his head smacked the stone floor. He didn't move. He didn't even twitch.

"Holy Jesus!" Willi said. "Did you kill him?"

Claude took the question seriously. He felt for the noncom's pulse. "He lives," he said laconically, and dropped Baatz's wrist. It fell back limply. Baatz might be alive, but he sure wasn't connected to the real world. The tapman looked to the other Germans at the corporal's table. "He hit me first. Please take him away. He is no more welcome here."

They didn't argue with him. Nobody in his right mind would have argued with Claude then—not without a Schmeisser in his hands, any-how. Arno Baatz was as boneless as an octopus as they dragged him out of the tavern.

One of the Frenchmen drinking there sent up smoke signals from his pipe. He said something in his own language. Claude shrugged a massive shrug, as if to say, *Well, what can you do?* Willi guessed the cus-tomer had warned him he would get in trouble.

"We'll say he started it," Willi volunteered.

"It's the truth," Wolfgang agreed.

"*Danke*," Claude said. "For official business, this is good. For not of-ficial business . . ." He spread his hands and let his voice trail away.

Willi understood that. If Arno Baatz and his friends—assuming he had any, which struck the biased Willi as improbable—decided to come back with weapons, what would the officers set over them do about it? Anything? Even if they did, how much would that help Claude after the fact?

"Maybe we'll go forward again soon. Blizzards can't last forever—I don't think," Wolfgang said. "Then Awful Arno will be out of your hair."

"*Ja.* Maybe," Claude said. It was the first time Willi had heard him even slightly enthusiastic about the prospect of a German advance. He was a Frenchmen. The Germans had maimed him in the last war. You couldn't blame him for not wishing them well. But you also couldn't blame him for wanting Corporal Baatz the hell out of Watigny, even if that meant the *Wehrmacht* went forward.

The tapman ducked into the back room for a little while, then came out again. A couple of minutes later, so did Michelle. She brought Willi a beer and Wolfgang a brandy they hadn't ordered. When they tried to pay for them, she wouldn't take their money.

"*Merci. Merci*," Willi said. It didn't seem enough, but it was the best he could do.

They finished the free drinks and left. After they got outside and closed the door behind them again, Wolfgang said, "If she *really* wanted to thank us, she could have taken us into that back room while Papa looked the other way."

"She's not that kind of girl," Willi said.

"Yeah. Ain't it a shame?" Wolfgang's breath smoked even though he didn't have a cigarette in his mouth. After a couple of steps, he brightened. "Could be worse, you know? Old Arno sure got his."

"Boy, did he ever!" Willi agreed enthusiastically. They walked on through the snow, toward the house where they were quartered.

FRENCH VILLAGERS STARED FEARFULLY AT Vaclav Jezek and the rest of the Czechs in his outfit. Vaclav knew why, too. Their uniforms weren't quite the right color, their helmets were the wrong shape, and they spoke some funny foreign language. To people who didn't know any better, that was plenty to turn them into Germans.

And, just to make things worse, they were coming from the east. If they were Germans, they would have smashed all the defenders ahead of them, but you couldn't expect civilians to think of things like that.

One of the locals came out with something. Vaclav had picked up a handful of French words, but not nearly enough to let him follow. "What did he say?" he asked the guy along as an interpreter.

Benjamin Halévy looked even less happy than he had before he heard the Frenchman's news. The Jewish sergeant pointed north and west. "Old geezer claims the Germans are already over there."

"Shit," Vaclav said. If that was true, they were in danger of getting cut off and surrounded. If . . . "Does he know his ass from a hole in the ground?"

He eyed the Frenchman. The guy was around fifty, and had some ugly scars on his jaw and left cheek. Maybe those weren't war wounds, but they sure looked like them. If this fellow had gone through the mill before, he wouldn't see a cow and imagine it was a German armored division.

Halévy went back and forth with him. After a last *"Merci,"* the sergeant returned to Czech: "Sure sounds like he does. They pushed through the woods over there. This guy says he saw a couple of armored cars, but no tanks."

"Bad enough," Vaclav muttered. Several of his countrymen nodded. He went on, "Where are our tanks? Where are our armored cars?" Nobody answered him. The Germans always seemed to have armor when they broke through. They used their armor *to* break through. The French scattered it up and down the line, which meant they never had enough where they needed it most. That was one reason they were falling back and the Nazis moving up.

Halévy gave Vaclav a crooked grin. "Hey, pal, that's why you've got your antitank rifle, right?"

Vaclav told him where he could put the antitank rifle. Halévy would have walked very straight if he'd tried. You could get your behind in a sling for telling off a noncom, but Vaclav's behind was already in a sling because he was up at the front, so what did he care?

He would have expected a Jew to get stuffy about that kind of thing, maybe to threaten him with official regulations. But Sergeant Halévy just laughed and said something about his mother and troopships. From another guy, or under different circumstances, Vaclav would have tried to rearrange his face. He laughed now, too. They'd been through it together. They'd earned the right to zing each other.

"Seriously, we ought to head up that way," Halévy said. "If your rifle can take out those cars, it'll do us some good."

Vaclav was no more enthusiastic about putting his dick on the chopping block than any other soldier in his right mind would have been. But he could see the need. "I'll try it," he said.

"Attaboy," Halévy told him. He clapped another Czech soldier on the back. "Dominik, take point."

"Right, Sergeant." Dominik didn't sound thrilled, but he never did.

He was little and skinny and nervous as a cat in a room full of Rottweilers—all of which made him a goddamn good point man. He carried a captured German submachine gun. If he ran into trouble, he could spray a lot of lead at it.

"Let's go," the sergeant said. He moved right behind Dominik. He didn't believe in staying away from trouble. None of the people who said Jews were a bunch of cowards had seen him in action. David had stayed right up there with everybody else, too, till he stopped one. And they both hated Nazis even more than Vaclav did, which he wouldn't have believed if he hadn't seen it with his own eyes.

"*Bonne chance,*" called the Frenchman who'd warned them about Germans. *Luck,* that meant, or something like it. Vaclav waved to the guy without looking back.

Trees and bushes and rocks. The western part of the Ardennes was as wild and rugged as anything in Czechoslovakia. Vaclav would have bet the Germans couldn't get any armor through here, but he would have lost if he had. He'd already escaped from tanks in these parts: Panzer Is and IIs, and also some captured Czech T-35s. Those infuriated him. Yes, everybody grabbed whatever he could get his hands on—his own antitank rifle and Dominik's machine pistol showed as much. But seeing Czech tanks fight against Czech soldiers made him want to cry.

Dominik waved urgently. Vaclav dove behind the closest bush. He didn't know what was up ahead, and he didn't want to find out the hard way. Sergeant Halévy twiddled fingers at him. Ever so cautiously, Vaclav slithered forward. He swore under his breath every time a knee or an elbow broke a twig.

Then he froze—German voices up ahead. The breeze swung, and he got a whiff of cigarette smoke. "God in heaven, I'm tired," one of the Fritzes said. "I could sleep for a month."

"Just a little going on, Klaus." If those dry tones didn't come from a sergeant, Vaclav would eat his boots.

"*Ja*," Klaus said, and then, "What the hell was that?"

That was Vaclav's antitank rifle scraping through some dry bushes. The goddamn thing was more than a meter and a half long—almost as long as he was tall. It wasn't just heavy; it was also unwieldy as all get-out. Jezek froze.

"I didn't hear anything," the noncom said.

"I sure thought I did," Klaus replied.

"Want to check it out?"

"Nah. I just want to sit here and grab a smoke."

"Sounds good to me. Let me bum one off you," the sergeant said.

Even more warily than before, Vaclav crawled forward. He spotted an armored car between a couple of chestnuts. Hoping the noise wouldn't give him away, he chambered a round. The Germans didn't have kittens, so he got away with it. A couple of those long, fat rounds through the engine compartment and that armored car wouldn't go anywhere for a while.

He waggled the fingers on his left hand to let Sergeant Halévy know he was in position. The rest of the Czechs opened up on the Germans. His noise covered by theirs, he punched one through the armored car's thin steel side and into the engine.

He was about to shoot at it again when a German with a subma-chine gun popped up out of nowhere. Vaclav shot him instead. A round designed to pierce armor did horrible things to flesh. It seemed to blow out half the German's insides. The poor bastard fell over with a grunt and never stirred after that. It was over fast for him, anyhow.

Shoulder aching—even with muzzle brake and padded stock, the antitank rifle kicked harder than a kangaroo—Vaclav reloaded. Here came the other armored car. He fired at where the driver would sit, once, twice. The car slid to the left and slammed into a tree.

That seemed to take the vinegar out of these Germans. They either ran off or gave up. "Good job!" Sergeant Halévy called to Vaclav. "Don't you wish it was this easy all the goddamn time?"

"Jesus!" Vaclav exclaimed. "I'm just glad it was this easy once." Halévy laughed, for all the world as if he were joking.

LIEUTENANT JULIUS LEMP STOOD AT stiff attention. When a rear admiral reamed you out, you had to stand there and take it and pretend it didn't hurt. The process was a lot like picking up dueling scars, except you had no sword of your own.

"You thick-skinned idiot!" Karl Dönitz didn't raise his voice, which only made things worse. "Did you *want* to drag the United States into this war?"

"No, sir," Lemp replied woodenly. He stared straight at a spot three centimeters in front of Dönitz's nose.

The round-faced chief of U-boat operations was not a man who stood out in a crowd. Dönitz was supposed to be a pretty good guy, too. He had a reputation for sticking up for his captains. But nobody would stick up for you when you screwed up the way Lemp had.

"U-boats brought the Americans in the last time," Dönitz said. "We try not to make the same mistakes twice, you know." He waited.

"Yes, sir." Again, something mechanical might have spoken through Lemp.

"I've had to calm down Goebbels and von Ribbentrop and the *Führer*," Dönitz said. "They all wanted your scalp." He waited.

What am I supposed to say now? Lemp wondered. He tried, "I'm honored, sir." In a way, he was. If the Propaganda Minister and the Foreign Minister and Hitler himself noticed you, you'd done something out of the ordinary, no doubt about it.

Rear Admiral Dönitz's pale eyes grew cold as the seas off Greenland. "I wouldn't be, if I were you," he said, and his voice was as icy as his face. "Dr. Goebbels had to put together a whole propaganda campaign to shift the blame away from us. Now there's some doubt about who sank the *Athenia*—but not among us, eh?"

"No, sir. I did it, all right." Lemp still didn't change expression. Yeah, sometimes you had to stand there and take it. This was one of those times.

"I'd run you out of my office if you told me anything else," Dönitz said. "If you screw up like this again, I won't be able to help you. Do you understand that?"

"Yes, sir." Men who served on U-boats weren't normally long on military discipline. This was one of those occasions where formality was mandatory, though. You took your abuse by the numbers.

"A notation about your error will go into your service jacket," Dönitz said, which meant Lemp would be a long time seeing another promotion.

"Yes, sir," Lemp said one more time. He couldn't get into more trouble as long as he kept saying that, and he was in plenty already.

"Next time we send you out, for God's sake try not to sink anything flying the Stars and Stripes," Dönitz said.

"I will, sir," Lemp replied. But he couldn't help adding, "You *are* going to send me out again?"

"Yes, yes." The commander of the *Kriegsmarine*'s U-boat forces sounded impatient. "You've proved you can hit what you aim at. We need that in our skippers. I have to dress you down, because you aimed at the wrong ship. I have my orders, too, you understand."

Did that mean he'd been going through the motions before? It sure sounded that way to Lemp. If he had, he could take his act on stage. He'd make more money with it than he ever could in a naval career. "I see," the U-boat skipper said cautiously—one more phrase that stayed pretty safe.

Dönitz looked altogether different when he smiled. "All right, then," he said. "Dismissed. And you can tell your crew we won't send them to a camp."

Lemp saluted. "Yes, sir. I'll do that. Some of them have been worried about it." Some of them had been scared shitless. You didn't want to say that to a rear admiral, though. Lemp didn't like the idea of living in a place where making an honest mistake could land you in this much trouble. But, no matter what else the *Vaterland* was, it was the *Vaterland*.

"Go on, go on." Dönitz had spent all the time with him he was going to. Stacks of papers smothered the admiral's desk. It wasn't as if he had nothing else going on.

After one more salute, Lemp made his escape. He was glad he'd worn his greatcoat. Germany had enough coal to keep furnaces going and heat buildings, but Wilhelmshaven was bloody cold outside. Screeching gulls wheeled overhead. The air smelled of the sea and, more faintly, of fuel oil—familiar odors to a U-boat skipper.

Dönitz's office wasn't far from the harbor, and from the seaside barracks that housed U-boat crewmen when they came in to port. Lemp made for the two-story red-brick building with dormer windows where the sailors from the U-30 were staying. A sailor wearing a *Stahlhelm* and carrying a rifle stood guard outside. He saluted Lemp. The skipper and his crew weren't quite under arrest—but they weren't quite *not* under arrest, either.

Returning the salute, Lemp said, "You can relax, Jochen. I think they'll give you some other duty soon."

"I wouldn't mind," Jochen said.

Lemp walked on in. The sailors crowded the wardroom, smoking and playing cards and reading newspapers. It wasn't nearly so crowded as the long steel tube of the U-30 would have been, though. Everything stopped when the men saw Lemp. They searched his face as anxiously as they would have searched the horizon when Royal Navy destroyers were in the neighborhood.

"It's over," Lemp said. "The admiral read me the riot act, but they'll let us put to sea again."

The sailors cheered. They stamped their feet. A couple of them whistled shrilly. Only later did Lemp wonder why. As long as they stayed in harbor, they were safe. Any time they went hunting, they laid their lives on the line. And they were glad to do it. If that wasn't madness . . .

Of course it was. He had a case of the same disease. So did the British sailors who tried to bring merchantmen into their harbors, and the other sailors who set out to sink U-boats. So did the soldiers in German *Feldgrau,* and so did the bastards in assorted shades of khaki who tried their best to stop the *Wehrmacht.*

Without that kind of madness, you couldn't have a war. Julius Lemp took it for granted. So did men far more important than he.

"What did Dönitz say?" asked a machinist's mate.

"That we were bad boys for sinking an American liner. That we could have got the *Reich* into all kinds of trouble. But we didn't," Lemp answered. "He also said he needed people who could shoot straight."

More cheers rose. These were so loud and raucous, Jochen stuck his nose into the wardroom to see what was going on. Nobody told him. Miffed, he slouched back outside. The soldiers started clapping and stomping again.

"We'll go out there and do some more straight shooting," Lemp said. The men shouted agreement. They were good fellows, all right—and crazy the same way he was.

Chapter 18

~~~~~~~~~~~~~~~~~~~~~~~~~~~~~~~~~~~~~

For more than two years, the war in Spain had electrified the world. Everybody could see it foretold what would happen when Fascism squared off against Marxism. Both sides threw what they could into the struggle. Italian troops, German planes, Russian tanks . . . Most of the bodies, on both sides, stayed Spanish.

Not all. Chaim Weinberg wouldn't have left New York City without a strong feeling that something had to be done to stop Fascism before it exploded all over Europe. He wasn't the only one: the International Brigades were proof of that. Outnumbered and outgunned, the Republic remained a going concern despite everything Marshal Sanjurjo could do to crush it.

And then, when the Internationals were about to get pulled from the line, the big war *did* break out in Europe. Spain's fight was suddenly Britain and France's fight, too. Matériel flooded south across the Pyrenees as the French border opened up. It seemed too good to be true.

It was. As soon as Hitler turned his troops on the Low Countries and France rather than Czechoslovakia, the flood didn't go back to being a trickle. It dried up altogether. Everything the French could make, they shipped northeast to shoot at the *Boches.*

Germany and Italy had already pretty much forgotten about Spain. With the French and English navies in the war, the Fascists had a much harder time getting through than they'd had before. And they needed their toys to use against the Western democracies.

So Spain went from being the cockpit of world attention to the war that everybody forgot. Everybody, that is, except the poor, sorry bastards still stuck fighting it.

Lately, Sanjurjo's men on an outpost a few hundred meters away had found themselves a new weapon: a loudspeaker system. It crackled to life now: "Come over to the winning side!" a Spaniard shouted, and the loudspeaker gave him something close to the voice of God. "Come over to us, and we'll feed you what we eat ourselves. It's lovely chicken stew tonight! Don't miss it!"

"Ha!" Chaim said, and turned to Mike Carroll. "You know how to make Sanjurjo's chicken stew?"

"First, you steal a chicken," Carroll answered wearily. "That's an old one. Got a smoke?"

"Yeah." Chaim gave him a Gauloise.

"Lovely chicken stew!" the Nationalist boomed again.

"Thanks. Tastes like shit, but thanks." Carroll puffed happily. Chaim agreed with him—the French tobacco did taste like shit. But Gauloises and Gitanes were better than no cigarettes at all—and better than roll-your-owns made from other people's (and your own) butts.

"Chicken stew—with dumplings!"

"Lying cocksucker," Chaim said without much rancor. Every so often, guys from the other side deserted. From what they said, the Nationalists were just as hungry, just as miserable, as the Republicans.

"Maybe their officers have chicken stew," Carroll said.

"Now you're talking," Chaim said. Republican officers ate and lived no better than the men they led. It was an article of faith on this side that the enemy's officers exploited their soldiers—they were fighting *for* class distinctions, after all. Some of what the deserters said supported that: some, but not all. The Republicans mostly discounted anything that disagreed with what they'd thought before.

"Wonderful chicken stew! All you can eat!"

Somebody in the Republican lines fired at the loudspeaker. If you were hungry and cold and miserable, talk of food could drive you nuts. And you had to be nuts to shoot like that. At long range, with the crappy rifles and cheap ammo most Republicans carried, how likely were you to hit what you aimed at? Even if you did, what kind of damage could you do? And besides . . .

Chaim pulled his entrenching tool off his belt. It was very well made; he'd taken it off a dead Italian. He started digging. "That stupid asshole's gonna bring some hate down on our heads."

"Tell me about it." Carroll's entrenching tool consisted of some scrap iron a smith had beaten flat and then bolted to a stick. But it moved dirt, too. He deepened his foxhole and added dirt to the parapet in front of it and the parados behind.

Sure as hell, the shot woke up the Nationalist artillery. Sanjurjo's men had more guns and better guns than the Republicans. Hitler and Mussolini had been lavish in supplying their Spanish friends till they got distracted. Nobody on the Republican side had ever been lavish with anything, not till the Czech fight started and not for long enough then.

Fragments wined and snarled overhead. Chaim dug like a mole, trying to make what vets of the last war called a bombproof. He should have done that a long time ago. He knew as much, but nobody liked to dig without need. Now the need was here.

Mike Carroll made dirt fly, too. They both stopped about the same time. Somebody not far away had been wounded, and was making a godawful racket. "I'd better go get him," Chaim said, though he could think of few things he wanted to do less. As if to convince himself, he added, "God knows I'd want somebody to pick me up if I got hit."

"Yeah." Carroll also scrambled out of his hole, even if he'd just improved it. Not being by himself above ground made Chaim a little less lonely. It also made him wonder if he'd have to try to make pickup for two. Well, if he stopped something himself, somebody was out there to make pickup on him.

He scuttled along like a pair of ragged claws—some damn poem picking the exact wrong moment to bounce around in his head. Like a snake would have been closer, because his belly hugged the ground every second. Off to his left, Mike also looked flattened by a steamroller.

To add to the joy, a couple of Nationalists started shooting at them with rifles. Luckily, none of the rounds came close. Spaniards, whether Nationalists or Republicans, made piss-poor riflemen. Chaim didn't know why that was true, but it sure seemed to be. The bullets got close enough to scare him cracking past, but no closer than that.

He crawled past some trench a shell hit had caved in and flopped down into the earthwork beyond with a sigh of relief. Mike Carroll made it, too. There lay the wounded guy, trying to clutch his chest and his leg at the same time and howling like a banshee. Two other men from the International Brigades were nothing but raw meat and blood—no blaming them for not helping their buddy, because nobody could ever help them again.

"Fuck," Carroll said hoarsely. "See who it is?"

Chaim hadn't noticed—one injured fighter sounded much like another, no matter which language he'd grown up speaking. Now he took a look. "Fuck," he echoed. "It's Milt."

Milton Wolff—*El Lobo* to the Spaniards on both sides—had led the Abraham Lincoln Battalion since Robert Merriman was lost the spring before. He'd kept them in the line no matter what Sanjurjo's goons threw at them. He wasn't just their heart; he was also a big part of their backbone.

And he was badly hurt. Fragments had shredded his left calf and thigh and laid open the left side of his chest. "Jesus," Chaim muttered. His stomach tried to turn over. He wouldn't let it.

"What do we do?" Carroll sounded as lost and horrified as Chaim felt. If you saw your father like that . . . "What *can* we do?"

"Try and patch him up. Try and get him back to the docs. Maybe they can pour some blood into him," Chaim answered. Republican doctors could do more with transfusions than just about anybody. That was one of the few places where the Republic worked well—if the crack mobile unit was anywhere within a few kilometers, anyhow.

They used their wound dressings. They used strips of cloth from their uniforms and from those of the dead men, who didn't care any more. One of the corpses had a miraculously unbroken syringe in a belt pouch. Chaim jabbed Wolff with it—it was the only painkiller he was likely to get.

Wolff was a big man—six-two, easy—which only made things worse. Manhandling him over to a communications trench that went back was no fun for Chaim or Mike Carroll or the wounded Abe Lincoln officer. Hauling him across bare, broken ground and praying the snipers didn't get lucky would have been even worse . . . Chaim supposed.

They were heading back instead of sideways when Wolff stopped screaming and asked, "Will I die?" He sounded amazingly calm. The morphine must have hit him all at once.

"I don't think so, Milt," Chaim answered, and hoped he wasn't lying. "We'll get you patched up."

"You bet," Mike agreed.

A Red Cross flag flew over an aid tent. In his bad Spanish, Chaim asked, "Is the blood truck close?"

"*¿Quién sabe?*" a harried-looking male nurse answered. He sounded like a fruit, but that was the least of Chaim's worries. And he did gasp when he found out who the wounded Abe Lincoln was. "*¿El Lobo? ¡Madre de Dios!*" He crossed himself.

By the way people went dashing out of the aid tent, Chaim got the idea they'd track down the blood truck as fast as they could. He wondered whether they would have done the same if he came in wounded. Actually, he didn't wonder: he knew damn well they wouldn't.

And he had a hard time getting pissed off about it. He was just a *soldado*. He had his uses, but their were plenty more like him. Milton Wolff was *El Lobo*. If he stayed out of action long, the Lincolns wouldn't be the same. And, while the rest of the world might have forgotten the Spanish Civil War, it remained brutally real to the people who went on fighting it.

HANS-ULRICH RUDEL WAS GETTING SICK of huddling in muddy slit trenches. This one was in western Belgium. It was two in the morning, and British bombers were overhead again. By the roar of their engines, they weren't very far overhead, either. RAF Whitleys and Hampdens couldn't fly very high no matter how much their pilots might wish they could.

And, at night, it hardly mattered. *Luftwaffe* night fighters found enemy planes more by luck than any other way. When German bombers struck England under cover of darkness, the RAF's night fighters had the same problem.

Bombs whistled down. Some of them landed close enough for the bursts to make Rudel's ears hurt. Blast could do horrible things to you even when fragments and flame didn't. He buried his face against the trench wall. He'd come out looking like the end man in a minstrel show, but he didn't care. As long as he came out.

More explosions, and the rending crash of something metal going to smithereens all at once. "Goddamn flying suitcases!" somebody a couple of meters away said.

"*Ja!*" Hans-Ulrich nodded, smelling mold and damp. Hampdens were a lot like *Luftwaffe* bombers, though more slab-sided than any of them—hence the nickname. Whitleys were bigger, slower, and clumsier, but carried more bombs. They could take a lot of punishment . . . and needed to, because they got it. Rudel wouldn't have wanted to fly one in the daytime. The British had tried that, but not for long.

Well, the *Luftwaffe* wasn't sending Stukas over England any more, either. Some things cost more than they were worth. Even biplane Gladiators were dangerous to the German dive-bombers. As for Hurricanes and the newer Spitfires . . . !

The real trouble was, Hurricanes and Spitfires chewed up Bf-110s almost as easily as they mulched Stukas. Bf-109s held their own against the top RAF fighters, but they had short range and couldn't linger long over England. And, when they had to escort the 110s as well as the bombers, they couldn't mix it up with the enemy the way they should.

From everything Rudel had heard, nobody in the *Luftwaffe* higher-ups had dreamt the 110 would show such weaknesses. War gave all kinds of surprises—including the nasty ones.

A few more bombs fell. Then things eased off; the drone of enemy engines faded in the west. Hans-Ulrich spat to get the taste of loam out of his mouth. "Well," he said brightly, "that was fun."

Several people in the trench told him what he could do with his fun. Somebody who knew his classics quoted Goethe's Götz von Berlichen: "*Du kannst mich mal am Arsch lechen.*" Even if it was poetry, *Lick my ass* got the point across.

He climbed out of the trench. Something was burning: a Stuka in a half-blasted revetment. The orange flames sent a dim, flickering light across the airstrip. "Got to put that out," a flyer said. "If the damned Englishmen see it, they're liable to come back."

Groundcrew men started playing a hose in the Ju-87. That would take a while to do any good. Gasoline and oil liked to keep burning. And the ammo in the Stuka's machine guns started cooking off. The popping seemed absurdly cheerful. "Hope none of those rounds hits anybody," Hans-Ulrich said.

"Jesus Maria!" somebody said—a Catholic, by the oath. "That'd be all we need."

Somebody else was exhausted, relentlessly pragmatic, or both: "Only thing I hope is, I can get back to sleep."

"Amen!" the Catholic said. Sure enough, he sounded like a Bavarian.

The burning dive-bomber gave just enough light to let Hans-Ulrich have an easy time going back to his tent. He lay down on the cot—and then remembered his face was muddy. If he hadn't been a minister's son, he might have quoted Götz von Berlichen himself. Being one, he knew that thinking the words was as bad as saying them. He sometimes swore in the heat of action, but never in cold blood—and he always regretted it afterwards.

When he got up and came out the next morning, the fellow in the next tent greeted him with, "Who's the nigger?"

"Funny, Manfred. Fun-ny," Hans-Ulrich said. "You should take it to the movies."

"Go drink some milk, preacher's son," Manfred jeered. "You'll feel better."

Hans-Ulrich's hands balled into fists. He took a step toward the other flyer. "Enough, both of you," a more senior officer said. "Do you want to get tossed in the clink? Save that *Scheisse* for the enemy, hear me?"

Reluctantly, Manfred nodded. Even more reluctantly, so did Hans-Ulrich. He was sick of being the white crow in the squadron. He couldn't even say that: somebody would have told him he was the white crow because he drank so much milk.

If he'd changed his ways and drunk schnapps, everybody would have liked him. The notion didn't cross his mind.

Other people razzed him about his dirty face, but not so viciously as Manfred had. Some other pilots and rear gunners had also got muddy, though none quite so muddy as Rudel. While they ate, a grunting bulldozer repaired damage to the airstrip.

German bombers—Spades and Flying Pencils—droned past overhead, bound for England. Bf-109s would protect the Heinkels and Dorniers from RAF fighters, and they could protect themselves better than Stukas. All the same, Hans-Ulrich wondered how much longer the *Luftwaffe* would go over the enemy island by day. Nighttime bombing was less accurate, but also much less expensive.

He wasn't sorry not to cross the North Sea again. He counted himself lucky to have made it back the times he'd tried it. Maybe the twin-engine bombers would have better luck. Maybe.

His own mission lay to the southwest. The French were bringing matériel up from Paris to the front that still shielded their capital from the *Wehrmacht*'s onslaught. If the *Luftwaffe* could smash up those trucks and trains, enemy troops would get less of what they needed to keep up the fight.

"Ready?" he asked Sergeant Dieselhorst.

The man in the rear seat looked at him. "Nah. I'll bug out as soon as we get airborne."

Rudel's ears heated. "Me and my big mouth. Let's go get 'em."

"Now you're talking," Dieselhorst said.

Bombed up, gassed up, their Stuka rumbled down the runway. Hans-Ulrich pulled back on the stick. The Stuka's nose lifted. The plane would never be pretty. Though the design was fairly new, plenty of aircraft looked more modern: the nonretractable landing gear made the Ju-87 seem older than it was. But the beast got the job done. Next to that, what were looks?

A few black puffs of smoke appeared in the sky as the Stuka squadron crossed over the front line, but only a few. This wasn't the kind of barrage that would have greeted the Germans over England—

nowhere close. The French didn't seem as serious about the war as the British. But they hadn't rolled belly-up yet, either. *We just have to keep thumping them till they do,* Hans-Ulrich thought.

Was that river glittering in the sun the Marne? Hans-Ulrich thought so: the farthest the Kaiser's armies reached in the last war. The *Wehrmacht* was almost there, too, though it had started rolling in dead of winter and had to take out Holland as well as Belgium.

Silver sausages gleamed above Paris: barrage balloons. The English used them over their towns, too. They didn't keep places from getting bombed. They did keep dive-bombers from stooping on targets. Hans-Ulrich shuddered, imagining what would happen if he tore off the Stuka's wing against a mooring cable. He'd feel like an idiot . . . but not for long.

Well, he didn't have to worry about that, anyhow—not yet. The squadron's targets lay in front of Paris. Captain Mehler's voice filled his earphones. "I think that's what we want down below," the new squadron leader said. "Let's hit 'em."

"Here we go," Hans-Ulrich said into the speaking tube, warning Sergeant Dieselhorst.

"*Jawohl,*" the gunner and radioman said. "I was listening, too."

Hans-Ulrich tipped the Ju-87 over into a dive. Acceleration slammed him back in his seat. It would be trying to tear Dieselhorst out of his. Hans-Ulrich had never heard of a rear gunner's straps and harness failing—a good thing, too. That wasn't pretty to think about.

Down below, the highway swelled. Yes, that was a truck convoy. As the shriek from the Stukas' sirens mounted, soldiers started bailing out and running like ants. Too late, fools. Too late.

Everything had a red tinge. Rudel was right on the edge of blacking out. He pulled the bomb-release lever, then yanked back on the stick as hard as he could to bring the Stuka out of its deadly plunge. Behind him, the *poilus* would just have discovered hell on earth.

"You all right?" Sergeant Dieselhorst's voice said he wasn't sure about himself, let alone Rudel.

"I—think so." Hans-Ulrich made himself nod. As they usually did after a steep dive, his thoughts needed a few seconds to come back to normal. He muzzily recalled the Stukas in Spain that had crashed before the *Luftwaffe* installed that gadget to pull out of dives if pilots didn't.

He fought for altitude. He'd got up to 2,500 meters when Dieselhorst's machine gun started chattering. "Dodge!" the gunner yelled. "French fighter!"

Hans-Ulrich threw the big, clumsy Ju-87 around the sky in ways the manufacturer never intended. An open-cockpit Dewoitine monoplane zoomed past—obsolescent, but flying. A 109 could have hacked it out of the air with the greatest of ease. It still outclassed a Stuka, though.

Here it came for another pass. Hans-Ulrich saw the skeleton with a harrow painted on its dark green flank. The machine guns firing through the Grim Reaper's propeller disk blazed. Rudel jinked again— right into the stream of bullets.

His engine coughed and quit and started smoking. A round punched through both sides of the cockpit in front of him before he had time to blink. "We've got to get out!" he yelled to Dieselhorst, praying the sergeant would answer.

"I was hoping you'd be here to tell me that," Dieselhorst said. "Sounds good to me. Are we still inside French territory, or did we make it back to our own lines?"

"Only one way to find out." Rudel eyed the gauges. "Don't waste time, either—we're losing altitude."

He yanked back on the canopy. The Stuka's glasshouse had two movable parts: one for the pilot, the other for the gunner-radioman. Hans-Ulrich hoped the bullet that almost nailed him hadn't messed up the track along which his part slid. He breathed a sigh of relief when it retracted smoothly enough.

Wind tore at him. It didn't want to let him get out. He fought his way clear of the cockpit. A quick glance told him Sergeant Dieselhorst was already gone. Rudel threw himself into space.

He missed smashing himself against the Stuka's upthrust tail: the first risk every pilot bailing out took. Then he counted down from ten and yanked the ripcord. *Wham!* The blow he took when the chute opened made him gray out for a second, the same as dive-bombing would have done. He came to faster than he would have pulling out of a dive, though.

He looked around. There was another canopy, below him and to the left. Dieselhorst hadn't hit the tail, either. Good.

Back in the last war, pilots hadn't worn parachutes. The powers that be thought having them would turn men into cowards. Soldiers had gone into that war without steel helmets, too. They'd learned better there sooner than they had with chutes.

The *Luftwaffe* model still left something to be desired. Hans-Ulrich dropped faster than he would have liked—but not nearly so fast as if the chute hadn't opened! He couldn't steer very well, either.

He bent his legs and tried to relax as the ground rushed up at him. He sprained an ankle anyway, but didn't think he broke it. He used his belt knife to cut away the canopy before it dragged him into some trees. He couldn't see where Sergeant Dieselhorst had come down.

"Hold it right there, shithead, or you're fucking dead meat!" somebody yelled. Hans-Ulrich needed a moment to realize he understood the obscenity-laced command. It was in German. He'd landed among friends.

Happily, he raised his hands. "I'm a Stuka pilot!" he shouted back. "My number two's around here somewhere."

Three men in field-gray cautiously emerged from those trees. "Get under cover, you *Dummkopf*," one of them said. "There's Frenchies only a few hundred meters from here."

Hans-Ulrich tried to stand. His ankle didn't want to let him. "My leg—" he said.

One of the soldiers had a machine pistol. He covered the other two, who were riflemen. They trotted forward and each got one of Rudel's arms over his shoulder. "We'll take you to an aid station," one of them said. They lugged him back to the woods.

A KNOCK ON THE DOOR. Up till now, Sarah Goldman hadn't known something so ordinary could be so terrifying. The ordinary police thumped. The *Gestapo* pounded. She could guess who was there from the different knocks, and she proved right most of the time. If only proving right would have done her the least bit of good!

This knock didn't seem quite so frightening. So Sarah told herself, anyway, as she went to the door. Maybe she was trying to find hope whether it was really there or not. She braced herself to face some scowling SS man all in black.

But no. "Oh! *Frau* Breisach!" she exclaimed in glad surprise. Even if Wilhelmina Breisach liked to grumble about every little thing, the people across the street had always got on well with the Goldmans till the Nazis started making things tough on Jews. And, naturally, no one from the neighborhood seemed eager to stop by after Saul did . . . what he did. Better to pretend you didn't have any idea who those people were than to have to explain why you wanted anything to do with them. So Sarah hesitated before asking, "Won't you come in?"

"No, thank you. Please excuse me, but I'd better not." *Frau* Breisach shook her head. She was a plump, reasonably pretty blond a few years younger than Sarah's mother. Now she thrust an envelope into Sarah's hand. "This was addressed to us, but I think it may be for you." She didn't wait for any answer from Sarah, but scurried away as if hoping no one had seen her come. She probably was hoping exactly that, too.

"Thank you," Sarah said, but she was talking to *Frau* Breisach's back.

She closed the door, scratching her head. "What was that all about?" her father asked.

"I don't know." Then Sarah looked down at the envelope, and she did. Ice and fire rippled through her, fractions of a heartbeat apart. She recognized the handwriting on the address. "I think maybe you'd better have a look at this. Mother, you, too."

Samuel and Hanna Goldman came out to see why she was fussing. Without a word, she handed her father the envelope. Behind his glasses, his eyes widened. So did those of Sarah's mother. Neither of them said much. They didn't know the *Gestapo* had put microphones in their house, but they also didn't know it hadn't. In Adolf Hitler's Germany in 1939, they didn't want to take any foolish chances.

Sarah's father took the letter out of the envelope. Sarah and her mother crowded close to read it with him. *Hello, Uncle, Aunt, and Cousin Elisabeth,* it said. *Just a note to let you know basic training is going well. Don't listen to the rubbish you hear from some people. We get plenty to eat. The work is hard and we are often tired, but this is no Strength through Joy cruise. We are getting ready for war. I may end up in panzers. The drill sergeants say I have the knack for them. I hope so. They hurt the* Reich's *enemies more than anything else does, I think. I must go now—more drills. Stay well.* Heil *Hitler!* The scrawled signature was *Adalbert.*

Sarah and her father and mother all eyed one another. That was Saul's handwriting. "How in the world did he—?" Sarah began, and left it right there.

"He must have got some identity papers," Samuel Goldman whispered. "And when he did . . ." The professor's chuckle was most unprofessorial. "Well, who would guess to look for him there?"

When Sarah thought of it like that, she started to laugh. The Nazis wouldn't believe Saul had joined the *Wehrmacht,* even if he and Father both tried to do it right after the war broke out. To the thugs who ruled Germany, Jews were nothing but a pack of cowards. And so, chances were, they'd go on combing through the sad, shabby civilian world, simply because they couldn't imagine a Jew would deliberately expose himself to danger.

Mother plucked the letter and the envelope from Father's fingers. She carried the papers off to the fireplace in the front room. No matter what the *Gestapo* said, they weren't going to report this. No, indeed! Jews got only cheap, smoky brown coal for their heating and cooking needs, and precious little of that. The fire on the grate was more a token gesture than anything else. Even so, the envelope and letter flamed for a moment, then curled to gray ash.

"There." Mother sounded pleased with herself. "That's taken care of, anyhow."

"So it is." Father nodded. "I wonder how he managed to . . ." His voice trailed away again.

Several pictures formed in Sarah's mind. Maybe one of the fellows on Saul's football club had connections and got him papers. Maybe, after he fled Münster, he went drinking with somebody named Adalbert and stole the identity documents he needed. Or maybe he ran into this Adalbert walking along a country road and knocked him over the head.

That would make Saul a real criminal, not just somebody who'd snapped because a gang boss wouldn't treat him like a human being. The thought should have horrified Sarah. Somehow, it didn't. Her brother never would have done anything like that if the Nazis hadn't pushed him over the line. Never.

"I hope he'll be all right," Mother said worriedly. "You can tell he's not an ordinary German, after all."

Father followed that faster than Sarah did. "Jews aren't the only ones who get circumcised," he said. "Sometimes it's medically necessary. What I wonder is how *Frau* Breisach knew that letter was really for us."

"Somebody must have recognized the handwriting." Sarah had no trouble figuring that out. "Saul used to go over there all the time to help the Breisach kids with their homework—back when you could without getting into too much trouble, I mean. I think he was sweet on Hildegarde Breisach for a while, but . . ." She didn't go on.

"Yes. But," her father said heavily. "I wouldn't have minded intermarriage very much. The all-wise, all-knowing, and all-powerful State"—you could hear the stress he gave the word—"is a different story. And Hildegarde would have been insane to take the chance."

"If the State really were all-wise and all-powerful, *Frau* Breisach would have taken Saul's letter straight to the *Gestapo*," Mother said. "Some people still remember what human decency means."

"Never mind human decency. The Breisachs know *us*," Father said. "That counts for more, I'd say. I wouldn't bet a pfenning that they'd help some strange Jew. But we've lived across the street from them since the last war. We aren't strangers—we're neighbors. People first, Jews second, you might say. All over Germany, gentiles are probably going, 'Well, I don't have a good word to say about most Jews, but Abraham down the street? He's all right.' "

"I wonder how much good it will do," Sarah said.

"Some, anyhow." Father nodded toward the now anonymous ashes in the fireplace. "And I'm jealous of your brother."

"For heaven's sake, why?" Mother got that out before Sarah could.

"He made it into the *Wehrmacht*," Father answered. "I fought for Germany before. I would have done it again. I *am* a German, dammit, whether the Nazis want to let me be one or not."

"Isn't getting shot once enough for Germany?" Mother asked pointedly.

"If I hadn't, the goons would have treated us even worse than they did," Father said. "Hitler says Jews haven't got any guts—but he can't say that about front-line soldiers from the last war. So we have it better than most Jews—not good, but better."

"Oh, joy," Sarah said in a hollow voice. "If this is better, I don't want worse."

Father nodded solemnly. "You'd better not. The difference between bad and worse is much bigger than the difference between good and better. So when you think about the difference between better and worse . . ."

He sounded like someone who knew what he was talking about. Chances were he did. What *had* life in the trenches been like? Sarah had read *All Quiet on the Western Front*—who hadn't? She'd seen the movie, too. But her father had really gone through all those things, and maybe more besides. It was probably like the difference between reading about kissing and kissing, only more so.

Mother started to laugh. "What's funny?" Sarah asked. *She* sure didn't see anything.

Still in a low voice to foil the microphones that might not be there at all, her mother answered, "Our only son's just gone into the *Wehrmacht*. And I'm happy! Happy! He has a better chance of staying safe there than he would if he were still running around the countryside somewhere."

Sarah laughed, too. When you put it that way, it *was* funny. Her father put things in perspective, the way he usually did: "If you have to go that far for a laugh, you've got more *tsuris* than you need."

He hardly ever dropped a Yiddish word into his German. It would have made him seem less German, more openly Jewish. It might even have made him seem that way to himself. Sarah stared at him now. She understood *tsuris,* of course—understood what the word meant and, these days, also understood the thing.

"We do have more *tsuris* than we need," Mother said. Neither Sarah nor Samuel Goldman tried to tell her she was wrong.

It could have been worse, though. If the *Gestapo* caught up with

Saul after he clouted that work boss . . . What would they have done to him? Whatever it was, Sarah made herself think about something else.

"Do you suppose the British bombers will come over tonight?" she said. That was something else, all right, but not a better something else.

"Let them." Her father sounded almost gay. "Bombs don't care if we're Jews. Bombs can fall on *Gestapo* headquarters, too . . . *alevai.*" Two Yiddish words from him in two minutes. What was the world coming to?

"Of course, the *Gestapo* men can run into a shelter," Sarah said.

"So what? Even that doesn't always help," Father said. And he was right. Sarah felt like a German, too, if not so strongly as Father did. But she had trouble believing any German would cry if a bunch of *Gestapo* men got blown up.

Chapter 19

German artillery crashed down on the French position. Luc Harcourt dug as hard as he could, trying to carve a cave into the front wall of his foxhole. If he could manage that, fragments would have a hard time biting him . . . barring a direct hit, of course. He wished he hadn't had that last thought, but it did make him dig faster than ever.

The ground was muddy—almost too muddy to let him make the shelter he wanted. A cave-in could kill him, too, and much more ignominiously than a shell would have. But artillery was a worse risk. Five months of war had taught Luc to fear artillery more than anything but tanks. And what were tanks but artillery on tracks?

Luc almost had the hole he wanted when the shelling let up as suddenly as it had begun. He knew what that meant. His entrenching tool went back on his belt. He grabbed his rifle.

"They'll be coming any second!" Sergeant Demange yelled from a trench near the foxhole, for the raw replacements and the idiots in his section. "Make 'em pay for it, that's all. We don't have a hell of a lot of room to back up in."

"Your sergeant is right." That was Lieutenant Marquet—Luc thought that was his name, anyhow. He'd replaced the previous company commander a few days earlier, after Captain Rémond stopped some shrapnel with his chest. He'd been alive when he went off to the aid station. Now, who could say? The lieutenant seemed brave enough. He did like to hear himself talk, though: "Three times in a lifetime, the *Boches* have attacked Paris. They took it once, to our shame. We held them the last time, to our everlasting glory. Which would you rather have now, my friends?"

All Luc wanted was to come through alive and in once piece. The only shame he worried about was letting his buddies down. They mattered to him. Paris? Next to the dirty, smelly, frightened men alongside of whom he fought, Paris wasn't so much of a much.

Small-arms fire picked up. The Germans knew what was going on as well as the Frenchmen they were trying to murder. They wanted to get into the French fieldworks as fast as they could, while the *poilus* were still woozy from the barrage.

If they do that, I'm dead. The thought was enough to make Luc stick his head up and bring his rifle to his shoulder. A bullet cracked past, too close for comfort. He wouldn't have had to worry about that if he'd stayed all nicely huddled in his young cave.

No, but then he would have had to worry about other things. Sure as hell, the Germans were loping forward. The men who ran straight up and down had less experience than the ones who folded themselves as small as they could. Most of the *Boches* did know enough to hit the dirt or dive behind something when French machine guns started chattering.

The Germans never got to Meaux the last time around. That meant all the damage in town was brand new. The thirteenth-century cathedral lay in ruins a couple of kilometers behind Luc. Guns and Stukas cared nothing for antiquities—and the French weren't shy about placing observers in the steeples. If the bastards in field-gray kept pressing forward, pretty soon French guns would start shelling Meaux—and the *Boches* would have put men with binoculars up in high places.

As if thinking of French guns had called them up, several batteries of quick-firing 75s started banging away at the Germans. They'd slaughtered the *Boches* by the thousands in 1914, and all through the last war. Things were tougher now. German 105s outranged them and delivered bigger shells. The enemy knew better than to advance in tight-packed ranks, too. But when you needed to drop a lot of artillery on some unlucky place in a hurry, 75s were still hard to beat.

German medics in Red Cross smocks and armbands ran around gathering up the wounded. Luc left them alone as much as he could. War was tough enough without making it worse.

He thought so, anyhow. A medic fell, and then another one. Another German wearing the Red Cross emblem pointed angrily toward the French line . . . right about toward where Sergeant Demange was lurking. A moment later, that medic ducked, which meant a bullet hadn't missed him by much. He could take a hint—he dove behind a battered stone wall.

"Naughty, Sergeant," Luc called.

"So's your mother," Demange answered, which wasn't exactly a ringing denial of anything.

Luc was in no position to tell him what to do. He had other things on his mind, anyway: "Have we got any tanks in the neighborhood? Do they?"

"Sure haven't seen any of ours," the sergeant said.

Since Luc hadn't, either, he asked the next important question: "Have we got any antitank guns?"

"Sure as hell hope so," Demange answered. That was also less encouraging than Luc wished it were.

Meaux lay in a loop of the Marne. Maybe the Germans were having trouble getting their armor across the river. They'd managed farther east with far fewer problems than he wished they'd had—probably far fewer than they should have had. With luck, the Allies were figuring out how to make those crossings tougher. Without luck, the *Boches* were feinting here so they could knock the crap out of the French and English defenders somewhere else.

Even without tanks, they hadn't given up in front of Meaux. More artillery came in, this barrage precisely aimed at the French forward positions. Luc cowered in his hole while hell fell all around him.

"Up!" Sergeant Demange screamed. "Up, you gutless assholes! They're coming!"

Luc didn't want to come up. Shell fragments did dreadful things. But he didn't want to get shot or bayoneted in his foxhole, either. The Germans aimed to make the French keep their heads down so they'd make easy meat. The French couldn't let them impose their will on the combat . . . Luc supposed.

He came up firing. A German had crawled to no more than thirty meters away. He had a potato-masher grenade in his right hand. Luc shot him before he could fling it. *"Heilige Scheisse!"* screamed the soldier in the coal-scuttle helmet. He clutched at himself. He must not have pulled the grenade's fuse cord, because it didn't go off after he dropped it.

Then French machine guns opened up, one of them from a spot where Luc hadn't known his side had a machine gun. The *Boches* hadn't known it was there, either. Several of them fell. Others ran back toward the river. Luc would have done the same thing in their boots. Flesh and blood had limits, and facing machine-gun fire out in the open went beyond them.

The German Luc had shot lay where he'd gone down. He wasn't dead; he kept thrashing around and yelling and swearing.

"Make him shut up," Sergeant Demange called. "Either blow his head off or go out there and bring him back."

Neither possibility appealed to Luc. Killing a wounded man in cold blood felt like murder. If he were lying there wounded, he wouldn't want the Germans taking pot shots at him.

But if he went out there to get the *Boche,* other soldiers in field-gray might nail him. He knew he had only a few seconds to make up his mind. Demange wouldn't hesitate longer than that before shooting the German himself. He wouldn't have second thoughts about it afterward, either.

"*Je suis dans le merde,*" Luc muttered. Up shit creek or not, he had to do *something.* He climbed out of the foxhole and crawled toward the wounded *Boche.*

Firing had slacked off. That could end any second, as he knew too well. None of the few rounds flying about came close—the Germans weren't aiming at him, anyway.

"I'll take you in," he called to the soldier in field-gray, hoping the fellow understood French. "We'll fix you up if we can."

"*Merci,*" the man answered in gutturally accented French. "Hurts."

"I bet," Luc said. The bullet had torn up the German's left leg. "Can you climb up on top of me?"

"I'll try." The *Boche* did it. He felt as if the fellow weighed a tonne—he was a bigger man than Luc, and weighted down with boots and helmet and equipment. Slowly—the only way he could—Luc crawled back toward the French line. Seeing what he was doing, the Germans paid him the courtesy of aiming away from him.

Other hands reached out to pull the wounded man off him. The German groaned as they got him down into the trenches. Luc had never been so glad to get under cover again himself. "Whew!" he said. "I felt naked out there."

"You did good, kid," Sergeant Demange said, and handed him a Gitane.

"Thanks." Luc leaned close for a light.

"You didn't go out there pretty damn quick, I was gonna plug the motherfucker," Demange said.

"Yeah, I figured. That's why I went." Luc's cheeks hollowed as he sucked in harsh smoke.

"Maybe they'll learn something off him," the noncom said. "He'll sing like a goddamn canary, and sergeants, they know stuff." Not without pride, he tapped his own chest.

"Was he a sergeant? I didn't notice," Luc said. Demange rolled his eyes. Grinning, Luc added, "If I'd known that, I would've shot him for sure."

"Funny man," Demange said scornfully. "You got that crappy hash mark on your sleeve, so you think you're entitled to be a goddamn funny man."

"Sergeant, if it meant I'd come through the war without getting shot, I'd never make another joke the rest of my life," Luc promised.

"Oh, yeah?" Sergeant Demange said. Luc's head bobbed up and down as if it were on springs. Demange spat out a tiny butt, crushed it underfoot, and lit a fresh Gitane. Then he returned to the business at hand: "Well, you don't need to worry about that, on account of it doesn't." Luc already knew as much. All the same, he wished Demange hadn't spelled it out.

ANASTAS MOURADIAN WAS DRUNK. Yes, a blizzard howled outside. Even so, a proper Soviet officer wasn't supposed to do any such thing. Sergei Yaroslavsky knew that perfect well. He would have been angrier at Mouradian if he weren't drunk himself.

They couldn't fly. They had plenty of vodka. What were they going to do—*not* drink it? Try as he would, Sergei couldn't come up with a good reason for leaving it alone.

Ivan Kuchkov was bound to be drinking with his fellow enlisted men. If the Chimp got smashed, the rest of the aircrew should, too. It showed solidarity between enlisted men and officers. It also showed that neither enlisted men nor officers had anything better to do when they couldn't get an SB-2 off the ground to save their lives.

"If Hitlerite bombers show up now, if we have to take shelter outside, we've got plenty of antifreeze in our blood," Sergei said.

"Never mind Hitlerite bombers. What about Hitlerite soldiers?" When Mouradian was sober, he spoke excellent Russian. He stayed fluent when he got drunk, but his Armenian accent turned thick enough to slice.

Sergei laughed and laughed. When he got drunk, everything was funny. "Where would Hitlerite soldiers come from?"

"Out of the sky. With parachutes. Like they did in Holland and Belgium." Anastas looked around the inside of the tent, his eyes big and round like an owl's: he might have expect Nazi parachutists to pop up any minute now.

That owlish stare only made Sergei laugh harder than ever. He looked around the inside of the tent, too. Enough of the wind outside got in to make the flame from the kerosene lamp flicker. That wasn't why his wide, high-cheekboned face registered dismay. "We're out of pelmeni! *And* pickled mushrooms! Where'd they go?"

Mouradian patted his stomach. "Good. Not spicy enough, but good." Being a southerner, he liked everything full of fire. As far as Sergei was concerned, the mushrooms and the meat dumplings were fine this way. Russians had all kinds of snacks that went with vodka. Even a half-skilled cook at a forward airstrip could do a decent job with some of them.

"We had a big plate of them," Sergei said sadly. The plate was still there. But for a couple of crumbs from the pelmeni, it was bare. Sergei sighed. He pointed at Anastas. "Not even the fucking Germans would be crazy enough to drop parachutists in this weather."

"God shouldn't have been crazy enough to make this weather." Mouradian must have been very drunk, or he wouldn't have talked about God so seriously. It gave Sergei a hold on him, which wasn't something anybody in the USSR wanted to give anyone else. Of course, there was something close to an even-money chance neither of them would remember anything about this come morning.

Even without dumplings or mushrooms, Sergei raised his tumbler. "*Za Stalina!*"

"To Stalin!" Anastas echoed. They both drank. The vodka was no better than it had to be. It went down as if Sergei were swallowing the lighted kerosene lamp. The really good stuff slid down your throat smooth as a kiss, then exploded in your stomach like a 500kg bomb. But this got you there, smooth or not.

Sergei sighed. If it was harsh now, he'd feel it worse in the morning. The good stuff didn't make you think elephants in hobnailed boots were marching on top of your skull.

"We have aspirins?" he asked.

"Somewhere," Mouradian said vaguely. Then he brightened. "We'll have more vodka."

"*Da.*" That cheered Sergei up, too: at least a little. Another dose of what made you feel bad could make you feel better. He reached for the bottle again. If he drank it now, he'd feel better right away.

"Leave me some," Anastas said.

"Leave me some, *sir,*" Sergei said. The drunker you got, the more important military discipline seemed . . . unless, of course, it didn't. He passed Mouradian the bottle. They drank till there was very little left to drink. They would have drunk till nothing was left to drink, but they both fell asleep first.

Getting up in the morning was as bad as Yaroslavsky had known it would be, or maybe a little worse. The first thing he did was drink half the remaining vodka. He would have drunk all of it, but Anastas snatched the bottle out of his hands. "To each according to his needs," the Armenian croaked, and no one in the USSR, no matter how hung over, dared quarrel with unadulterated Marx.

Fortunately, the aspirins turned up. Sergei dry-swallowed three of them. Mouradian took four. As sour as Sergei's stomach already was, the aspirins felt like a flamethrower in there. If he belched, he figured he could incinerate the whole airstrip.

Mouradian didn't look or sound much happier. "Breakfast," he said. The mere thought made Sergei groan. Then Anastas added, "They'll have tea—coffee, too, maybe."

"Well, maybe." Sergei peeled back the tent flap and looked out. The sun shone brilliantly off snow. He squinted at the alarming landscape. "Don't want to bleed to death through my eyeballs," he muttered.

"Tell me about it!" Mouradian said fervently.

Both being brave men, they made it to the field kitchen. *Shchi*—cabbage soup—seemed safe enough to Sergei. Anastas stuck to plain brown bread. The cooks had one battered samovar full of tea, another full of coffee. After getting outside of some of that—and after the aspirins took hold—Sergei decided he'd live. Eventually, he would decide he wanted to.

The radio blared out music. Mouradian turned it down. Sergei would have loved to turn it off, but he didn't dare. People might think you didn't want to listen to the news. If you didn't want to listen to the splendid achievements of the glorious Soviet state, people would wonder why not. Some of the people who wondered would have NKVD connections, too. And you'd be heading for a camp faster than you could blink.

Nobody complained about turning down the radio, though. Several other men eating breakfast had red-tracked eyes, sallow skin, and a hangdog expression. When it was snowing at an isolated airstrip, what were you going to do besides drink?

The song ended. An announcer gabbled about the overfulfillment of production norms at factories in Smolensk, Magnitogorsk, and Vladivostok. Not easy to imagine three more widely separated places. "Thus, despite the efforts of Fascists and other reactionaries, prosperity spreads throughout this great bulwark of the proletariat!" the announcer said.

Sergei had nothing against the bulwark of the proletariat. In his present fragile state, though, he didn't much want to hear about it. He made himself seem attentive even so, as he would have during a dull lecture in school. The penalty for obvious boredom then would have been a rap on the knuckles, or maybe a swat on the backside. He might pay more now.

Music returned. He didn't have to seem to be listening to that so closely. He couldn't ignore it altogether, however, or show he didn't like it. It wouldn't have gone out without some commissar's approval: without the state's approval, in other words. And if the state approved, citizens who knew what was good for them needed to do the same.

At the top of the hour, a different announcer came on the air. This fellow sounded better educated than the joker who'd been bragging about production norms. "And now the news!" the man said.

Several people with Red Air Force light blue on their collar tabs perked up. News from around the world mattered. "Soviet forces continue to punish the Polish reactionaries and the Nazi bandits who support them," the announcer crowed. "Over the past several days, Soviet infantrymen have driven another twenty kilometers deeper into Poland. Knowledgeable officers report that enemy resistance is beginning to crumble."

Nobody said anything. Nobody even raised an eyebrow. Sergei didn't think anyone actually fighting the Poles and Germans believed their resistance was crumbling. He knew damn well he didn't. That particular item had to be aimed at bucking up civilian morale hundreds if not thousands of kilometers from the front.

"Foreign Commissar Litvinov has protested to the Japanese government about its troop buildup between puppet Manchukuo and progressive Siberia," the announcer went on.

Hearing that made Sergei's headache get worse. This borderland between the USSR and Poland was nowhere in particular. He tried to imagine fighting a war at the eastern edge of Siberia. That was Nowhere in Particular with capital N and P. The only reason either the Soviet Union or Japan cared about it was because of strategy. Other than that, the whole area could go hang.

Vladivostok was the USSR's window on the Pacific. It was a window frozen shut several months a year, but never mind that. Vladivostok also sat on the end of the world's longest supply line: it was the place where the Trans-Siberian Railroad finally stopped. It wasn't a million kilometers from Moscow—it only seemed that way.

What would happen if the little yellow monkeys who lived in Japan tried to seize the railroad and cut the town's lifeline? How long before Vladivostok withered? How long before the Japanese could just walk in? Sergei was too young to remember the siege of Port Arthur and the Russo-Japanese War as a whole, but he knew about them. Few Soviet citizens didn't. Even though the Tsar's corrupt regime was to blame for the Russian defeat, it still rankled.

Brooding about it made him read some of what the radio newscaster was saying. When he started paying attention again, the man was saying, "And the French government has declared that the front is Paris. The French say they are determined to fight in the capital itself, and to fight on beyond it even if it falls. They did not have to do this during the last war. Whether they will live up to their promises, only time will tell."

"If they'd done better by Czechoslovakia when the war started, they might not be in this mess now," Anastas Mouradian said. "They'll probably expect us to pull their chestnuts off the fire for them, too."

"Too fucking bad if they do. We've got enough worries of our own," Sergei said.

"German radio reports that Adolf Hitler has indignantly denied any military coup was attempted against him," the announcer said. "Reliable sources inside Germany report that at least four prominent German generals have not been seen for several weeks, however."

No one eating breakfast said anything to that. No one imagined anything could be safe to say. No one even wanted to look at anyone else. The look on your face could betray you, too.

Soviet generals—far more than four of them—started disappearing in 1937. Like some of the Old Bolsheviks who started getting it in the neck at the same time, a few confessed to treason in show trials before they were executed. Others were simply put to death, or vanished into the camps, or just . . . disappeared.

It wasn't only generals, either. Officers of all ranks were purged. So were bureaucrats of all ranks, and so were doctors and professors and anyone who seemed dangerous to anyone else.

Now the same thing was happening in Germany? Sergei had sometimes thought that Communists and Nazis were mirror images of each other, one side's left being the other's right and conversely. He'd never shared that thought with anyone; had he tried, he would put his life in the other person's hands. He wished the idea had never crossed his mind. Just having certain notions was deadly dangerous. They might show up on your face without your even realizing it. And if they did, you were dead.

Or maybe worse.

So did the enemy have to worry about the kinds of things that had convulsed the Soviet Union for the past couple of years? *Good,* Sergei thought. If both sides were screwed up the same way, the one he was on looked to have a better chance.

LUDWIG ROTHE LIT A GITANE he'd got from a German infantryman who'd taken a pack from a dead French soldier. It was strong as the devil, but it tasted like real tobacco, not the hay and ersatz that went into German cigarettes these days.

"Have another one of those, Sergeant?" Fritz Bittenfeld asked plaintively.

"You look like a hungry baby blackbird trying to get a worm from its mama," Ludwig said. Fritz opened his mouth very wide, as if he really were a nestling. Laughing, Ludwig gave the panzer driver a Gitane.

"Chirp!" Theo Hossbach said, flapping his arms. "Chirp!" He got a cigarette, too.

They'd all smoked them down to tiny butts when a blackshirt who'd been prowling around the panzer park finally got to them. "Can I talk to you boys for a minute?" he asked, a little too casually.

His shoulder straps were plain gray, with two gold pips. That made him the SS equivalent of a captain. How could you say no? You couldn't. "What's up, sir?" Ludwig tried to keep his voice as normal as he could.

"You men have served under Major Koral for some time—isn't that so?" the SS man said.

"*Ja,*" Ludwig said. Fritz and Theo both nodded. No harm in admitting that, not when the blackshirt could check their records and find out for himself that Koral had led the panzer battalion since the war started.

"All right," the SS man said, in now-we're-getting-somewhere tones. "How often have you heard him express disloyalty toward the *Führer* and the *Reich*?"

"Disloyalty?" Ludwig echoed. He had trouble believing his ears. But the SS man nodded importantly. He seemed as full of his own righteousness as the more disagreeable kind of preacher. Picking his words with care, Ludwig said, "Sir, you do know, don't you, that Major Koral's already been wounded in action twice?"

"Yes, yes." The SS man nodded impatiently, as if that were of no account. To him, it probably wasn't. He went on, "I'm not talking about his military behavior. I'm talking about his political behavior." *You idiot,* his gaze added. *You're supposed to know things like that without being told.*

Sergeant Rothe bristled at so obviously being thought a moron. But then he chuckled to himself. If the blackshirt figured him for a *Dummkopf,* a *Dummkopf* he would be, by God. "Sir, the major just gives me orders. He doesn't waste his time talking politics with noncoms."

"What's going on, anyway?" Theo sounded as innocent as an un-weaned baby. His dreamy features let him get away with that more easily than Ludwig could have.

The SS man didn't hesitate before answering, "You will have heard that certain *Wehrmacht* generals betrayed their country by viciously plotting against the *Führer*?"

Ludwig had heard that, all right, from Hitler's own lips. Telling the SS man as much struck him as the very worst of bad ideas. "*Gott im Himmel!*" he exclaimed, as if it were a complete surprise. "I heard it, *ja*, but I thought it was only enemy propaganda." Beside him, Theo and Fritz nodded.

"It's true, all right," the blackshirt said. "They were disgraces to the uniform they wore, disgraces to the *Volk,* disgraces to the *Reich.* And so we must purify the army of all their associates and of everyone who might have shared their vicious views. Now do you understand why I am inquiring about Major Koral?"

"He wouldn't do anything like that," Fritz said. "He wouldn't put up with anybody else who did, either."

Theo nodded again. "That's right."

"I think so, too," Ludwig said.

"You might be surprised. You might be very surprised indeed," the SS man said. "We've found treason in some places where no one would have thought to look for it if these generals hadn't disgraced themselves."

If Ludwig hadn't heard it from the *Führer,* he would have wondered what that meant. He did wonder what the SS and the *Gestapo* were up to now. Had they sniffed out more real treason, or had they "discovered" it regardless of whether it was really there? He didn't ask this fellow that kind of question. That it could occur to him might be plenty to mark him as disloyal.

He did ask, "Why do you think Major Koral might be mixed up in this . . . this *Scheisse*?"

"*Scheisse* it is," the SS man agreed. He pulled a scrap of paper from the right beast pocket of his tunic. "He has . . . let me see . . . a long history of association with General Fritsche, and also with General Halder. He may have been a Social Democrat before 1933—the record is not completely clear about that, but it is worrisome. And one of his cousins was formerly married to a Jew."

If Fritsche and Halder were two of the generals who'd tried to overthrow the *Führer,* that might mean something. Or, of course, it might not. Ludwig had a long history of association with his cats, but he'd never wanted to eat mice himself. The rest didn't seem to mean much. The Social Democrats had been the biggest party in Germany during the Weimar Republic. They were about as exclusive as a blizzard. Ludwig had no great use for Jews, but he thought one of his cousins was married to one, too. He hoped to God the SS would never dig that out and use it against him.

"Sorry not to be more help, sir," he said insincerely.

"Like the sergeant said, Major Koral's always been brave in combat," Theo added. "Didn't he win the Iron Cross First Class? Didn't they put him up for the *Ritterkreuz*?"

The Iron Cross First Class—just like the Führer, Ludwig thought— one more thing he knew better than to say out loud. But the two awards weren't really comparable. Lots of officers got the Iron Cross First Class now. For a common soldier in the Kaiser's army to have won it the last time around was much more remarkable. Even the Knight's Cross in this war wasn't the same.

The SS man looked unhappy enough at Theo's mild questions. "That has nothing to do with anything," he said stiffly. "If you recall anything suspicious about him, report it to your superiors at once. At once, do you hear?" He tramped off, his back ramrod straight.

"Jesus Christ on roller skates!" Fritz said. "I think I'd sooner go to the dentist than get another little visit like that."

"You can spread that on toast and call it butter," Theo agreed. Ludwig supposed it was agreement, anyhow. The radioman came out with the strangest things sometimes.

Fritz Bittenfeld found a new question: "Should we go tell the major he's got hounds sniffing on his trail?"

"If we see him in the field, sure," Ludwig said. "But those fucking goons've got to be keeping an eye on him. If we go blab, what happens to us? We stick our dicks in the sausage grinder, that's what?"

"Oh, that smarts!" Theo said in shrill falsetto. Ludwig and Fritz both laughed. Better to laugh than to grab at yourself, which was what Ludwig's figure of speech made him want to do. Assuming it *was* a figure of speech, of course. With the SS, you could never be sure. And if they did it for real . . . Ludwig wanted to grab at himself again.

Bitterly, Fritz said, "It's a hell of a note when you find out combat's not the worst thing that can happen to you."

"Yeah, it's a hell of a note, all right," Ludwig said. "You going to tell me it isn't true? I can deal with the Czechs and the French and the English. I can even deal with the Russians if I have to. My old man fought in the East the last time around. Yeah, I can cope with that—bet your ass I can. But heaven help me if I've got to try and handle the cocksuckers who think they're on my side."

He kept his voice down. No one but his buddies could possibly have heard him. Only after the words were out of his mouth did he wonder if he could trust Fritz and Theo. They all trusted one another with their lives on the battlefield. But political matters were different—and, as Fritz had said, worse.

If he and the driver and the radioman *couldn't* trust one another . . . Ludwig swore under his breath. This was the nastiest thing the SS did, right here. If you weren't sure you could count on people who'd already saved your bacon more times than you could remember, then what?

You were screwed, that was what.

"We're as bad as the Russians, you know?" Theo said, which was too close for comfort to what Ludwig was thinking. The radio operator went on, "Pretty soon I'm going to start praying for cloudy weather."

"What the hell is *that* supposed to mean?" Ludwig demanded.

"Well, if my shadow isn't there, I don't have to worry that it'll betray me to the *Gestapo* when I'm not looking," Theo answered. That either made no sense at all or altogether too much.

"Maybe it isn't there *because* it's off betraying you to the *Gestapo.*" Later, Ludwig wondered about himself. At the time, what he said seemed logical enough—to him, anyhow.

It didn't faze Theo, either. "Nothing would surprise me any more," he said. "Shadows aren't to be trusted. No matter how much you feed 'em, they never get any fatter than you do. And have you ever seen one that wasn't as dark as a nigger, even when it was walking on a snow-bank?"

Fritz looked from one of his crewmates to the other. "I think you've both gone round the bend," he declared.

"*Zu befehl,*" Theo said—*at your service.* He clicked his heels, as if he were a Prussian grandee or an Austrian gentleman with more noble blood than he knew what to do with.

A battery of French 75s near Meaux started shelling the panzer park at extreme long range. Only a few shells came close enough to drive the Germans into the holes they'd dug. They *had* dug holes, of course; whenever they stopped for more than a few minutes, they dug. Anyone would have thought *Wehrmacht* men—and their French and English counterparts—descended from moles rather than monkeys.

"Wonder if the SS shithead has enough sense to take cover," Fritz remarked.

"Nobody'll miss him if he doesn't," Ludwig said. "With a little luck, even the Frenchmen won't miss him." Fritz and Theo both groaned. Neither tried to tell him he was wrong.

After a while, when the French guns didn't blow up any ammunition dumps or show other tangible evidence of success, they eased off. The panzer crews came up above ground. And there was the blackshirt, a pistol in hand, leading Major Koral to a waiting auto with a swastika flag flying above its right fender. Face pale and set, the major got in. The car sped away, back toward Germany.

"What is this world coming to?" Ludwig wondered out loud.

"Nothing good," Fritz answered. "Dammit, we've still got a war to fight."

"So does Major Koral," Theo added. Koral would likely lose his. And who would get the blame if the *Wehrmacht* also lost its?

Chapter 20

Paris in wartime. Alistair Walsh had seen the City of Light in 1918, too. Then, though, it had been pretty clear that the Kaiser's troops wouldn't make it this far. Bombers were only nuisances in those fondly remembered days.

Things were different now, not quite twenty-one years later. Maybe 1914 had felt like this: the sense of the field-gray Juggernaut's car bearing down on the city, with all the people in it wondering whether to run away or to grab what amusement they could before everything disappeared.

British money went a long way in France. Walsh remembered that from the last time around, and it still seemed true. He'd got buzzed at a bar where the fellow serving drinks—a man no more than a couple of years older than he was—had a patch over his left eye and walked with a limp. "You here before, Tommy?" the Frenchman asked in fair English.

"Oh, yes." Alistair brushed his wounded leg with one hand. "I caught a packet, too—not so bad as yours, but that's just bloody luck one way or the other."

"Yes. We could both be dead," the bartender agreed, handing him his whiskey and soda. "And you—you have another chance."

"Right." Walsh didn't like thinking about that, however true it was. "So do you, pal, come to that. Damned Germans bomb Paris every chance they get."

The Frenchman called his eastern neighbors several things unlikely to appear in dictionaries. Walsh hadn't learned a lot of French in his two stays on the Continent, but what he had learned was of that sort. "You bet," he said, and slid a shilling across the zinc-topped bar. "Here. Buy yourself one, too."

"*Merci.*" The barman made the silver coin vanish.

"Damn shame about the Eiffel Tower, too," Walsh added awkwardly.

"When the top part falls off—fell off—it should fall on the government's head," the French veteran said. "Then maybe it do some good. After we beat the *Boches,* we build it again."

"There you go." Alistair started to suggest that the Germans could pay for it, but he swallowed that. Reparations had been nothing but a farce after the last war. Why expect anything better this time around?

"Drink up, *mon ami,*" the Frenchman said. "You will look for other sport, eh? Night still comes too soon, especially with blackout."

"Too right it does." Walsh realized the barman really liked him. Otherwise, the fellow would have tried to keep him in there forever. But the man must have realized he'd do all right from his other customers. Soldiers wearing several different uniforms packed the place. As long as none of them was in German kit . . .

Walsh had to push through double blackout curtains to get out onto the street. A little light leaked out despite the curtains. A *flic* blew his whistle and shouted something irate. Since Alistair didn't understand it, he didn't have to answer. That was how he felt, anyhow. And it was already dark enough to let him fade into the crowd before the copper could get a good look at him.

He knew where he was going, or thought he did. The house was supposed to be around the corner and a couple of streets up. He figured it would be easy to find even in the dark: places like that always had queues—or, given French carelessness about such things, crowds—of horny soldiers outside waiting their turn for a go with one of the girls.

But he missed it. Maybe he walked past the corner in the gloom, or maybe the place wasn't where he thought it was. He wandered around, bumping into people and having others bump into him. "Excuse me," he said, and, *"Pardon."* It wasn't curfew time yet, and Paris kept going regardless of such tiresome regulations.

Cars honked like maniacs as they rattled along. They had headlamps masked with black paper or cloth so only a tiny slit of light came out: with luck, not enough to see from 20,000 feet. The faint glow wasn't enough to let drivers see much, either. Every so often, the sound of crunching bumpers and frantic cursing punctuated the night.

Another couple of steps and Alistair bumped into somebody else. "Excuse me," he repeated resignedly.

"Pardon," said his victim: a woman.

They both stepped forward again, trying to go around each other, and bumped once more. "Bloody hell," Walsh said. You could be as foul-mouthed as you pleased in a country where most people didn't know what you were talking about.

But the woman laughed. "I was thinking the same thing," she said, her English better than the barman's.

"Sorry," Alistair mumbled.

"Don't worry," she answered. "My husband would say that when he was alive. He was a soldier from the last war."

"You were married to a Tommy?" Walsh asked.

"That's right," she said. "My father was a butcher. My brother got killed at Verdun, and so Fred took over the business. Better than he could have done in England, he always said. But he died five years ago . . . and now we have war again."

"Too right we do." Walsh wondered what the hell to say next. Verdun was gone, lost, this time around, though not with the titanic bloodbath of 1916. He couldn't very well ask a woman where the *maison de tolerance* was. He wondered if he could talk her into taking him home with her. If she was used to British soldiers (though he was no damned Englishman—by the way she sounded, her Fred had come from Yorkshire or thereabouts) . . .

Before he could find anything, she said, "Maybe you should go left at the next corner. It's not far at all—only a few meters. Good luck, Tommy." Then she was nothing but fading footsteps on the street: this time, she stepped around him nimbly as a dancer.

Alistair laughed at himself. So she wasn't a widow who needed consoling—not from him, anyhow. "Too damned bad," he muttered. "She'd be better than what I could pay for." And then, thoughtfully, "Left, is it?"

He didn't think in meters, but he could make sense of them. You had to if you were going to fight on the Continent. He found the corner by stepping off the curb. He didn't fall on his face, which proved God loved drunks. He didn't get run over crossing the street, either—no thanks to the French drivers, most of whom tooled along as if they could see for miles, not six inches past their noses if they were lucky.

A long block down the street, he bumped into somebody else. " 'Ere, myte, watch yourself," growled an unmistakable Cockney.

"Oh, keep your hair on," Walsh retorted, not only showing he was from Britain himself but suggesting he had the bulge to deal with any ordinary soldier. He paused. He still couldn't see much, but his ears told him a long file of men stood here breathing and muttering and shuffling their feet. A light went on in his head, even if it illuminated nothing out here. "Is this the queue for—?"

"You fink Oi'd wyte loike this for anyfing else?" the Cockney answered.

"I suppose not," Walsh said. Fred's widow knew soldiers, all right, and knew what they'd be looking for. If she knew he also wouldn't have minded looking for her . . . well, that was how the cards came down. She might have been better, but this wouldn't be bad—not while it was going on, anyhow. Later, he'd likely wonder why he wasted his money on some tart who'd forget him as soon as he got off her.

But that would be later. The queue lurched forward a few feet. Somebody joined it behind Alistair, and then somebody else. He wished he could light a cigarette, but that was against the blackout rules, too. One more thing he'd have to wait for. Well, it wouldn't be long.

BREAKFAST AT THE AIRSTRIP WAS rolls and strong coffee. Hans-Ulrich Rudel longed for milk. By the way a lot of the Stuka pilots and rear gunners went on, they longed for schnapps or whiskey. He didn't care what they drank, as long as it didn't hurt what they did in the air. They sassed him unmercifully. He'd got used to that—by all the signs, he was the only teetotaler in the *Luftwaffe*. He didn't much like it, but he couldn't fight everybody all the time.

And then someone said something different to him: "What do you think of the new wing commander?"

"Colonel Steinbrenner?" Rudel shrugged. "He seems like a good enough officer—and I'm sure he's a good German patriot."

"Do you think Colonel Greim wasn't?" asked the other pilot, a new fish. Was he Maxi or Moritz? Moritz, that was it.

Hans-Ulrich shrugged again. "He'd still be in charge of the wing if the powers that be thought he was. Me, I say '*Heil* Hitler!' and I go about my business. What else can you do?"

Moritz started to say something, stopped, and then tried again: "The war hasn't gone the way everybody hoped it would when it started."

"And so?" Rudel gulped coffee. He needed help prying his eyelids open—like most flyers these days, he was chronically short on sleep. And this brew would do the trick, too, which meant it had to come from captured stock. But he could see some things even with his eyes closed. "How many wars *do* go just the way one side thinks they will beforehand? Do we toss out the *Führer* because things aren't perfect?"

"Of course not," Moritz said quickly.

"Of course not," Hans-Ulrich agreed. He hadn't expected his colleague to say anything else. That the other man might not dare say anything else never crossed his mind. He believed in *Führer* and Party at least as strongly as he believed in his father's stern Lutheran God. Till the latest political upheavals, he'd assumed everybody else felt the same way. "This foolishness isn't doing the war effort any good."

Moritz looked down into his coffee mug. Then he eyed Hans-Ulrich again. "Which foolishness?" he asked quietly. "The coup, or what's happening now to anybody who might have known anything about it?"

"Why, the coup, of course." Rudel's answer was as automatic as the mechanism that pulled a Stuka out of a dive. Only after it came out did he fully realize what the other man had said. "I could report you for that!" he exclaimed. He almost said, *I should report you for that!*

"*Ja.* I know," Moritz answered. "But think first. Would I go up there to get my ass shot off if I weren't loyal to the *Vaterland*?"

Nobody without a death wish would fly a Stuka if he weren't doing it for his country. Even so, Hans-Ulrich said, "You can't be loyal to the *Vaterland* if you're not loyal to the *Führer*. We'd lose for sure if anyone else tried to run the war, or if we bugged out of it. We'd stab ourselves in the back, the same way we did in 1918."

"No doubt," the other pilot said. Was that agreement, or was he just trying to get Hans-Ulrich out of his hair? Hans-Ulrich knew which way he'd bet. He didn't know what to do next. Anyone who wondered about vengeance was less loyal to the Party and the *Führer* than he should have been. But if you were a brave pilot, and you hurt the French and British every time you flew . . .

Rudel was still chewing on that when he headed off to hear Colonel Steinbrenner's morning briefing with the rest of the pilots. His ankle still hurt, but he could walk on it and use the Stuka's aileron controls. That was all that counted.

"If we can break through north of Paris, we have them," Steinbrenner declared. "Then we wheel around behind the city, the way we would have done it in 1914 if von Kluck hadn't run short of men and turned too soon."

He was in his forties—old enough to remember von Kluck's turn, maybe old enough to have been one of the footsloggers who made it and then got hurled back from the Marne. By the way he spoke, he still took it personally a generation later.

"We've done better this time than we did in 1914," he went on. "Thanks to the panzers and to you boys, we've got most of the French Channel ports. That makes it harder for England to send men and machines to the Continent. And who's to thank for the panzers and the Stukas and the rest of our toys? The *Führer,* that's who."

Hans-Ulrich nodded vigorously. So did most of the other men in the wing. He judged that some of them, like him, meant it from the bottom of their hearts. Others wanted to be seen nodding so the new wing commander would have no reason to doubt their loyalty. *Whited sepulchers,* he thought scornfully. His father had plenty of things to say about parishioners who acted pious in church but behaved like animals as soon as they got outside again.

And a few stubborn souls, Moritz among them, just sat there listening as if Colonel Steinbrenner were going on about the weather. Maybe they had the courage of their convictions. Some men did fight for *Vaterland* rather than *Führer.* Rudel didn't think the two were separable. He was willing to bet Germany's foes didn't, either.

After a moment, Steinbrenner resumed: "Your target is Chaumont. There's a railway viaduct there—it's more than six hundred meters long, and it crosses the Suize. Artillery hasn't been able to knock it out, and the enemy keeps sending men and matériel across it. Time to put a stop to that, by God!"

Now everybody nodded. Give the *Luftwaffe* a purely military problem, and it would handle things just fine. Even Hans-Ulrich was relieved that he wouldn't have to think about politics while he was flying. If any of the other men felt differently, he would have been very surprised.

Groundcrew men were already bombing up his Stuka and fueling it when he went out to the revetment. Sergeant Dieselhorst was grabbing a premission cigarette a safe distance away. "What's on the plate?" Dieselhorst asked.

"Chaumont. Railroad bridge," Hans-Ulrich said.

"*Ach, so.*" The sergeant's cheeks hollowed as he took one last drag. He crushed the butt underfoot. "Flak'll be thick enough to walk on," he said mournfully. "They know what those bridges are worth."

"You can always bow out," Hans-Ulrich said. The rear gunner sent him a reproachful look. Rudel gestured toward the Ju-87. "Well, come on, then. *Heil* Hitler!"

"*Heil!*" Dieselhorst echoed. Whatever he thought of the rumored coup, he didn't say much. He just did his job. That wasn't the worst attitude for a noncom—or anyone else—to have.

Inside the plane's cabin, he and Hans-Ulrich went through their preflight checks. Everything came up green. With all the flying the planes were doing, the groundcrews had to work miracles to keep so many of them airborne. So far, the mechanics and armorers seemed up to it.

A groundcrew man spun the prop. Hans-Ulrich fired up the engine. Another groundcrew man sat on the wing to help guide him as he taxied out of the revetment and onto the airstrip's chewed-up grass. The ground crewman hopped off with a wave. Rudel gave him one, too. When he got the takeoff signal, he gunned the Stuka. It bounced down the runway and lurched into the air. It might not have been pretty, but it flew, all right.

Chaumont wasn't far on the map, but it was far enough: farther than the Kaiser's army had ever got. "We have company," Sergeant Diesel-horst said, distracting Rudel.

He looked around, making sure he'd read the noncom's tone the right way. Yes, those were Messerschmitts flying with the Stukas, not Hurricanes or French fighters streaking in to attack them. Chaumont *was* important, then. Flights over France, unlike those across the Chan-nel, didn't always get escorts laid on.

Hans-Ulrich saw the flak well before he reached the target. It did look thick enough to walk on. Yes, the enemy also knew how important Chaumont was. Hans-Ulrich muttered to himself, but didn't say any-thing out loud. He didn't want Dieselhorst worrying any more than necessary. Worrying as much as proved necessary would likely be bad enough.

Hurricanes streaked at the Stukas maybe a minute and a half later. The 109s zoomed away to meet the British fighters. Hans-Ulrich had seen over England that that was the best way to hold off enemy planes. Sticking too close to the bombers you were escorting gave attackers a big edge.

Sometimes the enemy got through no matter what you did. Sergeant Dieselhorst's machine gun chattered. Rudel saw a couple of Stukas diving for the deck, hoping to outrun the Hurricanes on their tails. He wished them luck, and feared they'd need it.

He started his own dive for the railroad bridge sooner than he'd in-tended to, which also meant it had to be shallower. That gave the anti-aircraft gunners plenty of time to fire at him. Shells burst all around his Stuka. He hung on to the stick as tight as he could—it was like driving a car on a badly rutted dirt road. Puffs of evil black smoke came closer and closer. A few bits of shrapnel rattled off the plane or tore into it—luckily, only a few.

Trying not to think about anything else, Hans-Ulrich bored in on the bridge. The viaduct had three levels, towering more than fifty me-ters above the river it overleaped. Some plump, pipe-smoking, mustachioed French engineer of the last century must have been proud of himself for designing it. Rudel yanked at the bomb-release lever. With a little luck, he'd make that Frenchman's grandchildren unhappy.

As soon as the bombs fell free, the Stuka got faster and friskier. More flak burst behind it, in front of it, all around it. And Sergeant Dieselhorst's voice rang tinnily through the speaking tube: "You nailed the fucking bridge! It's going down!"

"*Danken Gott dafür!*" Rudel said. He sped back toward the east, keeping his gauges at the edge of the red till he was sure he'd made it to German-held territory. If one of the Hurricanes had chosen to chase him, red-lining the gauges wouldn't have done much good. The Stuka made a fine dive-bomber, but a poor tired donkey in a sprint on the flat.

He got down. To his surprise, Colonel Steinbrenner trotted up before his prop stopped spinning. "Rudel!" the colonel said. "They swore you'd got shot down again. They said nobody could go into that kind of fire and come out the other side in one piece."

They, whoever they were, hadn't tried it themselves. Hans-Ulrich shrugged. He hadn't thought—much—about going down. All he'd thought about was doing his job. Letting the other get in the way would have distracted him. It might have given him cold feet. Now that he'd made it through, he wondered why the devil it hadn't.

Shrugging again, he said, "I'm here. The bridge is down."

"There's an Iron Cross First Class!" Steinbrenner said.

Medals weren't the biggest thing on Rudel's mind—nowhere close. He did say, "Make sure Dieselhorst gets one, too. He kept the enemy fighters off my back."

"He'll be taken care of," the wing commander promised. Hans-Ulrich believed him. Back in the last war, enlisted men always got the shitty end of the stick. The *Führer* understood that—he'd seen it for himself, in four years at the front. He'd sworn things would be different this time around, and he'd meant it. Some of the *von*s left over from the last round might not like it, but too bad for them.

Hans-Ulrich climbed out of the cockpit. Behind him, Sergeant Dieselhorst was coming out, too. "Made it," the noncom said with a wry grin.

"*Ja.*" Hans-Ulrich nodded. "And do you know what we won? Besides the *Eisenkreuz,* I mean?"

"What's that?" Dieselhorst asked.

"A chance to have just as much fun again tomorrow, or maybe later on today," Rudel answered.

The rear gunner and radioman made a wry face. "Hot damn!" he said.

JOAQUIN DELGADILLO LOOKED ACROSS THE Straits of Gibraltar to Africa. That was better than looking at Gibraltar itself. The British had fought like fourteen different kinds of demon to hold on to the Rock. In the end, it didn't do them a peseta's worth of good. Spain's gold and scarlet flew over Gibraltar for the first time in more than two hundred years.

Posters slapped onto walls or fences still standing boasted of the return to Spanish sovereignty. OURS AGAIN! they shouted, and GOOD-BYE TO ENGLAND! Glum British POWs moped behind barbed wire. The people who'd lived in Gibraltar were mostly Spaniards. The ones left alive after the fight seemed just as disheartened as the enemy soldiers. General Sanjurjo's men were making them sorry they'd backed the Union Jack.

A couple of Condor Legion German airmen walked by, gabbing in their incomprehensible guttural language. Delgadillo wondered why they didn't choke to death every time they opened their mouths. One of them nodded to him and said, *"Buenos días."* Sound by sound, the words were in Spanish, but no one who heard them would have dreamt they came from a Spaniard's throat.

"Buenos días," Delgadillo answered politely. Even if they did talk as if their mouths were full of glue, they'd done Marshal Sanjurjo a lot of

good. German bombers had helped flatten the British defenses here, for instance, and made British battleships keep their distance.

That thought made Joaquin look west instead of south. If the Royal Navy wanted to cause trouble, it still could. And it might: not only to pay Spain back for reclaiming Gibraltar but to keep the Straits open so British and French ships could pass into and out of the Mediterranean.

He'd faced fire from big naval guns before German planes pounded them into silence. If he never had to do that again, he'd light a grateful candle in church. Once was twice too often. They were much, much worse than land-based artillery—and that was more than bad enough.

The Condor Legion men were looking out to sea, too. One of them—not the one who'd spoken before—asked, "Where is your engineering officer?" He spoke better—not well, but better.

Delgadillo pointed north. "That way, about a kilometer and a half. Why do you need him?" He would never have asked that of one of his own officers. Spanish common soldiers didn't ask their officers anything. They existed to do as they were told. But the Germans were so foreign, so exotic, they might not know that.

Sure enough, this one answered readily enough: "We need spare parts to discuss. Since the big war in Europe began, we have from a shortage of them suffered."

Why didn't he put his verbs where they would do him some good? Did he hide them in his own language, too? He must have, or he wouldn't have done it in Spanish.

"I don't know if he'll be able to help you, *Señor*." Delgadillo *was* polite. He didn't tell the Condor Legion men the engineering officer didn't have a chance in hell of doing them any good. Lieutenant Lopez tried hard. Sometimes he could come up with a new bolt or a spring for a rifle. He'd done yeoman's duty repairing the broken axle on a horse-drawn wagon. But he knew no more about airplane parts than a goat knew about the miracle of transubstantiation.

"Well, we will out find. Many thanks. Much obliged," the German said. He and his pal headed north. A Spaniard, on a mission bound to be futile, would have taken his time. The Germans marched away as if they were on a parade ground. Why anybody would be so diligent without some superior's eye on him was more than Delgadillo could fathom. He shrugged. The foreigners might be a little bit crazy, but they were good at what they did, and they were on his side.

He looked west again. No British battleships. No smoke in the distance. No enormous shells crashing down like the end of the world. Nothing but one Spanish soldier with the jitters.

Well, no. That wasn't quite true. A couple of hundred meters away, an officer with enormous, tripod-mounted binoculars scanned the horizon. Delgadillo knew there were observation posts up on the heights of the Rock, too. They could see farther from there.

If the battleships came and those Germans didn't have their spare parts . . . What would happen then? The same thing that would happen if there were no airplanes. The ships would pound the stuffing out of Gibraltar.

He laughed at himself. What could he do about it any which way? Jump into the closest foxhole, work his rosary for all it was worth, and pray to the Virgin to keep the guns from blowing him to dogmeat. A common soldier's life wasn't easy, but most of the time it was pretty simple.

Any common soldier, no matter whose army he belonged to, learned to look busy, even—often especially—when he wasn't. Sergeant Carrasquel turned his basilisk stare on Joaquin, but didn't put him to work. If you had a rag and a brush, you could look as if you were cleaning your rifle. No underofficer ever complained if he caught you doing that. And if you weren't so diligent as you might have been . . . well, how could a sergeant tell?

Having successfully evaded any real duty most of the day, Delgadillo queued up for supper with no small feeling of accomplishment. Food on the Rock was pretty good. Not the smallest reason was that much of it came from captured British supplies. The enemy had done his best to destroy what he could before Gibraltar fell, but the Spaniards took the place before he could ruin it all. Joaquin had heard that the Tommies scorned bully beef, but it beat the devil out of going empty.

Pride went before a fall. He got nabbed for kitchen police. Washing and drying and scrubbing weren't dangerous, but they weren't any fun, either. Pepe Rivera, the boss cook, was a top sergeant, and an evil-tempered son of a whore, too. No matter what Joaquin did, it wasn't good enough to suit him.

Delgadillo had just gone to bed when antiaircraft guns woke him up. He grabbed his helmet—a Spanish copy of the German model from the last war—and ran for the closest trench. "God damn the French to hell!" he said as he scrambled down into it.

"He will. He does," another soldier said. It wasn't the first time French bombers had crossed from Morocco to hit Gibraltar. They were only nuisance raids—nothing like the pounding the papers said the Germans were giving to London and Paris. But you could get killed in a nuisance raid, too, if you were careless or unlucky.

Bombs whistled down. They exploded, none of them especially close. The drone of aircraft engines overhead faded away. The antiaircraft guns kept hammering for another ten or fifteen minutes. Then they seemed satisfied and shut up.

"*Gracias a Dios y su Madre*," Joaquin said, climbing out of the trench. He yawned enormously. Maybe he could grab some sleep at last.

OUT ON THE STREETS OF MÜNSTER, away from any possible micro-phones, Sarah Goldman said, "I wish we'd get another letter." Even here, she named no names and gave no details. You never could tell who was listening. If people in Germany had learned anything since 1933, that was it.

Her mother nodded. "So do I. But we were lucky to get one, and *Frau* Breisach put herself in danger to bring it to us."

"I know. It was kind of her. Brave of her, too," Sarah said.

Propaganda posters sprouted like mold on walls and fences and tree trunks. Some showed jut-jawed, blue-eyed men in coal-scuttle helmets: recruiting posters for the *Wehrmacht* and the *Waffen*-SS. Sarah didn't mind those so much. Germany was at war, after all. Father and Saul would have joined if the country had let them. In spite of everything, Saul *had* joined.

There'd been more *Waffen*-SS posters lately, especially since the coup against Hitler failed. Sarah didn't like that, but she didn't know what she could do about it. No. Actually, she did know. She couldn't do a thing.

Other posters showed hook-nosed, flabby-lipped Jews pulling the strings on puppets of Chamberlain and Daladier, or a capitalist Jew in a morning coat and top hat shaking hands with a Communist Jew in overalls and a flat cloth cap above a woman's corpse labeled GERMANY. Still others carried a stark, simple message: THE JEWS ARE OUR MISFORTUNE.

"Why do they hate us so much?" Sarah whispered. The poison made her want to hate herself.

"I only wish I knew," Mother answered. "Then maybe I could do something about it." She sighed. Her breath smoked. Spring was supposed to be on the way, but it hadn't got here yet. "Or maybe knowing wouldn't make any difference. Sometimes things just are what they are, that's all."

"That's what I was afraid of," Sarah said. "If it made sense, though . . ." She shook her head in frustration. "If it had to make sense, the *goyim* wouldn't do it."

"They might. Sometimes people don't care what they do." Mother paused, then added, "And look at the name you just called them. If you could, you'd do worse than call them names, wouldn't you?"

"I wouldn't start anything," Sarah said. "But after all they've done to us, shouldn't we get even if we can?"

"An eye for an eye. A tooth for a tooth. And after a while everyone's blind and nobody has any teeth," Mother said sadly.

Laborers were still repairing British bomb damage and hauling away rubble one wheelbarrow at a time. The RAF wanted to make sure Germany had no eyes or teeth. Sarah had always thought of herself as a German, at least till the Nazis wouldn't let her any more, and the enemy bomber crews were trying to kill her, too. All the same, she wouldn't have shed a tear if one of their bombs blew up Hitler and Hess and Goebbels and Göring.

The laborers paused when Sarah and her mother went by. Sarah felt their eyes on her—and maybe on Mother, too. She tried to pretend the sweaty men in overalls weren't there: that was one more complication she didn't need.

And looking at them would have reminded her of Saul working in a gang just like this one . . . and of his shovel caving in the gang boss' skull. She wished she could forget she'd ever seen that. She wished she could forget she'd ever heard it, too.

"Hey, sweetheart!" one of the workmen called. He rocked his hips forward and back. His buddies laughed.

Sarah just kept walking. "They don't know we're Jews," she said in a low voice.

"A good thing, too. They'd be worse if they did," her mother answered. "I keep hearing they're going to make us put yellow stars on our clothes. Thank God it hasn't happened yet—that's all I can say."

"Like the ghetto in the old days." Sarah shivered.

"Not quite," Mother said. Sarah raised a questioning eyebrow. The older woman explained: "In the old days, they wouldn't have charged us ration points for the cloth we need to make the stars."

"Where did you hear that?" Sarah's heart sank. It had the ring of truth: exactly the kind of thing the Nazis, with their often maniacal drive for efficiency, would think of.

"I forget who told me. Maybe I don't want to remember." Mother's face twisted. "It sounds too much like something they'd do."

"I was thinking the same thing," Sarah said. "I was hoping you'd tell me I was crazy." She said *verrückt,* the proper German term. Back before the Nazis took over, or back at home even now, she would more likely have said *meshuggeh.* It was a friendlier, more comfortable word. But she didn't want to speak any Yiddish where Aryans might overhear.

Aryans! Her father had had several instructive things to say on that score. He tore *Mein Kampf*'s claims to little pieces and then stomped on the pieces. He really knew what he was talking about, where the half-educated Hitler cobbled together bits and pieces from pamphlets and political tracts and lying, outdated books he'd read. Hitler reassembled them into his own mosaic, which had precious little connection to real history.

Samuel Goldman was scholar enough to know as much. He could prove it, citing chapter and verse. All of which, of course, did him no good whatever. He wasn't going to change the Nazis' minds. Knowing how much of the Party's antisemitism was built on lie atop lie only gave him a sour stomach and heart palpitations.

With an effort, Sarah dragged her mind away from Father's frustrations. She had plenty of her own to dwell on. The most immediate came out: "I hope we'll be able to get what we need. I hope we'll be able to get *anything.*"

"Well, we haven't starved yet," Mother said, which was true but less than encouraging. With Jews able to shop only as things were about to close, and with their being unwelcome in so many shops anyhow, staying fed and clothed was even harder for them than for their German neighbors.

One clever Jew in Hamburg had given her family's ration coupons to a gentile friend, who used them to shop for her. The friend could have used the coupons for her own kin, but she hadn't done that. She'd played square—till someone betrayed them. The Jewish family got it in the neck for evading rationing regulations. And the gentiles got it in the neck for helping Jews.

For all Sarah knew, they had side-by-side bunks in the Dachau camp. Or maybe they'd all been shot. She wouldn't have been surprised. If you were a German Jew—or an Aryan rash enough to remember you were also a human being—you couldn't win.

A trolley rattled by. The motorman ignored Sarah and her mother, as they ignored him. Jews weren't supposed to ride streetcars, either, except going off to the work gangs in the morning or coming back from them at night. No, you couldn't win.

"I hope our soles will last," her mother said. Leather and even synthetics for shoe repairs were impossible to come by. Sarah nodded. She hoped her soul would last, too.

Chapter 21

Victory will come soon. So the official from the German department in charge of interned neutrals had assured Peggy Druce. Konrad Hoppe, that was the bastard's name. Well, *Herr* Hoppe wasn't as smart as he thought he was. Here it was a month later, and Germany was still fighting hard.

Here it is, a month later, Peggy thought. *More than a month. Pretty soon it'll be spring. And here I am, still stuck in goddamn Berlin.*

The RAF had come over several times. French planes had dropped bombs once or twice. Even the Russians had shown up, flying all the way across Poland and eastern Germany in bombers said to be bigger than anybody else's.

None of that had done a hell of a lot of actual damage. Berlin was a long way off for enemy planes—a long way off from anywhere civilized, in Peggy's biased opinion. The bombers had to carry extra fuel, which meant they couldn't carry so many bombs.

German searchlights ceaselessly probed the night sky, hunting marauders. German antiaircraft fire was like a million Fourths of July all folded into one. It didn't do much good, though.

That had to be part of why Berlin seemed so jumpy to Peggy. These days, Berliners talked about Hermann Call Me Meyer Göring as Hermann the Kike—but in low voices, to friends they trusted, in places where the *Gestapo* was unlikely to overhear. They were less discreet than they might have been, though. Peggy wouldn't have heard—and chuckled about—Hermann the Kike if they weren't.

But she was careful where she chuckled, too. She judged that most of Berlin's *Angst* came simply from victory deferred. Had the *Wehrmacht* paraded through Paris when *Herr* Hoppe thought it would, chances were the generals wouldn't have tried whatever they tried. Or had that happened earlier? Nobody officially admitted anything. After whatever it was didn't work, Peggy stopped hearing so many juicy jokes. Passing them on didn't just land you in trouble any more. You could, with the greatest of ease, end up dead.

SS men in black uniforms and soldiers in field-gray seemed to compete with one another in arresting people and hauling them off God knew where to do God knew what to them. Peggy had never been so glad she carried an American passport. It was sword and shield at the same time. You couldn't walk more than a block without somebody snapping, "Your papers!" at you.

And when you showed them, what a relief it was to pull out the leatherette folder stamped in gold with the gold old American eagle and olive branch rather than the German one holding a swastika in its claws. "Here you are," Peggy would say, and show off the passport with all the pride—and all the relief—she felt.

So far, the talisman had never failed. Whether she displayed it to SS man, *Abwehr* official, or ordinary Berlin cop, it always made him back off. "Oh," he would say, whoever *he* happened to be this time around. Sometimes the German would salute after that; sometimes he'd just turn away in disappointment, or maybe disgust. But he would always let her go on.

Then, three blocks farther along, some other jumped-up kraut reveling in his petty authority would growl, "Your papers!" The whole stupid farce would play out again.

Once, a particularly reptilian SS man—again, in Peggy's biased opinion—tried out his English on her, demanding, "What is an American doing in Berlin?"

"Trying to get out, pal. Nothing else but," Peggy answered from the bottom of her heart. "You want to send me home, I'll kiss your shiny boots." And were they ever. She could have put on her makeup using the highly polished black leather for a mirror.

For some reason, the SS man didn't like that, either. "It is a privilege to come to the capital of the *Reich,*" he spluttered.

"I'm sure the RAF thinks so, too," Peggy said sweetly.

The SS man was a fine, fair Aryan, which only made his flush more obvious. "Air pirates!" he said, proving he not only read but believed Goebbels' newspapers. "They murder innocent civilians—women and children."

"Sure," Peggy said, and then, incautiously, "What do you think your own bombers are doing?"

"We strike only military targets," the SS man insisted. The scary thing was, he plainly believed that, too.

Peggy wanted to yank off his high-crowned cap and beat him over the head with it, in the hope of knocking some sense into him. But she held back—it was bound to be a lost cause. If you were the kind of jerk who joined the SS, you had to be immune to sense. She contented herself with, "Can I go now?"

" 'May.' It should be 'may.' " Proud of winning a battle in her language, the SS man handed back her passport and waved her on.

She turned a corner—and walked straight into a police checkpoint.

"Your papers—at once!" a beer-bellied cop shouted. Peggy produced the American passport. The policeman recoiled like Bela Lugosi not seeing his reflection in a mirror. As the SS man had before him, he barked, "What are you doing in Berlin?"

And, as she had before, Peggy answered truthfully: "Trying to get out." Only later did she wonder about taking a big chance twice running. How many chances had she taken? Too damned many—she was sure of that. Hadn't she been proud of acting more mature? She sure couldn't prove it today.

But she got by with it one more time. "Pass," the cop said, writing a note on a sheet clipped to a flat board. Any *Gestapo* official who examined all the reports various Berlin security officials compiled could figure out everywhere she went. For all she knew, some *Gestapo* goon did that every day. If she were a spy, it might have meant something. But she was only an interned tourist with a big mouth.

She couldn't even have fun shopping. Window displays had nothing to do with what you could actually buy. And everything you *could* buy required ration coupons of one kind or another. She got enough for food to keep her going. For almost everything else, the Germans didn't seem to feel obligated to take care of her.

And, after the *Athenia* went down, she couldn't get out. She'd tried to arrange another train ticket to Copenhagen. She'd tried to arrange a plane ticket to Stockholm. Once she was in Scandinavia, she could get to England. Once she was in England, she could get to the States . . . if the Germans didn't torpedo her on the way. And if they did, well, going down with her ship sometimes seemed more appealing than staying in Berlin.

But they wouldn't let her out. She got "Your papers!" when she tried to buy her tickets, too. And when she flashed her passport then, it wasn't magic. It was more like poison. They would frown. They would check a list. Then they would say, "I am very sorry, but this is *verboten*." They liked saying *verboten*. Telling people no was much more fun than saying yes would have been. You got to watch your victims throw the most delightful tantrums.

Peggy refused to give them the satisfaction. She just walked away both times. After failing to get the plane ticket, she hied herself off to the U.S. embassy. If she couldn't get help there, she figured, she couldn't get help anywhere.

By all the signs, she couldn't get help anywhere. The embassy personnel spoke English, not German, but they might as well have clicked their heels and intoned, "*Verboten.*" What they did say amounted to, "Sorry, but we can't make the German government get off the dime."

"Why not?" Peggy snarled at an undersecretary—she'd made herself obnoxious enough at the embassy that the clerks had booted her upstairs to get rid of her. "Denmark's neutral. Sweden's neutral. *We're* neutral, for crying out loud. Why won't the Nazis let me out of this loony bin?"

The undersecretary—Jenkins, his name was, Constantine Jenkins—had shiny fingernails—painted with clear polish?—and a soft, well-modulated voice. Peggy guessed he was a fairy, not that that should have had anything to do with the price of beer. "Well, Mrs. Druce, the long answer is that the Germans say they're at war and they fear espionage," he replied. "That weakens any arguments we might make, because it means they can tell us, 'Sorry, emergency—we don't have to listen to you.' "

"Espionage, my ass!" Peggy blurted, which made the faggy undersecretary blink. She went on, "The only thing I've seen is what a horrible, run-down dump this place is."

"That *is* information the Germans would rather keep to themselves," Jenkins said seriously. "And besides, the short answer is, the Germans are just being Germans—sometimes they enjoy being difficult. And when they do, you can shout till you're blue in the face for all the good it does you."

"Being pissy, you mean. Shit," Peggy said. That made much more sense than she wished it did. She also made the American diplomat blink again, which was the most fun she'd had all day. She went on, "Can't I just sneak over the border somewhere? All I want to do is go home."

"I would not recommend it," he said seriously. "We can be of no assistance to anyone caught violating the regulations of the country in which she happens to find herself, and whether those regulations are just or humane is, I'm afraid, beside the point."

"Shit," she said again, and walked out of the embassy. A man standing across the street wrote something down. Were the Nazis keeping tabs on her in particular or on everybody who went in and out? What difference did it make, really?

They wouldn't let her go to Sweden. They wouldn't let her go to Denmark. They wouldn't let her go to Norway or Finland, either—she'd also found out that Oslo and Helsinki were off limits. The bastards wouldn't let her go anywhere decent, damn them to hell.

She thought about Warsaw. Regretfully, she didn't think about it long. Maybe she could get to Scandinavia or Romania from there, but she feared the odds weren't good. The Russians had pushed Poland right into bed with Germany. The Poles probably didn't want to land there, but what choice did they have when the Red Army jumped them? She wished Stalin such a horrible case of mange, it would make his soup-strainer mustache fall out. That'd teach him!

Then she had a brainstorm—or she hoped it was, anyway. She turned around and went back to the American embassy. The guy across the street scribbled some more. Maybe the *Gestapo* would have to issue him another pencil.

This time, Peggy didn't have to be so difficult to get to see the queer undersecretary. Constantine Jenkins eyed her as if *she* had a case of the mange. "What can I do for you now, Mrs. Druce?" he asked warily.

"Can you help me get to Budapest?" Peggy asked. Hungary wasn't exactly a nice place these days. Admiral Horthy's government (and wasn't that a kick in the ass? a landlocked country run by an admiral) was a hyena skulking along behind the German lion, feeding on scraps from the bigger beast's kill. When the Hungarian army helped Hitler dismantle Czechoslovakia, England and France promptly broke relations. So did Russia. But she didn't think any of them had gone and declared war on the Horthy regime. And if they hadn't . . . something might be arranged.

"Well," Jenkins said. "That's interesting, isn't it?"

"I hope so." Peggy sent him a reproachful stare. "Why didn't you think of it yourself?"

For his part, he looked affronted. "Because chances are the Germans won't let you go, even if Hungary is an ally. Because getting to Budapest doesn't mean all your troubles are over, or even that any of them are."

"If I can get into Hungary, I bet I can get out," Peggy said. "Romania—"

"Don't get your hopes up," the undersecretary warned. "Romanians and Hungarians like each other about as much as Frenchmen and Germans, and for most of the same reasons. Romanians spite Hungarians for the fun of it, and vice versa. But if you're trying to get out of Hungary, you need to worry about Marshal Antonescu's goons, not Admiral Horthy's."

"Oh." Peggy knew she sounded deflated. Hell, she felt deflated. She paused to visualize a map of southeastern Europe. "Well, if I could get into Yugoslavia, that would do the trick, too. Anywhere but this Nazi snake pit would."

"I don't suppose you want to hear that the Hungarians have territorial claims against Yugoslavia, too," Jenkins said.

"Jesus! Is there anybody the Hungarians *don't* have territorial claims against?" Peggy exclaimed.

"Iceland, possibly." Jenkins didn't sound as if he was joking. He explained why: "If you think Hitler hates the Treaty of Versailles—"

"I'm right," Peggy broke in.

"Yes. You are," he agreed. "But Horthy and the Hungarians hate the Treaty of Trianon even more—and with some reason, because Trianon cost them more territory than Versailles cost Germany. A lot of it wasn't territory where Hungarians lived, but some of it was . . . and they want the rest back, too. They aren't fussy, not about that."

"I'm sure." Peggy sighed. "People couldn't have screwed up the treaties at the end of the war much worse than they did, could they?"

"*Never* imagine things can't be screwed up worse than they are already," Constantine Jenkins replied. "But, that said, in this particular case I have trouble imagining how they could be."

"Right." Peggy sighed. She got to her feet. "Well, I'm going to give it a shot. What have I got to lose?"

"Good luck." For a wonder, the American diplomat didn't sound as if he meant *And the horse you rode in on, lady.*

So Peggy went off to the train station to try to get a ticket to Budapest. When she displayed her passport, the clerk said, "You will need an entry visa from the Hungarian embassy and an exit visa from the Foreign Ministry. I regret this, but it is strictly *verboten*"—that word again!—"to sell tickets without proper and complete documentation."

"Crap," she muttered in English, which made the clerk scratch his bald head. "It's a technical term," she explained helpfully, "meaning, well, *crap.*"

"I see," he said. By his tone, he didn't.

Peggy did, all too well. She went off to the Hungarian embassy at 8 Cornelius-Strasse. "Ah, yes—an interesting case," said the minor official who dealt with her. His native language gave his German a musical accent. Had he spoken English, she supposed he would have sounded like a vampire. Maybe, for once, German was better. He relieved her of fifty Deutschmarks and stamped her passport. So she was almost good to go.

Last stop, the Foreign Ministry. Nobody wanted to come right out and tell her no, but nobody wanted to give her an exit visa, either. And nobody did. Finally, one of Ribbentrop's flunkies sighed and squared his shoulders and said, "It is not practical at this time."

"Why the devil not?" Peggy blazed. "I'd think you'd be glad to get rid of me."

The man shrugged "My orders say this visa is not to be issued. I must, of course, follow them."

By the way he talked, it wasn't that something very bad would happen to him if he didn't—though something probably would. But not following an order was as dreadful to him as desecrating the sacrament would have been to a devout Catholic.

"Aw, shit," Peggy said, and that pretty much summed things up.

VACLAV JEZEK HAD NEVER LIKED quartermaster sergeants. As far as he was concerned, most of them were fat pricks. This miserable Frenchman was sure wide through the seat of his pants. And he was acting like a prick, all right. He thought he personally owned everything in the depot near the village of Hary.

Vaclav had been arguing with him through Benjamin Halévy, because he still hadn't picked up much French himself. Since that wasn't getting him anywhere, he fixed the French sergeant with a glare and asked him, "*Sprechen Sie Deutsch?*"

He got exactly what he hoped for: indignant sputters. Then the Frenchman spoke to the Jewish noncom doing the translating: "He wants to know why you think he should speak the enemy's language."

"Does he?" Vaclav pounced: "Tell the son of a bitch I figured he would because he's doing more to help the Nazis by sitting on his ammo till it hatches than he could any other way."

"Are you sure you want me to say that?" Halévy asked. "He *really* won't help you if I do."

"Fuck him. He's not helping me now. He's got rounds for my anti-tank rifle, and he won't turn them loose," Jezek said.

"All right. I'll try. I just wanted to make sure you knew what you were doing." In the Jew's French, Vaclav's insult sounded less nasty than it would have in Czech or German—French was better for kissing ass than for telling somebody off. No matter what it sounded like, the crack got home. The quartermaster went as hot—and as red—as iron in the forge. He said several things that sounded heartfelt.

"What's all that mean?" Vaclav asked with clinical curiosity.

"You'd break your piece over his head if you knew," Halévy said.

Vaclav laughed. "Not this goddamn thing." Antitank rifles were huge, heavy brutes. The heavier the weapon was, the less it kicked when it spat one of its honking big bullets. Jezek approved of that. As things were, his shoulder was sore all the time. You could stop an elephant with an antitank rifle. Sometimes, you could even stop a tank. Elephants couldn't grow more armor. Tanks, unfortunately, could. The rifle would be obsolete pretty soon, and you'd need a field gun to deal with enemy armor.

In the meantime, Vaclav wished he had a field gun to deal with this goddamn quartermaster sergeant. The Frenchman and the Jew went back and forth. Halévy chuckled. "He doesn't like you, Jezek."

"Suits me—in that case, we're even," Vaclav said. "I'm trying to defend his lousy country. It's more than he's doing, Christ knows. You can translate that, too."

Halévy did. The French sergeant didn't just sputter—he bleated. Then he sprang up from his folding chair. Vaclav thought the fellow was going to try and slug him. *Monsieur le Français* would get a dreadful surprise if he did; Jezek promised himself that.

But the quartermaster sergeant spun on his heel and stormed away. The view from the rear was no more appetizing than the one from the front. "If he's going after military policemen to haul you off—" Halévy began.

"They'll grab you, too, 'cause you're the one who said it in French," Vaclav said happily. The Jew seemed less delighted. *Too bad for him,* Vaclav thought. Just to be helpful, he added, "It's called shooting the messenger."

In Yiddish, French, and Czech, Halévy told him what he could do with a messenger. To listen to him, shooting was the least of it. Vaclav listened in admiration. He didn't understand everything Halévy said, but he wanted to remember some of what he did understand.

The quartermaster sergeant came back. A thunderstorm clouded his brow. He said several pungent things of his own. French might lack the guttural power of Czech or German when it came to swearing, but the sergeant did his damnedest. Vaclav hardly cared. At the same time as the Frenchman was cussing him out, he was also handing over half a dozen five-round clips of long, fat antitank-rifle cartridges.

"Tell him thanks," Jezek said to Benjamin Halévy.

"Sure." The Jew eyed him. "It won't do you any good, you know." He spoke in French. The quartermaster replied. Halévy translated for Vaclav: "He says you can shove a round up your ass and then hit yourself in the butt with a golf club to touch it off."

"A golf club?" Vaclav had to laugh. "Well, that's something different—fuck me if it's not."

"He'd say fuck you anyway," Halévy replied. "Let's get out of here before he decides he really does have to shaft us, just on general principles."

That seemed like good advice. Vaclav took it. The quartermaster offered a couple of poignant parting shots. Vaclav glanced toward Halévy. The polyglot Jew declined to translate. That was bound to be just as well.

Civilians streamed away from the front. They didn't want to get caught by bombs and shells and machine-gun bullets. Well, who in their right minds would have? Vaclav didn't, either. But when you put on a uniform, that was the chance you took.

Some of the Frenchmen and -women eyed the Czechs suspiciously. They weren't *poilus*. They weren't Tommies, either. British soldiers were familiar sights in France. The damnfool locals probably thought they were Germans—it wasn't as if that hadn't happened before farther east. Vaclav would have thought German uniforms were plenty familiar here, too. Maybe he was wrong.

Soldiers came back with the civilians. The ones who clutched wounds, pale and tight-lipped, were simply part of what war did. The ones who didn't seem hurt worried Vaclav more. He'd watched the Czech army fight till it couldn't fight any more. Then, when the Nazis kept the pressure on, the Czechs went to pieces.

Would the same thing happen here? As far as Vaclav could see, France was in better shape than Czechoslovakia had been. The country seemed united in its fight against the Nazis. Czechoslovakia sure hadn't been. Half the Slovaks—maybe more than half—wanted the state to come to pieces. Their precious Slovakia was supposed to be independent these days, but Hitler pulled the strings and made Father Tiso dance.

As for the Sudeten Germans, the miserable bastards who'd touched off the war . . . Vaclav muttered something foul. The Czechs had been pulling them out of the army because they were unreliable. He muttered something else. Too little, too late. Back right after the last war ended, Czechoslovakia should have shipped all those shitheads back to Germany. If they wanted to join the *Reich* so much, well, fine. So long.

It hadn't happened. Too goddamn bad.

A French captain spotted the enormous rifle Vaclav had slung over his left shoulder. He said something in his own language. Vaclav only shrugged and looked blank. "Do you want me to understand him?" Halévy asked—in Czech.

Vaclav didn't even have to think about it. "Nah," he said. "He'll pull me off to do something stupid that'll probably get me killed. I'd rather go on back to camp."

"Makes sense," the Jew agreed. Like Vaclav, he stared at the French officer as if he had no idea the fellow was talking to them. The Frenchman said something else. Vaclav and Halévy went right on impersonating idiots. The captain tried bad German. Jezek understood that. He also understood the captain did have something dangerous for him to try. He didn't let on that he understood one damn thing. He was willing to risk his life: as he'd thought before, that was why he wore the uniform. But he wasn't willing to get himself killed without much chance of hurting the enemy.

"Ah, screw you both," the captain said in German when the Czechs wouldn't admit they followed him. They went right on feigning ignorance. The Frenchman gave up. Vaclav had his ammo, and he didn't have to try anything idiotic. As far as he was concerned, the day was a victory so far.

ONCE UPON A TIME—probably not very long ago—the froggies had had themselves a big old supply dump outside a place called Hary. Willi Dernen eyed what was left of it with something not far from disgust. The Frenchmen had hauled away whatever they still had a use for, then poured gasoline on the rest and set fire to it. The stink of stale smoke was sour in his nostrils.

"Come on. Get moving," Arno Baatz growled. "Nothing worth grabbing in this miserable place."

"Right, Corporal," Willi said. Whenever Baatz talked to him these days, he had to fight like a son of a bitch to keep from giggling.

Every once in a while, that showed in the way he sounded. The underofficer favored him with his best glare. "Did I say something funny?"

"No, Corporal," Willi answered hastily, and bit down hard on the inside of his cheek so the pain would drive mirth from his voice. Awful Arno remembered getting slugged in the tavern back in Watigny. He knew it had happened, anyway—you couldn't very well *not* know when you woke up with an enormous bruise on your chin and a knot on the back of your head.

But Baatz showed no sign of remembering that Willi and Wolfgang Storch had been in there to see his piteous overthrow. He also didn't remember he'd been jealous because Michelle brought drinks to them but not to him. He'd stopped a good one, all right. And that was highly convenient. Since he didn't remember, he didn't blame them for the damaged state of his skull.

Lieutenant Erich Krantz had replaced Lieutenant Gross the same way Gross had replaced Neustadt. Gross had kept his arm after all; he might even come back to duty one day. Neustadt hadn't been so lucky. Krantz was here now—at least till *he* stopped something. Junior lieutenants seemed to have an unfortunate knack for doing that.

And, if the enemy didn't get them, they were liable to do themselves in. Krantz stooped and started to pick up a charred board. "Sir, you might want to be careful with that," Willi said, getting ready to shove the officer aside if Krantz didn't feel like listening.

But the lieutenant did hesitate. "What? Why?" he asked.

Corporal Baatz butted in: "Sir, Dernen's right." He didn't say that every day, so Willi let him go on: "The French pulled out of here just a little while ago. That's the kind of thing they might booby-trap."

"Is it?" Krantz looked surprised and intrigued. "Well, how about that? All right, I won't mess with it."

"That's a good idea, sir," Baatz said. His narrow, rather piggy eyes said Krantz should have figured this out for himself. Luckily for him, it wasn't easy to gig a man—especially a noncom—on account of the look on his face. And Baatz looked mean and scornful most of the time, so maybe the lieutenant didn't notice anything strange.

Krantz was looking south and west. "Now that we've driven the French out of here, we should be able to go on to Laon without much trouble."

We? As in you and your tapeworm? Willi thought. The way it looked to him, the froggies had hung on so hard at Hary because it shielded

Laon. They were probably digging in a little closer to the city even now—as well as anyone could in this miserable freezing weather.

Krantz was an officer. Wasn't he supposed to know stuff like that because he was an officer? He didn't have much experience, obviously. And if he kept poking around in a gutted supply dump, he wouldn't live long enough to get any, either. Willi didn't want to be standing close by when something Krantz was playing with went boom.

He couldn't say anything like that to the lieutenant. Yes, the *Führer*'s *Wehrmacht* was a much more democratic, easygoing place than the Kaiser's army had been. Old sweats who'd put in their time in the trenches in the last war all said so. Of course, Hitler was an old sweat himself. He'd fought almost from first to last without getting seriously wounded. The way things were on the Western Front from 1914 to 1918, that was either amazing luck or proof of the *Gott mit uns* on a *Landser*'s belt buckle. (But that was just the Prussian buckle the last time around, not the national one. Hitler had served in a Bavarian regiment, and would have had a different motto in front of his belly button.)

Yes, the *Wehrmacht* was more democratic now. Still, a private couldn't explain the facts of life to an officer. Not even Corporal Baatz could. A grizzled *Feldwebel* might have done it. But Sergeant Pieck was wounded, too, and hadn't been replaced. Krantz would have to learn on his own—if he lasted.

As if to show the platoon commander he wasn't ready for General Staff *Lampassen* on the outer seams of his trouser legs, the French put in a counterattack later that afternoon. Whether Krantz had or not, Willi'd been fearing one. He was no General Staff officer, either, but he could see what a long southern flank the Germans held. The *Wehrmacht* had gone around the Maginot Line to the north, not through it. Evidently, the generals had counted on keeping the enemy too busy up there to worry about down here. Unfortunately, what you counted on wasn't always what you got.

By the time the 75s started whistling in, Willi already had himself a foxhole. It had belonged to a *poilu,* who'd dug himself a cave in the northern wall to protect himself from German shells coming in from that direction. Willi hacked and scraped at the nearly frozen dirt in the southern wall of the hole with his entrenching tool to try to make himself the same kind of shelter from French artillery.

No splinters flayed his flesh or broke his bones, so he supposed he'd done well enough. No shells burst especially close to him, so he couldn't prove a thing. But proof didn't matter. All that mattered was, he didn't get hurt.

He wasn't sorry to let the Frenchmen come at him for a change. Sometimes—mostly when there were panzers around—attackers had the edge. More often, defenders crouched in the best shelter they could find or make and tried to murder the fellows coming at them.

His mouth went dry. He recognized that creaking, clanking rumble. As far as he knew, the Germans didn't have any panzers in the neighborhood. If the French did, it wasn't such a good day to crouch in a foxhole.

Boom! The report behind him was one of the sweetest sounds he'd ever heard. A split second later, he heard another one. That unmusical *Clang!* was an antitank round slamming into a French panzer. And the smaller *pops* and *blams* that followed marked ammunition cooking off inside the stricken machine. Willi wouldn't have wanted to be a French panzer crewman, not right then, not for anything.

He stood up and fired at the foot soldiers loping along with the hastily whitewashed French panzers. The *poilus* threw themselves flat and shot back at him. *Boom!* The 37mm antitank gun had found another target—found it and missed it. Behind their steel shield, the German artillerymen frantically reaimed and reloaded. Meanwhile, the French panzer's turret swung inexorably toward them.

Both guns spoke together, as near as made no difference. The enemy panzer slewed sideways and stopped with a track shot off. But its high-explosive shell ruined the German gunners. Their shield did some good against small-arms fire. If a shell burst behind it . . . well, tough luck.

But then another antitank gun off to the left fired two quick rounds. The crippled French panzer started to burn in earnest. Behind the line, German artillery woke up. Shells started raining down on the ground south of Hary. Willi ducked back into his hole. Some of those shells would fall short. Your own side could kill you, too—one more lesson he wondered whether Lieutenant Krantz had learned.

Before long, the French attack petered out. The froggies didn't seem to have had their hearts in it, not that that helped the crew of the anti-tank gun. Willi knew more than a little sympathy for the sorry bastards in Adrian helmets and worn khaki uniforms. Like him, they were at the mercy of officers who sent them forward and hoped something grand would come of it.

He lit a cigarette and stuck his head out for another look around. The two killed French panzers in front of him would burn for a long time. A few khaki-clad bodies lay on the snow-streaked ground. A raven glided down out of the sky and pecked at one. Scavengers never waited long.

And there was Lieutenant Krantz, peeking out of his own hole in the ground like a *Feldgrau* marmot. He'd come through another scrap. A few more and he'd start having an idea of what was going on out here. *As much as I do, anyway,* Willi thought. *As much as anybody does.* He took another drag and blew out a long, happy plume of smoke. He'd made it again.

THEO HOSSBACH WAS MESSING WITH the Panzer II's radio set again, methodically taking out one tube after another, replacing each with a fresh one, and trying the radio again. "How's it going?" Ludwig Rothe asked him.

Since Theo was wearing earphones, it wasn't surprising that he didn't follow. It also wasn't surprising that he didn't take them off so he could. Ludwig had often thought that Theo cared more about the radio than about either of his crewmates.

Direct action, then. Ludwig yanked the earphones off Theo's head. The radio operator gave him a wounded look. "What did you go and do that for?" he asked.

"So I could talk to you?" Ludwig suggested.

By the way Theo blinked, that hadn't occurred to him. "Are you a goddamn blackshirt, so you have to interrogate me right this fucking minute?"

"*Gott im Himmel!*" Ludwig's head might have been on a swivel as he looked around the panzer park. Nobody seemed to be paying attention to his panzer, for which he was duly grateful. "Are you out of your mind, Theo? Do you *want* them to haul you away?"

"Nah. If I did, I would've—" But even Theo stopped short, swallowing whatever he'd been about to come out with. He was definitely an idiot, but maybe—just maybe—he wasn't quite an imbecile.

Would've done what? Ludwig wondered. The first thing that sprang to mind was *would've plugged the* Führer *when I had the chance.* Ludwig didn't ask him if that was what he meant. For one thing, he feared Theo would say yes. For another, letting Theo know such a thought had crossed his own mind would give the radioman a hold on him.

And so Ludwig pointed to the set Theo was working on and asked his original question over again: "How's it going?"

"Haven't found the new bad tube yet." As Theo spoke, he extracted another one. "They give out faster when we bang all over the landscape, you know."

"Sure, but what am I supposed to do about it? Keep working. We're as deaf as the damned Frenchmen till you do." Ludwig had examined quite a few knocked-out French panzers. Most of them had no radios at all. French panzer leaders signaled their subordinates with wigwag disks. The Germans carried them, too, but only for emergencies. They worked well enough on the practice field. In real combat, with dust and dirt flying, they were much harder to make out. And, of course, a panzer commander who stood up in the cupola to semaphore with wigwag disks was as likely to get shot as any other suicidal damn fool.

Theo grunted and forgot about Ludwig. He put the earphones back on. After a moment, he nodded, not to Rothe but to the radio set. "You finally find the dead one?" Ludwig asked hopefully.

A moment later, he remembered Theo couldn't hear him any more. He didn't want to tear the earphones off the radioman's head again; that was pushing things, even for a sergeant.

For a wonder, Hossbach doffed the earphones of his own accord. "We're back in business," he reported.

"Outstanding!" Because Ludwig had given him a hard time before, he made himself sound enthusiastic now. Yes, Theo lived in his old little world and visited the real one as seldom as he could get away with, but he did his job pretty well anyhow. Ludwig had heard plenty of other panzer commanders bitch about their radiomen and drivers in terms that horrified him. All in all, he was more lucky than not.

French artillery came down about half a kilometer in front of the panzer park. Somebody was getting it in the neck—probably a bunch of poor, damned infantrymen, as usual—but the precious panzers stayed out of range of enemy guns when not actually fighting.

Planes buzzed by overhead. Ludwig looked up, more curious than worried. Sure enough, Stukas and Messerschmitts flew west to punish the French and the English. The enemy didn't use planes against German forces anywhere near so much. Ludwig was damned glad of it, too. He'd seen what air power could do to soldiers. He didn't want anybody doing that to him.

German 105s opened up. Maybe they were shooting at the French guns. Maybe they were softening up the *poilus* so the next German thrust could finally break through them instead of just pushing them back. Maybe . . . Ludwig laughed at himself. Not for the first time, he was pretending he'd joined the General Staff. No *Lampassen* on the legs of his black coveralls.

Something off in the distance blew up with a hell of a bang. Even Theo noticed. "Ammunition dump?" he said.

"Christ, I hope so," Ludwig answered. "Damned Frenchmen have already thrown more shit at us than we ever thought they had. The more we can get rid of, the less they're liable to hit us with."

Theo blinked in owlish surprise. "I hadn't thought of it like that."

"You're always off in Radioland," Ludwig said. "Half the time, I don't think you even remember there's a war on."

"Oh, I remember," Theo said. "I'd be doing something better than this if they hadn't stuck a uniform on me. So would you." He still looked like an owl, but a challenging owl now.

Getting that much of a rise out of him took Ludwig by surprise. "Watch your mouth!" the panzer commander said again. "The way things are, if anybody in the other blackshirts hears you go on like that, you're down the shitter." He was proud of those panzer coveralls, but wished the SS didn't wear the same color.

Theo nodded slowly. He seemed much more . . . engaged with the real world than he often did. He even looked around to make sure nobody was eavesdropping before he said, "Well, you're right about that, too. And things shouldn't work that way, either. You know damn well they shouldn't."

"We'll fix it after the war," Ludwig said. "We can't waste time worrying about it now. If France and England beat us again, we're screwed. Remember how it was when we were kids, when they occupied us and we needed a bushel of marks to get a bushel of turnips? Do you want to see those days back again?"

"Who would? Only a crazy man." But Theo looked around again. Softly, he added, "The other thing I don't want is, I don't want our own side fucking us over. And that's what we've got."

He'd just put his life in Ludwig's hands. If Ludwig reported him the way a dutiful sergeant was supposed to, he'd have a new radioman in short order. What would happen to Theo after that was none of his business. He would be better off *not* wondering about such things. Theo wouldn't, but he would.

But he didn't want a new radioman. Theo spent too much time in his own little world, but most days he did a good job. If he doubted whether Germany was always wise . . . well, so did Ludwig. Gruffly, the sergeant clapped the other man on the shoulder. "We'll take care of that after the war, too. They'll have to listen to us then."

"Nobody has to do anything." Theo spoke with unwonted conviction. But then he must have realized he'd taken things as far as they could go, or more likely a few centimeters farther. He seemed to shrink back into himself. "Well, we'd better worry about the Frenchies right this minute, eh?"

"Now you're talking!" Relief filled Ludwig's voice. Something else on—he hoped—the French side of the line went up with a hell of a bang. That relieved him, too. He knew how hideously vulnerable to antitank rounds the Panzer II was. As with the previous bang, the fewer of them the enemy could aim at him, the better.

The panzers rattled forward an hour or so later. Foot soldiers in *Feldgrau* loped along with the armor. One of them waved to Ludwig, who stood head and shoulders out of the cupola. He nodded back. Panzers could do things the infantry only dreamt about. Everybody knew that, and had known it all along. But the war had taught a different lesson: that panzers needed infantrymen, too. Without them, enemy soldiers could get in close and raise all kinds of hell with grenades and bottles full of blazing gasoline and whatever other lethal little toys they happened to carry.

Stukas screamed down out of the sky. Fire and smoke and dirt rose into the air a few hundred meters ahead. Even at that distance, blast from the big bombs rattled Ludwig's teeth. What it was doing to the bastards in khaki on whom the bombs fell . . . Ludwig felt a curious mixture of sympathy and hope that nobody up ahead was in any shape to fight any more.

A forlorn hope, and he knew it. Some of them would be dead. Some would be maimed, or too shellshocked to know sausage from Saturday. But there were always some lucky, stubborn assholes who'd . . . He hadn't even finished the thought before a French machine gun started banging away.

A *Landser* toppled, clutching at his chest. Other German foot soldiers hit the dirt. Ludwig was back inside the turret a split second before several bullets rattled off the panzer's armor. Small-arms ammo couldn't get through. That never stopped machine gunners from trying.

"*Scheisse,*" Fritz said. Like Ludwig, the driver must have hoped the Stukas would do all their work for them.

Ludwig swung the turret toward the closest French machine gun. He fired back, hot 20mm cartridge cases clattering down onto the fighting compartment's floor. The enemy Hotchkiss fell silent. The panzer pushed on.

Chapter 22

Meaux was gone. Luc Harcourt could see the smoke in the east, much of which came from the lost town. Maybe the *Boches* were celebrating by burning everything they couldn't steal. Or maybe French engineers had planted charges under everything they didn't want the enemy to use. German prisoners who spoke French had nothing but admiration for the engineers.

As far as Luc was concerned, who torched or blew up what hardly mattered any more. No matter who did it, France caught hell. All he cared about was staying in one piece till the war ended.

No guarantee of that. Sergeant Demange was commanding the company. No replacement officer had come forward since Lieutenant Marquet stopped an antitank round with his stomach. It cut him in half. The top half lived, and screamed, much longer than Luc wished it would have.

Luc had a squad himself. A private first class wasn't much of a noncom, but he'd gone this far without getting hit. That put him several long steps ahead of the scared conscripts he led.

The sergeant came by, his red-tracked eyes missing nothing. The Gitane in the corner of his mouth twitched as he snapped, "Don't let 'em lay there with their thumbs up their asses, Harcourt. Set the sorry sods to digging. They'll hate you now, but they'll thank you as soon as the Germans start shelling us again."

"Right, Sergeant," Luc said wearily. He knew Demange *was* right, too, but he wanted nothing more than to lie there himself, and who cared where his thumb went? With a sigh, he hauled himself to his feet. "Come on, you miserable lugs. You can rest once you've got foxholes to rest in."

They groaned. Some of them didn't even have hard hands yet; their palms blistered and bled when they used shovels or entrenching tools. But they'd seen dead men—both bloodied and astonished after meeting death unexpectedly and bloated and stinking from lying in the fields four or five days unburied. They didn't want anyone else seeing them like that: worse than getting caught naked. They weren't eager, but they dug.

So did Luc. He already had a scrape of sorts. He improved it as fast as he could. There seemed to be a lull now, but how long would it last? Another twenty minutes? Another twenty seconds? No time at all?

"Don't throw the dirt every which way!" he said in something not far from horror. "Sweet suffering Jesus, pile it in front of you! Don't they teach you anything in basic these days?"

"They teach us how to march and how to shoot," one of the new fish said. He had bloody hands and a pale, unweathered face. "From what they tell us, there isn't anything else—or if there is, we can pick it up at the front."

"They're sending you out to get slaughtered. They ought to see the *Boches* face-to-face themselves. That'd teach them something—the ones who come back from it," Luc said savagely.

Sure as hell, the shooting picked up before the soldiers finished their foxholes. They might be raw, but they weren't complete idiots. They knew enough to jump into the holes and keep on digging while inside them. Luc didn't think anybody got hit. He thanked the God in Whom he had more and more trouble believing.

He also thanked that God Who might or might not be there for sending nothing worse than small-arms fire his way. German machine guns fired faster than their French counterparts. Sergeant Demange said the same thing had been true the last time around, though both sides used different models now. Why couldn't the French have caught up with their longtime foes, especially since the Germans hadn't been allowed to mess with machine guns till they started laughing at the Treaty of Versailles?

Luc knew the answer to that. France hadn't wanted to believe another war would come. The Germans, by contrast, embraced battle the way a man embraced his girl . . . although fire from the flank could send them running, too. But they had the better tools with which to do their job.

"Is that a tank?" one of the rookies asked fearfully.

"No, my dear," Luc said after listening for a moment. "That's a truck—one of our trucks, by God. Maybe we've got reinforcements moving in. We could sure use some—I'll tell you that."

He almost shot one of the newcomers before he recognized the khaki greatcoat and the crested Adrian helmet. The French uniform had been modernized after 1918. It still looked old-fashioned next to what the Germans wore. The *Boches* seemed . . . streamlined, almost like oncoming diesel locomotives.

"Where are they?" shouted a corporal who sounded a hell of a lot like Sergeant Demange.

Demange himself gave an answer that was almost useful: "Look in the direction the bullets are coming from, *mon vieux*. You'll find the Germans, I promise."

"Funny," the corporal said. "You see? I laugh." And, having laughed a laugh that could have come straight off the cow on the label of a popular brand of cheese, he sent several shots toward the *Boches*.

A loop of the Marne—whose course was complicated in these parts—curled up toward the French position from the south. The enemy would have to cross the river twice to get in behind Luc and his comrades. As he'd seen to his sorrow, they were good at such things, but he could hope they would think two crossings were too much trouble here.

He popped up out of his hole to fire at an oncoming gray shape in a coal-scuttle helmet. The shape went down. Luc ducked before he could decide whether he'd hit it or not. Thinking of it as a shape, a target, meant not thinking of it as a human being he might just have killed. If he didn't think of it as a human being, he didn't have to think so much about what he was doing in this damned foxhole.

And ducking in a hurry meant that none of the other shapes in field-gray had the chance to draw a bead on a khaki shape and wonder whether he'd hit it. Luc didn't want some nice German young man to have him on his conscience.

The Nazis must also have decided that fording the Marne twice was more trouble than it was worth. But that didn't mean they stopped coming. If they couldn't go around the French here, they seemed determined to plow through them.

Sergeant Demange screamed for his men to hold fast till he realized they would all get killed or captured if they tried. One reason he made a good company commander was his aversion to dying. Luc shared the feeling. He wondered whether that would do him any good.

After fighting for a while in some woods, the French fell back into one of the riverside villages. Luc didn't know which one it was. There were lots of them, each Something-sur-Marne. The soldiers had fun with that, calling them things like Ammo-Dump-sur-Marne and

Blowjob-sur-Marne. A blowjob on the Marne would have been a hell of a lot more fun than what Luc was going through.

Most of the locals had long since bugged out. Luc would have, were he still a civilian. Nobody was paying those poor slobs to get shot at, and they didn't have the weapons to shoot back.

But a few stubborn souls always stuck around. He wished one of them would have been a teenage girl with legs up to there, but no such luck. Most were grizzled men who'd done their bit the last time around and weren't about to let a little gunfire drive them away from their stone houses and shops and farms. They were plenty tough. Their wives were even scarier, at least to Luc.

Several locals had varmint guns. They were ready to turn them against the *Boches.* "Big rats, but still gray," one of them said with a raspy chuckle.

Sergeant Demange didn't want them. "Dumb assholes won't take orders," he muttered to Luc. He was a little more polite to the embattled villagers and peasants, but only a little: "Let us do the job. You know what happens if the Germans catch a *franc-tireur*? The guy gets it, and then they shoot a bunch of hostages to remind everybody else to play by the rules."

"They shot my cousin like that in 1914," said another rifle-toting villager.

"Don't you think you paid 'em back after that?" Demange asked with surprising gentleness. The local had two fingers missing from his left hand and walked with a limp.

"Not enough," he said. "Never enough."

Demange could have argued with him. Instead, at his unobtrusive gesture, three soldiers sidled up to the man and forcibly disarmed him. The other locals muttered, which bothered the sergeant not a bit. "I told you—let us do the job," Demange said.

They might have squawked some more, but incoming artillery made everybody scramble for cover. A house that took a direct hit fell in on itself. A woman swore horribly. As soon as Luc saw that the house wouldn't catch fire, he ran for the ruins. You couldn't ask for better cover—and maybe, like lightning, 105s wouldn't strike the same place twice.

Here came the Germans. They must have had some new guys among them. Seeing a village that had just got shelled, they figured nobody would be waiting for them in there. One of them got close enough for Luc to see how surprised—and offended—he looked when he got shot. It was almost funny, although no doubt not to the poor *Boche*. Well, too bad for him.

His buddies, the ones who hadn't caught packets themselves, hit the dirt and started moving up the way they'd learned in training. Luc wished for a battery of 75s to tear them to pieces. Wishing didn't produce any French guns. Small-arms fire, then.

But damned if a couple of French tanks didn't show up a few minutes later. They were Renaults left over from the last war, without much armor and without much speed. Still, each one had a cannon and a machine gun, and there didn't seem to be any German armor around. The *Boches* didn't like getting shot up while unable to reply any better than anyone else would have. Luc would have bugged out, and so did the Germans.

"I'll be fucked," Sergeant Demange said. "Wasn't sure we'd get away with it this time. Well, I'd rather be lucky than good."

He *was* good, which meant he could afford to talk like that. But luck counted, too. If a shell came down on your hole, how good you were didn't matter. Luc shivered inside his own foxhole. He was still here. Maybe it was only fool luck, but he'd take it any which way.

SPRING SEEMED TO BE COMING early to eastern Poland and western Byelorussia. As far as Sergei Yaroslavsky was concerned, that was a mixed blessing. The warmer, clearer weather meant he could fly more often against the Poles and Germans. But it also meant the thaw would start pretty soon. And when it did, all the dirt airstrips in this part of the world would turn to mud. Nobody would do much flying till the ground dried out and hardened up again.

Rasputitsa. The mud time. Russian had a word for it. It came in both fall and spring; in fall because of rain, in spring from melting snow. The spring *rasputitsa* was worse, and lasted longer. Not just airplanes would be grounded. Armies would slow to a crawl, if they moved at all.

Sergei didn't think the Soviet generals had intended to keep on fighting the Poles till the *rasputitsa* came. He didn't think they'd intended to draw the Nazis in on the Poles' side, either.

He did keep what he thought to himself. If he said something like that out loud, he'd end up in a place where the spring thaw started in June . . . if it ever did. The USSR had plenty of places like that, and plenty of people had found out more about them than they ever wanted to know.

He had the feeling he wasn't the only one in his squadron thinking thoughts the NKVD wouldn't like. Meals became oddly constrained. Men seemed to be chewing on more than sausage and black bread, swallowing more than tea and vodka. You couldn't ask another pilot or navigator what was on his mind. If he told you, he proved himself a fool with a death wish. He was much more likely to say something innocuous and peg you for an informer. Sergei knew he didn't trust a couple of his fellow pilots. You had to watch out. If the enemy didn't get you, your own side would.

His bombardier had a simple solution. "Fuck 'em all," Ivan Kuchkov declared. "Fuck their mothers. Fuck their grannies, too, the filthy old cunts." To him, that wasn't *mat.* It was the way he talked. Maybe he didn't know where ordinary Russian stopped and *mat* started. Maybe he just didn't care.

"Some of these people you have to be careful around," Sergei said . . . carefully.

"I suppose," Kuchkov said with a noncom's sigh about the foibles of his superiors. "The guys who think they have big dicks are the guys who're big pricks, all right."

"Right." Yaroslavsky wondered why he bothered. He stood a better chance of talking a thunderstorm into changing its ways than he did of persuading Ivan.

But not even the NKVD could send a thunderstorm to a camp in Siberia. Ivan Kuchkov wasn't so lucky. The blocky bombardier amazed Sergei by winking at him. "Don't get your tit in a wringer, Captain," he said. "They never come after the likes of me. I'm not worth bothering with."

"How many other people have thought the same thing?" Sergei said. "How many of them turned out to be wrong?"

"Poor sorry fuckers," Kuchkov said. Sergei started to nod, then caught himself. He'd already said more to Ivan than to any of his fellow officers, even Anastas Mouradian. If Ivan was a fellow with a pipeline to the NKVD, he'd said more than enough to hang himself.

He eyed the bombardier's broad, rather stupid face. Ivan Kuchkov was a Russian peasant of purest ray serene. Surely he didn't have the brains to inform on anybody . . . did he?

You never could tell. That was the first rule. There was that iron-jawed commissar who looked even more like a village pig butcher than Kuchkov did. What was his name? Khrushchev, that was it. Yes, he sure seemed the type who'd take off his shoe and pound it on the bar if he got into an argument. And if that didn't work, he'd pound it on your head.

But, regardless of what he looked like, he was nobody's fool. He'd lived through the purges, after all, when so many hadn't. So maybe dear Ivan wasn't as dumb as he let on, either.

Their SB-2 got off the ground to fly a mission against a *Luftwaffe* airstrip in eastern Poland. As Sergei guided the bomber into formation with the others, he wondered when the *rasputitsa* would close down operations. Muck had flown from the Tupolev's tires as it roared down the strip, but it got airborne. Make the mud a little thicker, a little gooier, and it wouldn't.

One way to deal with the problem would have been to pave runways. That never crossed Yaroslavsky's mind. Soviet authorities didn't pave highways between towns, not least because invaders could have used paved roads, too. But if the highways weren't paved, airstrips weren't likely to be, either.

"Here's hoping we give the Nazis a nice surprise," Anastas Mouradian said.

"That would be good," Sergei agreed.

"Better than good," his copilot said. "If we don't surprise them, they're liable to surprise us, and getting surprised by a bunch of Germans doesn't sound like a whole lot of fun."

"Er—right." Sergei gave the Armenian a funny look. Did Mouradian talk that way because he was making a joke or because his Russian was slipping? Maybe it was both together; Anastas did like to make jokes, but they didn't always come out the way he wanted.

Maybe that was why Stalin and Beria and Mikoyan and the other formidable fellows from the Caucasus cut such a swath through Soviet politics—the Russians who were trying to deal with them couldn't figure out what the devil they were talking about till too late. Yaroslavsky didn't say that to Anastas. One more time—you never could tell. If the Armenian took it wrong, it might end up as a one-way ticket to a labor camp.

And then Sergei forgot about it. Me-109s tore into the Soviet bombers. The plane just in front of his spun down toward the dappled ground trailing flame from its left engine. Another SB-2, fortunately farther away, blew up in midair. That felt worse than a near miss from an antiaircraft shell; Sergei's bomber staggered as if bouncing off a wall.

One of the rear machine guns chattered. Kuchkov's voice came through the voice tube: "These pricks are all over everywhere like crabs on cunt hair! Do something about it, for Christ's sake!"

Off to Sergei's left, a Soviet bomber dropped its load over nothing in particular, broke formation, and scooted for Byelorussia. That looked like cowardice. Another SB-2 went down, and then another. However the Fascists had found out about this attack, they were all over it. What had seemed cowardice a moment before began to look more and more like good sense.

Sergei fired the forward machine gun at a 109. Tracers didn't come close. The German fighter flipped away with almost contemptuous ease. During the Spanish Civil War, the SB-2 outran and outclimbed Nationalist fighters. Everybody said so. But those German and Italian biplanes must have been mighty clumsy. As Yaroslavsky had first seen in Czechoslovakia, the bomber was no match for a Messerschmitt.

One more SB-2 tumbled in flames. That was enough—no, too much—for Sergei. "Dump the bombs, Ivan!" he yelled into the speaking tube. "We're heading for home!"

"Now you're talking, boss!" Kuchkov said. Grating metallic noises said he was opening the bay and pulling release levers as fast as he could. Half a dozen 220kg bombs whistled toward the ground. "They're bound to come down on some mother's head," Kuchkov called cheer-fully.

He wasn't even wrong; Sergei could console himself with that thought. He hauled the SB-2 around and roared east at full throttle. Maybe it could outrun an Italian Fiat. Next to a 109, he might have been piloting a garbage scow. The airspeed indicator said he was making bet-ter than 400 kilometers an hour. All the same, he felt nailed in place in the sky. When a Messerschmitt could get up over 550, how could any-body blame him, either?

Kuchkov's ventral machine gun barked again. The bombardier let out a shout of triumph—or was it surprise? "*Nailed* the fucker!" he roared.

"Damned if he didn't." Anastas Mouradian certainly sounded surprised. As bomb-aimer, he had a better view below than Sergei did. "The pilot managed to get out and hit the silk."

"Too bad. Only means he'll be flying against us again before too long," Sergei said. He tried to look every which way at once, including in his rearview mirror. German fighters were bad enough when you knew they were around. If they took you by surprise, you were dead. It was about that simple.

He flew over the Poles and Russians. Soldiers from both sides fired at the SB-2. That always happened. They weren't likely to hit anything.

"Won't it be wonderful," Mouradian said in his Armenian-accented Russian, "if we lead the Fascists to our airstrip and they shoot us up after we land?"

"Fucking wonderful," Sergei half-agreed. His superiors wouldn't love him for leading the *Luftwaffe* back to the field. But what could you do? His only other choice was putting down on the first open ground he saw. And if it was rough or muddy—and odds were it would be one or the other if not both—he was asking to go nose-up or dig a prop or a wingtip into the dirt. His superiors wouldn't love him for that, either.

There was the airstrip. Groundcrew men could get the plane under cover in a hurry. Sergei landed in a hurry, too—as much a controlled crash as a proper descent. His teeth clicked together when the landing gear smacked the ground. He tasted blood—he'd bitten his tongue. Anastas said something flavorful in Armenian that he didn't translate.

"You all right, Ivan?" Sergei asked the bombardier.

"I'm here, anyway," Kuchkov answered darkly.

That would do. Right now, anything would. They scrambled out of the plane. The groundcrew men hauled it towards a revetment. They'd drape camouflage netting over it. In minutes, it would be next to impossible to spot from the air. No 109s circled overhead or swooped low. All the same, Sergei decided he could hardly wait for the *rasputitsa* to kick in full bore.

THE FRONT WAS PARIS. Alistair Walsh would have known as much even if papers didn't scream it, even if posters weren't pasted to everything that didn't try to pick you up. Bomb craters and, now, shell hits from Nazi heavy artillery told their own story. When the 105s started reaching the City of Light, that would be real trouble.

No, Walsh thought. *When the* Boches *drive their tanks down the Champs-Élysées,* that's *real trouble.* Till it happened, he'd damn well enjoy Paris instead of fighting in it.

Or he hoped he would. This time, he didn't exactly have leave. His unit had fallen back into the eastern outskirts of town. Maybe they were supposed to be setting up somewhere, getting ready to hold back the next German push. If they were, though, nobody'd bothered to tell him about it.

In a way, that wasn't so good. It said orders from on high weren't getting where they needed to go. He would have been more upset were he less surprised. If the Germans kept pushing everybody else back, of course things would go to hell every so often. God only knew they had in 1918.

A lot of Parisians had already run away. On the other hand, a lot of provincials from the north and west had fled into Paris one step ahead of the invaders. You couldn't be sure whether the face that peered out a window at you belonged to a homeowner or a squatter who'd picked a lock or broken a window. If you were a Tommy, what the hell difference did it make, anyhow?

Plenty of bars stayed open. Most of the men who filled them were soldiers—French, English, or from heaven knew where. Walsh had run into Czechs before. Maybe the hard-drinking fellows who spat incomprehensible consonants at one another were more from that lot. Or maybe they were Yugoslav adventurers or White Russians or . . . But what the hell difference did that make, either?

One of the *poilus* had a concertina. When he started playing it, several other Frenchmen sang with more enthusiasm than tune. Walsh knew just enough of the language to recognize a dirty word or two every line. The barmaids pretended to be shocked. Their acting might have been even worse than the soldiers' singing.

Half a dozen military policemen stormed into the joint. The concertina squalled to a stop. The French MPs started hauling *poilus* out into the street. Then they grabbed one of the maybe-Czechs. He was in French uniform. He said something to them. It didn't help—they dragged him toward the door. Then he hit one of them in the face. The Frenchman went down with a groan. His buddy, unperturbed, hauled out a blackjack and coshed the Slav, who also crumpled. He might not have wanted to go wherever they were taking people, but he would.

Walsh's hand tightened on his mug of piss-sour, piss-thin beer. They wouldn't haul him off without a fight.

They didn't haul him off. One of them nodded his way, shrugged Gallically, and said, *"Eh bien, Monsieur le Anglais?"* He pointed to the flattened MP and soldier, as if to say, *Well, what can you do?*

"Just leave me alone, that's all." Walsh didn't loosen his grip on the mug. He didn't want to provoke the military police, but he also didn't want them taking him anywhere.

By the time they got through, they'd more than half emptied the dive. "Wot'll it be, mate?" the barman asked Walsh in English he might have picked up from an Australian in the last war.

"Another mug of the same." For what Walsh felt like spending, the wine would be urine, too, and the whiskey or brandy loaded with enough fusel oil in them to make him wish he were dead come morning.

"Right y'are." The barman was opening a bottle when Walsh heard the scream of a big shell in the air. Two wars' worth of reflexes threw him flat on the floor a split second before the shell burst in the street outside.

Plywood covered the plate-glass windows. But how much did that help when a 150—maybe even a 170—blew up far too close? Blast shoved in the plywood—and brought down part of the roof. Fist-sized chunks of jagged metal slammed through wood and glass. Not so many knifelike glass splinters spun through the air as would have without the plywood, but one as long as a pencil buried itself in the side of the bar about three inches in front of Walsh's nose.

More shells screamed in. He rolled himself into a ball, not that that would do him any good if his luck was out. Maybe it wasn't. None of the others hit close enough to do the tavern any more harm. After an eternity of ten or fifteen minutes, the bombardment stopped.

Walsh had to make himself unroll. He felt like a sowbug that had just escaped an elephant. As he dazedly picked himself up, he realized not everybody in the little bar had been so lucky. If he wanted that beer, he would have to get it himself. The barman's blood splashed broken bottles behind the bar. The stink of the spilled potables almost drowned the butcher-shop odor of blood.

Other soldiers were down, too. Walsh did what he could for them, which mostly consisted of pulling tables and chairs off them and using their wound dressings. He hoped he helped a little.

The door had been blasted open. The door, not to put too fine a point on it, had been blasted off its hinges, and lay in the middle of the floor. He stepped over it and out into the street, which now had a crater big enough to hold a horse. It was filling up with water from a broken main.

Staggering away, Walsh realized one thing was absolutely true—and absolutely terrifying. The front *was* Paris.

THE FRONT WAS THE USSURI RIVER. Northeastern Manchukuo was about as different from the Mongolian border region as anything Sergeant Hideki Fujita could imagine. Gone were waterless wastes with camels and wild asses running through them. Great forests of pine towered toward the sky here. Rain—and sometimes snow—poured down out of the sky. Japanese soldiers who'd been here longer than Fujita said tigers prowled these woods. He didn't know about that. He'd seen no sign of them himself. But he wouldn't have been surprised.

He did know there were Russians on the far side of the Ussuri. That was the same here as it had been 800 kilometers to the west.

Not far east of the Ussuri, the Russians' Trans-Siberian Railroad ran south toward Vladivostok. If Japan could get astride the railroad, the USSR's eastern port would fall into Japanese hands like a ripe fruit.

Fujita crouched in a log-roofed dugout artistically camouflaged with dirt and pine boughs and, now, the latest snowfall. He peered across the Ussuri toward the Red Army positions on the far bank. He couldn't see as much as he would have liked. The other side of the border was as thickly wooded as this one—and the Russians, damn them, were at least as good as his own people at hiding what they were up to.

"What do you see, Sergeant?" Lieutenant Kenji Hanafusa asked.

"Trees, sir. Snow," Fujita answered. "Not much else. No tigers. No Russians, either."

"They're there," the lieutenant said.

"Oh, yes, sir," Fujita agreed. "They're everywhere. The Mongols would have fallen over years ago if the Russians weren't propping them up."

"No, the Russians are *really* everywhere," Hanafusa said. "A quarter of the way around the world, they're fighting the Poles and the Germans. And that's why we're here. When things get cooking on this front, they'll be too busy in the west to do anything about it."

"Yes, sir," Fujita said resignedly. Japanese officers always figured enlisted men were hayseeds. The sergeant had figured out why his unit was transferring from the Mongolian border to the northeast as soon as it got the order. He knew what a map looked like. And if he'd never slept in a bed with a frame and legs till he got conscripted . . . Lieutenant Hanafusa didn't need to know that.

"As soon as the weather warms up and the snow melts, I think we'll move," Hanafusa said.

"Sounds good to me, sir," Fujita said. You needed as many clothes here in the winter as you did in Mongolia, and that was saying something.

Something buzzed by high overhead: an airplane. "Is that one of ours or one of theirs?" Hanafusa asked.

"Let me see, sir." Fujita raised the field glasses. The plane was too far off to let him make out whether it bore the Rising Sun or the Soviet red star. But he recognized the outline, and spoke confidently: "It's one of ours, sir."

"Well, good," Hanafusa said. Both sides sent up reconnaissance planes: each wanted to see what the other was up to. Every so often, one side would send up fighters to chase off the spies or shoot them down. Sometimes the other side would send up fighters of its own. Then the men on the ground could watch dogfights and cheer on the planes they thought were theirs.

Sergeant Fujita hoped the Russians would open up with their anti-aircraft guns. He didn't want them hitting the Japanese plane—that was the last thing he had in mind. But if they started shooting at it, his side could see where they'd positioned their guns. That would be worth knowing when the big fight started.

He wasn't much surprised when the guns stayed silent. The Russians were better at hiding their artillery till they really needed it than he'd imagined anyone could be. If you didn't think they had any guns nearby, half a dozen batteries were zeroed in on you. If you thought you knew about those half a dozen batteries, four wouldn't be where you expected them to be and you'd missed another half a dozen. You wouldn't find out about them, either, not till the Russians needed to show them to you.

He said as much to Lieutenant Hanafusa. Not all of the Kwantung Army had as much experience with the Russians as the men who'd fought them in Mongolia did. These fellows who'd been on the Ussuri or over by the Amur . . . well, what did they know? Not much, not so far as Fujita could see.

But Hanafusa nodded. "Thank you, Sergeant," he said. "We've seen that ourselves. There have been skirmishes along this frontier, too, you know. Even the Korean Army got into the act—but they had to ask us for help when the Russians turned out to have more than they expected."

"All right, sir." Fujita wasn't sure it was, but what could he say?

He did share Hanafusa's scorn for the Korean Army. The Kwantung Army was a power unto itself. It dictated policy for Japan as often as Tokyo told it what to do. The Kwantung Army had masterminded and spearheaded the Japanese thrust deep into China. Some people said there were men in the Cabinet back in Japan who didn't like that and wanted to pull back. If there were, those people were keeping their mouths shut and walking softly. Army officers had assassinated Cabinet ministers before. They could again, and everybody knew it.

The only force that had any chance of restraining the Kwantung Army wasn't the Cabinet. It was the Navy. Generals here saw the Russians looming over Manchukuo like the bears cartoonists drew them as. The admirals looked across the ocean and babbled about America—and, sometimes, England.

"Can the Americans give us trouble, sir?" Fujita blurted.

"What? Here on the Ussuri?" Lieutenant Hanafusa stared. "Don't be ridiculous."

Fujita's cheeks heated in spite of the chilly wind wailing down from Siberia. "No, sir, I didn't mean that. I meant, well, anywhere."

"Oh. I see." The lieutenant relaxed. "Mm, they won't jump in and pull the Russians' chestnuts out of the fire, the way they did in the Russo-Japanese War. I'm sure of that. The Communists don't have any friends. England and France are fighting Germany, too, but the two wars might as well be one on the moon, the other on the sun. They don't like Stalin any better than we do, and neither do the Americans."

"Yes, sir." That did help ease Fujita's mind. All the same, he went on, "I've talked to some guys who served in Peking. They say the United States doesn't like what we're doing in China."

"Who are these people?" Hanafusa asked softly.

Sergeant Fujita beat a hasty retreat: "I don't know their names, sir. Just some guys I was talking with waiting in line for comfort women." That wasn't exactly true, but Lieutenant Hanafusa would never prove it. You didn't rat on your friends.

"I see." The lieutenant had to know it was a lie, but he also had to know he wouldn't get anything more. His snort sent steam jetting from his nostrils. "Your brothel buddies aren't too smart—that's all I've got to say. The Americans go right on selling us fuel oil and scrap metal, no matter what's happening in China. As long as they keep doing that, they don't much care—right?"

"Oh, yes, sir." Fujita knew he wasn't the smartest guy ever born. But he wasn't dumb enough to get into an argument with an officer. If you were that dumb . . . He shook his head. He couldn't imagine anybody that dumb, not in the Japanese Army.

Chapter 23

Julius Lemp scowled at U-30. "What the hell have you done to my boat?" he demanded of the engineering officer standing with him on the quay at Kiel.

"It's a Dutch invention," that worthy answered. "We captured several of their subs that use it. We're calling it a snorkel—well, some of the guys who install it call it a snort, but you know how mechanics are."

"Ugliest goddamn thing I've ever seen," Lemp said. "It looks like the boat's got a hard-on."

The engineering officer chuckled. "Well, I've never heard that one before."

He couldn't appease Lemp so easily. "All you have to do is put it on. I'm the poor son of a bitch who has to take it to sea. Why the hell did you pick on me?"

"I couldn't say anything about that. I got my orders and I carried them out," the engineering officer replied. He wasn't chuckling any more. "If you've really got your tits in a wringer about it, go talk to Admiral Dönitz."

That shut Lemp up with a snap. He'd done more talking with the head of the U-boat force than he ever wanted to, and about less pleasant subjects. Sinking an American liner when the *Reich* wasn't at war with the USA would do that to you. German propaganda loudly insisted England had lowered the boom on the *Athenia*. Lemp and Dönitz both knew better.

And despite all that, it could have been worse. Lemp hadn't got demoted. He did have that reprimand sitting in his promotion jacket like a big, stinking turd, but nobody'd said a word about putting him on the beach and letting him fill out forms for the rest of the war. A good thing, too, because he wanted nothing more than to go to sea.

But . . . The *Kriegsmarine* had its ways of showing it was unhappy with an officer, all right. Loading down his boat with experimental equipment was one of them. You didn't want a skipper you really cared about to play the guinea pig. Oh, no. In that case, you'd lose somebody you wanted to keep if the—the goddamn snort, that's what it was—didn't work as advertised. But if that happened in U-30 . . .

Poor old Lemp, people in the know would say. *First the liner and now this. He wasn't lucky, was he?*

Poor old Lemp, poor old Lemp thought. He was stuck with it, all right. "I don't need to talk to the admiral," he mumbled after a long silence.

"No? Good." The engineering officer paused in the middle of lighting a cigarette. A chilly breeze blew off the Baltic, but it didn't faze him. He was one of those people who could keep a match alive in any weather with no more than his cupped hands. It was a useful knack for submariners, who had to come up onto the conning tower to smoke. Some guys had it and some didn't; that was all there was to it. Happily puffing away, the engineering officer went on, "You'll take two engineers to sea with you this cruise."

"*Wunderbar,*" Lemp said. A U-boat needed a second engineer the way a fighter plane needed an extra prop in its tail. The only reason you took one was to train him so he could become the engineer on a new boat his next time out.

Or so Lemp thought, till the engineering officer told him, "*Leutnant* Beilharz is an expert on using the snorkel." Lemp would have liked that better if he hadn't tempered it with, "If anybody is, of course." Still, maybe it meant the powers that be didn't actively hope he'd sink. Maybe.

Gerhart Beilharz proved improbably young and improbably enthusiastic. He also proved improbably tall: within a centimeter either way of two meters. Type VII boats—hell, all submarines—were cramped enough if you were short. With all the pipes and conduits running along just above the level of most people's heads . . . "You're asking to get your skull split," Lemp said.

"I know," Beilharz said. He pulled an infantryman's *Stahlhelm* out of his duffel bag. "I got this from my cousin. He's somewhere in France right now. I'm pretty good at remembering to duck, but maybe the helmet'll keep me from knocking my brains out when I forget."

"That'd be nice," Lemp agreed dryly. "Try not to smash up the valves and such when you go blundering through the boat, if you don't mind."

"*Jawohl!*" Gerhart Beilharz said—he really was an eager puppy.

And he knew things worth knowing. Or he was supposed to, anyhow. "Tell me about the snort," Lemp urged.

"You've heard that, sir, have you? Good," the young engineer said. "It's a wonderful gizmo, honest to God it is. You can charge your batteries without surfacing. That's what the Dutch were mostly using it for. But you can cruise along submerged, too, and you're much harder to spot than you would be on the surface."

"But how am I supposed to spot targets if I do that?" Lemp asked. "If I'm puttering along at three or four knots—"

"You can do eight easily, sir," Beilharz broke in. "You can get up to thirteen, but that sets up vibrations you'd rather not have."

"Can I get the periscope up high enough to look out with it while I'm running with the snorkel on?" Lemp asked.

"*Aber natürlich!*" Beilharz sounded offended that he could doubt.

True believers always sounded offended when you doubted. They sounded that way because they were. That was what made them true believers. Lemp was also a true believer, in his way. He believed in going out and sinking as many ships bound for England as he could. Anything that could help him sink those ships, he approved of. Anything that didn't . . . He eyed the ungainly snorkel one more time.

"Well, we'll give it a try," he said. "The North Sea is rough. Will the snort suck all the air out of the boat if the nozzle goes under water?"

"That's not supposed to happen," *Leutnant* Beilharz said stiffly.

Lemp concluded that it could, whether it was supposed to or not. What happened then? Did it vent exhaust back *into* the boat? That might not be much fun. He wished he'd never set eyes on the miserable *Athenia.* Then they'd have fitted the goddamn experimental whatsit onto somebody else's U-boat.

Well, he was stuck with it. He tried it out before the U-30 left the calm waters of Kiel Bay. It worked as advertised. The diesels chugged along with the whole boat—but for the tip of the snorkel tube—submerged. Gerhart Beilharz seemed as proud as a new papa showing off his firstborn son.

What happens when the little bugger pisses in your eye after you take his diaper off to change him? Lemp wondered sourly. He stayed surfaced through the Kiel Canal and out into the North Sea. Away from the sheltered bay, the ocean showed some of what it could do. Several sailors went a delicate green. Puke in the bilges would remind the crew it was there all through the cruise.

"Ride's smoother down below," Beilharz suggested.

"*Nein.*" Lemp shook his head. "I'll use the snort when I have to, but not for this. I want to get out there and go hunting, dammit. Even eight knots is only half what I can make on the surface, so we'll stay up here." The second engineer looked aggrieved, but that was all he could do. Lemp had the power to bind and to loose, to rise and to sink.

He cruised along at fifteen knots, heading up toward the gap between Scotland and Norway. The Royal Navy patrolled the gap, of course—they didn't want subs getting loose in the Atlantic. They laid minefields in the North Sea, too. A lot of U-boat skippers stuck close to the Norwegian coast. Some even—most unofficially—ducked into Norwegian territorial waters to stay away from the Royal Navy. Sometimes—also most unofficially—the limeys steamed into Norwegian waters after them.

Lemp steered straight for the narrower gap between the Orkneys and the Shetlands. As far as he was concerned, the Norwegian dogleg only wasted fuel. He prided himself on being a hard-charging skipper. (Sometimes, these days, he wondered how proud he should be. Would he have torpedoed the *Athenia* if he'd waited longer to make sure of what she was? But he couldn't dwell on that, not if he wanted to do his job.) And the North Sea was plenty wide. Chances were he wouldn't hit a mine or get spotted by a destroyer. And if he did get spotted, he told himself, it was at least as much the destroyer's worry as his.

He kept four men up on the conning tower all the time during the day. Their Zeiss binoculars scanned from side to side and went higher up into the sky to make sure the watchmen spotted a plane before it saw the U-boat. *Leutnant* Beilharz took his turn up there. Why not? It was the only time when he could stand up straight.

His disapproval of the way Lemp used—or rather, didn't use—the snorkel stuck out like a hedgehog's spines. Finally, Lemp pulled him into his own tiny cabin. Only a sheet of canvas separated it from the main passageway, but it gave him more privacy than anyone else on the sub enjoyed.

Quietly, he said, "We have the gadget. If we need it, we know what to do with it. Till then, I don't intend to break routine. Have you got that?"

"Yes, sir," Gerhart Beilharz answered sourly. U-boat discipline was on the easygoing side—enough to threaten to give officers from the surface navy a stroke. That formal response felt like, and was, a reproach.

Where the conversation would have gone from there was anybody's guess. *Downhill* was Lemp's. But somebody yelled, "Smoke on the horizon!"

"It'll keep," Lemp said as he jumped to his feet.

"*Ja.*" Beilharz sprang up, too. He wore his cousin's helmet all the time inside the U-boat—and needed it, too. It scraped on something overhead as he trotted along behind Lemp. He might make a submariner yet, even if he was oversized. Lemp would have thought hard about chucking him overboard had he tried to waste time.

The big, pole-mounted field glasses were aimed northwest when Lemp stepped out onto the top of the conning tower. "What is it?" he demanded.

"Looks like a light cruiser, skipper," the bosun answered.

"Well, well," Lemp muttered, peering through the powerful binoculars. It was indeed a warship: maybe a cruiser, maybe only a destroyer. He would rather have seen a fat freighter out there, but. . . . Before he did anything else, he scanned the horizon himself. If it was a cruiser, it was likely to have destroyers escorting it. Ignoring them while making a run at the bigger ship could prove embarrassing, to say the least.

"Shall we stalk it?" Beilharz asked, all but panting at the chance. "It'll give you a chance to try the snort in action."

Lemp didn't answer right away. Only after he'd gone through 360 degrees without spotting any more smoke or another hull did he slowly nod. "*Ja,*" he said. "We'll do it." He heard the odd reluctance in his own voice, whether the junior engineer did or not. Beilharz could afford to be eager. To him, this was like playing with toys. But Lemp had to be careful. U-30 and the crew were all on his shoulders, a burden that sometimes felt heavier than the one Atlas bore. He muttered something the wind blew away. Then he clapped Beilharz on the shoulder. "Let's go below. We'll see what we can do with your precious gadget."

He didn't submerge right away. He still wanted to get as close as he could on the surface, where he had the best turn of speed. When he did go under, he could still make the eight knots Beilharz had promised, and he would have been down to half that on battery power. The extra speed helped him maneuver into a good firing position.

He launched two torpedoes at the cruiser—he still thought it was one—from a little more than 800 meters. The British warship never changed course, which meant no one aboard saw them at all. One hit up near the bow, the other just abaft of amidship. Like a man bludgeoned from behind, the ship never knew what hit it. It shuddered to a stop, rolled steeply to starboard, and sank inside of fifteen minutes.

Cheers dinned through the long, hollow steel cigar of the U-30's hull. Lemp went to his tiny cabin and pulled out the bottle of schnapps he used to congratulate sailors on a job well done. He thrust it at *Leutnant* Beilharz. "Here you go, Gerhart. Take a big slug," he said. "You've earned it, you and your snort."

Beilharz drank and then coughed; Lemp got the idea the young man didn't take undiluted spirits very often. Well, if he stayed in U-boats long, he would. After a sailor pounded Beilharz on the back, he said, "Pretty soon, I bet every boat in the *Kriegsmarine* will mount a snorkel. But us, we've got ours now!" Everybody cheered some more. Why not? They'd just given the Royal Navy a damn good shot in the teeth.

STAFF SERGEANT ALISTAIR WALSH SHIVERED inside a house that once upon a time had kept an upper-middle-class French family warm and dry and snug. That family was gone now. So were the glass from the windows, a wall and a half, and most of the roof. What was left of the two-story house gave Walsh and several other British soldiers a good firing position from which to try to stop the Germans pushing down from the northeast.

He wasn't sure whether he was technically in Paris or in one of the

French capital's countless suburbs. They blended smoothly into one another. Maybe the fine details mattered to a Frenchman. Walsh didn't much care.

All he cared about right now was whether the side that mostly wore khaki could hold off the side in field-gray. If the French were determined to fight, Paris could swallow up an army. Seizing the place block by block, house by house . . . Walsh wouldn't have wanted to try it. And he would have bet the Germans weren't what anyone would call keen on the notion, either.

If they got around Paris to the north and came in behind it, the jig was up. They'd tried that in the last war, but hadn't quite brought it off. They were trying it again now. Walsh worried that they would make it this time. But he couldn't do anything about that. All he could do was make life as rough as he could for any *Boches* who got within a few hundred yards of him.

More *Boches* were trying to do that than he would have liked. Germans had always been aggressive soldiers; he'd seen that the last time around, and it hadn't changed a bit in the generation since. And they had their peckers up now, the way they hadn't in 1918. They thought they were winning, and they wanted to keep right on doing it.

The Tommies who huddled with Walsh weren't so sure how their side was doing. They'd all started out in different regiments, but here they were, thrown together by the fortunes or misfortunes of war. One of them—Walsh thought his name was Bill—said, "Where do we go if we have to fall back from here, Sergeant?"

"Beats me," Walsh answered, more cheerfully than he felt. "They want us to hold where we are, so we'll do that as long as we can."

He peered out through a hole that had been a window. The bomb that had mashed this house had leveled three on the far side of the street. As far as Walsh was concerned, that was all to the good: it let him see farther than he could have if they still stood. Some British infantrymen were setting up a Bren gun over there, using the rubble to conceal and strengthen their position. That wouldn't protect them from artillery the way a concrete emplacement would, but it was a damn sight better than nothing.

And Walsh liked having machine guns around. They stretched an ordinary rifleman's life expectancy. Not only did they chew up enemy foot soldiers, they also drew fire, which meant the Germans wouldn't be shooting anywhere else so much—say, at the precious and irreplaceable carcass of one Staff Sergeant Alistair Walsh.

Artillery probably based somewhere inside of Paris thundered behind the British position. The shells came down a few hundred yards in front of Walsh. A short round burst much too close to the Bren gunners. One of them turned and shook his fist in the direction of his own gunners.

Walsh would have done the same thing. Artillerymen and foot soldiers often brawled when they came together in taverns behind the line. The artillerymen seemed to wonder why. Not the infantry. They knew, all right.

"Can't win, can you, Sergeant?" a different private said. His name was Nigel, and he talked like an educated man.

"Oh, I don't know. Look at it the right way and we're all winners so far," Walsh replied.

Nigel looked puzzled. "How's that? This isn't a holiday on the fucking Riviera." His wave encompassed the shattered house and the wreckage all around.

"Too bloody right it's not," Walsh agreed. "But you're still here to piss and moan about it, eh? They haven't thrown you in a hole in the ground with your rifle and tin hat for a headstone. They haven't taken your leg off with a strap to bite on 'cause they ran out of ether with the last poor bloke. If you're not a winner on account of that, chum, what would you call it?"

"Heh." Nigel chuckled sheepishly. "Put it like that and you've got something, all right. Taken all in all, though, I do believe I'd sooner win the Irish Sweepstakes." He lit a Navy Cut and passed around the packet. He might talk like a toff, but he didn't act like one.

With one of Nigel's fags in his mouth, Walsh didn't feel like arguing any more. Sure as hell, a cigarette was better than a soft answer for turning away wrath. Then the German artillery woke up, and he forgot about everything else.

He hoped the Fritzes were sending back counterbattery fire. If they wanted to drop some on his own gunners' heads, he didn't mind . . . too much. But no such luck. The first shells burst a little closer to his position than the German rounds had. Then they walked west.

"Christ, we're for it this time!" he shouted, and dove under the dining-room table. It was the best shelter around. The other Tommies knew what they were doing, too. They all ended up in a mad tangle under there. That table, a great, solid hunk of oak, had to date back to the last century. It would keep the rest of the roof and the ceiling from coming down on their heads if anything could.

If anything could. That table wouldn't stop a shell burst on the house or right outside of it from filling them with fragments. Walsh knew that painfully well—and, with somebody's boot in his eye, somebody else's elbow in his stomach, and somebody else altogether squashing him flat, *painfully* was *le môt juste*.

An explosion to the right. Another to the left. Two more behind the house. Bits and pieces of things came down. Something about the size of a football thumped on top of the table and banged away. Another chunk of the ceiling? Whatever it was, Walsh wouldn't have wanted it landing on him. But it didn't. That table might have let a tank run over him, not that he was anxious to find out by experiment.

The bombardment pressed on, deeper into the Allied position. It was almost like the walking barrages the British had used in the last go. That memory galvanized Walsh. "Up!" he shouted urgently, lifting his face from the small of—he thought—Nigel's back. "Get up! We'll be arse-deep in *Boches* any second now!"

Getting out from under the table was more complicated than getting in there had been. They'd packed themselves in too tightly. After mighty wrigglings and much bad language, they got loose. Bill had a gash on his left leg. It might have come from broken glass on the floor or a graze by a fragment. In civilian times, Walsh would have thought it was nasty. Neither he nor Bill got excited about it now.

Walsh ran up to the top floor. Sure as dammit, here came the Fritzes. Their storm troops had submachine guns and lots of grenades. They'd learned that stunt in 1918. They'd bring real machine guns along, too. The current models were more portable than Maxims had been back then. And they were Fritzes. That alone gave Walsh a healthy respect for their talents.

He took a quick look at the Bren-gun position across the street. It didn't seem to have taken a hit, but the gun stayed quiet. With luck, the crew was playing possum, luring the *Boches* forward to be mown down. Without luck, somebody else would have to get over there—if he could—and use the Bren.

An unwary German (yes, there were such things: just not enough of them) showed himself for rather too long. Walsh's Enfield jumped to his shoulder almost of its own accord. The stock slammed him when he pulled the trigger. The German went down. By the boneless way he fell, Walsh didn't think he'd get up again.

"Now they know we're here," Nigel called from downstairs. He didn't sound critical—he was reminding Walsh of something he needed to remember.

"We couldn't have kept it secret much longer," the veteran noncom answered. "As long as they haven't got any tanks, winkling us out'll take a bit of work." He hadn't seen any mechanical monsters right around here. They did less well in built-up places than out in the open. They grew vulnerable to grenades and flaming bottles of petrol and other dirty tricks.

A machine gun started barking from most of a mile away. Bullets slammed into the east-facing stone wall. It wasn't aimed fire, but it made the Englishmen keep their heads down. A rifle could hit at that range only by luck. The machine gun stayed dangerous not because it was more accurate but because it spat so many rounds.

German infantry advanced under cover of that machine-gun fire. Walsh had been sure the *Boches* would. They knew what was what. And then, like the cavalry riding to the rescue in an American Western, the Bren gun in the wreckage across the street opened up. Walsh heard the Fritzes shout in dismay as they dove for cover. This wouldn't be so easy as they'd thought.

The machine gun that had been firing at Walsh and his chums forgot about them and went after the more dangerous Bren gun. The Germans didn't use light machine guns in this war. They had a general-purpose weapon that filled both the light and heavy roles. It wasn't ideal for either. But, being belt-fed, it could go longer than a box-fed Bren.

Not that that did the advancing *Landsers* much good. The Bren-gun position was secure against small-arms fire. The Tommies manning it ignored the other machine gun and kept the foot soldiers in field-gray at a respectful distance.

And Walsh and his pals and the other riflemen in the half-wrecked suburb made the Germans pay whenever they stuck their heads up. The only thing he dreaded was that the German artillery would come back. It didn't. After half an hour or so, the attack petered out. The Fritzes had taken a good many casualties, and Walsh couldn't see that they'd gained an inch of ground.

Nigel passed around the packet of Navy Cuts again. Bill found a bottle of wine the French family had forgotten. They passed that around, too. It didn't take long to empty. Once it ran dry, Walsh set it aside. If he got the chance, he'd make a petrol bomb out of it. He opened a tin of steak-and-kidney pudding—the best ration the Army made. A smoke, some wine, a tin of food . . . He was happy as a sheep in clover. A soldier could be satisfied with next to nothing, and often was.

· · ·

WHEN MILT WOLFF WENT DOWN, Harvey Jacoby took command of the Abraham Lincoln Battalion. He'd been a labor organizer in Seattle before he came to Spain. Chaim Weinberg thought he was a pretty good guy. He was brave and smart. But nobody would ever call him anything like *El Lobo*. He had neither the name nor the personality for it—he ran things with brains and common sense.

He came back from a meeting of International Brigade officers muttering to himself. "They're going to pull us out of the line here," he announced, his tone declaring that it wasn't his idea and he didn't like it for hell, but he couldn't do anything about it.

He must have known the news would bring a storm of protest, and it did. "What for?" Chaim yelped, his voice one among many. "We can hold the Ebro line forever! *¡No pasarán!*"

"The Republic is going to transfer the International Brigades to where they need us more," Jacoby said, picking his words with obvious care.

That only made the Abe Lincolns hotter than ever. Next to Chaim, Mike Carroll called, "They can't do that! The Party wouldn't like it!" Again, he was far from the only man with the same thought.

"They can. They are." Jacoby held up a hand, which slowed but didn't stop the torrent of vituperation. At last, something resembling quiet except for being much noisier prevailed. It was enough to satisfy Jacoby, anyhow. "Listen to me," he said, and then again, louder, "*Listen to me*, goddammit! Things aren't the way they used to be, and we'd better get used to it."

"What's so different?" Chaim challenged.

"Here's what—the Republic doesn't have to worry about the Party line any more," Jacoby answered. "Back when we were getting most of our stuff from the Soviets, the government had to pay attention to what the Party wanted. But when's the last time a Russian ship tied up in Barcelona?"

Chaim knew the answer to that: just before the big European war started. Since then, that supply line had dried up. All the supply lines for both sides had dried up. Nationalists and Republicans were fighting with what they had left from before and with what they could make for themselves. That that might affect policy hadn't occurred to him up till now.

But it did. "The Party isn't the tail that wags the dog any more," Harvey Jacoby said regretfully. "Russian officers can't tell the Spaniards what to do and how to do things." His grin was crooked. "Well, they can, but the Spaniards have quit listening."

Chaim's chuckle sounded forced. In his time with the Internationals, he'd seen that Russians could be as obnoxious and arrogant as Germans. Firmly convinced they were the wave of the future, they ordered people around to suit themselves and had as much give as so many snapping turtles. Somebody—Chaim had forgotten who—had said, "If the fuckers weren't on our side, there'd be a bounty on 'em." That about summed things up.

"We're tougher'n any outfit the Republic has," someone told Jacoby. "If we don't want to move, they can't make us."

"They want us to move *because* we're tough," the new leader said. "Way it sounds to me is, they're going to push the Fascists back from Madrid, and they want troops who know what they're doing."

A different kind of murmur ran through the troops who'd volunteered to come to Spain. There was a time, early in the civil war, when Marshal Sanjurjo could have taken Madrid easily. But he chose instead to rescue Colonel Moscardó, besieged in the fortress at Toledo with a small garrison. He succeeded, but he gave the Republic time to fortify the capital. The Internationals had taken gruesome casualties keeping it in Republican hands. Getting on toward three years later, it still was.

Mike turned to Chaim. "Think we can move the bastards?"

"Damned if I know—depends on just where we go and what we've gotta do," Chaim answered. "Even getting there'll be a bitch kitty—know what I mean?"

"Fuck! I don't want to think about that," Mike said with feeling. The Republic's railway net had more holes than a cheap sock. The roads might have been in worse shape yet, even assuming the quartermasters could scrape together enough trucks to move all the Internationals and enough gas to keep them moving. Chaim wanted to march from the Ebro to Madrid like he wanted a hole in the head. He'd signed up to give Sanjurjo a black eye, not to walk his own legs off.

"Madrid!" Jacoby said again, as if the name carried magic all by itself. And damned if it didn't. He went on, "Do you want to keep on fighting for chicken coops and frozen hills here, or do you want to fight for a place that really counts?"

Madrid had magic, yes. Another thoughtful murmur rose from the Abe Lincolns. But even magic was worth only so much to veterans. "Cut the crap, Harvey!" said a guy who could only have come from New York City. "Fighting's fighting. It's all shitty, no matter where you do it."

"You can cry if you want to," Jacoby said. "You can go home if you want to—and if the commissars and border guards let you get away with it. But if you stick with the Abe Lincolns, you're damn well going to Madrid. So what'll it be, Izzy?"

"Oh, I'll go," Izzy answered. "I still want to kick these Fascist assholes around the block, same like the rest of us. But you got to let us blow off steam first."

"What do you think I'm doing?" Jacoby said. "I know how hot the boilers run on some of you guys."

Chaim found himself nodding. The new CO'd hit that nail right on the head. A meeting of the Abe Lincolns—a meeting of any group from the International Brigades—was more like a workers' soviet than a typical military gathering. Or such meetings always had been like that, anyway. Not everybody who came to Spain to fight for the International Brigades was a Red, but most of the men were. And the Reds had always dominated the way things went.

They had, yes. How long could they keep on doing it? As Jacoby had said, the Party's stock was down. Chaim snorted. There was a capitalist figure of speech for you! Well, everybody else's stock in Spain was down, too. The war still mattered to the people who had to fight it. The rest of the world cared only for what was happening near Paris.

Spanish anarchist militiamen came forward to take the International Brigades' place on the Ebro line. They had a sprinkling of foreigners with them, too; as Chaim trudged toward the railhead down in Tortosa, he exchanged nods with a tall, pale, skinny fellow with a dark mustache and hair who had to come from England or Ireland.

The Internationals were a raggedy bunch: Americans (many of them Jews), anti-Nazi Germans, anti-Fascist Italians, Frenchmen who remembered the ideals of the Revolution, Englishmen, Magyars who hated Horthy, and Poles and Romanians and Greeks and God knew who all else who couldn't stand their local strongmen. There were even a couple of Chinamen and a Jap. They were raggedy, all right, but they could fight.

Bombs cratered the approaches to the bridge across the Ebro. Plenty of bombs must have gone into the river, too. But the bridge still stood. Aerial bombardment was no fun, but it wasn't the war-winning monster people had feared it would be. There weren't enough bombs, and the planes couldn't place them accurately enough to do everything the generals wanted.

The train that chuffed into Tortosa for the fighters had seen better days, better years, better decades. The locomotive wheezed asthmatically. The cars seemed to be missing half their windows. Once Chaim squeezed inside, he discovered the compartments had nothing but hard benches. He was lucky to get to sit down at all; the Internationals were packed in tight as sardines, without the benefit of olive oil to grease the spaces between them.

"Boy, this is fun," he said to nobody in particular.

"*Scheisse*," declared the tall, skinny, blond German wedged in beside him. "My ass." The guy looked as if he ought to belong in the SS, but his heart was in the right place. He took a pack of Gitanes from his breast pocket and offered it to Chaim. "*Zigarette?*"

"Thanks," Chaim said. He shared the red wine in his canteen with the young blond fellow. They talked in a weird mixture of English, German, Yiddish, and Spanish. The German's name was Wladimir—he insisted on the W at the front, even if it sounded like a V—Diehl. Chaim could think of only one reason why a German his age would be called Wladimir. "Your folks name you for Lenin?"

"You betcha," Diehl answered, a phrase he must have picked up from an American. "They tried to help the Red revolution in Bavaria. My father, I think, was lucky to live. They fought Hitler's goons in the streets when the Nazis were new and no one thought they would ever amount to anything. My father and mother have been fighting the Nazis longer than almost anyone." He spoke with somber pride. And well he might: among the Internationals, that was something to be proud of.

If anything, the locomotive seemed even wheezier pulling out of Tortosa than it had coming in. Chaim knew why: it was pulling all these cars stuffed with soldiers. And it had to take the long way to Madrid. If the Republicans hadn't recaptured the corridor to the sea from the Nationalists, there would have been no direct route through their territory from the upper Ebro to the city. They would have had to go to Barcelona, take ship, land in Valencia or some other port, and then head west from there. And they probably would have arrived just too late to do the cause any good.

Nobody bothered to feed the Internationals on the train. Along with the wine in his canteen, Chaim had enough bread and garlicky sausage to keep from getting too hungry for a couple of days. He'd been in Spain long enough to assume inefficiency would rear up and try to bite him in the ass. Wladimir carried stewed beans and smoked herrings instead. They swapped some of their iron rations. What Chaim got was no better than what he gave away, but at least it was different.

They didn't go very fast. Again, he was anything but surprised. It wasn't all the poor spavined engine's fault. The Spanish railroad net had been ramshackle to begin with, at least by American standards (and German ones—what Wladimir had to say put out more high-pressure steam than the locomotive's boiler; Harvey Jacoby'd known what he was talking about, all right). Two and a half years of war, two and a half years of bad maintenance—often of no maintenance—did nothing to improve matters.

Everybody had to get out and walk a couple of miles outside the little town of Villar. Jacoby and other International Brigade big shots promised that another train would be waiting at the depot. Chaim marched past a break in the track. Fascist saboteurs? Or just an ancient railroad line coming apart at the seams? He couldn't tell. He wasn't sure it mattered. Any which way, the line was fucked up.

And sleepy Villar might never have seen a train since the beginning of time. A few small boys stared at the Internationals as they slogged up to the yawningly empty depot. None of the other locals seemed to want to show their faces. Chaim would have been angrier had he believed the officers' promises to begin with. He'd been in Spain too long to trust anybody or anything any more.

The train did show up ... fourteen hours later, in the middle of the night. The locals had emerged by then, to offer food and drink at inflated prices. The Internationals proposed a different bargain: if they got fed, they wouldn't sack the town. Upon hasty consideration, the people of Villar agreed. "God protect us from our friends," Wladimir said, and Chaim nodded.

When somebody shook him awake, he didn't want to get up. He really didn't want to get on another train. As usual, nobody cared what he wanted. He managed to snag another seat. It was hard and cramped and uncomfortable, but inside of ten minutes he was snoring again.

He dozed till an hour past sunup. Not even artillery bursts around the station as the Internationals disembarked in Madrid got him very excited. It was a big city, and it already looked like hell. The Nationalists had battered it with guns and bombs ever since the war was young.

But the International Brigades were here to do what they'd done before—to help make sure Madrid stayed with the Republic. And, somewhere, Chaim would find a warm place to sleep.

Chapter 24

Joaquin Delgadillo didn't know what to make of Major Bernardo Uribe. His new battalion commander was recklessly brave. You had to be, to keep going forward into the shelling the British laid down in their defense of Gibraltar. Uribe hadn't hung back. He'd even won Sergeant Carrasquel's grudging respect—and Carrasquel gave no other kind.

But if the major wasn't a *maricón*, Joaquin had never seen anybody who was. Uribe smelled of rose water regardless of the hour. He was always shaved smooth as a woman—this among soldiers for whom scruffiness was a mark of pride. And he exaggerated the Castilian lisp into something beyond both effeminacy and self-parody.

If he ever tries rubbing up against me, I'll break my rifle over his head, by God! Delgadillo thought. But Uribe never did. Virile machismo virtually defined the Nationalist cause. Major Uribe cared nothing for machismo—unless it made him hot—but in his own strange way he was worth more to Marshal Sanjurjo than a lot of hard-drinking, hard-wenching officers.

"We are going back to Madrid," he told his soldiers, flouncing atop a kitchen table he was using for a podium. "We are. We'll take it away from the Republican beasts once and for all this time. And do you know what I've heard? Have you got any idea, my dears?" He waited expectantly, one hand cupped behind his ear.

"What is it, *Señor*?" the soldiers chorused, Joaquin loud among them.

"I've heard the International Brigades are back in Madrid. Isn't that jolly?" the major shrilled.

"No, *por Dios*," Sergeant Carrasquel muttered beside Joaquin. "They may be a bunch of fucking Reds, but they can fight. I ran up against those cocksuckers in '36, and once was plenty, thank you very much."

Up on his rickety platform, Uribe turned the sergeant's argument upside down and inside out: "People say they make good soldiers, and I guess that's true. But they're a pack of filthy, godless Communists. They kill priests and they rape nuns for the fun of it. The sooner we kill every one of them, the sooner we make Spain a clean place to live again."

Some of the Nationalist soldiers cheered. Most of those, Joaquin saw, were men new to the battalion. How much did they know about hard fighting? Sergeant Carrasquel, who knew as much as anybody in the world these days, did some more muttering: "That's all great, but how many of us are those assholes going to kill?"

"Victory will be ours," Major Uribe insisted. "Ours! Spain's! Germany and Italy have other scores to settle. But we—the honest people of Spain, the pious people of Spain—*we* will give the Red Republic what it deserves. *¡Muerte a la República! ¡Viva la muerte!*"

"*¡Viva la muerte!*" the troops shouted back. *Long live death!*—the battle cry of the Spanish Foreign Legion—sounded ferocious when they yelled it. In Major Uribe's full-lipped mouth, it seemed more like an endearment.

Uribe, of course, was not speaking for himself alone. He was passing on orders he'd got from the officers above him. If those officers said the battalion was going to Madrid, to Madrid it would go. The only other choice was desertion. And if Marshal Sanjurjo's men caught you after you sneaked away or—ever so much worse—went over to the Republic . . . They wouldn't waste a cigarette on you before they stood you against the closest wall. They might not even waste a firing squad's worth of bullets on you. Why should they, when they could bash in your skull with a brick or hang you upside down, cut your throat, and bleed you like a stuck pig?

Joaquin didn't want to go over to the Republic. He hated Communists and anarchists and freethinkers, and he had a low opinion of Catalans, too. Even if he hadn't hated all those people when the war started, all the fighting he'd done would have turned his heart to stone against them. And deserting was too risky. A healthy man of military age, without papers to prove he really ought to be a civilian, wouldn't last long.

And so, resignedly, Delgadillo climbed aboard a beat-up train with the rest of the men in the battalion and clattered north from Gibraltar. Sergeant Carrasquel checked the soldiers off one by one as they got on in front of him. Trying to skedaddle with the sergeant's beady black eyes on you was worse than hopeless. If you started thinking about getting out of line, Carrasquel knew it before you did.

Hillsides were starting to turn green. Down in the south, spring came early. The calendar insisted it was still winter. Up on the far side of the Pyrenees—maybe even up in Madrid—it would be. But the warm breezes blowing up from Africa made the southern coast of Spain almost tropical.

"You wait," somebody said. "When we get over the mountains, it'll be raining." Sure as the devil, it was—and a cold, nasty rain at that. Yes, winter still ruled most of Europe.

The closer they got to Madrid, the more Sergeant Carrasquel fidgeted. "Damned Russian planes shot us up last time I was here," he said. "They shot us and bombed us, and not a fucking thing we could do about it but pray."

"Will they do it again?" Joaquin asked. Getting attacked from the air was even more terrifying than moving up under artillery fire. He thought so while no one was shelling him, anyhow.

Sergeant Carrasquel only shrugged and lit a Canaria. Like everything else, the local brand wasn't what it had been before the war. He blew out a stream of smoke before answering, "I'm sure God knows, *amigo,* but He hasn't told me yet. When He does, I promise I'll pass it along."

Ears burning, Joaquin shut up. The train rattled along. One good thing about the rain: those gray clouds scudding along overhead meant enemy aircraft couldn't get off the ground no matter how much their pilots might want to. They also meant Marshal Sanjurjo's planes couldn't fly, but that didn't worry Joaquin so much.

The train came in after dark, so it got closer to the city—closer to the Promised Land, so to speak—than he'd thought it could. Rain still pattered down, but it wasn't the only reason he couldn't see the great city he'd come to take. Both sides observed a stringent blackout. If anyone showed a light, someone else would fire at it.

Even in the absence of light, the Republicans' artillery lobbed a few shells at the train. Somebody asked Carrasquel how they could know where it was. He gave the poor naïve fellow the horse laugh. "Did your *mamacita* tell you where babies come from?" he jeered. "They've got spies, same as we do. Sometimes I think every fourth guy in Spain is a spy for one side or the other—or maybe both."

He was kidding on the square. When the civil war broke out, how many Spaniards had ended up stuck behind the lines in a part of the country ruled by the faction they despised? Millions, surely. And lots of them would do what they could for their side when they found the chance. Early on, General Mola had bragged that he had four columns moving on Madrid and a fifth inside the city ready to help as soon as the Nationalist troops got closer. The same held true all over the country. When the Republicans advanced, as they sometimes did, they could find traitors to help them, too.

General Mola's four columns hadn't taken Madrid. The fifth column inside hadn't given enough help. And the Reds who held the city had massacred all the Nationalist sympathizers they could get their hands on—thousands of them, people said. It wasn't as if the Nationalist martyrs hadn't been avenged, either.

Marshal Sanjurjo's authorities here must have known reinforcements were coming up from the south. Odds were the reinforcements had come because authorities here asked for them. Joaquin was no marshal, but he could see that plain as day. He'd figured the authorities would have barracks ready for the newcomers, or at least tents pitched in a field.

The muddy field was here. So was the dripping night. Along with all his buddies, Joaquin got to wrap himself in a blanket and try to stay dry. "This is an embarrassment," Major Uribe said angrily. "On behalf of my superiors, men, I apologize to you."

He apologized because his superiors never would. Joaquin could see that, too. Sergeant Carrasquel said, "This is the kind of shit that makes people go over to the other side. They ought to whale the stuffing out of whoever couldn't be bothered to take care of us."

Joaquin whistled softly. Anybody who opened his mouth that wide was liable to fall right in. Carrasquel had to know as much, too. But he didn't keep quiet. You had to admire him for that.

Rain or no rain, mud or no mud, Joaquin fell asleep. When he woke up, the clouds had blown away and the sun was shining brightly. And he could see Madrid. He took a good look . . . and winced, and turned away. It was too much like looking at the half-rotted corpse of what had been a beautiful woman. Two and a half years of bombing and shelling left Madrid a skeletal wreck of its former self.

Guns boomed, there in the ruins. A salvo of shells screamed toward the Nationalists' miserable encampment. They burst well short, but even so . . . Madrid might not be alive any more, but, like some movie monster, it wasn't dead, either. Marshal Sanjurjo's men had to take it and drive a stake through its heart. If they could . . .

SAMUEL GOLDMAN STARED MOROSELY AT the bandages across the palms of his hands. He was a wounded war veteran. He walked with a limp because he was a wounded war veteran. Except during the last war, he'd never done hard physical labor.

None of that mattered to the Nazis who ran Münster. Jews went into work gangs. That was what they were for. It was so mean, so unfair, it made Sarah Goldman want to grind her teeth and scream at the same time.

You couldn't scream very well while you were grinding your teeth, but that was beside the point. Instead of letting out a shriek that would have brought the neighbors and the police, she asked, "Do you want to put on more ointment, Papa?"

He shook his head. "No. I need to toughen up my hands. Pretty soon, they'll have calluses. Then everything will be all right."

"No, it won't!" Sarah exclaimed.

Her father's chuckle was also a wheeze. "Well, you're right, sweetheart. But it will as far as that goes, anyhow. I can't do anything about the rest."

"Somebody should be able to," she said.

"What do you want me to do?" Samuel Goldman asked. "Write a letter to the *Führer*?"

"Why not? What have you got to lose? You were a front-line soldier, just like him. Maybe he'd listen to you. You've said it yourself: things aren't as bad for veterans as they are for other Jews."

"Mm . . . That's true." For a moment, Sarah thought her father would pull out a piece of paper and start writing. But he shook his head instead. He looked even older and more tired than he had when he first came home from the labor gang. "What have I got to lose? If I were just any Jewish veteran, I think I *would* send him a letter, because I wouldn't have anything. But with Saul . . . With Saul, I would do better not to remind the authorities about us. Or do you think I'm wrong?"

He meant the question seriously. Sarah respected him for that. If she could find a reason to make him change his mind, he would. She respected him for that, too. But she saw at once that she couldn't find a reason like that. "No. I just wish I did," she said sadly. "Everything's gone wrong, and we can't do anything about it."

"Not everything," her father said. "We're all still here, and three of us are together. And if Saul isn't, he isn't anywhere the Nazis are likely to look for him, either. I'll tell you something else, too."

"What?"

"The *Führer* isn't the first ruler who hardened his heart against the Jews. Pharaoh did the same thing in Egypt more than three thousand years ago, and look what it got him. *Pesach* isn't far away, you know."

Sarah eyed him in something not far from astonishment. She didn't think she'd ever heard him call the holiday *Pesach* before; when he said anything, he said *Passover*. And it wasn't as if they were a religious or an observant family. They ate pork. They'd never bothered with matzoh during Passover. They didn't go to the synagogue even on the High Holy Days.

Her surprise must have shown. Samuel Goldman laughed softly. "You're right," he said. "I never cared much about being a Jew before. So I was Jewish and Friedrich Lauterbach was Lutheran. So what? We were both Germans, weren't we?"

"As a matter of fact, no," Sarah said.

"As a matter of fact, yes. As a matter of policy, no." Even now, Father was relentlessly precise. "But if, as a matter of policy, the Nazis won't let me be a German, what else can I be? Only a Jew. And do you know what else?"

"What?" Sarah whispered again, fascinated and intrigued.

Her father smiled a sad, crooked smile. "I find I rather like it, that's what. I wish I'd been more of a Jew when I had more of a choice. I wish we'd raised you and Saul more in the faith. Hitler made me less assimilated than I thought I was, and part of me wants to thank him for it. Isn't that funny?"

Sarah bent down and kissed him on the cheek. He needed a shave; his beard was rough under her lips. "Oh, good!" she exclaimed.

"Good?" He looked at her over the tops of his spectacles. "Why?"

"Because that means I'm not the only one who feels the same way," she said.

"Very often, you don't understand what something is worth till you run into someone who tries to tell you it isn't worth anything," Samuel Goldman said. "And, very often, that turns out to be too late. I can only hope it won't here. If I thought it would do any good, I would pray, but"—he spread his hands in apology to her, or perhaps to God—"I still can't make myself imagine it helps."

"Make yourself believe it helps," Sarah corrected.

He smiled again, more broadly this time. "Make myself believe it helps," he agreed. "That's what I meant to say. I believe I am a Jew, all right. Whether I can believe I am a believing Jew . . . I am the kind of Jew who enjoys making paradoxes like that, which is probably not the kind of Jew God had in mind when He made us."

"Well, why did He make us the way we are, then? Why did He make so many of us like that?"

"Stubborn and cross-grained, you mean?" Now Father was grinning from ear to ear, something he hardly ever did. "He made us in His own image, didn't He? No wonder we're this way."

"You're having more fun playing with this than you ever did with the Greeks and Romans." Sarah made it half an accusation.

And her father, to her astonishment, went from grinning to blushing like a schoolgirl. "I sure am," he said. "I didn't know it showed so much. I've even started brushing up my Hebrew, and I haven't cared a pfennig for it since my father and mother made me get bar-mitzvahed. Know what I'm thinking of trying next?"

"Tell me," Sarah urged. She was fascinated in spite of herself, and had the feeling her father felt the same way.

"Aramaic," Samuel Goldman said in a low voice. He might have been someone who dabbled in drugs confessing that he planned to start shooting morphine into his veins.

All Sarah knew about Aramaic was that it was an ancient language. Growing up in a family that prided itself on its secularism, on its Germanness, she hadn't learned much more about Hebrew. Maybe that was why she blurted, "Teach me!"

"Teach . . . you?" her father echoed. The idea might never have occurred to him before. No, no *might* about it: plainly, the idea never *had* occurred to him before.

But she nodded. "I'm not a blockhead, you know. I could learn it. And you taught from the end of the last war till the Nazis wouldn't let you do it any more. You liked doing it, too, and everybody always said you were good at it."

"What on earth would you do with Aramaic, dear?" Samuel Goldman asked. "Or even Hebrew, come to that?"

"Beats me," Sarah said cheerfully. "What'll *you* do with them?"

Father blinked. Then he started to laugh. "To tell you the truth, I don't know, either. I just thought learning something new would help me pass the time. Of course, pick-and-shovel work is liable to take care of that."

Sarah nodded. "If you're able to go on with it yourself. If you're not too tired."

"A bargain." Her father held out one abused hand. She solemnly clasped it. He hesitated, then went on, "I have found one possible use for all this."

"Oh?" Sarah couldn't see any, not at first. Then she thought she did: "You mean going to Palestine, if we ever got the chance?"

"Mm, that, too, for Hebrew—if we ever got the chance." By the way Father sounded, he didn't think they would. "But that isn't what I meant. I was thinking that, if I asked God in one of His own languages why He was doing this to us, I might possibly get an answer." With a sigh of regret—or exhaustion—he shook his head. "Too much to hope for, isn't it?"

She wished she could tell him no. But, almost of its own accord, her head bobbed up and down. "I'm sorry, but I'm afraid it is."

PETE MCGILL LISTENED TO MAX WEINSTEIN spit out singsong syllables at Wang. Wang answered; damned if he didn't. McGill stared at Max. Like most of the Marines at the American Legation in Peking, he'd picked up a few Chinese words and phrases himself, most of them foul. But he'd never imagined he'd be able to sling the lingo the way Max did. He'd never imagined he would want to, either.

"What are you going back and forth with him about?" he asked. "Has he got a nice, clean sister?"

"Shit, McGill, drag your mind out of the gutter, why doncha?" Max said. "Me and Wang, we were talking about Mao Tse-tung."

"About who? About what?" For a second, the name was just another singsong noise in Pete's ears. Then it rang a bell. He looked disgusted. He sounded that way, too, as he went on, "Jesus Christ on a fuckin' pogo stick! You go to all the trouble of learning that dumb language, and what do you want to talk about? A lousy Red! My aching back, man! Worry about the important stuff first." As far as he was a concerned, women and food topped the list, with weapons running a strong third. He was a Marine's Marine.

Nobody ever said Max couldn't hold his own in brawling and drinking. He wasn't big, but he didn't back away from anybody. "Mao's no lousy Red," he said. "Mao's the straight goods. If anybody in this crappy country can give the Japs grief, Mao's the guy."

"Chiang Kai-shek—" Pete McGill began.

"My ass," Weinstein said, and then, " 'Scuse me. My ass, *Corporal*. See, the difference is, Chiang's all about Chiang, first, last, and always. Mao's about China instead. Ain't that right, Wang?"

"What you say?" Wang wasn't about to admit he understood enough English to make sense of that. But Max started spouting Chinese and waving his arms. Even in his own language, Wang answered cautiously. Pete knew why: if Wang sounded like a Red, he'd lose his cushy post at the Legation. He'd have to try to make an honest living instead, if there was any such thing in China these days.

"He's not telling me everything he's thinking," Max complained.

"He's smarter'n you are, that's why," Pete said, and explained his own reasoning.

"Oh." Max grunted. "Yeah, I bet you're right. That's just how the re-actionaries who run the Corps would respond to constructive, class-centered criticism."

"Give it a rest, willya?" Pete said, rolling his eyes. "I bet you even sound like a Communist recruiting pamphlet when you're getting laid." He did his best to imitate a pompous Red proselytizer: "The triumph of the waddayacallit, the proletariat, cannot be denied—and wiggle your tongue a little over to the left, sweetheart."

He laughed himself silly. He thought that was funny whether Max did or not. After a second, the Jewish Marine laughed, too. "Ah, fuck you, McGill," he said between chuckles. Then he got serious again. "You ever hear of a hooker in the States or here who *wasn't* from the prole-tariat? Gals who can find any other way to make a living . . . well, they do."

"You get an extra charge out of feeling guilty when you screw 'em?" McGill asked. Max couldn't claim he didn't lay Chinese whores. If he tried, Pete would call him a liar to his face, even if that started a fight. Weinstein was one of the horniest Marines in Peking, and that was say-ing something.

He gave Pete the finger. Aside from that, he didn't try to answer. Wang said something in Chinese. Max replied in the same language. Pete didn't know just what he said, but it sounded like a phrase that was definitely raunchy. Whatever it was, Wang giggled. Then he said something that set Max snickering.

"C'mon, man—give," Pete urged.

"He says Mao's the really horny son of a bitch," Max answered. "Mao's gotta be up near fifty, but he likes his broads young—eighteen, twenty, twenty-two, like that. Wang says he likes a bunch of 'em in bed with him all at the same time, too."

"What a dirty old man!" Pete said. It wasn't that that didn't sound like fun, and it wasn't that he didn't like young women, either. But he was young himself. Imagining a Chinaman old enough to be his father in the middle of an orgy made him want to puke, or at least to trade places. After a few seconds, he asked, "Does Captain Horner know about this shit?" Then he started laughing again, this time on account of the captain's name.

"Well, I never told him—I know that," Max got out between snickers of his own. He went back and forth with Wang in Chinese again. "Wang says he never talked about it with any other round-eye. I believe him. He doesn't know enough English to do it, and how many leathernecks speak Chinese?"

"You make one, and everybody knows you're a queer duck," McGill said. Max flipped him off again. Ignoring that, Pete went on, "You really ought to pass this stuff to the captain. He picks up as much intelligence as he can on the Chinese and the Japs."

"Yeah, yeah," Max said.

Pete knew what that meant, or thought he did. "Listen, I don't care if you don't feel like telling 'cause it'll make one of your precious Red heroes look bad. But I don't give a shit about that, so if you don't pass it on, I damn well will."

"All right, already. Shut up," Weinstein said.

Shut up Pete did—then. Three days later, he quietly went up to Captain Horner. The officer listened, then nodded. "I heard some of this from Weinstein, but not all of it," he said. "It's interesting. I'm not sure what I can do with it—hell, I'm not sure what the United States can do with it, assuming it's true—but it is interesting."

"Yes, sir." Pete had hoped to get a bigger rise out of him. Maybe what Horner had already heard from Max took the edge off of it.

And maybe the captain had other things on his mind. That didn't occur to Pete till the following Wednesday, when a bombshell hit the American Legation: more than half the Marines in the garrison would be transferred to Shanghai, effective immediately.

"There are many more foreigners—not just Americans, but also Europeans—in Shanghai than in Peking," Horner told the assembled leathernecks. "We can be more useful there. Also, Shanghai is a port, with direct connections to the United States." He paused, looking unhappy. "If the war between Japan and China keeps getting worse, moving our men between here and the coast may prove neither easy nor safe. Better to reduce our presence in Peking now, when we don't lose face by doing it under duress."

That sounded to Pete as if the United States had to react to what was going on around it—as if the country had little choice. He would rather the USA dictated circumstances and didn't have to respond to them. Sometimes, though, you had to play the hand you were dealt even if it was a bad one.

Captain Horner displayed a couple of typewritten sheets of names, several columns' worth on each. "I shall post these as soon as we finish here," he said. "If your name is on the list, pack your kit and be ready to move tomorrow. The Japanese authorities have promised there will be no difficulties as we march to the train station." He looked as if he were biting down on something nasty as he spoke. That American Marines should need Japanese permission to move through Peking—! But they did. At least they had it. "Questions?" the captain asked.

Nobody had any. If the other Marines were anything like McGill, their only question was whether their name had made the list. As soon as Captain Horner posted it, everybody swarmed forward to see.

Pete's was there. So were those of most of his buddies. "Misery loves company," he said, and he wasn't joking. He had a day to boil everything he'd picked up in Peking into a duffel's worth of stuff. Some of the residue he could mail back to his folks: jade and enamelwork and the like. The rest . . . He set it out for the Marines who were staying behind. "Take whatever you want and pitch the rest," he told them. He wasn't the only guy saying that, either—not even close. Somebody who stayed in Peking would hit the jackpot with what other Marines thought was junk. Whether he'd get the chance to enjoy it might be a different question.

Japanese and Chinese stared at the leathernecks marching through the city. Some of the Chinamen pointed and exclaimed. The Japs showed better discipline. "Eyes—front!" Sergeant Larry Koenig bawled. McGill's head went to the front. He kept looking around, though. Koenig wouldn't catch him at it—and he didn't.

The train flew American flags and had the Stars and Stripes painted on, and on top of, every car. No one wanted another incident like the gunboat *Panay*'s misfortune. Pete knew damn well he didn't. He climbed onto the train. His corporal's stripes assured him of a seat. The whistle screeched. The train started to roll. In a day or so . . . Shanghai. *Well, it'll be different, anyhow,* Pete thought, and lit up an Old Gold.

HIDEKI FUJITA WOULD HAVE LIKED to see better weather before Japan unleashed its attack along the Ussuri. Other sergeants who'd been stationed along this stretch of the border between Manchukuo and the Soviet Union longer than he had laughed at him for saying so. He would have bet even privates who'd been stationed here a while laughed at him. They knew better than to do it where he could catch them, though.

He would have made them sorry. He couldn't thump other sergeants. As long as he didn't do anything permanent, he could knock privates around as he pleased.

The hell of it was, the laughing sergeants and even the laughing privates might be right. This was the kind of place that had about twenty minutes of summer every year, with a half hour of spring to warn you it was coming and another half hour of fall to warn you it was going. If the army waited for perfect weather in which to strike, it might still be waiting in 1943.

This weather was a lot of things. Perfect it wasn't, not unless you were a polar bear. One blizzard after another howled down from Siberia. The swirling snow did let the Japanese hide the men and matériel they brought forward for the attack. Of course, it also made bringing troops and guns and munitions forward that much harder. But if you complained about every little thing . . .

Sergeant Fujita did wonder whether the horrible weather also let the Russians bring up reinforcements and guns. When he mentioned that to Lieutenant Hanafusa, the platoon commander indulged in what seemed to be everybody's favorite sport: he laughed at Fujita. "Not likely, Sergeant!" Hanafusa said. "The Russians are too busy fighting the Poles and the Germans to even worry about us."

"Yes, sir," Fujita said woodenly, and dropped the subject like a live grenade. He wasn't an educated man or anything. He couldn't hold his own in an argument against somebody who was. But he knew his own country was up to its armpits in China. That didn't keep anybody from starting this new adventure. Russia was bigger than Japan, a hell of a lot bigger. Why shouldn't it also be able to pat its head and rub its stomach at the same time?

After a while, snow started melting faster than it fell. More and more bare ground appeared; white no longer cloaked the pines and firs and spruces on both sides of the Ussuri. Here and there, flowers started blooming. They sprouted with what struck Fujita as frantic haste, as if they knew they wouldn't have long to do whatever they did. He wouldn't have called this spring in Japan, but it looked to be as much as the Ussuri country had to offer.

Lieutenant Hanafusa seemed delighted. "Spring comes early this year!" he exclaimed. "Even the weather *kami* are on our side."

No one told him he was wrong. Fujita only hoped the spirits in charge of the weather knew what they were doing. No, not *only*. He hoped the people in charge of the Kwantung Army knew what they were doing, too.

Whenever he got the chance, he peered across the Ussuri with field glasses. He rarely glimpsed Russians. Whatever the Red Army had over there, it was concealed. The Japanese would find out when they crossed the river—no sooner.

He kept hoping the people in charge of things would change their minds. Hope was cheap—no, free. And one of the big reasons it was free was that it was so unreliable. Men and guns kept right on moving up toward the Ussuri. Fujita presumed planes did, too, but the airstrips were farther back, so he didn't see them.

Superior Private Shinjiro Hayashi said, "Please excuse me, Sergeant-*san,* but do our superiors believe the Russians *don't* know we're preparing an attack?" His education didn't keep him from seeing what also looked all too obvious to Fujita.

"If you think our superiors tell me what they believe, Hayashi, you're dumber than I give you credit for, and that isn't easy," Fujita snapped. He quashed the university student without showing how worried he was himself. He hoped he didn't show it, anyhow. If Hayashi had suspicions, he also had the common sense to keep quiet about them.

The Japanese got a start hour—0530 on 1 April 1939. The last couple of days dragged along. Everybody got ready and did his best to make sure the Red Army went on thinking everything was normal . . . if that was what the Red Army thought.

"When we detach Vladivostok from the Communists, the Emperor will be proud of us," Lieutenant Hanafusa told his platoon as they waited for the barrage to begin. Sergeant Fujita imagined marching into Vladivostok. He imagined the Emperor pinning a medal on him with his own divine hand. He imagined his heart bursting in his chest from pride.

The shelling opened right on time. The noise was titanic. The Kwantung Army was firing everything it had, and firing as fast as it could—so it seemed to Fujita, anyhow.

Hanafusa's whistle shrilled. "Let's go!" he said. They raced out of the dugouts and ran for the boats waiting on the river. As soon as they got in, got over, and got out, they could start fighting a more ordinary kind of war.

Russian shells were already dropping on the Japanese side of the Ussuri. The barrage hadn't stunned all the Reds, then. Too bad, even if Fujita hadn't really believed it would. The Russians were just too good at covering up and digging in. Well, no help for it. He jumped into his assigned boat. The whole squad made it in. He cut the rope that tied the boat to the riverbank. "Come on!" he yelled, and started paddling like a man possessed. The rest of the soldiers paddled with him.

He didn't want to go into the river. With the heavy pack on his back, he'd sink like a stone. And the water that splashed up onto him said it was bitterly cold even now. Russian machine guns on the far bank yammered out death. Tracers snarled past the boat. Bullets kicked up rows of splashes in the stream. One holed the boat, miraculously without hitting anybody. Water jetted in.

"Stuff something into that!" Fujita shouted to the closest soldier. The man did. Fujita didn't see what. He didn't care. As long as the leak slowed, nobody would.

Mud grated under the boat's keel. The Japanese soldiers jumped out. They ran toward the closest machine-gun nest. The sooner they knocked out those deadly toys, the longer they were likely to live. One of them exploded into red mist fifty meters from the enemy strongpoint. "Mines!" everybody else yelled. Fujita wanted to run very fast and to stand very still, both at the same time. He might have guessed the Russians would use mines to protect their positions, but he didn't have to like it.

A couple of more men went down before the Japanese chucked grenades into the dugout through the firing slit. Even that didn't do for all the Russians. One fellow staggered out all bloody, his uniform shredded. He raised his hands over his head. "*Tovarishchi!*" he choked out. Fujita had heard that in Mongolia. *Comrades!*, it meant.

He shot the Russian in the face. "You can't shoot at us and then quit, bastard," he said. From everything he'd heard, machine gunners everywhere had a hard time giving up. And he might even have done the Russian a favor. He was inclined to think so. What greater disgrace than surrender was there?

Japanese soldiers stormed into the woods. They soon discovered their artillery hadn't done everything it might have. The Russians had more machine guns farther back from the Ussuri. They had snipers in camouflage smocks high up in the trees. They'd hidden more mines to slow and to channel the Japanese advance. And they had riflemen waiting in rear-facing foxholes invisible from the front, men who stayed quiet till the Japanese went by and then shot them in the back. Those fellows had as much trouble surrendering as machine gunners did.

Airplanes dueled overhead. In among the trees, Fujita couldn't see how the aerial combat went. When bombs fell on the Red Army positions ahead, he felt like cheering. When explosions came too close to his own men, he swore. He thought the Russians were taking more punishment than they were giving out, but he wasn't sure. Maybe he was just rooting for his own team.

Halfway through that mad afternoon, a runner told him, "You're in command of the platoon."

"Huh?" he said. "What happened to Lieutenant Hanafusa?"

"He caught two in the chest," the other soldier answered. "Maybe he'll make it, but . . ." A shrug said the odds were bad.

Fujita sure wouldn't have wanted to catch two in the chest, or even one in the toe. But if the platoon was his—at least till another officer showed up—he had to do his best with it. They were still at least a kilometer from the day's planned stop line. He needed to find out what was up with the other squads, too. "Forward!" he called. That was never wrong.

Chapter 25

"Moscow speaking," the radio announced. It was 0600. Sergei Yaroslavsky drank a glass of sugared tea, hot from the samovar. Pilots and navigators jammed the ready room at the Byelorussian airstrip. A Stuka could have taken out the whole squadron with a well-aimed bomb. The Nazis were sleeping late—or later, anyhow. The Soviet flyers hungered for news, not least because it might tell them what they would be doing next.

Smoke from almost as many *papirosi* as there were Red Air Force officers in the ready room blued the air. Somebody got up and made the radio louder. When he sat down, someone else patted him on the back, as if to say *Good job!* Yes, they were all jumpy this early morning.

"Comrades! Soviet citizens! Our motherland has been invaded!" the news reader said solemnly. "Without provocation, without warning, the Empire of Japan has launched a multipronged attack against the Siberian districts of the Russian Federated Soviet Socialist Republic of the peace-loving USSR. Severe fighting is reported in several areas. All drives against the Trans-Siberian Railroad have already been blunted or soon will be—so Red Army commanders in the field have assured General Secretary Stalin. Under his leadership, victory of the Soviet workers and peasants is assured."

Sergei nodded. So did almost everybody else in the ready room. Some officers, he was sure, had no doubts that what was coming out of the radio was the truth, the whole truth, and nothing but the truth. And if you *did* have doubts, looking as if you didn't was even more important. People couldn't suspect what they didn't see.

The announcer went on and on about towns bombed from the air, atrocities on the ground, and numbers of Japanese soldiers killed. Except for civilians, he said not a word about Soviet casualties. There must have been some; chances were they were heavy. Sergei was sure he wasn't the only one to notice the omission. Notice or not, the Red Air Force officers went right on nodding.

"Foreign Commissar Litvinov has pledged that this war against the Japanese will have a result different from that of the Tsar's corrupt regime in 1905," the newsreader finished. Sergei cheered and clapped his hands. So did everyone else. Nobody could be proud of Russia's performance in the Russo-Japanese War.

After a pause, the announcer talked about fighting in the Soviet west. "The *rasputitsa* has made movement difficult for both sides," he admitted. That wasn't the smallest understatement Sergei had ever heard. Eastern Poland and western Byelorussia were somewhere between swamp and bog. The Germans still occasionally flew off paved runways. The Red Air Force was grounded.

"In western Europe, the fighting in France has reached what the Germans call a decisive phase," the fellow went on. "The French government denies German claims that there is fighting inside the Paris city limits. The French and English admit heavy fighting continues east and northeast and even north of the French capital. They state they still hope to halt and eventually repel the latest German thrust, however."

He spoke with an air of prissy disapproval, like an important man's plump wife talking about the facts of life. As far as the USSR was concerned, the imperialists were hardly better than the Fascists. But the Soviet Union and England and France had the same enemies at the moment. Expedience could trump ideology.

And, sure enough, the newsreader sounded a little warmer when he said, "British and French bombing of German territory seems to be picking up—judging, at least, by the outraged bleats emanating from *Herr* Goebbels. If one listens to the Germans, their opponents take care to bomb only schoolhouses, orphanages, and hospitals."

Sergei chuckled. Then he wondered why he was laughing. Yes, German propaganda was pretty ham-fisted. But wasn't what poured out of Soviet radios just as clumsy?

That was something a good Soviet citizen wasn't supposed to notice. After all, didn't *Pravda* mean *Truth*? Maybe only someone who was serving in the military—maybe only someone serving in the military who'd spent some time in a foreign country—would notice the discrepancies. Once you spotted a few lies, though, you started wondering what else you heard was malarkey.

Across the table, Anastas Mouradian sat there smoking *papirosi* one after another. Did irony fill his liquid black eyes, or was that only Sergei's imagination? Anastas was going to get in trouble one of these days. Anybody who looked ironic in the middle of the morning news was bound to get noticed. The only surprise was, it had already taken this long.

When the announcer shifted to increased production and overfulfillment of the Five-Year Plan's norms, the officers started to relax. This was only fluff; they'd already got the meat from the news. If you were careful, you could smile about this stuff without risking too much.

At last, music replaced the news. "Two fronts," remarked the flyer from Siberia, the guy who came from a thousand kilometers north of Irkutsk and laughed at the cold weather here. Quickly, Bogdan Koroteyev added, "It's not what we wanted, of course, but it's what we've got."

"We'll win anyhow," Anastas Mouradian said. Sergei nodded vigorously. He grinned at his crewmate. That was how you were supposed to talk! He had his doubts whether Anastas meant it, but what did that have to do with anything? The picture you showed the outside world was more important (to your survival, anyhow) than whatever you carried deep inside your heart.

"You'd better believe we will," Lieutenant Colonel Borisov boomed. "We can whip the little yellow monkeys with one hand tied behind our back, and as soon as things are dry here we'll show the Nazis and Poles what we can do."

No one argued with the squadron commander. For one thing, he *was* the squadron commander. For another, what he said was bound to be the Party line. Russia hadn't beaten the Japanese the last time around, but it was easy to blame that on Tsarist corruption, as the radio announcer had. The Red Army *had* performed well in recent border clashes.

Well, it had if you believed the news. Sergei wished he hadn't started wondering about what he heard on the radio and read in the papers. It made him wonder about everything. Oh, well. What could you do? Doubting the official stories might give you a better notion of what was really going on. What was the phrase in the Bible? You saw through a glass, darkly—that was it. In the USSR, that was likely to be your closest approach to truth.

No enemy planes came overhead. If German or Polish bombers had taken off from paved runways, they were harassing other Soviet fields. And the SB-2s here couldn't fly even if the pilots wanted to. As with the winter blizzards, the flyers had nothing to do but sit around and wait.

Somebody pulled out a bottle of vodka. It was early to start drinking. Sergei thought so, anyhow. By the way Bogdan Koroteyev tilted back the bottle, he started at this heathen hour all the time—or maybe he hadn't stopped from the night before. Sergei took a swig, too, when the bottle came his way. Why not? You didn't want to look like a wet blanket or anything.

NEWSBOYS HAWKED THE *VÖLKISCHER BEOBACHTER* on every street corner in Berlin. "Decisive battle in France!" they yelled. DECISIVE BATTLE IN FRANCE! the newspaper headline shouted in what had to be 144-point type. The photo under the headline showed three *Wehrmacht* men, rifles in hand, leaping over some obstacle in unison. Except for the weapons and helmets, they might have been Olympic hurdlers. NOTHING CAN STOP OUR INFANTRY! the subhead boasted.

"Paper, lady?" asked a towheaded kid of about fourteen. If the war lasted long enough, he'd put on the same uniform the soldiers on the front page were wearing.

See how you like it then, you little son of a bitch, Peggy Druce thought. Aloud, all she said was, *"Nein, danke."* In another block or two, she knew she'd have to do it again.

Boys, old men, women . . . The only men of military age were cops, soldiers and sailors on leave, and middle-aged fellows who'd been too badly wounded in the last war to have to wear the uniform this time around. She supposed some farmers and doctors and factory workers were also exempt, but she didn't see them. Whatever jobs they had, they were busy doing them.

Another newsboy cried a different headline: "Soviet Russia now encircled in a ring of steel!" Several people stopped to pay a few pfennigs for his paper. The Germans like that idea. When they thought about it, they didn't have to think that the *Reich* was fighting a two-front war.

Peggy wouldn't have called a half-assed fight over here and what might be a bigger, more serious one way the hell over there a ring of steel. A ring with gaps so big would fall off your finger pretty damn quick. But the Goebbels school of newspaper writing had perpetrated far worse atrocities. Even a Hearst headline man might have come up with this one.

A big, beefy cop came out of his tavern. He was in his fifties, with a big mustache he'd probably grown before the last war and never bothered to shave off. At the moment, he was using a prehensile lower lip to suck beer foam out of it. He saw Peggy watching him do it. To cover his embarrassment, he did just what she'd known he would: he held out his hand and said, *"Papieren, bitte!"*

Out came her American passport. "Here," she said. "I'm a neutral, as you see."

He scowled at the passport, and at her. "In the struggle against Bolshevism and world Jewry, there can be no neutrals," he declared. Some Germans really did talk that way, the same as some Communists really did parrot the Moscow line. Then he said, "Come to the station with me, so my captain can decide what to do with you."

"To the station?" Peggy yelped. "You've got no right!"

"I am an officer of police," the cop said importantly. "Of course I have the right." In Hitler's Germany, he damn well did, too. He touched the billy club on his belt. "Do you defy my authority?" *I'll bust your head open if you do.*

"No," she said. "But let me see *your* papers, please. I will complain to my embassy, and I want to know who you are."

"Ha! Much good it will do you!" He showed her his ID willingly enough. His name was Lorenz Müller. Peggy wrote it down. She didn't think the embassy would be able to do anything, either, but it was the only card she had, so she played it with as much panache as she could.

The station was only a couple of blocks away. Except for his uniform and haircut, the desk sergeant looked like a desk sergeant back in the States: fat and bored but wary, in other words. Müller spewed out a stream of German, too fast for Peggy to follow it. The sergeant listened, then turned to her. "What happened?" he asked.

"I said I was a neutral, and I am—I'm an American. And he got angry at me and brought me here," Peggy answered.

"An American? Let me see your passport, please." When the desk sergeant said *please*, he sounded as if he meant it. Peggy handed him the passport. After studying it, he gave it back. "Yes, it is in order. *Danke schön.* You may go."

"What?" Lorenz Müller spluttered furiously—for about a second and a half. Then, without raising his voice, the desk sergeant gave him the most thorough reaming out Peggy had ever heard. She understood maybe one word in three, but that was plenty. Müller would've needed to get plopped into a specimen jar as soon as he was born to be as congenitally idiotic as the sergeant claimed, and he would have had to be 165 years old to have acquired all the vices the sergeant imputed to him. By the time the man got done, nothing was left of Müller but a demoralized puddle of goo on the floor. So it seemed to Peggy, anyhow.

"I am sorry you ran into this . . . individual," the desk sergeant told her. She'd never dreamt the word could sound so filthy. "By all means visit your embassy. A formal complaint will go into his record, which is good."

By then, she didn't want to. She found herself pitying Müller, which she wouldn't have dreamt possible a few minutes earlier. As she walked out of the station, the sergeant tore into the cop again—something about getting the *Reich* in bad with an important neutral power. *Let's hear it for the Red, White, and Blue,* Peggy thought. *Yeah! Let's!*

In the end, she did go by the embassy. The underlings quickly shunted her up to Constantine Jenkins, whose job probably included dealing with obstreperous tourists. He heard her out and then said, "Sounds like the sergeant did worse to this fellow than we could manage in a month of Sundays."

"Ain't it the truth!" she said. "All the same, I do want you to make a formal complaint."

"Just remember that the official head of the Prussian police is Hermann Göring," Jenkins said. "He won't listen. If he does listen, he won't care."

"I understand all that," Peggy said. "I still want to get it on the record."

"Okay. I'll do it," Jenkins promised. "Maybe it'll keep some other American from getting dragged to a police station because he runs into a cop in a lousy mood."

"That'd be good," Peggy said. "See? I'm a public benefactor." She'd been a lot of things in her time, but that was a new one.

Undersecretary Jenkins gave her a look that would have been fishy if not for the half-hidden amusement she spotted. "What you are is a troublemaker," he said accurately. "And you enjoy making trouble for the Third *Reich*, too."

"Who, me?" Peggy couldn't possibly have been as innocent as she sounded. And, as a matter of fact, she wasn't.

HANS-ULRICH RUDEL GULPED FROM a big mug of steaming black coffee. Plenty of pilots in the squadron were keeping themselves going with benzedrine. Hans-Ulrich thought pills were even more unnatural than alcohol. He didn't want to use them. If he had to, though, if it meant victory for the *Reich* . . .

And any one mission might. He knew that. They were so close, *so* close. The radio kept going on about the Battle of France, the decisive battle. If they could break through the enemy's lines, he'd never be able to form new ones. Maybe nobody in the whole battle could see that as well as the flyers who went after the French strongpoints.

He wondered whether the Allied fighter pilots had that same sense of seeing the whole chessboard at once when they looked down from five or six thousand meters. Or were they just trying to spot the Stukas before the German dive-bombers roared down and blasted another bridge or train or battery of 75s to hell and gone?

He shrugged. He had more immediate things to worry about. The German attack had accomplished a lot. It had knocked the Low Countries out of the war. It had pushed French and English ground forces back from the middle of Belgium to the outskirts of Paris. The enemy was on the ropes.

But he wasn't out, worse luck. And, while German supply lines had got longer and thinner, those of the Allies had contracted. The irony facing the Germans was that success made further success harder. Nobody on the other side could be in much doubt about what the *Wehrmacht* and the *Luftwaffe* had in mind any more, either. That made planning easier for the forces in khaki.

Which didn't mean the forces in *Feldgrau* couldn't still win. Hans-Ulrich was flying off an airstrip in northern France. Not long before, it had been a French strip. A couple of smashed French fighters still lay alongside the runway. German technicians had cannibalized them for usable parts—they were just scrap metal now.

Off in the distance, artillery rumbled. Rudel hoped it came from his own side, giving the Allies hell. Otherwise, French and English guns would be pounding the *Landsers*. He thanked God he was no foot soldier. He slept soft, and in a real bed—a cot, anyway. He ate well. Most of the time, he was in no danger. The enemy could still kill him. That came with any kind of military life. But he wouldn't be hungry and filthy and lousy when it happened, if it happened. He wasn't scared all the time, either.

Of course, when he was, he was about as scared as any human being could be. That also held true for the infantry, though. It was true for the ground pounders a lot more often than it was for him, too.

Sergeant Dieselhorst came by, a cigarette dangling from the corner of his mouth. He sketched a salute and asked, "Have they told you what we're doing next?"

"Not yet." Hans-Ulrich pointed toward Major Bleyle's tent. "As soon as the boss lets me know, I'll tell you."

"If they haven't hauled him off in the middle of the night," Dieselhorst remarked.

Hans-Ulrich looked around in all directions. Nobody stood close to them, and nobody seemed to be paying any attention to what they were saying. Even so, he wagged a finger at the rear gunner. "If you aren't careful, they'll haul *you* off in the middle of the night," he warned.

"Yeah, I know." Dieselhorst made a sour face. "That's not what I signed up for, dammit."

"Neither did I," Rudel said. "Who would have dreamt so many traitors to the *Vaterland* were still running around loose?"

"Yeah. Who?" Dieselhorst said tonelessly. The cigarette twitched as he eyed Hans-Ulrich. At last, almost against his better judgment, he went on, "Who knows how many of them really are traitors, too?"

"What else would they be, if the government arrested them?" Hans-Ulrich exclaimed.

Sergeant Dieselhorst's cigarette jerked again. "That's right. You're the milk drinker." He might have been reminding himself. "Sometimes people get arrested because they tell friends the truth. Sometimes they get arrested because somebody with pull doesn't like them. And sometimes, by God, they get arrested for no reason at all."

"Dirty traitors tried to overthrow the *Führer* and stab us in the back again!" Rudel said hotly. "Where would we be if they'd got away with it?"

"Better off?" Albert Dieselhorst suggested. Then he held up his hand. "And if you don't care for that, go tell one of the pigdogs in a black shirt about it. You'll have a new gunner faster than you can fart."

"I don't want a new gunner. I want—"

Before Hans-Ulrich could say what he wanted, Dieselhorst did it for him: "You want a good little boy who never makes trouble and never looks past the end of his nose unless he's aiming at the enemy. You want somebody just like you. I wish I were, Lieutenant—you can bet your ass it'd make my life simpler. But I've got pals—better Germans than I'll ever be—in concentration camps or dead because those SS bastards hauled 'em out of bed in the middle of the night. This isn't Russia, dammit. This is a civilized country, or it's supposed to be."

Had a flyer Rudel didn't know well said anything like that, he would have reported the man to the SS without the least hesitation. But he was alive not least because Sergeant Dieselhorst was good at what he did. By any reasonable definition, Dieselhorst was a good German, a patriotic German. If he was talking this way . . .

"You're upset. You're not yourself," Hans-Ulrich said.

Dieselhorst stamped out the cigarette. "I'm not crazy, if that's what you're trying to say. This whole war is a lot more fucked up than you've figured out yet. And some of the people who're running it—"

"Don't say any more. I don't want to listen to it," Rudel said. "All I have to do is fly. The same with you, too."

"Christ, Lieutenant, flying is the easy part—any jerk with an airplane can do that," Dieselhorst said. "Trying to steer clear of the shit that pours down from on high, that's where the going gets tough."

"Well, let's see what we have to do, that's all." Hans-Ulrich was grateful for the chance to turn away. As far as Sergeant Dieselhorst was concerned, *he* was part of the shit that poured down from on high. They'd gone through much too much together for Hans-Ulrich to feel easy about turning in the sergeant now. He'd keep his mouth shut—for the moment, anyway.

"Gisors," Major Bleyle said a few minutes later. "They're pushing supplies through there to the front near Beauvais." He whacked a map with a pointer. "Gisors is about seventy kilometers northwest of Paris. You'll recognize it by the castle and the cathedral. Here are some photos." He passed around the reconnaissance shots. "Railroad and highway. Pick your targets when we get there. We'll try to knock out both routes. Questions?" He waited. Nobody raised a hand. "All right, then. Good luck, everybody."

Rudel and Dieselhorst stuck to business as the pilot taxied the Stuka out of the revetment and got it into the air. Hans-Ulrich felt bruised by their earlier encounter. He wondered if Dieselhorst did, too. One more thing he couldn't ask . . .

Messerschmitt 109s accompanied the Ju-87s as they flew west. Hans-Ulrich hadn't seen a 110 for quite a while. The two-engined fighters hadn't lived up to expectations over the North Sea and England. Maybe they'd gone back to the shop for retooling. Or maybe the idea wasn't as good as the high foreheads in the design bureau thought it would be.

Antiaircraft fire came up as soon as they crossed the front. It was heavy and alarmingly accurate. The Allies had more and more guns shooting at the *Luftwaffe*. They knew what was at stake here as well as the Germans did. French and British fighters attacked, too. The 109s darted away to take them on. Then more fighters jumped the dive-bombers.

They were French machines, not too fast and not too heavily armed. The 109s outclassed them. Stukas, unfortunately, didn't. Hans-Ulrich threw his all over the sky, trying to dodge the enemy fighters. It was like trying to make a rhinoceros dance. Even when you did it, the result was none too graceful. Sergeant Dieselhorst's machine gun chattered again and again.

"How you doing back there?" Rudel asked him.

"They haven't shot me yet. That's something, anyway," the rear gunner answered. "How are *we* doing?"

It was a fair question—several bullets had hit the Stuka. "Everything shows green," Hans-Ulrich said. A Ju-87 could take a lot of punishment. The war had shown that the dive-bomber needed to. Rudel's head might have been on a swivel. "Now which way is Gisors?" He'd done so much frantic jinking, he didn't know north from sauerkraut.

He spotted what he thought was the cathedral steeple a moment before Major Bleyle's voice dinned in his earphones: "Abort! Break off! We're losing too many planes!"

"Devil take me if I will," Hans-Ulrich muttered to himself. To Sergeant Dieselhorst, he added, "I have the target. I'm going into my dive."

"What about Bleyle's orders?"

"What about 'em?" Rudel shoved the control column forward. The Stuka's nose went down. Acceleration slammed him back against the armored seat. Damned if that wasn't a truck column on the road. Even if this wasn't Gisors after all—plenty of little French towns had cathedrals—he'd do some damage. He yanked at the bomb-release lever, then pulled up for all he was worth.

In the rear seat, Sergeant Dieselhorst whooped. "What a fireworks show! They must have been hauling ammo!"

"*Gut. Sehr gut,*" Hans-Ulrich said. "Officially, of course, I never heard the major's order to withdraw."

"What order was that, sir?" Dieselhorst said innocently. Rudel laughed, then grimaced. Ignoring orders, disobeying orders . . . Once such things started, where did they stop? With trying to overthrow the *Führer*?

But I helped the Reich *more than I would have by obeying,* he thought. Maybe the conspirators had felt the same way. He shrugged. He was loyal. He knew it. His superiors did, too.

Pretty soon, they'd refill the Stuka's gas tank and bomb her up again, and he and Dieselhorst would go off and try this again. And, if they came back from that run, they'd do it one more time, and one more after that, till the war was won and they didn't have to worry about it any more. As long as you looked at things the right way, they were pretty simple.

SOMEBODY KICKED WILLI DERNEN IN the ribs. He grunted and folded up on himself and tried to go back to sleep. After a few seconds, the German marching boot thudded into him again. He grunted once more, louder this time. Reluctantly, his eyes opened.

"There you go," Corporal Baatz said. "Time to get moving again."

"Your mother, Arno," Dernen said. With great determination, he screwed his eyes shut again.

Arno Baatz kicked him yet again, this time with real malice. He knew just where to put a boot to make it hurt most. Willi wondered how he knew. Had he learned in noncom school along with other bastardry, or maybe from an SS interrogator? Or was it just natural talent? It worked the same any which way. Willi sat up, clutching at the injured part. As with Macbeth, Baatz had murdered sleep. "Get it in gear," he snapped. "Nobody put you on leave."

Willi staggered to the bushes to take a leak. He was still yawning when he came back. No one who hadn't been through a campaign had the faintest notion of how exhausting war was. Some men could get kicked almost to death without waking up, let alone marching. The mechanism simply wore down. Willi wasn't there yet, but he wasn't far from that dreadful place.

Maybe breakfast would help. Then again, maybe it wouldn't. He took out his mess tin and advanced on the field kitchen. The cooks spooned the tin full of slop. They called it porridge, but that gave it too much credit. They took everything remotely edible they could find and boiled it all together in a giant kettle. It ended up tasting the way library paste smelled.

The coffee, by contrast was pretty good. That was because it wasn't *Wehrmacht* issue. Like the cigarettes the *Landsers* smoked, it was the good stuff, foraged from French farms and villages—and, no doubt, corpses. Wolfgang Storch already had a tin cup's worth. "You know you're beat to shit when even this stuff won't make your heart turn over," he said sadly.

"Tell me about it," Willi agreed. He gulped the coffee anyway. He certainly didn't move slower with it inside him. If he moved any slower, he'd be dead. The stink that fouled what should have been a fine spring morning reminded him how easy dying was these days. The *Wehrmacht* was still pushing forward, so what he smelled were mostly dead Frenchmen. Dead Germans were no sweeter to the nose, though.

Lieutenant Krantz took advantage of having most of his men gathered together. "We have to get through," the platoon commander said earnestly. "We aren't as far along as we ought to be. The more we fall behind schedule, the better the chance we give the enemy. If he stops us here, he can reinforce his positions north of Paris. That wouldn't be good—not a bit."

A few of the soldiers eating breakfast and smoking managed weary nods. Willi didn't have the energy. He knew too damned well why they hadn't come farther or gone faster. Anybody with a gram of sense did. The terrain in the Ardennes sucked, and they didn't have enough panzers along to punch through the Frenchmen and their friends blocking the way west. Most of the goodies—and most of the air support—went to the right wing, the one punching ahead somewhere to the northwest. The plan had almost worked in the last war. The High Command had decided it just needed to make the fist a little bigger this time around.

And maybe the High Command knew what it was doing, and maybe it had its head up it ass. One reason you fought wars was to find out things like that.

Willi washed out his mess tin and stowed it on his belt. He put on his helmet and picked up his Mauser. The rifle was just over four kilos; it only seemed to weigh a tonne. He couldn't even sling it. He had to carry it instead—the French were too damned close.

As if to remind him of that, a Hotchkiss machine gun stuttered awake. The malign rattle made his asshole pucker. Somewhere up ahead lay Laon, which the Germans had been bombing and shelling for days. How many French soldiers still crouched in the ruins with rifles and machine guns and grenades—waiting?

"Come on," Lieutenant Krantz said. "We've got to move up, and that damned gun is in the way."

Well, I'm awake now, Willi thought as he heaved himself to his feet. Raw terror burned away exhaustion. And anybody who had to stalk a well-sited machine gun—and this one would be, because the Frenchies knew how to play the game, too—made an intimate acquaintance with terror.

Farms in these parts were small. Stone fences separated one from another. *Poilus* lurked behind the fences. Every so often, one of them would pop up and shoot. Or a mortar team would lob a couple of bombs from God knew where. Willi hated mortars. You couldn't hear the rounds coming till they got right on top of you, which was just exactly too late.

"There!" Wolfgang pointed. The machine gun was firing from a stone farmhouse's window narrowed to a slit with more building stones. Willi swore under his breath. This one would be a bitch and a half to get rid of. The position was shielded against anything this side of an antitank gun.

Or maybe it wasn't. Lieutenant Krantz spoke into the radio set a lance-corporal got to lug. Fifteen minutes later, a fellow with a couple of tanks on his back and a sinister-looking nozzle in his hand came forward. Everyone shied away from him. He didn't seem to care, or maybe he was used to the response by now.

"Keep them busy, all right?" he said. The German soldiers nodded. You wanted a flamethrower man on your side to succeed, but you felt faintly guilty when he did. Nobody mourned a flamethrower man who got roasted by his own hellish device, either. And Willi had never heard of anyone who managed to surrender with that apparatus on his back.

But that wasn't his worry, except at one remove. He raised up from behind a boulder and took a shot at the machine gun's firing slit. He ducked back down as soon as he'd pulled the trigger—and a good thing, too, because the Hotchkiss promptly spat lead his way. The froggies in the farmhouse were mighty alert. Willi hoped the miserable bastard with the flamethrower had his life insurance paid up.

One of his buddies groaned. Somebody else yelled for a medic. If you poked a bear in its den, you were liable to get clawed. The last thing Willi wanted was to rise up again and shoot at the slit. He did it anyway, which proved what a strong thing *Wehrmacht* training was— and, even more, how powerful was his fear of looking bad in front of his squadmates. Without that fundamental fear, nobody could have fought a war.

When he rose up one more time, the muzzle of the Hotchkiss was pointing straight at him. Before the Frenchies could shoot him, though, the flamethrower man used his toy. *Foomp!* Even across several hundred meters, Willi heard the man-made dragon's noise. Fire engulfed the machine gun and the firing slit—and whoever had the bad luck to be right behind them.

German soldiers whooped. Even so, nobody seemed especially eager to show himself. Maybe more Frenchmen had dragged their charred friends away from the trigger and were waiting to give optimists or fools—assuming there was a difference—a nasty surprise.

The flamethrower man solved that problem. He crawled right up to the farmhouse, stuck his nozzle into the firing slit, and . . . *Foomp!* He cocked his head to one side, as if listening. Then he waved. *No more trouble here,* the gesture said.

Willi still wasn't enthusiastic about standing up, but he did. The soldiers trotted forward as smoke rose from the farmhouse. The breeze came out of the west, as it commonly did. Willi's nose wrinkled. Along with woodsmoke, he caught the reek of burnt meat. The flamethrower had done its job, all right.

Even so, nobody wanted much to do with the fellow who carried it. He stood there, a little more smoke trailing from the snout of his infernal machine. Again, he didn't seem particularly surprised or disappointed. Well, why would he? How many times had he seen this same response by now?

Lieutenant Krantz pointed toward Laon. His officer's whistle squealed. "Come on!" he yelled. "Not far now! Follow me!"

An officer who said that made his troops want to do it. All the same, the infantrymen hesitated. That rattling clatter out of the east, getting louder now . . . "Panzers!" Willi said in delight. "*Our* panzers!" He hadn't seen many of them.

These two little Panzer Is were no more than mobile machine-gun nests. Better than a poke in the eye with a carrot, though. Both panzer commanders stood up in their turrets. They waved to the foot soldiers, who returned the compliment. "Come with us," one of the men in black coveralls shouted over engine noise. "Keep the French pigdogs away."

"And you keep them away from us," Lieutenant Krantz said. The panzer commander who'd spoken before nodded. Everybody needed help now and then.

Willi loped along to the left of the panzers. A French machine gun fired at them, which was stupid. Its bullets couldn't hurt them. One of the panzers crushed the sandbagged position, turning back and forth and round and round on top of it to make sure nothing in there survived.

Then a rifle of a sort Willi hadn't heard before went off—a big boom that would have set anyone's teeth on edge. What followed wasn't the ping of a ricochet, either. That round punched clear on through the baby panzer's thin frontal armor. The machine kept going in a straight line till it rammed a big oak and stopped. *Driver's hit,* Willi realized. German had antitank rifles, too, but you didn't expect to run up against one right after you'd finally picked up some armor.

War wasn't what you expected. It was what you got. What the surviving panzer got was out of there. Its crew knew that antitank rifle could do for them, too. And it did. Two rounds into the engine compartment turned the panzer into an immobile machine-gun nest. "We go on regardless," Lieutenant Krantz declared. Willi was still willing to advance. Able? He'd just have to see.

Chapter 26

Vaclav Jezek sprawled behind a chunk of chimney that a shell hit had detached from a nearby house. He chambered another round in his antitank rifle and waited. The crew of that disabled Panzer I wouldn't stay inside long. A hit from any kind of artillery would mangle them and torch them at the same time. A couple of more hits from the antitank rifle might set the tank on fire.

Sure enough, the commander clambered out of the turret. The Czech was ready. Despite a muzzle brake and a padded stock, the antitank rifle slammed his shoulder when he pulled the trigger. He'd already seen that, although these 13mm armor-piercing rounds weren't designed to kill mere human beings, they did one hell of a job. The German in black coveralls never knew what hit him. He tumbled off the tank and lay still.

The driver was sneakier, or maybe smarter. He scuttled out and kept the tank's carcass between him and Jezek till he bolted for some trees. Jezek shot at him, too, but missed. "Shit!" he said in disgust.

Sergeant Halévy had dug himself a foxhole a few meters away, and fronted it with bricks and stones from the ruined house. "Don't get yourself in an uproar," he said. "You did what you were supposed to do. Neither one of those tanks'll bother us any more."

"Fuck it," Vaclav said. "I should have finished the other cocksucker, too."

"You can't kill all of them by yourself," the Jew said. "Remember, you've got to leave some for me."

"Heh," Jezek said. Before the shooting started, he'd had doubts about how well Jews would fight. Yeah, Hitler was giving them a hard time, but they were still Jews, weren't they? Once they had rifles in their hands, they seemed to do just fine.

"You'd better dig in," Halévy said. "If the tanks couldn't do for us, they'll see how the artillery works."

Without raising his head, Vaclav pulled the entrenching tool off his belt and started scraping out a foxhole of his own. Halévy knew how the Germans operated, all right. Even now, some junior officer with a radio or a field telephone was probably talking to his regimental HQ, telling the gunners at which map square the trouble lay. Fifteen minutes of 105 fire ought to soften things up, he'd say.

And he'd get that artillery fire, too. The Germans were mighty damn slick about such things. Vaclav had seen as much in Czechoslovakia and here in France. They wouldn't have been half so dangerous if they weren't so blasted good at what they did.

He wondered how good the defenders were. Czechs, Frenchmen, Belgians driven back from their own country, Englishmen, Negro troops from some colony or other . . . Whatever the French marshals didn't urgently need somewhere else seemed to be jammed into a military sausage around Laon. Now if the casing didn't split and spill soldiers all over everywhere . . .

Sure as hell, here came the guns. Huddling in his scrape, Vaclav wished it were twice as deep, or even four times. He hated artillery more than anything else. German infantry made a fair fight. You could even face panzers. His monster rifle helped even the odds. But what could you do with artillerymen? Hope your own side's guns slaughtered them—that was all. It didn't seem enough.

Most of the shells were long—not very long, but Jezek took whatever he could get. If the troops a little farther back had hell coming down on their heads, he didn't. He could think of plenty of times when the Nazis' artillery had been right on target.

As soon as the shelling stopped, he came up out of his trench ready to fight. The Germans counted on stunning their opponents, at least for a little while. He kept an eye on the tank whose driver he'd shot, the one that had slammed into the oak. If the Germans could get the other driver into the machine, it might come back to life. He wouldn't have wanted to sit down on a seat soaked with his predecessor's blood, but war made you do all kinds of things you didn't want to.

"We can do it!" Sergeant Halévy shouted in Czech. Then he said what was probably the same thing in French. In Czech, he went on, "They've got to be at the end of their tether. If we stop them, they're really stopped."

How could he know that? Nobody in the middle of a battle knew a damn thing. It sure sounded good, though.

The Germans came forward. Vaclav had known they would. They were bastards, but they were brave bastards. And they exposed themselves as little as they could, which made them smart bastards.

No new panzers rolled up, for which he thanked the God in Whom he had more and more trouble believing. He wasn't thrilled about using the antitank rifle as an oversized sniper's piece—the fight with the French quartermaster sergeant lingered painfully in his memory—but he wasn't thrilled about getting killed in his hole, either.

He could, literally, have killed elephants with this rifle. Knocking over a few Nazis while they were still a long way off would make the rest go to ground and not move forward so fast. It would also make him wish some quartermaster sergeant could issue him a new shoulder, but that was one more thing he'd worry about later.

It worked out just the way he'd hoped. That stood out, because it happened so rarely in this war. He hit two Germans with four shots, which slowed the rest of them down to an amazing degree. Then, of course, the antitank rifle's loud roar and big blast of fire from every round drew the enemy's concentrated attention. Ordinary Mausers weren't especially accurate out close to a kilometer off, but they made him keep down. And he could have done without the machine gun probing for him.

He *really* could have done without the mortar bombs that started raining down on the Allied front. They did their best to make up for the artillery's poor performance. If one of them landed in your hole, you were dead, because you couldn't do anything about it.

But then, for a wonder, Allied—probably French—mortars closer to Laon opened up on the Germans. So did a couple of batteries of 75s that had stayed quiet and hidden up till now. Those 75s were weapons from the last war, and outclassed these days—which didn't mean they couldn't kill you if they got the chance.

The German mortars quit firing, quite suddenly. Thus encouraged, Vaclav stuck his head up—and plugged a soldier in field-gray who'd made the mistake of coming out from behind the dead cow he'd been using for cover. Jezek ducked down again right away. A good thing, too, because nothing had taken out that German machine gun. It sent a long, angry burst after him.

"Fuck me!" Sergeant Halévy called from his nearby hole. "Maybe we really will stop these assholes." He hadn't believed it before, then. Well, who could blame him? Vaclav hadn't believed it, either. He still wasn't sure he did.

More French troops came up to join the ragtag and bobtail on the front line. They wore khaki instead of the last war's horizon blue, but their uniforms still looked old-fashioned next to those the enemy wore. Still and all, Jezek wasn't inclined to fuss. Old-fashioned or not, they were here and they were shooting at the Germans. What more could you want?

And the Germans themselves weren't what they had been when the war broke out. They remained consummate professionals, and he'd remembered a moment before how brave they were. But they were also flesh and blood. They were every bit as worn out and ragged as the Allied troops they faced. It was like the later rounds of a championship prize fight. Both sides were bloodied, both half out on their feet, but they kept slugging away. The prize here was even sweeter than money. This fight was for power.

Damned if one of the German mortars didn't start up again. Several of the Frenchmen who'd just come up screamed like damned souls. The butcher's bill rose again. Thus encouraged, the men in field-gray put in another attack.

Vaclav blew the head right off one of them with the antitank rifle. And those Frenchmen had brought along several machine guns. The German weapon might be better, but the Hotchkiss sufficed for all ordinary purposes of slaughter. No infantry, no matter how good, could advance in the face of fire like that. Sullenly, taking as many of their wounded with them as they could, the Germans drew back.

When Vaclav reached for another clip, he discovered he'd run dry. Well, he had a pistol, and at least one of those Frenchmen didn't need his rifle any more. Any which way, it didn't look as if the *Wehrmacht* could break into Laon.

ALISTAIR WALSH GAVE THE JUNIOR LIEUTENANT who brought the order a hard look. He wanted to pretend he hadn't heard it, or at least hadn't understood it. "We're going to do what . . . sir?" he said.

Normally, that tone from a staff sergeant old enough to be his father would have wilted a subaltern. But this youngster, just up to the front from somewhere to let him keep his uniform clean and even pressed, was strengthened by the Holy Writ from Headquarters. "We're going to counterattack," he repeated brightly. "Can't very well let the *Boches* have their own way all the time, eh?"

"Counterattack with *what*?" Walsh demanded. "Christ on His cross, it's everything we can do"—*and a little more besides,* he added silently— "to hang on where we are."

"Forces to be committed include—" The subaltern rattled off several regiments, British and French. "Those should be plenty to shift the Germans hereabouts, don't you think?"

"Well, they would be," Walsh said.

He finally got a frown from the young officer. "What do you mean? Aren't they in this vicinity? This is where they are reported to be."

"Oh, bloody hell," Walsh muttered. He did his best to explain the facts of life: "Well, sir, pieces of them are, you might say. What's left of them after the *Boches* spent these past weeks banging on them with hammers and rocks."

"What is your estimate of their relative combat effectiveness?" the subaltern asked.

"Sir, I'm just a sergeant," Walsh said. A staff sergeant who'd served in the last war wasn't *just* a sergeant. Walsh wondered whether the second lieutenant understood that. About even money, he guessed. With a mental sigh, he went on, "The only reason we haven't come to pieces, near as I can see, is that the Germans have it about as bad as we do." He had much more sympathy for the Fritzes in the front line—poor bloody infantry just like him—than he did for the starched, gormless creature standing before him now. No matter what you thought, a single pip on each shoulder strap didn't turn you into God's anointed.

"I . . . see," the subaltern said slowly. Maybe he did have some notion of Walsh's station after all. Or maybe not: "I am here to deliver these orders, not to adjust them. The attack *will* go in. Is that clear?"

"Sir, it's bleeding madness," Walsh said. The lieutenant only waited. Walsh sighed and swore. God's anointed or not, those pips meant the youngster could break him like a rotten stick . . . after which the attack would go in anyway. Sure as hell, sometimes the real enemy wore the same uniform as you. A precise salute. "Yes, sir. I'll tell the men": an equally precise reproach.

The subaltern's cheeks reddened, as if he'd been slapped. He felt that, all right. "I should be honored to go forward with you," he said.

"Never mind, sir," Walsh said wearily. "It's not your fault. It's just war."

When Bill got the word, he grimaced and shrugged. "Well, we're fucked now." In his broad northern accent, it came out *fooked,* which only added to the point.

"It's bloody murder, is what it is," Nigel said. "I thought Field Marshal Haig did his worst in the last war." He had an education, all right—he hadn't been born when Haig was doing his worst.

Walsh, who'd lost a slightly older cousin in the mud at Passchendaele, was inclined to agree. What could he do, though? Not a damned thing except go forward as long as the German guns let him. "No help for it," he said. "Maybe the Germans really are on the ropes."

"Maybe babies really do come from under cabbage leaves, too," Nigel said. "Not likely, though."

"We wouldn't have so much fun makin' 'em if they did," Bill said.

Walsh laughed at that. "Barrage should start at 1500. It's"—he paused to look at his watch—"1310 now. As soon as the guns let up, we go forward—and may God go with us."

On the Western Front in the last war, barrages sometimes lasted a week. They were supposed to kill all the enemy soldiers and flatten all the wire between the side doing the bombarding and a breakthrough. Well, theory was wonderful. Long barrages warned an attack was coming. They didn't kill enough defenders, and the ones who lived always got to their machine guns before the attackers reached their line. One reason was that bombardments didn't flatten enough wire, but did tear up the ground so attacking troops couldn't move fast even when they most needed to.

Short and sweet worked better. Even in 1918, they'd figured that out. Enough to shock, enough to wound, not enough to throw away surprise. And then the infantry—and the tanks, when there were tanks—would go in and clean up the mess. They *had* driven the Germans back . . . in 1918.

Bill had a flask of applejack. He passed it around. Walsh took a nip with the other waiting British soldiers. A little Dutch courage never hurt anybody.

At 1500 on the dot, guns back in Paris opened up on the Germans in the suburbs. German counterbattery fire started right away. Walsh didn't mind. As long as those 105s were shooting at the Allied guns, they weren't pounding the front lines.

After not quite half an hour, the bombardment stopped. Up and down the front, officers' whistles screeched. Walsh's heart thuttered in his chest. He was probably pale as paste. He told himself it wouldn't be so bad as going over the top. But he'd been a kid then. Now he knew all the nasty things that could happen to you. He didn't want to get shot again. But he didn't want to seem a coward in front of his men, either.

"Let's go," he said hoarsely, and they went.

He'd barely crossed the street before a Mauser round cracked past him. No, the bombardment hadn't got everybody. How many Fritzes waited in foxholes and shattered buildings? Too damned many—he was sure of that.

He almost stumbled over a German crouching behind some rubble. The man was trying to bandage one hand with the other. He threw up both of them and bleated, "*Kamerad!*" when he saw Walsh.

Who would take care of prisoners? Anybody? Or would people behind the lines shoot them to save themselves the bother? Walsh knew such things happened. He bent down and threw the wounded German's rifle into some bushes. Gesturing with his own weapon, he said, "Go on, go on." What happened later wasn't his worry.

"*Danke!*" the Fritz said. Off he went, both hands still above his head.

Walsh forgot about him as soon as he was gone. Plenty of other Germans ahead, and not all the bastards would be bleeding. He was glad to hear Bren guns banging away. They brought real firepower right up to the front. You could carry one and fire from the hip, or even from the shoulder.

You couldn't move forward fast, not in this smashed suburb. Wreckage slowed you down too much. Stubborn Germans lurking in the wreckage were liable to slow you down for good. But the enemy seemed less stubborn than usual. Maybe the counterattack had surprised and dismayed them as much as it had Walsh. Stranger things must have happened, though he couldn't come up with one offhand.

Something warned him to throw himself down behind a burnt-out Citroën. Only a few seconds after he did, two Germans with Schmeissers came out of what was left of a house. Walsh pulled the pin on a grenade and rose up onto his knees to send it flying. A soft thump, a guttural cry of alarm, and a bang, all packed close together. Shrieks followed. Both Fritzes were down. Walsh shot them one after the other to make sure they didn't get up again. He scurried forward and grabbed a submachine gun and as many clips as the Germans carried. He slung his rifle so he could go forward carrying the Schmeisser. At close quarters, he wanted to be able to spray a lot of lead around.

Nigel came up and took the other German weapon. Walsh shared ammunition with him. "This is going better than I expected," the youngster remarked.

"I was thinking the same thing." In lieu of knocking wood, Walsh rapped his knuckles on his own tin hat. Nigel managed a haggard grin. Walsh gave him a Gitane—what he had—lit one of his own, and tramped ahead again.

He found one German fast asleep on what had been some French merchant's bed. The artillery hadn't wakened him; neither had the Allied infantry assault. Walsh knew just how the poor bugger felt: he'd felt that way himself. He carried away the German's Mauser and dropped it in the mud. He left the man alone. Without a weapon, the fellow was no threat to anybody. And this would be Allied ground by the time he woke up.

"Damned if it won't," Walsh said in tones of wonder. Maybe the generals and even that snot-nosed subaltern knew what they were up to after all. And if they did, wasn't that the strangest thing of all? Schmeisser at the ready, Walsh pressed on.

GERHARD ELSNER STRODE OVER TO Ludwig Rothe, who was adding oil to his panzer's crankcase. "Still running all right?" the company CO asked anxiously—there'd been a lot of wear and tear in the drive across the Low Countries and France.

But Rothe answered, "You bet, Captain."

"Good. That's what I want to hear," Elsner said. "Tomorrow morning we smash them. We go through south of Beauvais—between there and a village called Alonne. Three or four kilometers of open ground. We won't have to fight in built-up places. That's what they tell me, anyhow."

"Here's hoping they're right—whoever *they* are. That gets expensive fast," Rothe said. He turned to his driver and radioman. "But we'll be ready, right?"

Fritz Bittenfeld and Theo Hossbach both nodded. Then Theo yawned. Everybody was beat. Ludwig was running on looted French coffee and on pills he'd got from a medic. The pills were supposed to keep a dead man going for a day and a half. Ludwig still wanted to hole up somewhere and go to sleep, so he figured he was about two steps worse off than dead.

"This is the breakthrough—*the* breakthrough," Captain Elsner said.

He ignored the yawn. He was running on nerves and maybe drugs, too, same as everyone else. "We crack the line, we pour through, we wheel around behind Paris, and we make every old fart who remembers 1914 sick-jealous of us. We can do it. We can, and we will. *Heil* Hitler!" His right arm shot up and out.

"*Heil* Hitler!" Ludwig echoed. He imitated the Party salute. So did Fritz and Theo. If Theo was a beat late—and he was—Captain Elsner pretended not to see that, too. He was a good officer. He cut some slack for any man who was good in the field, and Theo was. As far as Ludwig was concerned, all the *Heil*-ing was a bunch of *Quatsch*. But you'd get your head handed to you if you said that out loud. The failed coup against the *Führer* left everybody jumpy.

Then Theo stopped being dreamy and asked a sharp question: "When we go in, will we have infantry support?"

"As much of it as there is," Captain Elsner answered. Panze-grenadiers in half-tracks and trucks could keep up with armor. Ordinary ground-pounders couldn't. The panzers were supposed to pierce the enemy lines and let the foot-bound infantry pour through after them. Panzers helped infantry enormously. What they'd found out in Czechoslovakia and here in the west, though, was that infantry support also helped panzers. Foot soldiers moving up along with the armor stopped plenty of unpleasant surprises.

The attack was scheduled for 0530. Morning gave attackers the most daylight in which to do what they could. And morning also let the Germans come out of the rising sun, which made them tougher targets. Ludwig approved of that. He knew better than most people how vulnerable his steel chariot was.

As in the attack on Czechoslovakia and the one that launched this campaign, white tapes guided the panzers to their start line in the dark. But this operation wouldn't be anywhere near so strong. Establishment strength for a panzer company was thirty-two machines. They'd been pretty much up to snuff before. After this grinding campaign across the

Low Countries and France, Captain Elsner's company had thirteen runners, and it was in better shape than a lot of others.

Well, the enemy's taken his licks, too, Ludwig thought. All through the advance, he'd driven past Dutch and Belgian and French and British wreckage. He'd breathed air thick with the smells of death and burnt rubber and scorched paint and hot iron. That stench was in his coveralls now. Not even washing—not that he'd had much chance to wash—got rid of it.

Behind them, the sky lightened. Gray and then blue spread west. Rothe checked his watch. He'd synchronized it with the captain's before they moved up. Any second now . . . *Now!* The eastern horizon blazed with light: not the sun, but muzzle flashes from the artillery pounding the *poilus* and Tommies up ahead.

"Get a move on, Fritz!" Ludwig shouted into the speaking tube.

"Right you are, boss!" Bittenfeld put the panzer in gear. Tracks rattling and clanking, it growled forward. Because of the crew's experience, they took point for their platoon. Ludwig could have done without the honor. The point man commonly discovered trouble by smashing his face against it.

French 75s and occasional 105s answered the German barrage. Ludwig didn't want to duck down into the turret so soon—he couldn't see out nearly so well. But, with fragments sparking off the panzer's side armor, he didn't want to get sliced up, either. You acquired experience by *not* getting killed.

"They're alert today," Fritz remarked.

"They would be," Ludwig agreed gloomily.

"I'm going to miss the waitress at that *estaminet* in Fouquerolles." The driver cheerfully mangled the French word and the name of the village where they'd stayed not long before. "Limber as an eel, she was."

"Can't you think of anything but pussy?" Ludwig asked, knowing the answer was no.

Machine-gun bullets clattered off the right side of the turret. "*Guten Morgen!*" Theo said from his seat in the back of the fighting compartment.

"I'll give *them* a good morning, by God!" Rothe said, and then, to Bittenfeld, "Panzer halt!"

"Halting," Fritz responded, and the Panzer II shuddered to a stop. Ludwig traversed the turret. There was the gun, still spitting bullets. Machine gunners never learned. You could fire at a panzer till everything turned blue, and you still wouldn't penetrate the armor. Of course, each crew that made the mistake lived to regret it—but rarely for long.

Ludwig fired several rounds from the 20mm cannon. Those would punch through whatever sandbags protected the machine gun. They'd punch through the soldiers serving the gun, too. Sure as hell, it shut up. Maybe the crew was lying low. More likely, those men wouldn't fire that piece again, not at a panzer and not at horribly vulnerable infantrymen, either.

But Ludwig also saw a burning Panzer II a few hundred meters away. A machine gun couldn't do for one, but anything bigger damn well could. And if an antitank-gun crew was drawing a bead on this stopped panzer . . . "Get moving!" Ludwig yipped into the speaking tube.

A 135-horsepower engine wasn't supposed to be able to throw 8,900 kilos of steel around like a Bugatti at Le Mans. All the same, when Fritz hit the gas the panzer jumped like one of the many barmaids he'd goosed. Ludwig almost got thrown out of his seat.

He spied armored shapes up ahead. Their lines were rounder than those of Germany's slab-sided panzers. "Get on the horn, Theo," he said. "Tell the captain the enemy's got armor in the neighborhood."

"I'm doing it," Hossbach said, "but I bet he already knows."

Elsner hadn't known when he briefed the company. Maybe one of those French machines had taken out the other Panzer II. They had more armor and bigger guns than most German panzers—they were easily a match for the Czechs' tanks.

Well, we beat those, Rothe thought. The next interesting question was what French armor was doing right at the *Schwerpunkt* here. Was it dumb luck, or had the enemy guessed much too right? If the breakthrough was going to happen, it would have to be a breakthrough indeed. "Panzer halt!" Rothe commanded again.

He fired at the closest enemy panzer. Yes, he was outgunned, but the 20mm could break a French *char's* armored carapace. The enemy machine caught fire. The crew bailed out. He gunned them down with the coaxial machine gun as they ran for cover. An ordinary machine gun was plenty to kill ordinary soldiers.

"Step on it, Fritz!" he said—not a command in the manual, but also not one easy to mistake. Again, the driver did his best to pretend he was at the Grand Prix.

That might have been why the antitank round slammed into the engine and not the fighting compartment. All three crewmen screamed *"Scheisse!"* at the same time. The panzer stopped. It wouldn't go anywhere again.

"Get out!" Ludwig yelled. The French or British gunners were bound to be reloading. When they did . . . He didn't want to be there.

Theo opened the hatch behind the turret. Then he slammed it shut again. "Fire!" he said.

"Follow me out, then," Rothe told him. He jumped out the turret hatch on the side away from that deadly round.

Theo and Fritz both made it out after him. Bullets cracking past them said *out* wasn't the best place to be, not when it was in the middle of a horribly bare field. Ludwig pointed to some bushes a couple of hundred meters away. Crouching low, zigzagging, the panzer crewmen ran for them. Not much of a hope, but some.

Ludwig didn't understand why he crashed to the ground. Then he did, because it started to hurt. He shrieked and clutched at himself. It was a bad one. He knew that right away. Then he groaned again, because Fritz went down, too. Damned if Theo didn't make it to the bushes. Sometimes you'd rather be lucky than good.

"Medic!" Ludwig cried. "Med—" Another bullet caught him, and he didn't hurt at all after that.

LUC HARCOURT CROUCHED IN A FOXHOLE. All around him, French and German tanks blazed away at one another—and at any poor damned infantrymen their crews happened to spot. He felt like a tiny ratlike ancient mammal stuck in the middle of a horde of battling dinosaurs. They might kill him without even realizing he was there.

Well, he'd had at least some small share of revenge. When a Panzer II started burning, the crew tried to make it out. They escaped the tank, but he shot one of them before the bastard could find a hole and pull it in after himself.

"How many of us did you get, you fucker?" he muttered as he slapped a fresh clip onto his rifle. "You won't get any more."

He wanted to huddle there, not moving, not looking up, rolled into a ball like a pillbug so he made as small a target as he could. He wanted to, but he didn't. If the *Boches* got this far, they'd kill him as easily as if they were squashing a pillbug. What they said in training turned out to be true: your best chance of living was acting like a soldier. He'd thought it was a bunch of patriotic crap when he heard it the first time, but no.

Speaking of crap, his drawers were clean—well, not dirty on account of that, even if he couldn't remember the last time he changed them. He knew the modest pride of going through fear and coming out the other side. He'd fouled himself before, yes, but not now. Like Sergeant Demange, he was past that . . . till the next time things got even worse than this, anyhow.

A French tank stopped not far from his hole. The commander

popped out of the cupola like a jack-in-the-box. He pointed at the Germans. "Advance!" he yelled. "If we stop them here, we can break them!" He disappeared again. The tank fired its cannon at, well, something. Luc didn't pop up himself to see what. The noise all around was worse than loud. It made his brain want to explode out through his ears.

The tank fired again. The machine gun in its bow also banged away—again, Luc couldn't see what it was shooting at. Then the tank rumbled forward. The commander hadn't urged him to do anything the man wasn't willing to try himself. Of course, he had twenty or thirty millimeters of hardened steel shielding him from the unpleasant outside world. But, to be fair, he also had worse things aimed at him than foot soldiers were likely to face.

Still . . . Advance? It almost seemed a word in a foreign language. The French Army and the BEF had got booted out of Belgium and beaten back across northern France. They'd given up more ground than their fathers (or, more often, their mourned uncles who hadn't lived to sire children) did in 1914. The Channel ports were lost, which meant the Tommies would have a harder time getting into the fight. Advance? After all that?

If they kept retreating, the *Boches* would win. Luc hated that thought. The Germans were good at what they did. On the whole, they fought clean—or no dirtier than the French. But so what? They were still *Boches.*

He popped up and fired at some Germans. They dove for cover. That was all he'd wanted—they were too far off for him to have much chance of hitting them. But if they were hiding behind trees or digging new scrapes for themselves, they weren't advancing against the defenders here.

Defenders? That wasn't one tank commanded by a homicidal—or suicidal—maniac. More French armor was going forward against the troops in field-gray. A crew of artillerymen manhandled a 37mm anti-tank gun into a position a couple of hundred meters farther east than it had held before. Even khaki-clad infantrymen—no great swarm of them, but some—were climbing out of their holes and trenches and moving toward the *Boches.*

Maybe twenty meters away, Sergeant Demange was watching the show from his foxhole. He looked as astonished as Luc felt. He looked almost astonished enough to let the Gitane fall out of his mouth: almost, but not quite. He caught Luc's eye. "This is something you don't see every day," he shouted. He had to say it two or three times before Luc understood.

"It sure is," Luc answered. "Do you want to join the party?" Were he a new fish, he would have waved—and given a German sniper or machine gunner something to draw a bead on. He knew better now.

"Do I look that fucking stupid?" Demange said. Luc wanted to tell him yes, but didn't have the nerve. Sure as the devil, a sergeant who scared you more than the *Boches* did wasn't the worst thing to have around. Then the veteran didn't just surprise Luc: he flabbergasted him. He scrambled from his foxhole and scurried toward a crater a bursting 105 had dug. As soon as he got there, he called, "Somebody's got to do it, right?"

No doubt somebody did. Luc wondered whether one of the somebodies had to be him. Regretfully, he decided he couldn't hang back when even a cold-blooded pragmatist like Demange was advancing.

Coming up out of a hole felt like a snail shedding its shell and turning into a slug. Luc grimaced and shook his head as he ran for a crater of his own. No, he didn't want to think about slugs, not when the lead variety were snarling all over the place.

His dive into the shell hole would have won no worse than a bronze at the last Olympics. Luc shook his head again. Those were Hitler's games, and to hell with him.

Time for another look around. German and French tanks burned nearby. The thick black smoke that rose from them hid the field as well as any barrage of smoke shells German artillery laid down.

Luc fired at another *Boche*. Again, he had no idea whether he hit him. In a way, that wasn't so bad. One less fellow on his conscience. He wished that particular organ had a switch he could flick or a plug he could pull. He didn't like to think about all the things he'd done, but sometimes they bubbled up whether he wanted them to or not.

"Come on!" Sergeant Demange rasped. "What did that American Marine say in the last war? 'Do you want to live forever?' "

Airplanes swooped low over the battlefield, machine guns yammering. Luc had started to move, but froze again, not that that would do him any good if those probing bullets found him.

They didn't. The fighters weren't Messerschmitts. They were English Hurricanes, the roundels on their broad wings looking inside out to Luc because the red was in the center instead of the blue. And they were shooting up the Germans.

"See how you like it, *cochons, salauds!*" he whooped joyously. He'd been on the other end of strafing too many times. Here as so many other places in war, it was better to give than to receive. Now . . . Did the English have anything like the Stuka, so they could *really* give the Germans what-for?

They didn't seem to, but maybe what they did have was enough. The *Boches* enjoyed air attack no more than anybody else. Only a few of them ran—they were good troops. But it took the starch out of them just the same. And, a moment after the Hurricanes roared away, a French tank knocked out what had to be the enemy's command vehicle. From then on, the few German tanks still moving didn't work together so smoothly any more.

"Come on!" Sergeant Demange said again, more urgently this time. "It was like this in the summer of '18, too. If we hit 'em a good lick, we'll get 'em." *We'll get 'em—on les aura.* The slogan from the last war should have seemed as dated as ground-scraping skirts. Somehow, it didn't.

Luc scrambled out of the shell hole and trotted forward. Sure as hell, the Germans were pulling back. Yes, they were pros. They had rear guards with machine guns to make sure nobody chased them hard. But they *were* pulling back. They weren't breaking through. They wouldn't break through. And if they wouldn't, they wouldn't win the war in a hurry. What would happen once they saw that, too? Luc lit a Gauloise. That was their worry, not his. He kept on advancing.

Read on for an excerpt from

The War That Came Early: West and East

by Harry Turtledove

Published by Del Rey Books

Theo Hossbach lay on a cot in a military hospital in Cambrai. All of him was fine except for the last two joints on the ring finger of his left hand. He wouldn't see those again until and unless the Resurrection of the Flesh preachers liked to talk about turned out to be the straight goods. Theo doubted it—Theo doubted almost everything people in authority said—but you never could tell.

One thing Theo didn't doubt was that he was lucky to be there, or anywhere. Along with the commander and driver, he'd bailed out of a burning Panzer II. They'd all run for some bushes a couple of hundred meters away. He'd made it. Ludwig and Fritz hadn't. It was about that simple.

The bullet that amputated those last two joints came later. He didn't know whether it was aimed at him in particular or just one of the random bullets always flying around a battlefield. The one by Beauvais seemed to have had more of them than most. Theo might have been prejudiced; he'd never had to bail out of a panzer before.

Or he might not have been. The French and English had stopped the *Wehrmacht*'s drive at Beauvais, and it hadn't got started again. This made two wars in a row where the Schlieffen Plan didn't quite work. Hitler's generals came closer to pulling it off than the Kaiser's had, but what was that worth?

A nurse came by. She took his temperature. "Normal. Very good," she said as she wrote it down. "Do you need another pain pill?"

"Yes, please," he answered. Those two missing joints seemed to hurt worse than the stub he had left. *Phantom pain*, the doctor who cleaned up the wound called it. He could afford to dismiss it like that; it wasn't his hand.

"Here." The nurse gave Theo the pill, watched while he swallowed it, and wrote that down, too. He figured it was codeine; it made him a little woozy, and it constipated him. It also left him less interested in the nurse, who wasn't bad looking, than he would have been if he weren't taking them every four to six hours. But it pushed away the pain, both real and phantom.

Most of the soldiers in the ward with him had nastier wounds. Most, but not all: the fellow two beds down wore a cast on his ankle because he'd tripped over his own feet and broken it. "I wasn't even drunk," he complained to anyone who'd listen. "Just fucking clumsy."

Woozy turned to drowsy. Theo was dozing when hearing his own name brought him back to himself. The nurse was leading a captain over to his cot. The pink *Waffenfarbe* on the man's *Totenkopf* collar patches and edging his shoulder straps said he was a panzer man, too. "You are, uh, Theodor Hossbach?" he said.

"Theodosios Hossbach, sir," Theo said resignedly. How was he supposed to explain that his father had been slogging through a translation of Gibbon's *The Decline and Fall of the Roman Empire* at just the wrong time?

He got the panzer captain's attention, anyhow. "Theodosios? Well, well. No wonder you go by Theo."

"No wonder at all, sir," Theo agreed.

"You are a radio operator. You are familiar with the operation of the Fu5 radio set?"

"Yes, sir." Theo knew he still sounded resigned. Every panzer in the *Wehrmacht* used the Fu5 except commanders' vehicles, which carried the longer-range Fu10. If he was a panzer radioman, he'd damn well better know how to use the standard set. A pfennig's worth of thought . . . was evidently too much to hope for.

Then the captain got to the point: "Can you return to duty? A radio operator in a Panzer II is not required to do much with his left hand."

That was true, and then again it wasn't. A radioman didn't need to do much with his left hand to operate the radio. When it came to things like engine repairs or remounting a thrown track, though . . . Theo knew he could have said no. His hand was swathed in enough bandages to wrap a Christmas present, or maybe a mummy. He hesitated no more than a heartbeat. "As long as they give me a jar of those little white pills, sir, I'm good to go."

"They will," the captain said, with a glance toward the nurse that warned someone's head would roll if they didn't. "You'll have it by the time I come back for you, in half an hour or so. A couple of other fellows here I want to scoop up if I can."

A doctor gave Theo the codeine and a reproachful look. "You should stay longer. You're nowhere near healed."

"I'll manage," Theo said. "I'm sick of laying around."

"Lying," the doctor said automatically.

"No, sir. I'm telling the truth."

"Right." The doctor looked more reproachful yet. Theo hadn't thought he could. "Maybe we're lucky to get rid of you."

"Maybe you are. Most of me doesn't need the bed—only my hand."

When the panzer captain came back for Theo, he had one other fellow (who walked with a limp) in tow and a discontented expression on his face. "The last guy I want is shirking," he growled. "I'd bet my last mark on it even if I can't prove it. Well, I just have to make do with you two. Let's go."

They'd laundered Theo's black coveralls. Putting them on again did feel good. The other panzer crewman, whose name was Paul, seemed to feel the same way. Once he had the black on, he stood taller and straighter and seemed to move more fluidly.

The captain bundled them both into a Citroën he'd got somewhere or other and headed west. They drove past and through the wreckage of a nearly successful campaign. Dead panzers—German, French, and British—littered the landscape, along with burnt-out trucks and shot-up autos. Here and there, German technicians salvaged what they could from the metal carcasses.

Just outside of Mondidier, the captain stopped. "You boys get out here," he said. "We're regrouping for a fresh go at the pigdogs. They'll fit you into new crews."

"What'll you do, sir?" Theo asked.

"Head for another hospital and see how many men I can pry loose there," the officer answered. "The more, the better. We can use experienced people, God knows."

Theo felt shy about joining a new crew. He'd spent his whole military career—he'd spent the whole war—with Ludwig and Fritz. They'd understood him as well as anybody did. They'd put up with him. If another driver and commander had lost their radioman . . . He made a sour face. He'd feel like a woman marrying a widower and trying to live up to the standard his first wife had set.

To his relief, he didn't have to do that. The personnel sergeant assigned him to what would be a brand new crew. The commander was a sergeant called Heinz Naumann. He had bandages on his neck and his left hand—and maybe in between, too. "Burns. Getting better," he said laconically. On his coveralls he wore the Iron Cross First Class and a wound badge. Sooner or later, Theo knew, a wound badge would also catch up with him.

By contrast, the driver was just out of training. His coveralls weren't faded and shapeless; you could cut yourself on their creases. He was a big fellow with dark hair who moved like an athlete. His name was Adalbert Stoss.

Theo was from Breslau, way off in the east. Naumann came from Vienna. Stoss hailed from Greven, a small town outside of Münster. "It's a wonder we can understand each other," he said with a grin.

Grin or not, he wasn't kidding. As far as Theo was concerned, Stoss and Naumann had different strange accents. They probably thought he talked funny, too. "We'll manage," Heinz said.

"Oh, sure." Adalbert went on grinning. He seemed happy as could be to have escaped basic and come out to join the grown-ups at—or at least near—the front. Theo had seen that reaction before. Most of the time, it wore off as soon as the rookie saw his first body with the head blown off. Training was hard work, to say nothing of dull, but you hardly ever got killed there. In real war, on the other hand . . .

"I was hoping they'd give me a Panzer III," Naumann said. "But no—it's another II." He eyed Theo's bandaged finger. "You aren't complaining, though, are you?"

"Not right now," Theo allowed. In a Panzer III, the radioman sat up front, next to the driver. He also served a hull-mounted machine gun. That wouldn't be much fun with a bad hand. Then again . . ."A Panzer III, now, that's a real fighting machine."

"I know, I know. That's why I wanted one," the sergeant said. Along with two machine guns, a Panzer III mounted a 37mm cannon. Unlike the Panzer II's 20mm gun, which fired only armor-piercing ammo, the bigger weapon had high-explosive shells, too. That made it a lot more useful against infantry out in the open.

A Panzer III also carried thicker armor, and boasted a more powerful engine. A Panzer III was a real panzer. A Panzer II was a training vehicle. Oh, you could fight with it. The *Wehrmacht* had been fighting with it, and with the even smaller, lighter Panzer I, ever since the *Führer* gave the order to march into Czechoslovakia, more than six months ago now. But it would be nice to have a fighting vehicle that matched the ones the enemy used.

Would have been nice. Panzer IIIs were still scarce, while there were lots of IIs and, even these days, quite a few little obsolete Is. (There were also Panzer IVs, which carried a short-barreled 75mm gun and were designed to support infantry, not to attack enemy armor. There were supposed to be Panzer IVs, anyhow. Theo didn't think he'd ever seen one.)

"I know what I'm doing in a II," Stoss said. "They never let us drive a III in training. Most of the practice we got was in those turretless Panzer I chassis—you guys know the ones I mean."

Theo nodded. So did Heinz Naumann. What you used in training was as cheap as the *Wehrmacht* could get away with and still do the job. Theo doubted whether any Panzer IIIs were within a hundred kilometers of a training base. You didn't practice with those babies—you got them into the fight.

Eager as a puppy, Adalbert asked, "You know where they're going to throw us in, Sergeant?"

"Nope," Naumann answered. "Far as the generals are concerned, we're just a bullet. Point us at the enemy, and we knock him over."

Or he knocks us over. Theo remembered the antitank round slamming into his old Panzer II's engine compartment. He remembered opening his escape hatch and seeing nothing but flames. He'd followed his panzer commander out the turret hatch instead. Ludwig hadn't made it much farther. Theo had—which didn't stop that bullet from finding him a little later on.

The new Panzer II looked like the one that had burned. Theo's station was behind the turret, just in front of the bulkhead that separated the fighting compartment from the one housing the engine. He couldn't see out. The smells were familiar: oil, gasoline, cordite, leather, metal, sweat. He didn't smell much lingering fear, which argued that this panzer hadn't seen a lot of action.

He started fiddling with the radio. No matter what the manufacturer claimed, every set was different. Heinz Naumann said something. Theo ignored it. Indeed, he hardly heard it: like the radio, he was good at tuning out anything that didn't directly concern him.

Sometimes, he tuned out things that *did* concern him. Naumann spoke again: "I *said*, is it up to snuff?"

"Uh, it seems to be." Theo came back to the world.

"Good. Pay some attention next time, all right?"

"Whatever you say, Sergeant," Theo answered. Ludwig had tried to keep him connected, too. Sometimes it worked, sometimes it didn't. When Theo got interested in a radio, or in whatever was going on inside his own head, everything else could go hang.

They motored west, toward the front, the next morning. Naumann rode along standing up with his head and shoulders out of the turret. That was how a panzer commander was supposed to do things when not in combat. A lot of commanders looked out even when their machine was in action. The vision ports in the turret just didn't let you see enough. There was talk of building a Panzer II with a proper cupola for the commander. The Panzer III had one. So did a lot of foreign panzers. Not the II, not yet.

Theo had another reason for liking the way Heinz did things. With the hatch open, some of the mild spring air got down to him. Then a bullet cracked past Naumann. The commander dove back inside the turret faster than you could fart. "Panzer halt!" he shouted.

"Halting," Adalbert Stoss said, and hit the brakes. Instead of using the traversing gear, Heinz manhandled the turret into position with the two handgrips on the inside. The machine gun snarled several short bursts at . . . something, at . . . somebody. Theo couldn't see out, so except for the gunshot he had no idea what was going on. Not counting his earphones, the radioman on a Panzer II was always the last to know.

"Maybe I got him. Maybe not," Sergeant Naumann muttered. Then he spoke into the tube that carried his voice to Adalbert's seat: "Forward!"

"Forward, *ja*," Stoss agreed. As the panzer got moving again, the driver asked, "A soldier behind our lines, or a *franc-tireur*?"

"Don't know. I never saw enough of him to tell whether he had a uniform," Heinz said. After a pause for thought, he added, "Sounded like a military rifle, though—not a little varmint gun."

"Are the Frenchies trying to infiltrate us? That wouldn't be so good," Adalbert said.

"No. It wouldn't." Heinz thought some more. Then he said, "Hossbach! Report this back to regimental HQ. If it's not just one guy with a gun, the higher-ups need to know about it. We're in map square K-4, just west of Avrigny. Got that?"

"K-4. West of Avrigny," Theo repeated. He sighed as he made the connection and delivered the message. Ludwig had always been on him because he was happier with his own thoughts that with the rest of the world. Now Naumann had figured out the same thing in about a minute and a half.

Theo would have liked to do something about that. But doing something about it would have involved changing, and he didn't care to change. His panzer commanders would just have to cope with it . . . and so would he.

From Greasy to Messy. Staff Sergeant Alistair Walsh nodded in weary approval. The Anglo-French counterattack, pushing east from the outskirts of Paris, was still making progress. Greasy was actually the hamlet of Gressy, a few miles west of where Walsh was now. Where Walsh was now was in Messy, which looked exactly the way its name made you think it would.

Messy had good reason for looking that way. Only a few weeks earlier, the Germans had bombed and shelled the place to chase the Allied defenders back toward Paris. And then, after the German attack ran out of steam both here and up near Beauvais, English and French guns pounded Messy to push back the *Boches*. A few buildings were still standing and didn't seem too badly damaged, but that wasn't from lack of effort on either side.

Hardly anyone lived in the ruins. People who could get out had done so before the Germans arrived. They hadn't come back to reclaim whatever might be left of their homes and property. A lingering sick-sweet stench said not everybody'd got away. Or Walsh might have been getting a whiff of dead Germans. After three days, everybody—and every body—smelled the same.

As much to blunt the reek as for any other reason, Walsh lit a Navy Cut. Beside him, Second Lieutenant Herman Cavendish looked around and said, "So this is victory."

Walsh hadn't liked the subaltern ever since Cavendish brought the first order to counterattack. The Anglo-French strike had worked, which didn't make the veteran noncom like the very young officer any better. "Sir, when you set this against 1918, it looks like a rest cure," Walsh said.

Maybe Cavendish had been born in 1918, maybe not. If he had, he was still making messes in his nappies. He hadn't seen—or, for that matter, smelled—the Western Front. He hadn't got shot there, either. Walsh had done all of those things, however much he wished he hadn't.

For a wonder, Cavendish heard the reproach in his voice. The youngster blushed like a schoolgirl. "I know you've been through a good deal, Sergeant," he said stiffly, "but I do believe I am gaining on you when it comes to experience."

That he could come out with such claptrap straight-faced only proved how much experience he didn't have yet. Telling him so would have been pointless precisely because he lacked the experience that would have let him understand what an idiot he was being.

Walsh didn't even try. "Whatever you say, sir," he answered. One of the things staff sergeants did was ride herd on subalterns till their nominal superiors were fit to go around a battlefield by themselves without getting too many of the soldiers under their command killed for no reason.

Cavendish might have been doing his best to prove he hadn't

reached that point yet. Pointing east, he said, "Well, we've given the *Boches* a proper what-for this time, eh?"

His posh accent only made that sound even stupider than it would have otherwise. Walsh wouldn't have thought such a thing possible, but Cavendish proved him wrong. "Sir, the Germans came from their own border all the way to Paris. We've come from Paris all the way to Messy," Walsh said. "If you want to call that a proper what-for, well, go ahead."

"There are times when I doubt you have the proper attitude," Sergeant," Cavendish said. "Would you sooner be fighting behind Paris?"

"No, sir. Not a bit of it." Walsh's own accent was buzzing Welsh, and lower-class Welsh at that. What else to expect from a miner's son? He went on, "I'd sooner be fighting in bloody Germany, is what I'd sooner be doing. But that doesn't look like it's in the cards, does it?"

"In—Germany?" By the way the subaltern said it, the possibility had never crossed his mind. "Don't you think that's asking a bit much?"

"Evidently, sir." Walsh left it right there. If the French generals—to say nothing of the British generals (which was about what they deserved to have said of them)—were worth the paper they were printed on, the German High Command wouldn't have been able to impose its will on them with such effortless ease. That had happened the last time around, too. The *Boches* ran out of men and matériel then, while the Yanks gave the Allies all they needed.

No Yanks in the picture now, worse luck. Just the German generals against their British and French counterparts. *Christ help us*, Walsh thought.

As if to remind people who'd forgotten (Second Lieutenant Herman Cavendish, for instance) that they hadn't gone away, German gunners began lobbing shells into Messy. When they started landing too close for comfort, Walsh jumped into the nearest hole in the ground. It wasn't as if he didn't have plenty of choices.

He thought Cavendish would stay upright and make a brave little speech about command responsibility—till a flying fragment did something dreadful to him. But no: the subaltern dove for cover, too. He'd learned *something*, anyhow. Walsh wouldn't have bet more than tuppence ha'penny on it.

After ten minutes or so, the bombardment eased off. Walsh cradled the Schmeisser he'd taken off a dead *Boche*—for throwing a lot of lead around at close quarters, nothing beat a submachine gun. If the Germans decided they wanted Messy back, he was ready to argue with them.

But no hunched-over figures wearing field-gray and coal-scuttle helmets loped forward. This was just harassing fire: hate, they would have called it in the last war. Somebody off in the distance was yelling for a medic, so the bastards serving a 105 had earned their salary this morning.

Lieutenant Cavendish went off to inflict his leadership on someone else. Walsh lit a fresh Navy Cut. He climbed out of the hole to see what the shelling had done to the hamlet.

A skinny little stubble-cheeked French sergeant puffing on a pipe emerged from cover about the same time he did. The Frenchman waved. "*Ça va*, Tommy?" he called.

"*Va bien. Et tu?*" Walsh ran through a good part of his clean French with that. He waved toward the east, then spat.

The French noncom nodded. "Fucking *Boche*," he said. His English was probably was filthy as most of Walsh's *Français*. A couple of his men came out. He started yelling at them. He was a sergeant, all right.

Walsh checked on the soldiers in his own section. The fellow who'd bought part of a plot came from a different company. That was something, anyhow. After nodding rather smugly, Walsh wondered why it should be. The British army was no better off because the wounded man wasn't from his outfit. And that other company was weakened instead of his. In the larger scheme of things, so what?

But it was a bloke Walsh didn't know, not one he did. You didn't want one of *your* mates to stop one. Maybe that was a reminder you were too bloody liable to stop one yourself. Of course, you had to be an idiot not to know as much already. Still, there was a difference—whether there should have been or not—between knowing something and getting your nose rubbed in it.

"Are we supposed to move up again, Sergeant?" asked a soldier named Nigel. Like Lieutenant Cavendish, he spoke like an educated man. He didn't sound toffee-nosed doing it, though.

"Nobody's told me if we are," Walsh answered. "You can bet your last quid the lieutenant would have, too."

He wasn't supposed to speak ill of officers. He was supposed to let the men in his charge form their unflattering opinions all by themselves. By the way Nigel and Bill and the others chuckled, they needed no help from him.

"He's a bit gormless, ain't he?" Bill said. *He* came from the Yorkshire dales, and sounded like it. The word wasn't one Staff Sergeant Walsh would have chosen. It wasn't one he'd heard before he took the King's shilling more than half a lifetime ago. Well, he'd heard—and used—a lot of words he'd never imagined back in his civilian days. *Gormless* was one you could actually repeat in polite company.

"Oh, maybe a bit," Walsh said, and they chuckled again. He added, "Say what you want about him, though—he is brave."

"Well, yes, but so are the Germans," Nigel said. "Even some of the Frenchmen . . . I suppose."

"They are. We'd be a lot worse off if they weren't," Walsh said.

"Half of them are Bolshies, though. Can you imagine what would happen if the Nazis and Reds were on the same side?" Nigel plainly could. By the way he rolled his eyes, he didn't fancy the notion. "Some Communist official would say, 'The Germans are the workers' friends,' and all the fellow-travelers would decide they didn't feel like fighting any more."

"It's not going to happen, chum," Walsh declared, not without relief.

"They're slanging away at each other on the far edge of Poland. You ask me, anyone who wants Poland enough to fight over it has to be daft."

"Anyone who's not a Pole, you mean," Nigel said.

"Them, too," Walsh said with more than a little heat. "Look at that bloody Bosnian maniac Princip in 1914. He got millions and millions killed because he couldn't stand the damned Austrian Archduke. Suppose that was worth it, do you? Just as bloody fucking stupid to go to war over Poland."

"There you go." Bill grinned at him from under the dented brim of his tin hat. "Now you've solved all the world's problems, you have. Go tell the *Boches* to quit shooting at us—'twas all a misunderstanding, like. Then get on your airplane and fly off to wherever the hell you go to pick up your Nobel Prize."

Walsh told him where the hell he could go, and where he could stuff the Nobel Prize. They all laughed. They smoked another cigarette or two. And then they were ready to get on with the war again.

Sergeant Hideki Fujita had spent more time than he cared to remember in Manchukuo. He'd got used to all kinds of noises he never would have heard in Japan. Wolves could howl. Foxes could yip. If he was wrapped in a blanket out where the steppe gave way to the desert, he'd fall asleep regardless. And he'd stay asleep no matter what kind of racket the animals made. Out there, he lived like an animal himself.

He also lived like an animal here in the pine woods on the Russian side of the Ussuri, the river that formed the northeastern border between Manchukuo and the Soviet Union. He dug himself a hole, he jumped down into it, and he slept. Howling wolves? Yipping foxes? Hooting owls? They didn't bother him a bit.

Tigers? Tigers were a different story. When a tiger roared or screamed, even gunfire seemed to hesitate for a moment. Those noises always woke him up, too, though he'd sleep through gunshots or through artillery that didn't come too close. You had to learn to fear gunshots. Not tigers. If you heard that roar, you *were* afraid, and on the double.

Fujita quickly found out he wasn't the only one who felt the same way. One of the superior privates in his squad, a student called Shinjiro Hayashi, said, "Something deep down inside your head knows that whatever makes that noise wants to eat people."

"*Hai!*" Fujita exclaimed. "That's just it!" He came off a farm himself. He often had the feeling that Hayashi looked down his nose at him, though a Japanese private who let his sergeant know for sure that he looked down his nose at him was asking for all the trouble in the world and a little more besides. Hayashi wasn't dumb enough to do that. And there were times when having a guy who knew things came in handy: Hayashi spoke some Chinese, for instance.

"When we came here from the Mongolian border, they said there'd be tigers here," said Shigeru Nakayama, another private. "I thought it was more of the same old crap they always give new people, but they meant it."

A major in the regiment had had his men drag in an enormous tiger carcass. He hadn't killed it; Russian artillery had. But he took possession of the hide—and of the innards. A tiger's gall bladder was worth plenty to the people who cooked up Chinese and Japanese medicines. You could probably get something for the rest of the organs, too.

But Hayashi spoke another truth when he said, "The tiger will make noise to let you know it's there. You never hear the damn Russian who puts a bullet in your back."

As if on cue, Russian mortar bombs started landing on the Japanese position. Like any soldier with even a little experience in the field, Fujita hated mortars. You couldn't hear them coming till they were almost there. Then they sliced you up like a sashimi chef taking a knife to a fine chunk of *toro*. Unlike the tuna belly, you weren't dead before they started. You sure could be by the time they got done, though.

Fujita jumped into a hole. He had more uses for them than sleep alone. Fragments snarled by overhead. A couple of hundred meters away, a Japanese soldier started screaming as if a tiger had clamped its jaws on his leg. Several rifle shots rang out a few seconds later. Another soldier shrieked.

"*Zakennayo!*" Fujita muttered under his breath. The Russians sent elaborately camouflaged snipers high up into pines that overlooked Japanese positions. Soldiers must have come out to pick up the man the mortars wounded—whereupon the snipers did more damage.

In the Russo-Japanese War, the Japanese had accepted surrenders and treated enemy prisoners as well as any of the soft Western powers did, even if yielding was a disgrace in Japanese eyes. Things hadn't worked like that on the Mongolian border. If you gave up there, you took your chances. And the Mongolians and Soviets weren't what anybody would call gentle, either.

The game was rough here, too. For that matter, Fujita didn't think any army in the world casually accepted surrenders from snipers, any more than most soldiers were willing to let machine gunners give up.

Japanese guns began to move. The Russians had the edge in artillery here, as they did on the edge of the Gobi. The Soviets might not believe in God, but they believed in firepower. And some of the dugouts they built would take a direct hit without collapsing. What they didn't know about field fortifications wasn't worth knowing. They got to show that off in this forest fighting, too.

Somewhere up ahead lay the Trans-Siberian Railroad and victory. Cut the railroad line, and Vladivostok would start to wither away. That would leave the USSR without its great Pacific port, which was exactly what Japan had in mind.

Unfortunately, the Russians could read maps, too. They were going to defend the railway line with everything they had. And if they didn't have more than the generals in the Kwantung Army thought before they started this war, Fujita would have been amazed.

Somewhere up ahead lay Hill 391, the latest strong point the Japanese needed to subdue before they pushed on toward the two parallel lengths of iron track that were the main reason for the attack. Main reason? Sergeant Fujita shook his head. Absent the railroad, this was terrain only tiger hunters would ever want to visit.

The Russians had more of their seemingly limitless cannon up at the top of Hill 391. Down toward the bottom, they had machine-gun nests, barbed wire to guide troops into the machine guns' lines of fire, and minefields to maim any soldiers the machine guns happened to miss. Fujita had already stormed one of the Red Army's fortified hills. He didn't want to do it again. Of course, his superiors cared not a sen's worth about what he or any other enlisted man wanted. Enlisted men were tools, to be used—or used up—as officers saw fit.

Airplane engines droned overhead. Fujita could see only bits of sky through the tall pines and firs and spruces and other trees he had trouble naming. He couldn't make out what was going on up there. Japanese planes had an engine note different from that of their Russian foes: a little higher, a little thinner. Everybody said so. Fujita believed it, but he had trouble hearing it himself.

When bombs started bursting on top of Hill 391 and on the west-facing slope, he felt like cheering. That would give the Russians something to think about! Airplanes full of bombs could counteract their superiority in cannon.

His excitement didn't last long. Once the planes got done pounding the Russian position, what would happen next? Infantry would go forward and try to clean it out—that was what. And then all the Red Army men the bombs hadn't killed would grab their rifles and wait at their machine guns and slaughter as many Japanese as they could.

Sure enough, Lieutenant Hanafusa's whistle squealed. "Come on!" the platoon leader shouted. "Time to dig them out! We can do it! May the Emperor live ten thousand years!" He trotted forward.

"*Banzai!*" Fujita echoed as he scrambled out of his hole. He didn't care about living 10,000 years himself, though he certainly hoped the

Emperor would. He did hope he would last another thirty or forty. Going up against another one of these hills made that a lot less likely.

But he couldn't hang back. It wasn't just that his own superiors would do worse to him than anything the Russians could dream up. They would, yes, but that wasn't what got him moving. You couldn't seem a slacker in front of your men. You were brave because they watched you being brave. And they were brave because you had your eye on them—and because they didn't want to let their buddies down.

Ahead, machine guns started hammering. Fujita shook his head as he dodged around trees. No, the bombers hadn't cleared out everybody on the ground. They never did. By the nature of things, they couldn't. That was up to the infantry.

Red Army khaki was a little darker, a little browner, than the color the Japanese used. Neither was very well suited to the deep greens and browns of these pine woods. Fujita scrambled behind a tree. He raised his rifle, made sure that the helmet had an unfamiliar outline, and pulled the trigger.

Down went the Russian. *One less round-eyed barbarian to worry about*, Fujita thought. Somebody ran past him, toward the higher ground ahead. A moment later, the Japanese soldier wailed in despair. He was hung up on barbed wire cleverly concealed among the ferns and bushes that grew under the trees. The way he jerked and struggled reminded Fujita of a bug trapped on flypaper.

A trapped bug might struggle for quite a while. One of the Russian machine guns soon found the Japanese soldier. He didn't jerk any more after that, but hung limply, like a dead fly.

Fujita shivered. That could have been him, as easily as not. If that private hadn't rushed forward, he might have done it himself. Rushing forward was what the Japanese Army taught its soldiers. Aggressiveness won battles. If it also got people killed, that was just part of the cost of doing business.

"*Urra!*" The Russian shout rang through the woods. A submachine gun stuttered, somewhere off to Fujita's left. The Japanese preferred rifles because of their longer range. The Russians liked weapons that could fire rapidly at close quarters. A lot of the fighting in these woods was at very close quarters, because half the time you didn't see the other guy till you fell over him—or he fell over you.

"Advance toward the rear!" an officer shouted. The Japanese had no command for retreat. That one did the job, though. Hill 391 wouldn't fall today. Neither would the railroad line—not here, anyhow.

PHOTO: © M. C. VALADA

HARRY TURTLEDOVE is the award-winning author of the alternate-history works *The Man with the Iron Heart; The Guns of the South; How Few Remain* (winner of the Sidewise Award for Best Novel); the Worldwar saga: *In the Balance, Tilting the Balance, Upsetting the Balance,* and *Striking the Balance;* the Colonization books: *Second Contact, Down to Earth,* and *Aftershocks;* the Great War epics: *American Front, Walk in Hell,* and *Breakthroughs;* the American Empire novels: *Blood & Iron, The Center Cannot Hold,* and *Victorious Opposition;* and the Settling Accounts series: *Return Engagement, Drive to the East, The Grapple,* and *In at the Death.* Turtledove is married to fellow novelist Laura Frankos. They have three daughters: Alison, Rachel, and Rebecca.